Enso

The Journey Beyond

Book IV

Richard Howe

Copyrights

This novel is entirely a work of fiction. The names, places, characters, and incidents are either the product of the author's imagination or are used fictitiously and are not to be construed as real. Any resemblance to any actual persons, living or dead, organizations, events or locales is entirely coincidental.

Table of Contents

Enso

The Journey Beyond

***

Dedicated

**To my cat Qing Qing,
who has brought me many joyous moments.**

Sources

This is a *fictional* novel. In my life of reading and research, I have read many books ... fictional and non-fictional by many great authors. I owe everything I write to them. Thank you.

On my website (**http://www.rhowe-haozi.com/Sources.html**) is a partial list of books I have drawn inspiration from for the books in this series. This is not an all-inclusive list as that would be impossible ... physically and mentally. In the end ... *life is all just a story ...*

Language & Words Selection

Many of the words and references come from ancient texts and usage in a specific area at a specific time. For me, to use them in a fictional book, would be ... ridiculous ... as only 1-2 people in the planet can read and understand these long-forgotten languages. Instead, I opted for a broader audience and used modern terms, phrases, and usage. For example, I have chosen to use the modern term "consciousness", for something the ancients described in different forms and words.

Author's Preface to Book IV

One day I was climbing through a hilly forest, near my home in the mountains of western Fujian when suddenly a large flying squirrel flew past me high up in the tree line. It was so majestic, soaring and weaving around the trees until it found the branch it was looking for. It landed, looked around, sniffed the winds, and launched itself off again, gliding further down the mountain on an invisible pathway, guided by some inner lodestone, known only to it. It was one of those moments in the forests that stayed with me.

There have been many similar special moments in forests where time seems to stand still ... a pathway through birch trees with leaves floating down on invisible breaths of forest air ... rushing waters carrying leaves down a timeless stream. At these times, I realize that life is not some continuum made up of linear time ... but rather, life is a series of moments ... *connected* moments ... filling in spaces of some imperceptible design ... which is almost finished, for me.

As I mentioned in my earlier books, I had a translation assignment a few years ago with a local publishing house. In it I tried to sense the essence of the text and put it into words and phrases, that I thought English readers could better understand. This new book is taking that treatment a step further. Through the years I have read hundreds upon hundreds of books and articles focusing on the mysteries of the universe ... from ancient texts to quantum physics ... the meanings of which are often obscure, hidden, or incomprehensible.

So, I have undertaken to *rephrase* the essence of these ancient/modern teachings into something more accessible. I hope you will enjoy this new book.

Richard Howe

Time

Some current quantum physicists and some ancient philosophers suggest that the human *perception of time* in terms of past, present, and future is illusory.

Einstein himself held this view. At the funeral of his friend Besso, Einstein is supposed to have said, "Now Besso has departed from this world a little ahead of me. That means nothing. People like us, who believe in physics, know that the distinction between past, present, and future is only a stubbornly persistent illusion."

Siddhartha asked his old friend, "Have you also learned the secret of the river, that there is no such thing as time?"

"Yes, Siddhartha, is this what you mean? The river is everywhere at the same time. At the source and at the mouth. At the waterfall, at the ferry, at the current in motion, and in the mountains ... Everywhere." "The present only exists for it, not the shadow of the past nor the shadow of the future."

"That is it," said Siddhartha.

"And then I learned that as I reviewed my life, it is also a river. Siddhartha the boy, Siddhartha the mature man, and Siddhartha the old man ...

are only separated by shadows ... not by reality."
"Time is a child of consciousness."

The Theory of Conscious Agents

Consciousness is often defined as *the state of being aware of one's surroundings and experiences. The Theory of Conscious Agents* proposes that consciousness is not just a product of physical matter, but rather the fundamental building block of the universe. It suggests that consciousness is not simply a passive observer of reality, but an active participant in its creation.

According to the *Theory of Conscious Agents*, conscious agents interact with each other to create the perception of reality. These interactions are based on information exchange and can be both cooperative and competitive. This means that our perception of reality is constantly changing as conscious agents interact with each other.

The Theory of Conscious Agents has implications for the concepts of free will and causality. It suggests that consciousness plays an active role in the creation of reality, which means that we may have more control over our experiences than we previously thought. It also suggests that causality may not be as straightforward as we once believed, as the interactions of conscious agents can create unexpected outcomes.

The Theory of Conscious Agents proposes that quantum mechanics and consciousness are intimately linked. It suggests that the collapse of the wave function in quantum mechanics is a result of conscious observation. This means that consciousness is not just an emergent property of physical matter, but a fundamental aspect of the universe.

Information plays a crucial role in the *Theory of Conscious Agents*. It is through the exchange of information that conscious agents interact with each other to create the perception of reality. This means that information is not just a passive component of reality, but an active participant in its creation.

Therefore, the very language of our visual perception and all of our senses is the wrong language to describe objective reality.

Galileo talks about a wine's good taste not belonging to the objective determination of the wine ... and hence of an object, even the object as an appearance, but *the special character is the sense in the subject who is enjoying its taste. That everything that we perceive is in some sense just a creation of our senses (minds).*

Reality is a mind device to navigate this illusion ...

Donald D. Hoffman, Department of Cognitive Sciences. University of California, Irvine USA (2014)

PART 1 – AVARGA

***

LF (Little Feili)

Walking in the mountains you may encounter one of nature's fascinating creatures, the flying squirrel. In the mountains of Fujian, they are somewhat larger, and the locals call them 'feili'.
Panda found an orphaned feili and named her, 'little feili' ... later she shortened it to 'LF',

Life ...It is all just a story ...

The Tale of the Two Legendary Immortals
Whose destinies were entangled for Eternity.
(By Granny Panda, Hong Xiongmao, (Yuan Dynasty)

"Granny Panda ... who is this little girl here in the tapestry?"

"That's their daughter, Hong Xiongmao ... come and sit here in front of the tapestry so you can follow the golden threads of their journey ..."

The children all gather in a semi-circle in front of the large tapestry which is finally all coming together ... it depicts the adventures of the Two Legendary Heroes ... and their daughter, Hong Xiongmao (Red Panda).

"So where did I leave off yesterday?"

"They went back to their cabin in the Snowy Mountains to live peacefully ever after ..."

Granny sighs, "If only life was so easy ..."

"In any event, the gods allowed them a few years of peace so they could raise their daughter ... and she was a special child."

"What do you mean Granny Panda? Could she fly? Could she lift up a mountain like Sun Wukong?"

Granny laughs, "Those are just fairy tales, child ... real heroes have no superpowers ... they are like you and me."

When she says that, some of the other women working on their tapestries smile.

"Can you tell us the story of the little girl?"

"Okay, do you all want to hear the story of little Panda?"

The children all shout, "YES!"

"Okay then ... when she was little, she had a keen interest for the animals and birds in the forest around the cabin ... one time when she was ..."

Just then a soldier barges into the room.

"Elder Grandmother, the Khan wants to see you immediately!"

She smirks, "I'm teaching the children right now ... I'll come when I am done."

The soldier couldn't believe his ears. (What? This is a request from the great Khan! To refuse is to seek death.)

"Grandmother please come with me ... it really is urgent ..." then he whispers, "It's between war and peace with the ..." then he finishes by saying,

"If you don't come, they will kill me and my families for three generations."

Granny Hong shrugs, looks at the children and tells them, "Children I must go, but I will be back soon ... maybe you go outside and play until I return?"

They all agree, and she follows the soldier to see the great Khan.

***

In the great hall, the Great Kublai Kahn, the most powerful emperor in the world, sits on a golden bejeweled throne on an elevated dais. Before him are several ministers from various provinces, his generals, and other aides. When Granny Panda enters, he looks up, smiles, and motions with his horse-tail whip for the others to leave. Once they are gone, Granny Panda approaches the Khan and bows in obeisance.

The Khan walks to her and raises her up, "Rise ... rise ... you know you only need to do that when the others are present."

"How can I help you Great Khan?"

"Great Khan? I am not your 'little rascal' anymore?"

Granny laughs, "You haven't been my little rascal for many years ... you are a Great Khan."

"Not the least bit, because of your wise advice through the years."

"How may I help you today 'little rascal', do you still wear my wolf bracelet?"

The Khan holds out his wrist with the wolf hair bracelet made many years before.

Then his face changes and he says,

"It's the Japanese. They keep raiding and pirating along the coast. My generals and ministers want me to launch a costly naval expedition against them."

"Granny Panda, what do you sense will happen if I undertake such an expedition."

"*Great Khan, you have asked me this before, and I told you, I see only disaster for your armies ... your armies are the mightiest mounted warriors of the steppes ... but horses don't gallop over the seas.*"

"*But the governors from the coastal regions, the admirals in my new navy, the generals in the armies all promise victory.*"

"*And the gods of the heavens? What does the Blue-Sky Tengri promise?*"

"*I have found a shaman that predicts victory.*"

"*Ha! How many did you have to consult before you found one to tell you what you wanted to hear?*"

The elder woman takes out two pieces of paper and writes on each. Then she turns them face down and tells the Khan,

"*Pick one and turn it over.*"

He picks one and turns it over. The woman reads it.

"*Disaster.*"

Then she shows him the other which had 'Victory' written on it.

Granny Panda approaches him and rests her hand on his arm, a gesture no one else can do.

"*Great Khan. Have I ever given you bad advice ... in all these years to you and before you, to your mother?*"

The mentioning of his mother strikes a heartfelt nerve, the great man softens and rises and leads her out.

"*You have always given me and my family the best advice ... and I appreciate it ... now go back to your weavers and my grandchildren ... I will ponder your advice carefully.*"

Granny Panda bows and returns to the weaving room, but her heart senses disaster approaching.

***

Later back in the weaving room ... the children gather around.

"*Now where was I before I left?*"

"*You were starting to tell the story of this little girl in the tapestry, their daughter.*"

"*Ah ... yes now I remember ...*"

[She continues to tell the story of the little girl to the children for most of the afternoon.]

"Okay, children, let's take a break here ... do you have any questions?"

One of the princesses' points to a section of the tapestry and asks,

"Granny, what's this little brown animal flying to the girl?"

Granny staggers ... a woman close to her helps her to sit down. There is a huge transformation in Granny's face, from the visage of a warm loving grandmother to the drooping face of a sad old woman ...

The children are silent ... the assistant finds some pills and Granny washes them down.

The woman turns to the children, "Granny is tired now, let's finish the story tomorrow ... okay?"

They all agree and as they leave there is a huge commotion outside the workroom.

An aide enters and announces, "The Great Khan has decided to invade Japan!"

Granny Panda slumps further in the chair ... and shakes her head.

A woman enters the room ... the weavers have seen her before with Granny, but they are not sure who she is except that she is a close friend or relative of Granny.

She sees Granny slumped in the chair and rushes up to her.

"What pills have you given her?"

The attendant shows her the bottle and say, "Three of these."

"Help me to bring her to her room."

They lift the old woman up and as they carry her; the attendant overhears the new woman whisper to Granny.

"Don't be sad, Panda, you have done all you could ... let it go."

Granny nods and feels the warmth from this person (a relative?).

After the attendant helps bring Granny Panda to her rooms and lays her down on her bed, the new woman tells her,

"You can leave now, I'll take care of her ... thank you for your help ... keep this private, okay?"

The assistant nods and leaves. The new woman turns back at Granny Panda who is crying.

"What is it daughter?"

Through her sobs, she unloads the frustrations on trying to direct the Great Khan on righteous paths.

"Daughter, I know ... we have been doing this for many years ... but you can't take the defeats inside you ..."

"I know ... but there was something else that happened today, right before we heard the news ..."

"What?"

"A long-buried memory ... one I thought I had buried forever ... rose to the surface of my mind and an overwhelming sadness and fear gripped me .... I don't know why ... after all these years ..."

"What was the memory?" her mother asks, thinking of the many tragedies that they experienced through the years ... the many friends and relatives who have been killed or passed away ... was it Tariq?

"The deaths of friends and family have never bothered me ... I know their spirits live on ... and that in many ways, their deaths were pre-destined."

"Then what?"

"One of the princess asked me about Little Feili ..."

"And a wall shattered inside my heart ... she was an innocent spirit."

The mother understands and comforts her daughter.

But it was a forewarning of disaster ... not for Granny but for the Khan.

The sole aim of every individual's life energies is ...
to touch the One Consciousness.
To awaken to the very core of our existence,
and to realize your immortal nature.
Most people search all their lives in the wrong places.
The problem is mind ...

1 Prologue Feili & The Kurultai

Seeking is not about looking for something ...
it is seeking in a different way.
By changing your perception.

By 1206, Temujin, the leader of one of the many Mongol tribes, had defeated all his rivals, and in the great Mongol kurultai (leader selection) meeting that year, he was chosen as the new khan (supreme leader). He took the name Genghis Khan ...

The beginning of the greatest land conquest in history.

To most ... his invasions, massacres, plundering, and destructions were like a terrible plague, but to a few ...

Genghis Khan was the cure ... not the disease.

Meanwhile in a small valley in the Dali kingdom (present day Yunnan, in SW China), sheltered by the towering Snowy Mountains, our legendary heroes, Yufeng and Yufei, live peaceably ... raising their daughter, Hong Xiongmao (Red Panda).

This day, the father, Yufei, is making a log playhouse for Panda.

When she decides she needs curtains ... she runs to her mother, Yufeng, and tells her excitedly,

"Mother we need to go to the village for some material for my curtains."

"Can it wait until market day?"

"Mother ... this is important!"

Yufeng smiles ... okay, I'm not busy today ... go tell your father."

"He knows, I already told him."

Wrinkling her eyebrows, Yufeng thinks,

(*when did she do that?*)

Mother and daughter gather their baskets and stroll to the small village not too far from their mountain hideaway.

In the small town, there is really only one main street, with wooden storefronts flanking each side of the narrow dirt street. Some of the storefronts have pennants to explain their wares ... baskets, dried herbs, cloth, embroidered cloth, etc.

The women selling the cloth are dressed elegantly in their native costumes ... and behind them bright blue and red colored sheaths of cloth hanging everywhere on rods.

Panda is looking through them and then she glances outside and becomes very excited, and grabs her mother's tunic, and started pointing at a middle-aged Tibetan monk down the street with his begging bowl held out to passer byes.

"Mama ... over there!" she said, pointing.

Her mother turned to look where she was pointing but only saw a nondescript Tibetan monk wearing a worn robe, like hundreds of others that she had seen through the years, talking to a local granny ... then something strange happened. The granny he was talking to smiled and pointed at her and Panda!

(*Was he asking about us?*)

(*And even more surprising, the monk is walking towards us!*)

(*Where's Yufei and why is Panda so excited?*)

The words that came out of Panda's mouth explained it all.

"Gugu!"

Yufeng is more confused now ... not just by the monk approaching but by Panda's words ...

(*That was her pet name for Gonggong, the old caretaker from ZhuXi's Academy in Wuyi ... but he died years ago! And this young monk looks the same age as Yufei!*)

The monk is wearing a traditional Tibetan Buddhist monks' robe, pantaloons, and tied hemp sandals ... his head is shaved, and he has a warm smile on his face as Panda runs up to him. Panda hugs him and he lifts her up to swing her around.

"Gugu!" she cries out for all to hear.

"Little Panda ... long time no see!"

Then he turns to Yufeng, and she looks into his eyes and probes his spirit ... and then she knows what Panda knew at first glance ... it is Gonggong!

(But, in a new body!)

It is then that she showers him with her warmest smile and *almost* hugs him ...

(*Oooops, can't hug monks in public places!*)

"Gugu ... as you once said to me, *you are like an insect returning to life after death!*"

The monk ... Gugu ... smiles and offers the traditional Buddhist vertical hand greeting gesture.

"A mi tou fo"

Yufeng returns the greeting and asks, "What brings you to our little village, master?"

He smiles, looks at Panda, and says, "I came to play with Princess Panda."

Panda smiles and asks, "Really?" then she looks at her mother.

"Can he stay with us Mother?"

Yufeng smiles a mischievous grin.

"Well, we'll have to ask your father ... he can be a ferocious old goat sometimes."

Panda crooks her head and wrinkles her eyebrows, "Baba ... an old goat?"

Then she and Gugu laugh, and they walk out of the village back to their secluded valley ... as the villagers whisper and spread new stories of the immortals who live in the *valley of laughing spirits* ... where their daughter *talks to the animals.*

***

When they get back to their cabin, Yufei is still outside working on the new playhouse for Panda. He had already sensed their return, so he doesn't look up when they approach him. Then he senses someone else ... someone familiar ... but when he looks up, he wonders ... *who is this strange monk?*

Usually he is wary of strangers, but he sees how comfortable Yufeng and Panda are, so he relaxes and greets the monk.

"A mi tuo fo."

Gugu returns the greeting, and the two men just stare at each other for a few moments ... until Panda breaks the ice,

"It's Gugu, Baba!"

Then Yufei's eyes open wide, and a huge smile covers his face ... and then ... he hugs his old mentor, with tears in his eyes.

Panda asks her mother,

"Mama ... why is Baba crying?"

Then she sees that her mother is crying also.

"Because he is happy to see Gugu ... so very happy."

2 Panda's World

They make up the guest room for Gugu and since monks travel frugally, it only took a few minutes for him to get settled in ... which entailed all of putting his begging bowl on a shelf.

He laughs,

"There, I'm settled in."

Which was fortunate because Panda was anxious to show him *her world*.

First, she showed him her new playhouse that Yufei had just finished near their garden. Even though it was just a playhouse, Yufei had built it from sturdy logs to survive the heavy snows of winter. It was 2 meters wide and 3 meters long ... inside were shelves, a window facing east, a door facing south, and a small table with two stools.

"What are these small openings for ... near the door and window?" Gugu asks.

"My *friends*." Panda replied as though she fully answered his question.

"Friends?"

Curling her eyebrows like talking to a child, Panda explained ...

"Well, there's LF and ..."

"LF?"

"Little Feili ... wait I'll call her ..."

Panda goes to the window and makes a strange clicking sound. Almost immediately there is a return clicking sound from the forest trees ... then Panda makes a similar but a little different clicking ... then she backs away from the window a step, explaining ...

"Sometimes she misjudges the glide path."

Gugu is both mystified and entranced. (*glide path*?)

In a couple of minutes, a large flying squirrel glides through the window with an *almost* perfect landing on the table.

Gugu is speechless.

"Mother says they are bigger here than in our Wuyi hometown."

Gugu stumbles with his next question.

"You talk to it?"

Panda crooks her head and wrinkles her eyebrows at the monk,

"Of course ..." she says, then adds,

"But ... it's not an *it*, it's a *she* ... do you want to pet her ... she will let you."

Gingerly, Gugu reaches out and pets the animal on her soft back fur. LF purrs inside ... a little like a cat that Gugu vaguely remembers from his past life.

"She's friendly!" Gugu says, as though it's news to the world.

Panda smiles, "Most animals are friendly."

"How did you learn to talk to her?"

Panda doesn't quite understand his question, so he tries another way.

"Did your mother teach you to how to talk to her?"

Panda is still confused, so he drops it and asks another question,

"What other animal friends do you have?"

The girl's eyes light up.

"Come ... follow me." And she grabs his hand to lead him outside and up a small trail.

As they walk, Panda makes different animal calls ... several different bird calls, a monkey call, and several animals that Gugu wasn't sure of ... and the forest comes alive with returning calls.

"What are you saying to them?"

"First I'm telling them good morning ... then I'm telling them that I have a new friend with me, and you are a good person...."

"Thanks ... and what are they saying?"

"They say good morning and they are happy to meet you."

They approach a cluster of low growing bushes and Panda gently pushes some branches aside, revealing a ground nest of a partridge-looking bird who is guarding her new hatchlings.

"Don't go too close, they just hatched, and she is protective."

The bird calls out a sharp song.

"What did she say to you?"

"Not me ... she was calling to her mate to hurry and bring back some food ... the babies are hungry."

Just then the bird's mate flies in and passes the food he had gathered to the mother, who portions it out to each of the babies.

Pando lets the bushes fold back in to cover them.

Gugu says,

"Maybe we should be going back for our breakfast too."

Panda smiles, "Okay" and they retrace their steps back down the path to the main cabin ... watching Panda glide down the path, Gugu is fascinated as Panda's feet, like her mother's feet from a memory many years ago, don't seem to touch the forest floor.

***

Yufeng has breakfast laid out on the main table ... eggs, porridge, fruits, and breads. Yufei is on his way inside after washing his hands in the outside sink that he fashioned from hollowed out bamboo tubes stretching from the stream. Then they all sit around the table for a hearty breakfast and talk.

Yufeng asks Panda,

"Did you introduce Gugu to your little friends?"

"Yes ... Mama ... and he saw the new brown-bird babies."

Yufei asks Gugu,

"Did you like her house?"

"It's beautiful ... can you build one for me?"

Yufei looks at Yufeng first.

"It depends ... how long are you planning on staying?"

Gugu smiles and looks at Panda.

"I don't know ... it depends on Panda ... what do you think?"

Panda smiles and shouts, "A long time ..."

They all laugh ... and then Yufei and Yufeng get into the obvious unasked questions. Yufei starts ...

"Where did you travel from?"

Gugu understands their query ... but the question is like his question to Panda about learning the animal language ... it has no answer in this language.

"Here and there ... the Western Mountains ..."

"Mt. Kailash?" Yufeng asks and Gugu nods.

Yufei continues, "Why?"

Gugu gets up, looks outside and then closes the door.

"Sorry ... old habits about the walls have ears ..."

Yufeng assures him,

"Don't worry, the villagers are afraid to come into our canyon ... and if there was a stranger, Panda's little friends would warn us and Yufei has some toys to protect us."

Gugu smiles and returns to his stool.

"Sorry ... okay, let me tell you the short story ..."

First, he talks about large scale events ... the Song invaded the Jin, the Jin defeated them and received renewed tribute and Chief Councilor Han's head. The new leadership in Hangzhou is more stable. The Xi Xia tribes control the Gansu corridor and the Silk Road but that may end soon. The Khwarizmi Moslems are threatening the Western regions of the Kara Khitans and Uighurs ... but the most important events concern the Mongols.

"They just had their kurultai ... the big meeting to select their new leader ... and they selected Temujin, who took the name Genghis Khan. He has united the various tribes under one banner."

"Is that good?"

"We think so."

"We?"

"The elders ... the grandmothers."

Yufei smiles at Yufeng. Meanwhile Panda is fascinated by a stream of ants on the floor. She tries to communicate with them but so far, she's unsuccessful.

Panda asks Yufeng,

"Mother, do ants have hearts, and ears, and eyes?"

"Yes, dear ... and different things too."

"Mama, how come my heart beats and my eyes, see?"

"It's not your heart or eyes, it's your heart spirit that beats, it's your eye spirit that sees, dear."

"Oh ..." Panda says.

Yufeng ponders this. *(she understands immediately!)*

"Does LF see things like I do?"

"Probably a little different."

"Why?"

"To help her survive in the forest, especially at night."

Yufeng continues,

"And she can see things that we can't ... birds, and animals, and fish have different senses to see this world differently."

'How?"

"Do you remember we talked about all the invisible spirits (*conscious spirits*) that make up things?"

Panda nods.

"The animals can sense these invisible conscious spirits better than humans."

"But I can sense them ..."

"You are different, Panda ... you are special."

Changing the subject, Yufei asks,

"What are they planning ... the elders?"

Gugu shakes his head ...

"You will need to ask them ... I only know a part of the plan ... the part I am playing now ... my assignment."

Yufeng wrinkles her brow as she rolls her head and looks at Yufei.

Yufei asks the elephant question in the room.

"Your assignment?"

***

3 Gugu's Assignment

How can Consciousness describe itself?
How can a knife cut itself?
How to use physical terms
to describe the non-physical?

Gugu stands up and pours another cup of tea from the handmade clay tea pot which is steaming over a small clay charcoal burner. As he walks, and gathers his thoughts, the others watch him.

Then, as though his internal debate has been resolved, he sits back down and explains.

"I'm here to be a *guide* for you ... the *three* of you ... if you allow me to."

Yufei and Yufeng look at each other and Yufeng asks.

"Guide us in what way?"

Gugu sighs and starts to explain as best that he can ...

"It's difficult to explain in our language ... first because it is spiritual rather than physical and secondly, because I won't know the pathway until we start down the road ... or up the road, as it may be ..."

"What do you mean?"

"The guidance ... the teachings ... the insight ... will come to us when it is the right time ... just as your enlightenment came to you when you were ready ... not the other way around."

"What *do* you know?"

"I know that you two ... you *three* ... have been chosen ... from before time ... to play an important part in the Divine Plan."

"The Divine Plan?"

"As you discovered on your last journey, there are powerful dark forces whose manifestations seek to destroy this world. One part of the Divine Plan is to defeat those dark manifestations."

"And you've been guiding me since I was a child?"

"Kind of ... subtly ... invisibly ... but now that you've crossed over the waters ... your talents can be enhanced to a higher level ... *if you want.*"

"And Panda?"

"When she is older, and her skills honed ... she will have the opportunity to accept or reject her assignment. But let me ask you something ...."

"How would you evaluate her present skills ... her inner skills?"

They look at each other and then look over at Panda who is still trying to communicate with the ants. Yufeng tells him,

"In some ways she is far ahead of us ... she has inherited all my inner abilities and Yufei's ... maybe two times or three times stronger ... "

"The talking to the animals ... who taught her that?"

"She did it herself ... as though it was as natural as talking to us."

"Why does she have all those bruises on her body?"

Yufeng laughs, "She thinks she is like LF and can fly through the trees ... she discovered slowly her body is different ... but she is a stubborn little girl and didn't give up so easy."

They all laugh, and Panda looks up.

"Nothing honey ... we are just talking about old times."

Yufei asks,

"Speaking of old times ... in your new body, can you remember everything from before?"

Gugu rolls his head, Indian style.

"Yes and no ... I'll try to explain ... when I died, I discarded my mind and my body ... that included all my memories ... when I acquired this new body, I had access, if needed, to everything that ever happened to my old body ..."

"Access?"

"If I need some information, it'll come to me ... I don't need to search for it ..."

"How did you get this body? Was it a recently deceased monk?"

Gugu shrugs, "I don't know the process ... whether it was like you said ... or it was just created ... I've stopped wondering long ago."

"The grannies have stories about *shapeshifters* ... is that what you are?"

He shrugs, "I don't know."

"Do you know any more about what *our* assignment is?"

"Not much ... they will tell you if you go to the mountain."

"So, we don't have to agree to the assignment now?'

"No ... that will be later with the elders ... now you just need to agree to accept me into your home and accept my ... *teachings* on certain things."

"Things?"

"Like *deep consciousness traveling* ... in the void and beyond ... learning to exchange information with conscious spirits and guiding *potential* happenings into *probable* happenings ..."

"Any others?"

Gugu laughs, "Oh ... maybe a hundred or more ... like more quickly recognizing the dark manifestations and defeating them ... like consciously bringing up those future images you only randomly saw before ... time traveling ... a few others."

Yufei holds up his hand,

"Okay ... enough ... before answering you, Yufeng and I would like to go outside and talk about this ... maybe you can help guide Panda in ant communication."

He stifles a laugh as Gugu frowns.

"Okay but before you talk about it, there's something else you should know."

"What?"

"My journey here was not as invisible as I would have liked."

"Were you followed?"

"Possibly."

"Were you attacked?"

"Several times."

"What happened?"

'Luckily, I sensed them coming and *disappeared*."

"Disappeared?"

"It's one of the skills I can teach you ... your body becomes almost transparent ... it's still there but if you are standing in front of a tree ... all they see is the tree."

"Do you think they followed you here?"

"I'm not sure ... I thought I lost them several times ... but they seem to find me."

Yufeng stands and speaks to Panda,

"Panda, Baba and I need to go outside for a minute ... can you explain your ant experiments to Uncle?"

Panda smiles, "Okay Mama ... Uncle ... come here and I'll explain ... do you see those tiny, pointed things on the ants' heads ..."

4 A Decision

Outside, they walk to the stream. Yufei has built a small dam which created an artificial pond under some shade trees. The pond is small but there are lotus flowers and fish in the pond, and it provides endless hours of amusement for Panda.

Yufei reaches for a small pebble and drops it into the pond ... they both watch its pathway to the bottom.

Yufeng looks up at Yufei.

"Like us ... it seems to know already."

Yufei nods,

"Like it's happened before ... or ..."

Yufeng wrinkles her eyes questioningly.

"The rock seems to *know ... to have traveled all the routes before* ... and then retravels the best one."

She nods.

"I know ... sometimes I feel like we have already traveled on this pathway ... but it still feels like the water is pushing against us."

Yufei nods ... then adds,

"I've always felt we are on the Way ... but the dark manifestations are pushing against us from taking the right way." then Yufei asks,

"Do you want to tell him that we agree?"

"I think he already knows."

"Then what's bothering you?"

"Panda."

"Panda?"

"You and I have journeyed to the other shore ... in a way, we know more about the dangers he is describing and can make our own decision ... but Panda ..."

Yufei nods, "I understand ... she is a child ... but still, she should make her own decision."

Yufeng nods.

"What do you think?" Yufei asks.

"Let's cross the stream one stone at a time ... receive his lessons ... learn what the elders plan ... and later we'll let her make her own decision."

He nods and hugs her tenderly.

Just then Panda runs out with Gugu following closely behind.

"I talked to them Mama ... the ants!"

Yufeng smiles, "That's wonderful princess..."

"Let me show you!"

Yufeng motions her head to Yufei to go for a walk with Gugu. Yufei says to Gugu,

"Oh ... Uncle ... if you are going to be living here for a while ... let me show you, our defenses.

He takes Gugu's arm and first they stroll down the canyon.

Yufei points high up one side, "Can you see those bushes?"

Gugu nods.

"Behind them is a large caisson of boulders which I can release with a rope tied to that tree and close off the canyon."

"But won't that trap you?"

Yufei smiles, "Patience old friend, the tour is just starting ..."

And they walk on ...

***

Later ... further up the canyon, behind the cabin, they come to a sheer rock wall.

Gugu looks around.

"Let me guess ... you wanted to show me that you can't be attacked easily from the rear."

Yufei smiles, "That was one of the things ..."

Then he goes up to the rock face and moves aside some bamboo trees stacked against the rock wall. Behind it is the entrance to a cave.

"Wow! Where does it lead?"

"Some interesting places ... but for now I just wanted to show you our back door in case we are attacked."

Gugu nods approvingly and they replace the bamboo covering.

As they walk back down the canyon Gugu asks,

"So, what have you two been doing these past few years?"

"Beside raising Panda and taking care of the household things, Yufeng has continued her medical and herbal studies ... but be careful."

Gugu stops walking and turns to Yufei.

"About what?"

'Asking about the local healing herbs."

"Why?"

Yufei says, "My wife has never seen a plant she doesn't love ... so when we go for walks, she stops every 2 feet to inspect every new plant ... "

Gugu smiles, "So your walks are learning experiences?"

Yufei laughs, "And now Panda does the same thing with plants and her animals ... I am their prisoner ... but now they have someone new to torture ... I mean teach." Yufei smiles at Gugu.

Gugu laughs and they continue back to the cabin.

5 Traveling in the Beyond

Later around the table, drinking Yufeng's home-grown tea, Gugu gives them their first of many lessons ... about *traveling* in the void.

"As you know, in the void, you can't use your physical bodies ... you can't walk or move your arms to try to *swim* ... but most important you can't use your mind ... don't even try."

The two adults look at each other and then at Panda.

Gugu understands and asks,

"Has she gone into the void?"

Yufeng smiles, "You can ask her."

Looking at Panda, Gugu asks, "Panda, have you gone into the void?"

Panda looks at him as though he had asked if she knows how to walk outside. She looks at her mother, who nods.

"Yes, uncle ... why do you ask such a simple question?"

Embarrassed, Gugu just shrugs, "No reason ... just making sure ... some children don't learn it until they are much older."

"But Baba told me he did it when he was my age ..."

"Yes, well, your father was special ... anyway, let me ask another question."

"When you go into the void, have you ever tried to go somewhere?"

Panda thinks about that, then answers, "Once."

Yufeng and Yufei are surprised to learn this and Yufeng asks,

"Panda, where did you try to go?"

"Back."

"Back?"

"One night, after the first snow, I had a dream ... you and father were there ... we were in a palace, and there were two others lying in beds ..."

Yufeng asks, "You dreamt about grandpa and auntie?"

Panda nods.

"Later, I tried to find them again ... I didn't want their memory to fade away."

Gugu reaches over and pats Yufeng's hand, then asks Panda,

"What happened?"

"At first I was sad, because I couldn't find them ... and then they came to me."

"Both of them?"

"Yes ... and another lady."

Yufei looks over at her and his eyes start to water. (*my mother?*)

Yufeng notices Yufei' reaction and holds his hand and asks Panda,

"And then what happened?"

"We all held hands ... like in a circle and I could feel their love."

Gugu says, "But in the void you have no hands."

Panda looks at him strangely, "*You don't?*"

Yufeng asks her, "Then what happened?"

"Grandpa said not to worry, that they would always be close by to watch over me ... and then I came out of the emptiness."

The adults are all silent ... as though holding their breaths ... then the tension relaxes, and they all reach for their teacups at the same time ... each one lost in their own thoughts.

Yufei stands and goes outside for a walk ... alone.

After a few moments, Yufeng follows after him.

***

Outside, she sees him by the pond ... staring into the water. She comes up to him silently and puts her arms around him.

"Did she ever tell you this before?"

"No ... I don't like to pry too deeply ... she usually tells me these things when she wants to ... when she's ready ... are you okay?"

He nods, then asks,

"Have you felt your hands before ... in the void?"

She thinks for a minute, then shakes her head, "No ... except that one time, when you came to save me ... I felt *something* pulling my spirit back ... but I didn't know what it was ... what about you?"

"Yes and no ... I need to talk to Gugu more ... let's go back inside."

"Wait ... there's something else bothering you ... tell me."

"I've tried hundreds of time to find my father ... but ..."

"No luck?"

He shakes his head and rises to walk inside.

***

Meanwhile inside, Gugu and Panda are having a standing-on-one-leg contest ... with neither one showing any signs of discomfort. When the two return though, it is Gugu who puts his other leg down first ... relieved.

"Ah ... you have come back ... good."

They all sit down and Yufei asks,

"Gugu, before, you mentioned that when we enter the void ... or when someone dies, they drop their body and their mind."

Gugu nods.

"Then my question is this ... when I am in the void, I *feel* like I still have a body, I *feel* like I am thinking ... just like Panda just described ... but if we have no mind, and no body, how can that be?"

"Good question ... that's what I was getting to before ... you know that our eyes are just windows ... and behind our eyes is our original conscious spirit."

They nod and he continues.

"But this thing you call *your* conscious spirit is like a wave ... it only *seems* real ... really only the ocean is real, the one Consciousness spirit."

They look questioningly at him.

"Your mind is not your conscious spirit ... it is just an organ to help you navigate this world."

They nod.

"When you enter the void, your mind doesn't go there ... just the wave, your conscious spirit ... think of the wave as your conscious spirit."

Yufeng looks up and asks, "And the ocean is an ocean of conscious spirits?"

Gugu nods, "Yes and no .... it is the One Consciousness underlying everything, which includes an ocean of conscious spirits."

And Panda nods too, as though she already sensed this.

Yufei asks the obvious, "And the universe?"

Panda smiles and says, "A universe of infinite consciousness spirits."

They all look at her ... then laugh.

31

Yufeng smiles at Yufei, "Of course ... didn't you know that?"

Yufei rolls his eyes and asks Gugu,

"So, what we thought was our mind in the void ... was really our conscious spirit."

Gugu nods.

"So, we use our conscious spirits to navigate in the boundaryless Consciousness."

"Yes, and that's one thing you need to work on ... using your consciousness ... *not* your mind ... it's like thinking without thinking."

Yufeng asks him, "I have a question ... Panda mentioned holding hands in the void?"

Gugu smiles, "It wasn't her physical hands ... she felt her *spirit* hands ..."

Gugu pauses and drinks some tea.

"It's difficult to describe in our language which is based upon visual perceptions and physical senses ... our language is the wrong language to describe things on the non-physical side ... in the void you only have your spirit body. You can't use your physical senses ... you use your inner senses ... your *non-physical* spirit senses."

Yufei asks, "So, getting back to your original travelling method ... in the void, if we don't walk, swim, or fly ... how do we get to where we are supposed to go?"

"Use your conscious spirit ... like when you went in to save Yufeng that time ... it wasn't your mind directing you, or your legs carrying you ... it was your inner senses ... being directed by the one Consciousness ... it's like when you are aware that you are in a dream ... and in the dream you are *moving but not moving ... seeing but not seeing* ... do you understand?"

They nod.

"Kind of ..."

Yufeng starts to ask, "But how ..."

Gugu holds up his hand, "It's impossible to explain in words ... you can only experience it ... that is why I am here ... to help you experience this and more."

Pointing to a shelf full of medical books, he says,

"It's like all the wisdom in all the medical books in the world are just preparation for when a sick patient comes in and you start to sense their qi energy channels inside ... it's your experience, and your instincts that will heal the person ... not the books."

"So, clear your mind; become aware (conscious) of the universal consciousness; aware inside, and the Way will open up to you."

"And remember this ... everything that we perceive here is just a creation of the conscious spirits ... this life is just an illusion... by conscious spirits in a world created by the interaction of conscious spirits."

"But why?"

Gugu smiles.

"That you will learn from the grandmothers."

"In Gobekli Tepe?"

Gugu nods.

Yufei looks at Yufeng and they both know ...

This is a continuing thread of our destiny.
Infinity is closing in on us ...

6 The Dark Forces

Gugu rises stretches and sits back down ... then he asks them ... mostly the two adults ...

"I want to talk a little about the dark forces ... both of you have mentioned times when you *didn't* sense the dark forces ... that the darkness was somehow hidden ...*cloaked*?"

Yufei nods, "Yes ... once on the trail we didn't sense a Jin patrol ... it was strange."

Yufeng adds, "And once in Basra, I didn't sense the darkness in the old woman, who helped the soldiers to capture me."

Gugu asks, "Both times, you didn't sense anything?"

They look at each other and shake their heads.

Then Panda surprises them,

"I sensed a blurring ... like looking through a paper window instead of an open window."

They all turn towards her. Yufeng asks,

"When did this happen?"

"Last year before the snows ... in the village."

"Why didn't you tell me?"

A little embarrassed, Panda says,

"I didn't know what it was, and I didn't sense danger ... so I just forgot it ... until you just mentioned *cloaking*."

"What was it?"

"An old woman shaman traveling through town ... she was dressed shabbily."

"What happened?"

"Nothing ... I turned to a merchant selling some birds in cages and forgot about it."

They laugh, then Gugu tells her,

"If it happens again, tell one of us ... okay?"

"Okay."

Yufei asks, "The cloaking ... it cloaks their dark spirits?"

Gugu nods.

"So, whenever we sense a cloaking phenomenon, we must be on our guard."

Gugu nods again and looks at Panda.

Pando nods, "I know."

Yufei asks, "Does this have to do with our assignment?"

"I'm not sure what your assignment is ... but it has to do with your survival ... and in defeating the dark manifestations ... like you learned before at Gobekli Tepe and Kailash."

Just then Yufei senses something with Yufeng ... he turns, and she has tears in her eyes. Panda notices them also and asks her,

"Mama what is wrong ... why are you crying?"

Yufeng wipes her eyes with her tunic sleeve, "It's nothing dear ... mommy just remembered something."

Yufei knows. (*It's her father, Wang Mingde, she still blames herself for his death.*)

Sensing this, Yufei asks Gugu, "Can you explain something to us?"

"Sure ... if I can ... what is it?"

"What happens after death?"

Yufeng looks up and then turns to Gugu, who shrugs, "Okay ... it was on my list ... so, we might as well get that behind us."

"Death ... is just a *word* ... and not a good word, that people use to describe something they don't understand ... in reality, it is just a natural rite of passage ... for every plant, every animal, and every human ... transiting from one form of existence ... to a formless existence which merges back with the Cosmic Consciousness ... I really wish they had chosen a different word ..."

"But what about reincarnation ... does that really happen?"

"Yes ... for some ... but not all."

"I don't understand."

"I once read in an ancient book ... *The sole aim of every individual's life energies is to reunite with the infinite ... the very core of our making.*"

"The goal then is to awaken *your* original consciousness, to realize its' immortal nature with the One Consciousness. Most people search all their lives in the wrong places ... the problem is mind."

Then Yufei asks the bigger question.

"But where do we fit in it all? What do you know about the One Consciousness, the Soul, and our individual conscious spirits?"

Gugu tries to explain the inexplicable.

"The One Consciousness is an intelligent Consciousness, spread throughout the vacuum of the universe ... and even beyond."

"What you call the Soul appears to be resonant energy reflections of this Consciousness ... like a tuning fork."

"What you call your individual Conscious spirit is an illusion caused by the interaction of the mind with the Soul."

Yufei asks, "So, then ... who are we?"

"In physical language, *we are an awareness in the infinite Consciousness of space ... like a conscious wave in a conscious ocean.*"

Yufei looks at Yufeng knowingly, having shared this thought before.

"But this thing called the *Soul is* not an *entity ... it's just a reflection, like the moon in the water ...* but without it, there is no awareness. So, without the Soul, there are no sentient beings."

"The *Soul's* main purpose is the manifestation of knowledge (*information*) into material form."

"The Soul speaks to your consciousness through the heart and intuition ... and vice versa."

Everything that we perceive is a creation of conscious spirits interacting through the mind, creating this illusion before us." As he sweeps his hand in a wide arc.

"The mind, through the physical senses, can only see physical manifestations, ... *illusion only sees illusion.*"

Yufeng asks,

"So, if 'I' am an illusionary reflection of an immortal soul ... and reality is an illusion for our experiential growth, then there can be no death ... just an *illusionary passage.*"

And then she starts to home in on her question.

Yufeng asks about the heart, "And if someone is a good person ... just not spiritually educated ... like a farmer ... what about them?"

"It's not the education ... it's their heart ... you remember that temple in Egypt?"

Yufeng remembers but Panda doesn't so she tells her the story of the Goddess Maat.

"Panda, the ancient Egyptians believed in a Goddess Maat who weighed our souls to discern the goodness ... against the weight of a feather ..."

Yufei then asks Gugu what Yufeng is hesitant to ask.

"Gugu ... what about the fate of Yufeng's father. Can you give her any insight?"

He understands now, "Ah ... you have nothing to worry ... his spirit is fine ... in fact ... you will probably be visited by him before too long."

This startles Yufeng, "Really?"

Gugu smiles and looks at Yufei, "Just as Panda did that time."

Yufei and Yufeng look at each other with an incredible closeness ... as though a burden has finally lifted after many years.

Yufeng asks, "Do you think my father will be reincarnated?"

"I don't know ... but many spirits with good hearts, who never had the opportunity in their time to gain experience in spiritual things, are reborn in another time where they will have that opportunity ... *but then it will be up to them.*"

"And us?"

"Ah ... that is a question really for the grandmothers ... perhaps that's enough for today."

7 What About Us?

Outside Yufeng tells Panda to get her medical kit ready for tomorrow.

"Okay mama!"

She leaves and runs inside to her mother's medical storage area ... and a moment later she is carrying a wicker kit to another shed built into the back of the cabin.

Gugu asks,

"You'll go to the village tomorrow?"

"Yes ... every market day we go to the village and set up a makeshift clinic and herbal shop. Before we came here the medical treatment in the village was handled by an aging physician with limited abilities ... and unfortunately, soon after Panda was born, he passed away and I started treating a few villagers until Panda was old enough to help me ... now we have a regular clinic and while I am treating patients, I am also training Panda."

"But she is so young!"

Yufeng smiles and shakes her head, "Come with us tomorrow and watch ... she will amaze you as she has amazed the both of us."

"What is she doing in that shed?"

"She's gathering the herbs that we will bring tomorrow and carefully filling the small drawers in my medical kit."

"And she knows ..." spreading his hands out, "all about the herbs?"

Yufei stifles a laugh.

"She senses things even I can't ... anyway, let's get back to what you wanted to tell us."

"Okay ... about what *may* be in store for you two ... on a divine pathway."

"You've heard the legends of Immortals?"

Yufei laughs, "That's what they call us in Wuyi now."

"Well, they may be closer to the truth than you realize."

Yufeng looks at him and asks, "You mean, there really were Immortals in the past?"

He smiles and says, "And in the present and in the future."

"But I thought those were mostly old granny folk tales."

"Most of those you heard are just made-up tales ... but some are not ... and many you don't hear about ... they are secret on purpose ... let me explain ..."

Gugu talks for an hour about real immortals ... real people selected for their spirituality and wisdom ... watched over and guided through several lives to where they are given an opportunity to become immortal and serve the divine purpose for longer periods ... the elders realized it made little sense in training spiritual guides, only to have them die after few years. Yufei asks, "So they slow their body's aging?"

Gugu nods.

"Some ... others come back like me."

"Can they be killed?"

"Yes ... but later they may evolve into another form."

"Another form?"

"In the beyond, we are all formless, but in this world, we all take forms ... but there are different types of forms ... some forms have energy, blood, flesh and bones ... some just have energy and substances which *resemble* bodies ... but if you shoot an arrow at them, the arrow just passes through."

"Are you ..."

"No, no ... this body can be killed and die ... those other forms are special, and I am not even sure how one becomes one."

"The elders?"

"They are like me ... but some will come back in another body and still retain their access to the infinite wisdom."

"And us?"

"I only know part ... you will be offered the ability to access infinite wisdom ... as well as other skills ... to aid you in your assignments."

He pauses, looks at both of them, and then continues,

"These assignments ... at first are to defeat the dark manifestations locally ... to *nudge* possibilities into probabilities ... and then, probabilities into actualized events."

Yufeng rolls her eyes, "You lost me there."

"Okay let me try to explain better but I must use some metaphors because there are no words."

"We can't change the past, but we can indirectly change the future ... we can influence *possibilities* in the present (it's possible this *could* happen) to become *probabilities* (it probably *will* happen) and thus to change the future ..."

He picks up a leaf and holds it at the edge of the pond.

"When I drop this leaf, it will float down to the water or the grass ... *two possibilities*. But if I blow it towards the water, I've increased the *probability* that it *will* fall into the water."

He drops it and as it floats down, he blows it toward the water ... where it softly lands.

Yufei and Yufeng smile in acknowledgement.

Gugu continues,

"Usually, it's information that causes the change."

"Information?"

"Remember on your first journey to the west and you *saw* Yufeng getting an arrow before it happened?"

Yufei nods.

"That was information, which caused you to try to change the future ... and you did. *Information is exchanged by the conscious spirits to change the possibilities into new probabilities and the new probabilities into actualized events.*"

Then Gugu gets more serious.

"As you know there have been massive invasions, slaughters, and enslavements in many parts of the world. To the Immortal Sisters, these are all dark manifestations, which they have dedicated their lives to try to defeat ... but ..."

"What?"

"Up until now, the dark forces have proven more powerful. Either intentionally or unintentionally."

"Unintentionally?"

"Some probabilities have been realized accidentally ... when there is no one fighting against them."

"What's new now?"

"The sisters have been cultivating the Mongols for many years ... now the Mongols are on the move."

"But we hear they are worse than the others ... slaughtering entire cities ..."

Gugu shakes his head, "We all wish there was another way ... but the dark manifestation has infected the entire world, and it must be purged."

"When storm lightning causes fires on the steppe grasslands, it may seem bad at that time, but by the next season, the ashes have rejuvenated the soils so that healthy new grasses grow in the spring."

"But ..."

"We understand ... but there is no other way. You learned from the grandmothers in Gobekli what happened ... "

He pauses, picks up a rock and tosses it into the pond.

"In the western mountains they dig a mineral out of the ground and beat it into fibers to make a fireproof cloak."

Yufei nods, "We've seen it."

"In time, it gets infested with lice, mites, and soils ... to clean it, they toss it into a fire. The fire burns off the impurities and the coat comes out clean ... that is what will happen soon."

"The Mongols are the cleansing fire?"

"In a way ... and in the aftermath, we hope it will be a better world."

Just then Panda runs up and tells Yufeng, "All done mama ... do you want to check?"

Yufeng smiles, "No, I trust you ..."

Panda smiles as LF runs up on her shoulder.

"Can LF come with us tomorrow?"

"Maybe not tomorrow ... there will be a lot of new people and they may be afraid of her."

"Afraid?"

"Yes dear, some people are afraid of strange new animals ... even if they are harmless like LF ... just tell her not this time."

"Okay." She says and turns to LF and starts chirping ... LF lowers his head ... almost sadly.

Then she chirps some more, and the animal brightens up and waves her tail.

Curious, Gugu asks her,

"What did you just tell her?"

Smiling, she says, "I told her I'd get some of her favorite nuts from town for her."

They all laugh.

Gugu turns to Yufeng and asks,

"How did you gain the villager's trust for the healing?"

"One day we were going into town and a young boy was unconscious by the trail ... he had fallen from a tree. We brought him into town, and I rebalanced his qi and set his broken arm. After that the villagers started to trust me."

Yufei smiles and adds, "And the visit to the king and queen helped."

Gugu looks to Yufeng for clarification.

"He means the Dali king and queen ... someone heard about my abilities and a maid of the queen came one day and asked me if I could come and see the queen."

Yufeng stops the narrative until Gugu prods her, "And ..."

"It's confidential ... she had a woman's problem ... caused by blockage of the qi ... I was able to help her."

"And that's it?"

Yufei adds, "And then there were other visits to the queen and royal gifts ... when the villagers saw all this, they were even more stunned by our presence in their village. They asked if they could come to our canyon, but we didn't want that, so Yufeng sets up the mobile clinic in the village on market days ... it's worked out good for everyone ... the villagers get treatment and Yufeng gains experience ... and Panda learns too."

"Sounds great ... I'm looking forward to seeing all this tomorrow!"

8 Market Day Clinic

A skillful physician and a beautiful ornament
Are everywhere esteemed.
Sakya Pandita

The next day they get up while it is still dark to do their morning yoga exercises, meditate, have an early breakfast, pack up, and then start down the trail as the sun is just rising over some low mountains.

Their small cart is pulled by one of their horses. On this day, the men walk beside the horse while mother and daughter ride in the cart. The back of the cart is loaded with cabinets of small drawers filled with various herbs and medical accessories ... acupuncture needles, moxibustion herbs, splints for setting broken bones, and various vials of medicines. Yufeng's most prized possessions are her books and her medical journal, in which she keeps track of all her cases.

She often tells Yufei, "If we ever go back to Damascus, I want to show Moses (Maimonides) my journal."

Yufei would always nod as though it was bound to happen ... someday.

As they rode down the valley, Yufeng never lost a moment to teach Panda about some herb or procedure. Lately she has been more cautious ... ever since that day about a month ago when she stumbled upon Panda operating on one of her animal friends.

Startled she shouted at her to stop ... but Panda ignored her and told her mother, "If I don't untwist her insides, she will die."

"Did you try the oil?"

"Yes, of course."

"But how do you know where it is twisted."

"I looked inside."

"After you cut her open?"

"Before."

(What?)

She watched as Panda carefully reached inside the unconscious animal's midsection to find the twisted intestine and untwist it, so the blockage was opened. She carefully put the organs back in place and asked her mother to sew up the small opening.

"Mama, can you sew it? You are better at sewing than me."

Yufeng sewed up the stomach and then wrapped the wound with bandage. When the animal started to wake, Yufeng gave it some herb to keep it sleeping for a while longer, to allow time to heal. Then Panda put it in a small cage.

Later inside the cabin, Yufeng wanted to talk to Panda and so they sat on stools near the table.

"Panda, tell me again how you saw *inside* the animal."

"It's hard to explain ... remember when you were teaching me how you probe inside a sick person to sense the imbalance of the qi?"

Yufeng nods.

"Shortly after that, I was trying it with LF... only when I probed inside, I could see all her internal organs. After that it didn't take long to see the problem ones."

Then Yufeng had an idea and told her,

"The next time that happens, tell me ... I want to learn how you go inside to help the animals ... maybe we can help people that way too."

Panda brightens, "Okay mama!"

And over the following few months they had several occasions to hone their knifeless inner observation skills.

Their cart enters the village and goes to the market stall area where there is an empty tent canopy waiting for them ... and a line of anxious patients. Yufei and Gugu help get everything unloaded and set up while Yufeng and Panda start talking to the villagers who are seeking their medical help. They select the most serious cases first and then work their way through the rest.

The first two hours are non-stop busy as there are over 20 villagers needing some kind of medical assistance. For some it was a simple herbal prescription, but there were 3 that needed to lie down on some blankets while Yufeng applied acupuncture needles and Panda followed with moxibustion, placing smoldering wormwood at the qi meridian points.

As they worked on the patients, Yufeng would whisper to Panda to ty to probe inside and then tell her what she saw or sensed. Many times, this would lead to further discussions between mother and daughter. Sometimes, Yufeng would retrieve one of her thick medical books and show Panda an illustration ... after which Panda would smile and point to it. Then Yufeng would read more from the book and then they would retrieve some herbs from the cabinet and explain to the patient how to make a decoction (soup-like mixture).

Gugu is in awe and asks Yufei if this happens often.

"Lately ... ever since Panda realized her ability to see inside a person."

Gugu turns to him, "See inside?"

Yufei shrugs, "You'll have to ask her ..."

"How old is she?"

"Eight? Nine? I'm not sure... she seems like eighteen."

They both laugh. Yufei sees the patient load is thinning and says to Yufeng,

"We'll start to pack up while you finish these last ones ... then we'll take Gugu around the market and shops."

"Okay."

***

Later, as they walk around the market, Yufeng often stops to check on a former patient's health or look at some herbs the grannies are selling ... usually she will include Panda in these discussions.

Gugu notices that one alleyway looks different ... first, it is filled entirely by women ... second, their clothes are very colorful, almost as though they are going to a wedding ... and last their handcrafts are beautiful ... woven fabrics, beaded necklaces, and hairpieces ... Gugu asks Yufeng about them.

"Yufeng, who are those people?"

"They are the Naxi tribe, they live near the big lake."

"Why are only the women here?"

Yufei laughs softly and Yufeng slaps him, then she explains.

"The women are in charge of almost everything ... the household, the crops, the weaving, raising the children ..."

45

"What do the men do?"

"The hunting, drinking their home brewed *sulima*, and boasting." she says with a snicker.

"The women are in charge?"

"The head of the house is the *Ah mi*, the matriarch. She controls everything."

"What about the husband ... the father of the children?"

"That's interesting ... the Naxi custom is called *zou hun* (walking marriage)."

"Walking marriage? What is that?"

"The women determines if a man can enter her house at night for a conjugal visit. He enters the house at night and leaves before sunrise. If a child is born, he has no obligation. The mother's brothers will help raise the children."

"So, he or she can sleep with whomever?"

"Yes."

"And that's accepted by everyone?"

"Yes ... think about it for a moment ... without the baggage of obligations, there are few arguments, and almost no child rearing disputes. The people are very content and peaceful ... it works ... for them."

Gugu looks at Yufei. Yufei smiles at Yufeng, who says,

"Don't even think about it!"

Then they all laugh.

Panda asks her father if she can have one of the small colorful knitted animals the grandmother is selling.

"Sure, Panda." Then turning to Gugu he says,

"See, I am controlled by two women also."

As they start to walk away from this area, several of the Naxi women, come up, bow and hand Yufeng some gifts of food, dried pork, nuts, and other specialties.

Gugu asks Yufei, "What was that about?"

"Yufeng has treated many of the Naxi grandmothers and they revere her. Not only because of her medical help, but also because they share a deep reverence for the Mother Goddess in their *daba* beliefs. They see Yufeng and Panda as reincarnations of their spiritual gods."

Then looking behind the grannies, Yufei says, "We should go now."

Gugu looks around, "Why? Is something wrong?"

"See those daba priests (shamans) over there ... they are afraid Yufeng's influence is diminishing their authority ... they tolerate her to a point because the grandmothers insist, but it is an uneasy truce."

Gugu ponders this and adds prophetically as they leave, "It happens elsewhere."

Panda is happy ... now that she has LF's favorite nuts ... so she chirps a feili song.

Some of the Naxi children following her, chirp back.

But dark eyes follow them ... and messages are sent.

9 The Canyon of Laughing Spirits

Time goes by fast in the canyon as there is always something to do. Stacking firewood for the winters; drying game, vegetables, and herbs; putting tubers in the root cellar; exercising the horses and building up a healthy supply of winter fodder ... and a hundred more everyday farm chores ... added on top of the medical training, reading, and writing, philosophy, and martial arts lessons.

Every market day follows a similar pattern ... treat the villagers, walk around the market, buy certain goods that they don't raise themselves, etc.

One day in the market, Panda asks her mother,

"Do you smell that?"

Yufeng sniffs but can't detect anything at first.

"Try again mama, breathe it in and hold it, then out back through your nose."

When she does this her eyes open wide, and she calls over to Yufei.

"What is it?"

"There's an slight essence of the darkness lingering here ... try to find out if any strangers came through lately."

"Okay."

He and Gugu walk around casually asking questions. They learn that a few days earlier, a strangely dressed "shaman" woman came through. She asked a lot of questions, but few people talked to her ... even the villagers could sense something evil about the old woman.

Yufeng asks,

"Then what happened?"

"Apparently, the woman didn't find what she was looking for, so she left."

"Did they tell you what she was looking for?"

"Yes." then looking at Gugu.

"A Tibetan monk, new in the area."

They look at Gugu but decide there is little they can do now ... just be more alert.

As they work at home, Gugu teaches ... about traveling in the void and Panda tries to teach Gugu how to communicate with LF ... unfortunately many of LF's dialogue is with her tail which she can move in endless directions ... each signifying something else, which only Panda has deciphered.

At least once a week, they have an art day ... Yufeng teaches Panda on the traditional Chinese ink while Yufei and Panda draw countless Enso circles with a thicker brush.

Gugu is adept at drawing the Enso also and has his own individual strength in his strokes ... but he is intrigued at Panda's Enso ... because in each of her Enso's, which are beautiful, she puts a dot in the center. When Gugu asked about the dot, Panda replies simply,

"That's me."

"But why do you place it in there."

She thinks for a while, then answers,

"When I drew my first Enso, I automatically placed a dot there ... I didn't know why ... just instincts ... since then I have always done it ... inwardly, I feel there is a significance to it."

She ponders it some more, "In the void it is dark and boundaryless ... until things appear ... the dot is like an anchor to this world ... maybe someday I will not need it ... but for now it gives me a feeling of connection."

"Connection?"

"To my mama and baba ... oh ... and LF." who is sitting on her shoulder watching her draw.

"Tell me more about your Enso ... what is this circle?"

Panda wrinkles her eyebrows and asks, "What circle?"

Perplexed, Gugu asks,

"What do you see?"

"Emptiness inside and emptiness outside ... "

"Then what are you drawing?"

"Conscious spirits ... but there is no line between the outside and the inside ..."

Then wrinkling her nose and eyebrows, she looks at him and asks,

"How could there be?"

Gugu smiles, then asks, "What do you think of my Enso?"

"It's different than mine ... more like baba's."

"What do you mean ... how is it different ... they look the same."

Panda crooks her head and purses her lips, "Uncle! Don't tease me! It's completely different ... look there (pointing) and there and the brush stroke ..."

The monk smiles, thinking ...

(The problem is mind.)

The circle ... the idea of separation ... represents the illusion of this life.

Taoist & Vedanta teach that there is no gap between the two realms.

There is just One Consciousness.

Your senses give you the impression that you are experiencing the world.

Your perception is focused outward - the very basis of existence is within you.

And just as we experience things in this temporal world,

our immortal spirits experience things in the timeless world ...

10 Captain Prtt and Princess Dorjie

The winter snow comes and goes and comes again ... the training continues ... their skills become enhanced in all areas experienced.

One sunny late Spring day, Yufeng is near the pond, painting a bamboo scene, while Panda, is playing with her small animal friends who come to see her every day for a treat ... Panda runs over and looks at her mother as she paints and asks,

"Mother, what are all those marks on your arms?"

Yufeng keeps painting, "Oh ... nothing ... just mosquitos bites ... don't worry, your baba will teach you how to swat them when you are older."

Then the child screams.

Yufeng looks at her and asks, "What is it?"

"Uncle Prtt and the Princess are coming!" she laughs as she jumps in joy and twirls around.

Yufeng looks around but can't see anything. She calls to Yufei, "Honey ... we have guests coming."

Yufeng puts away her paints, Yufei and Gugu stop what they were building, brush off their clothes and prepare to meet their guests.

When Chen Er and Princess Dorjie arrive, Panda runs into the Princess' arms. Yufei asks, "What is happening?"

Chen Er motions at the Princess who is holding little Panda and smiles,

"The Princess wanted to introduce me to her parents."

"And you agreed?" Yufei asks, smirking incredulously ...

"Well, my idea was to find a nice secluded tropical island with servant girls to cater to all my needs ... away from everything ...."

Chen smiles, then laughs "Maybe after this trip I can convince her...haha."

Yufei turns to Gugu, "See ... another man controlled by his woman!"

"Oh ... Chen Er, Princess Dorjie, let me introduce our friend, a Tibetan Buddhist wandering monk ... we call him, Gugu."

Dorjie looks at him curiously and asks,

"Which sect do you belong to?"

Caught off guard ... Yufei comes to his aid.

"Sects? ... haha ... *which* sect is not important, we all follow the Great Buddha ... come inside and rest."

Inside they all sit around the table. Princess Dorjie and Panda are renewing an old bond.

"Princess Panda, you have grown into a big girl ... and so beautiful ..."

Panda just laughs, "Come outside I will show you my house and my friends and my toys and my ..."

Yufeng motions with her hands, "Calm down Panda ... let them rest ... there is plenty of time for that."

As they drink tea, they fill each other in on their news. Chen Er and Princess Dorjie keep glancing at Gugu ... but for different reasons ... but they are content when they see the close relationship that they all have with this strange monk.

Finally, after telling them about their current plans to go to Lhasa, Chen Er smiles and asks, "Do you want to join us for a trip to Lhasa?"

They smile and look at Panda who laughs ... "Yes!"

Yufeng says to the Princess,

"Oh ... thank you for taking care of that thing in the capital."

Princess Dorjie smiles, "It was my pleasure."

"Oh ... here is a gift from the elders ... first they gave it to me ... and now I give it to you ..."

She hands the real fire jewel to Yufeng who smiles and bows.

"But I heard you gave it to the emperor ...?"

The Princess smiles, "My pirate friend switched it with a fake one ... we thought ... why waste a perfectly good fire crystal on idiots?"

Then they all laugh ... especially Panda.

Chen Er laughs,

"Before he lost his head, Minister Han spent many weeks trying to recreate the fire ray ... haha."

Then Yufeng looks first at Chen Er and then asks the Princess,

"So, you finally got this snake to shed his old skin?"

"I think so ... but we will see ... I always have my whip." the two women laugh.

The two men look over, "What is that about?"

"Just girl talk ... not important ... right Panda?"

Panda laughs ... (*foolish old men*).

As they say ...

> *You need companions to travel,*
> *to the Isle of immortals,*
> *it is hard to climb,*
> *the Azure cliffs alone.*

"Oh, here's a letter for you ... from Tarem in Kucha."

Yufei reads it and tells Yufei,

"Tarem and Beersheba invite us to come to Kucha ... business has been good, and he has more children."

Yufei looks at Yufeng and they don't need words to discuss their plan.

So, first we visit Lhasa, then the elders at Mt Kailash, and then to Kucha.

Then they look down at Panda who also is part of their unspoken communication.

"What do you think Panda?"

Panda shouts, "We go!" then she hesitates and asks, "Can LF come with us?"

Chen Er asks, "Who is LF?"

Panda chirps and the flying squirrel glides through the window onto her shoulder.

"This is LF ... my best friend."

Dorjie reaches out her hand and LF sniffs it, then wags her tail.

Panda explains, "She says hello, nice to meet you."

Chen asks,

"You can talk with it?"

Panda curls her mouth dismissively,

"Of course!" (*foolish old men!*)

11 Dark Travels the Night

They enjoy a large welcome meal and break out some of Yufei's aging homemade local rice wine. The women refrain from drinking, but the men make up for their reticence until they can barely walk to their bedding.

In a short while, they were all fast asleep and that's when silently, several black robed assailants creep through their compound.

Unfortunately for them, LF was alert and silently glided through the open window to alert Panda of the danger. Panda immediately understands and sensing the danger, quietly alerts her parents, who silently awaken the others.

They are all experienced with this sort of danger, but still take precautions to have Panda conceal herself behind a thick wooden table that they turn on its side.

Chen asked Yufei,

"How many are there?"

Yufei turned to Panda, who held up her thumb and small finger (six).

"Where?"

Panda held up two fingers to the front, two to each side.

Yufei reaches into his waistband and hands Panda his killing knife. Then he grabs his short sword from a shelf,

Yufei hands Dorjie and Gugu crossbows. Chen always has his small sword by his side, Dorjie had often complained about this but after tonight the complaints are fewer. Finally, Yufeng grabbed her two killing knives and some throwing darts.

They were ready for an army ... the 6 assailants didn't realize the hornets' nest before them ... a nest they would never leave.

The assailant's plan was to split up and when the others on the side windows heard the front door crash open, they would jump through the windows ... but they found out quickly that the best laid plans don't always go as they would have liked.

When the first two crashed open the front door, they were immediately brought down by a flurry of arrows. And when the others jumped through the darkened windows, they were cut down by Yufei and Chen's swords and Yufeng's killing knives.

One tried to escape back out the window, but LF jumped on his face, clawing his eyes before Yufei cut him down.

Panda chirped and LF jumped back to protect her.

"Good girl ... LF ... good girl."

They lit some candles, tried to interrogate the killers but they were all dead from the battle or self-inflicted poisons.

They dragged the bodies out and buried them outside the canyon entrance, not wanting to contaminate their consecrated valley.

Yufei and Yufeng scouted around but found no evidence of others.

When they returned, they had a meeting.

Chen stated the obvious.

"Maybe we should think about leaving soon."

The others agreed.

Yufeng says,

"I'll go into the village to check on my patients, ask around about any other strangers in town, and also buy a horse for Gugu for the journey. Dorjie and Panda can go with me."

Yufei adds,

"Chen, Gugu, and I will get everything stored away and also get everything ready to go for the journey up the trail."

Then looking at the others and each other, Yufei silently asks Yufeng,

(How long will we be gone?)

Yufeng shrugs and shakes her head.

(I sense it may be a long trip.)

Then sadly she looks around, thinking it may be the last time she will be in their home.

Only Panda is privy to their silent conversation ... but she knows what she must do and starts to make a list of things to bring for herself and LF.

.

12 To Lhasa

"When you change the way you look at things,
the things you look at change."
Max Planck

In town, they purchase a horse for Gugu and also two wicker saddle baskets for Panda's smaller horse ... one for LF to sleep and ride ... the other for her food, medicines, and other supplies.

Yufeng already has a smaller version of her medical kit that rides in packs on either side of her medical pack horse.

Near the entrance to the canyon lives a family that they are more close to, and they tell them of their trip (but not revealing their destination) and ask them to watch after things while they are gone ... this is the only family that they regularly allow into their inner sanctum (*the laughing spirits canyon*) ... but even they only enter when invited.

In the few days of preparation, Chen Er gets Yufei and Yufeng caught up on the news from the Chinese capital, Quanzhou, and Wuyi ... after the debacle of Minister Han's invasion, things have been restored to normal and the Song empire is prospering.

Although they are aware of the Mongol invasion of the Xi Xia and forays against the Jin ... the Mongol threat seems too distant for most people to concern themselves.

As they prepare for the journey, Chen Er pulls Yufei aside one day and asks,

"This Tibetan monk ... Gugu ... he *seems* familiar ... did I meet him before somewhere?"

"I don't know ... did you?"

"I mean did we meet him together somewhere ... before?"

"Him?" glancing with his eyes at Gugu, "I don't think so. I never saw that man before he came here."

"Then how did he become a close member of your family? You are not a sociably inclusive person."

"What? I'm very sociable ... I'm offended." Yufei motions with his eyes to Yufeng to rescue him. She understands and comes to ask Chen Er questions about her family.

"Chen Er, tell me again how's my sister doing? Any more babies? How's my mother? How's the tea business?"

Yufeng drags Chen Er away as he relates all the news.

Gugu and Panda walk up to Yufei. Yufei tells them.

"Maybe it's best if we keep your past identity a secret ... some people wouldn't understand."

The monk nods and they look at Panda.

"Panda, maybe you don't tell other people who this monk was before ... it'll be our secret ... okay?"

"Okay Baba ... what about LF?"

"Yufei smiles, "Well ... LF is okay, I think she probably already knows, and you are the only one that speaks her language."

Panda has a million questions for her father ...

"What's it like in Lhasa? Is it a big city? Are there many people? Do they have animals and temples for animals, and ..."

Yufei smiles and looks at Dorjie,

"Maybe you should ask Princess Dorjie ... she lived there all her life."

"Okay" she says and runs off to find Princess Dorjie.

Yufei turns to Gugu.

"What do you know about Lhasa?"

Gugu smiles, "Everything."

"How does that work? Accessing this library of universal knowledge?"

"Let's go talk over there." pointing to the stores of fodder near the stable.

***

Motioning with his hand, Gugu says,

"It's a lot like that fodder ... when the horses need food, they walk over here and eat ... they don't think .... And you can't push them to eat ... it's instinct."

"*Our brains are just a device, to help us navigate this illusion* ... a device, like reins to guide your horse, so we can use these things to gain experiences, learn wisdom ... and evolve."

"In this universe, *conscious spirits* provide the *illusion of seemingly real experiences* (reality). Even the people are illusions... who have illusionary experiences ... *that feel real*."

"The secret is to simply *know* what you want ... *without thinking* ... it's *the knowing* ... not some piece of knowledge."

"Sankara said, "*One becomes brahman simply by knowing brahman*."

Yufei asks,

"Is it like what the Indians call *moksa*?"

"No ... *mokṣa* appears to be a *future* attainment rather than a recognition of present reality. This false premise lures one into action with the intent to gain or become *brahman*, but *one cannot attain again what one has already attained*."

"Action is superfluous to accomplish an already accomplished fact."

"In fact, the more one attempts to gain, reach, or experience liberation while mistakenly presupposing its distance, the further it recedes like running after the horizon."

"It's the same about accessing the universal wisdom ... you don't seek ... *seeking is just illusions in your mind ... discerning clearly beyond the illusion is the challenge* ... just follow your instincts, enter the void, and the information you need will come to you."

"Automatically?"

"Kind of. It's different for everyone ... for me it is like the hidden library we had at the Wuyi academy ... for you it may be the same or that lost Tang library or some similar *imaginary library*."

"And the answers I may seek?"

"You don't have to search for it ... whatever answers you need, that information will come to you."

"Just appear ... in the air ... before me?"

The monk nods.

"In your mind ..."

"I don't understand ..."

"Okay, let me give you an example ... before I came here, I wanted to know where you were and what were the conditions here."

"I pondered this and then meditated and went into the void. Inside the void, our old hidden library appeared, and I floated to my old desk where there was a picture book open. As I scanned the pages, I could see everything."

"Wait ... you could see us in a picture book? Not reading words?"

"I could see you ... it was like a picture book ... with moving images."

Yufei's head jolts up and he confronts Gugu.

"What? You saw real life images ... in a book?"

"Yes ... the book was different ... there were no words printed on the pages ... just images."

Yufei shakes his head in amazement.

"Sounds impossible."

Meanwhile Panda is asking Princess Dorjie a thousand questions ... finally Yufeng comes to her rescue.

"Panda ... relax ... we have a long journey ahead, there will be plenty of time for the Princess to tell you all about Lhasa ..."

The Princess smiles and confides in Panda.

"And I have a great adventure tale to tell you ... the greatest adventure legend of our people ... The Epic of King Gesar!"

Panda is very excited and starts to ask a hundred questions about King Gesar ...

"Who was King Gesar? Where did he ..."

The two older women smile at each other and roll their eyes.

13 On the trail with King Gesar

Finally, after a few days, everything is ready for an early morning start. The horses are loaded, everyone is mounted, even LF is in her wicker basket peeking out ... inside, with her, is a cricket friend in a small cage also.

For the initial part, through the village to the foothills, they ride two abreast ... Yufei and Gugu in the lead and the three females and two pack horses following ... and Chen following up the rear ... resembling a wolf pack journeying across the steppes.

In and through the village they keep relatively silent as to not draw too much attention ... it is still dark because the mountains make for a late sunrise in the valleys. When they get past the village and approach the foothills, the sun's rays warm them and illuminate the colors of the trees of the beautiful mountains and countryside.

Dorjie says to Yufeng,

"You are fortunate to live in a peaceful beautiful valley like this ..."

"What about your life Princess? What places have you lived?"

"Mostly in my family's palaces in the city, Lhasa, or out in lavish tents on the high plateau grasslands."

Panda asks, "What does your palace look like?"

Dorjie starts to say.

"You were ..." but then remembering the circumstances of her first visit, she stops and changes.

"It's beautiful ... with many rooms and servants."

"What is a servant?"

"It's someone who lives and works in the palace to help the royal family."

"Is that where King Gesar lives?"

"Haha ... no, King Gesar lived a long time ago ..."

And so, the journey up the tea-horse trail became a journey back in time ... many hundreds of years ago ... in the eastern area of Tibet ... in the kingdom called Ling, which bordered on the kingdom of Hor.

Princess Dorjie starts to sing about Gesar but pauses.

"Why are you singing aunty?"

"Because the legend of Gesar is not written down ... it is really a long ballad, sung by inspired singers ... singers who sing from a deep memory pool."

"Will you sing the whole epic?'

"Haha ... no Panda ... I am not qualified ... but I will tell you the story ... just as I was taught when I was your age ... there are three parts .... The first part follows the creation of the world and then there was a bad period where bad spirits and demons took over the world. To fix this the gods decided to send a superhuman warrior to defeat the bad spirits and demons. His Tibetan name was *don grub*, but everyone knows him as Gesar."

"Was he a good child ... like me?"

Dorjie laughs and shakes her head, "No ... in fact, he was a naughty boy ... always getting into fights and trouble. In fact, he was so wild, that he and his mother were banished from their tribe."

"What happened ... was his mother sad?"

"At first she was angry at him ... but he consoled her and told her not to worry, that one of his uncles had told him that someday he would be king."

"Where did they go?"

"They went north into a wilderness near the headwaters of the great Yellow River, where they hunted small game. The mother made clothes from the skins and even a hat for Gesar with antelope horns."

"And when Gesar was about 12 or 13 years old, the tribe had a horse race contest in Ling ... and they announced that the winner would be the new king and get to marry the beautiful daughter of a neighboring tribe, *Brug mo*."

"What happened? Did he win the race?"

"Yes ... and he took the title *Gesar* and married the beautiful *Brug mo*."

"And did they live happily ever after?" Panda laughs "That's how Mama's stories always end."

Dorjie shakes her head, "Sadly it didn't work that way ... on his first campaign as king he fought against a terrible demon but after killing the demon, the demon's wife put a spell on Gesar, and he forgot everything for six years!"

"Everything ... even his mother and his wife?"

"Everything! And what was worse was that while he was away, the evil king of Hor kidnapped Gesar's beautiful wife."

They are now on the narrow mountain trail and Panda is riding ahead of Princess Dorjie. Panda keeps turning in her saddle, looking back over her shoulder at Dorjie.

"Really? What happened to her?"

Yufeng calls out to her,

"Panda! Watch where you are riding! This trail is very dangerous."

Panda turns around quickly, "Sorry Mama."

Dorjie says, "Maybe we should wait until we get past this narrow part and camp for the night."

Yufeng quickly agrees, "Yes ... that might be best."

So, for the rest of that day, they ride cautiously with Panda anticipating the continuation of the story in the evening.

Yufeng is happier too as she remembers the rockfall accident that she suffered on the trail the first time. Fortunately, the crickets aren't singing ... *not yet* anyway.

After a full day of riding up the narrow trail, they come to an open wooded grove where travelers have camped before. They decide to camp there for the night.

Panda is happy for several reasons. First LF can run around, climb a few trees, and fly around a little ... and she hopes Princess Dorjie will renew her story of Gesar.

***

While the others make camp, Yufei talks to Chen and Yufeng ... then he climbs up a precipice and looks back down the trail with his telescope. Seeing and sensing that no one has followed them, he climbs down and rejoins the campers getting ready to eat.

Chen and Yufeng look over to him, but he casually shakes his head to reassure them ... but inside, he senses a distant darkness stalking their journey.

He would be even more concerned if he knew what was happening back at their home. The night after they left, a second band of assassins raided the compound but found nothing ... except the decomposing bodies of their companions. Then they went to the family at the head of the canyon, and upon learning that they had all left, they killed them all, including their children ... venting their anger against the innocent and defenseless.

14 Gesar retrieves his wife

After they hobbled the horses and fixed the camp for the night, they cooked a light dinner with dried game, breads, and vegetables they brought with them. Then they sit around the campfire.

Panda excitedly retells parts of the story of Gesar to her father who pretends to hear it for the first time.

Yufei asks, "And then what?"

Panda crooks her head, looks at Princess Dorjie.

Princess Dorjie smiles.

"Well, I guess we are safe here ... and I can continue ... where was I?" pretending forgetfulness.

Panda quickly reminds her, "Gesar has lost his memory and the evil king of Hor has captured his wife, the beautiful Brug Mo."

"Ah ... yes ... when Gesar recovers his memory, he uses magic to enter the king of Hor's palace, kills the king, and saves his wife."

"Then what?"

"His life is full of adventures and campaigns against the four enemy kings with dozens of fortresses... in order to unite all the people on the high Tibetan plateau."

"The people sing the song and there are many poems and other stories from this one ancient legend ... one of my favorite stanzas goes something like this ..."

When a raindrop falls into a still pond,
It dissolves and disappears on its own.
As though nothing has happened.
But the same raindrop can fall into the same pond,
And ripples radiate out over the water.

[*Little did Dorjie realize it was the same poem Qime told Scorpion in the ice cave that fateful night.*]

"What's the meaning, Dorjie?"

"Panda ... two people may see the same event in different ways ... Gesar and his wife, Brug Mo, saw their experience one way, some others saw it another way."

Gugu tries to explain to Panda.

"Panda, you are not your body. And once you know that you are not the body, your life changes completely. When you are not the body, then you have a different perception of life. The center is different. Now you exist in the world as a conscious spirit, not as a body. If you exist as a body, then your world is of desire, greed, anger, etc. You have created a false world around you ... a body-centric world. Gesar and his wife did not follow that path of blame and guilt."

"And once they knew they were not the body, that world disappeared. A different world arose which was non-physical and spiritual. The center was shifted, not in the body anymore ... in the consciousness. That is the message of the story."

Panda is confused and looks to her mother,

"Mama, how do you know if you are seeing things the same as baba?"

"You need to look inside ..." but then she stops suddenly as an image appears.

"What is it?" Yufei asks.

"Nothing ... nothing ..."

Yufei ponders this and the others wonder if she senses storm clouds just on the other side of the protective mountains.

***

Later, when they are covering Panda up with furs for the night, Panda looks at her father and asks,

"Baba, have you fought demons before?"

Yufei looks at Yufeng, who wrinkles her lips and rolls her head and smiles.

"Panda, your baba and I have killed many demons ... it is our duty ... and even Princess Dorjie killed an evil demon at the Song emperor's palace!"

Panda's eyes go wide and turns to Princess Dorjie,

"Really ... was it a big demon with fire coming out of its mouth?"

Dorjie laughs, "No, Panda, demons all look different ... this demon at the palace was a black witch ... you must be careful of these, because they have dark powers."

Gugu, who understands more than the others, looks at Panda and hopes she can remember these lessons.

As they walk to their sleeping furs, Dorjie asks Yufeng,

"Is she ready for all this?"

Yufeng shakes her head,

"Are any of us ever ready?" she pauses, then continuing,

"She is stronger than I was at her age ... sometimes she travels even deeper than Yufei ..."

"We are all tested in our own ways ... once when I was younger, I wandered out on the desert and a black sandstorm came up suddenly ... in times like that, you find your inner strength."

Yufeng nods,

"Good night, Princess."

"Good night Yufeng."

***

Riding carefully and slowly, it takes the group several days to ride up through the mountain passes.

One day, just before the last pass, they pass a crevice in the mountain wall. Yufei stops his horse and seems distant. Yufeng rides closer and asks him,

"What is it? Do you sense danger?"

"No ... something else."

He looks around and spots the crevice. He dismounts and hands the reins to Yufeng.

"Hold these a minute."

As he walks to the crevice, the others just watch. He enters the small defile and looks around. There is little to see ... scraps of flotsam, burned ashes, nothing remaining of what happened there years earlier. But as he turns to walk out ... he sees it. On the rock wall is an etched image of the Enso.

He drops to his knees as tears fill his eyes. His body shudders, but he doesn't have a seizure ... just an overwhelming sadness overcomes him. Yufeng dismounts and hands the two reins to Chen Er.

"You and the others wait here ... don't come in there."

She rushes to him ... still not knowing what is wrong. She puts her arms around him and waits ... finally he points to the wall etching and she understands ... this is where his father and Qime sheltered that fateful night during the late blizzard.

Panda can sense the tremendous sadness in her father and without any other concern, leaps from her horse ... luckily Gugu is close and catches her reins. She rushes to her father, and even without being told, knows what has happened.

"Baba don't cry ... YeYe and Aiyi are fine ..."

Yufeng looks at her, "How do you know?"

"They came to me last night ... and just now as I sat on my horse, they told me to tell you not to be sad."

This doesn't stop Yufei's tears, but the sadness starts to dissipate ... Yufeng holds Panda's hand, and they stand up.

Yufei takes out his killing knife and carves an Enso next to his father's, then he holds out the knife to Panda, who does the same ... only with a dot in the center.

Yufeng meanwhile has placed several mani stones in a pile near the crevice.

Finally, with a sharp rock, Yufeng consecrates the ground with a circle.

And then they leave.

And in the ether, two spirits watch and smile.

Everything happens for a reason ... every thread is connected to another ... and then another ...

As they ride, Yufei keeps thinking back to the Enso that his father had carved into the rock.

***

(There was something different about it ... what was it Gugu said?)

To communicate with the Consciousness, we must use our non-physical senses ... like a mystic merging with the universe.

15 Lhasa and the Royal Palace

They ride over the last pass, down the backside foothills, through several villages, across two rivers, and, a week later, arrive in Lhasa ... to a festive welcome by Dorjie's parents and royal officials. Panda is also feted as a royal princess and is in awe of all the luxuries in the palaces.

Yufei, Yufeng, and Panda (and LF) are given their own guest palace in the compound and Chen Er has his own guest palace nearby also.

Panda is renamed the *Laughing Princess of the Flying Animals*.

At that time, most of the resident monks are of the Yellow Hat Sect and they look strangely at Gugu, who avoids all their inquiries.

The first days are spent largely getting to know the palace grounds and enjoying various welcome banquets. The food and drinks are all new to them and they eat and drink sparingly ... that is, everyone except Panda and Gugu who can't seem to eat enough.

The King and Queen and other royals (Dorjie's brothers, sisters, nieces, and nephews) are all relieved to see their favorite princess safely home ... although a bit curious about her Chinese *companion*.

Princess Dorjie and Chen Er talk to the Chief Advisor one day and introduce Chen Er ... his fleet of seafaring ships, his illustrious family, his father, Lord Chen, who is now one of the most influential ministers in the Song government, etc.,

This Chief Advisor, Tsonga Ru, then privately informs and assures the royals and relatives so as to provide Dorjie and Chen Er some degree of privacy.

Like any (*former*) kingdom with a large ruling family, there are princely rivalries, but on the whole most of the royals' love Princess Dorjie because she has been universally unselfish to all of them and never seeks position or power.

Remarking on this one evening over dinner, Chen Er observes.

"It's strange but in all the ancient writings, we read of the dark deeds of this person and that person ... as though that is what determines history. They tell of the strongest taking what they want and destroying the rest."

Yufeng nods and adds, "Yes ... caring for others does not seem to deserve chronicles."

Gugu smiles and says something strange, "Maybe ..."

Yufei turns to ask Dorjie,

"Princess ... in Lhasa these days, what is the current spiritual beliefs about the universe and existence?"

She laughs, "It is beyond me. You will have to ask our spiritual leaders ... I can have our Chief Religious Minister arrange some interviews with the spiritual leaders of the different sects ... would you like that?"

Yufei smiles and say, "Yes ... I would."

Then, the Princess turns to Yufeng and asks, "You too?"

Yufeng laughs, "No, no ... that is my husband's passion ... mine is medicine ... maybe I could talk to your top healers about their practices?"

"It's done ... and little Panda ... what do you want to see in Lhasa?"

Panda doesn't pause to think, just shouts, "Everything!"

They all laugh and Chen Er says, "I'm with Panda!"

Gugu says, "I'll go with Yufei."

Princes Dorjie says, "Good ... and I'll go with Panda too." (*and my wandering-eyed lover*)

Then looking at Chen Er, the Princess adds with a smile,

"So, maybe we should retire early tonight."

The adults catch the silent message and know it's time for them to retire also.

***

The next day, Panda and LF are the first one at breakfast, while Yufei and Yufeng are still practicing their yoga. Chen Er is there but the others haven't arrived ... so it is just him, Panda, LF, and a mountain of food.

Chen Er looks at Panda and then the mountain of food and asks,

"I'll eat half and you eat half ... okay?"

Panda laughs, "Okay!"

While they are devouring the mountain of food, the others start to roll in to join them. When she sees her mother, Panda shouts,

"Mama look! ...It's all so delicious!"

Surveying the lavish spread of food, Yufeng smiles and asks,

"What should I try first?"

Panda hands her a fried biscuit, "Try this ... but dip it in that sauce first ... so delicious."

"Okay." Yufeng grabs it, dips it in the sauce and eats it ... but then her face changes ... and turning to Yufei, warns him, as her eyes start to water.

"Oh ... Yufei be careful ... the sauce is a little spicy."

Chen Er laughs, "Your little princess can eat the spiciest foods ... some of the sauces bring tears to my eyes too, but she just enjoys them all."

Yufeng explains, "She immediately senses the properties of the ingredients, and then her body assimilates to the spices."

(*Just as she can sense inside an animal or person.*)

The last person to arrive is Princes Dorjie, who apparently has already eaten. With her are two older men ... ministers apparently ... one obviously a spiritual person by his Buddhist robes and the other an elderly scholar.

"So, are we all ready for our adventures?" They all nod, and Panda shouts,

"Ready!"

Dorjie introduces the scholar to Yufeng, "Yufeng, this is Gonpo, the court physician ... he is available to you for the entire day ... he has a plan to show you his clinic, his pharmacy and laboratory."

Yufeng bows to the man, "Master ... I am your humble student."

The elder physician leads her away.

Next Dorjie introduces the Tibetan monk to Yufei, "Yufei this is Sakiya, he is a new spiritual minister. He will be your spiritual guide today."

The monk offers the traditional extended palm greeting ... Yufei and Gugu return the gesture. Then those two walk off, leaving just Chen Er, Dorjie and Panda.

Dorjie looks at the two and asks,

Are you ready to explore the wonders of my city?"

Panda shouts, "Ready!" and Chen Er and Dorjie smile.

16 Tibetan Medicine

Yufeng and Royal Physician Gonpo stroll through the palace and come to his clinic and workshop. Inside, there are many essential equipment similar to a traditional clinic, pharmacy, and laboratory in China or India. Distilling equipment, stoves, small vials, and endless small drawers containing herbs from many regions ... not just Tibet.

"Go ahead, take a look." he says, waving his hand in a sweeping gesture. As they walk, Yufeng feels an open sincere spirit inside this older man, and she feels comfortable talking with him.

"What epidemics do you have here in the mountains?"

"Not many ... I think the air and altitude is not conducive to their spreading. We have had smallpox and some lesser diseases. Our main ailments here concern the air element ... breathing ... the lungs can't get enough air energy ... and the heart has problems pumping more blood."

"Your historical knowledge base is ... Tibetan?"

"At first it came from the ancient people and their knowledge of local plants, animal parts, and waters which helped people ... and this knowledge was passed down. Have you been to Mt Kailash?"

This startles Yufeng, but she recovers quickly and says, "Yes, several years ago, why?"

"That area in the west, what is now the Guge Kingdom, was the home of our most ancient people, called the Xiang Xiong (Zhangzhung) ... they are the ancestors of all Tibetans. Over time, they started to record their medical knowledge and these books were periodically updated and handed down."

Gonpo looks through some rolled up books in his shelves, finds one, blows the dust off and unrolls it.

"This is from the time of the first Tibetan king ..." he ponders, then continues,

"Over 1400 years ago ... (pointing in the text) ... in this physical realm there are six points of concern ... spirits, interfering spirits, mountain dwelling spirits, divisive spells, poisons ... and wild yaks!" he finishes ... laughing.

"According to their healing advice ... most important is a balanced diet, then if there are internal injuries, molten butter can repair wounds to the blood vessels ..."

Going to another shelf he sweeps his hand at several more shelves of books.

"During the reign of one of our great kings, Songtsen Gampo, medical scholars were invited from three different countries to introduce their medical systems ... the Persian Greek-Moslem Unami system, the Indian Ayurveda (and Siddhi) system, and the Chinese Classical Traditional medicine systems."

Yufeng asks, "Which system did they prefer?"

"Well, even though the Chinese Princess Wencheng (Songtsen Gampo's wife) brought Chinese physicians, the Greek system was most like the ancient Bon ... they both focus on the 3 main causes of diseases ...bile, phlegm, and blood disorders ... also pulse diagnosis and urine analysis were important."

"But with the spread of Buddhism ... the Indian system gained the most prominence while retaining our ancient Tibetan Bon practices. A later king invited two prominent Indian physicians to move to Tibet, which they did and passed their knowledge to their sons and grandsons, who became royal physicians."

Yufeng asks, "Are you related to them?"

"No, no, no ... that was too long ago, and many political upheavals have changed our country since then."

Yufeng tries to move past the history, "What do you use now?"

Gonpo smiles, "I thought you would never ask ..." he strides to his desk and opens several newly prepared texts.

"I call this my Sowa-Rigpa system ... it combines the best of all the systems ... lists of the most common symptoms, diagnosis techniques like urinalysis and pulse, natural herbal medicines and physical therapies like acupuncture and moxibustion."

"What do you use as the basis for your system?"

"Mostly I used the 4 tantras, which is a native Tibetan system including Indian, Chinese and Greco-Persian traditions ... simply ... it's focus is to keep the body's humors in balance ... the lungs, bile and phlegm."

"What are the 4 tantras?"

"It's a little long to describe ... the first tantra is called the Root Tantra ..."

***

This discussion lasts several hours but Yufeng is not bored as she mentally compares it to her vast medical knowledge acquired from her travels, her own experiences, and her readings. Many of the treatments are the same or a little different, giving her some new ideas for treatments.

"Tell me about your herbal treatments."

"Okay, come to my pharmaceutical area ... depending on the symptoms and the individual, I will usually prescribe 2 or 3 herbs ... but in special cases, up to over 100 herbs per formulation. As you know the health of the human body is based upon the balance of the five elements ... earth, water, fire, air, and space ... and the three humors (the lungs, bile, and phlegm)."

"How do you diagnose a patient?' she asks.

"I think most of the systems we studied are similar ... first we interview the patient and observe him or her ... taking into account their physical condition, living conditions and medical history."

"Then we will examine the urine, analyze it and get a better understanding of the nature of the illness to help with our diagnosis."

"Then we will conduct a 12-pulse diagnosis ... six from each wrist ... which will help clarify any problems in the internal organs ... finally we will inspect the tongue, the eyes, and any sensitive pressure points on the body."

"When this is all completed, I will formulate the medicines and treatments ..."

"Is that it?"

"Oh ... there is one more thing ... Tibetan physicians strongly believe that the mind affects the physical health of patients ... and can be the primary causes of diseases."

"The mind?"

"Yes ... the mind is connected to matter and matter is energy ... it is all inter-connected. Every illness has a cause. So, the key is to find the cause, isolate it, and help heal the patient."

Yufeng considers his last words ...

Every illness has a cause...

On the way back to her quarters, Yufeng strolls casually down the street, looking at the street peddlers. One particular peddler catches her attention ... a peddler with an elaborate medicine cart. She talks to the "street physician" for several minutes and inspects his medicine cart ... comparing it to her cart at home, this one is more elaborate and better organized, with folding out cabinets, and myriad smaller labeled drawers for herbs and medicines. One folding shelf door has multiple gourds hanging on hooks ... the opposite door has small shelves, with a horizontal rod to hold small vials from falling out. The peddler slides a desk top out as a table to mix decoctions in an array of cups and saucers. The ends of the cart open up too, to expose additional drawers and door shelves.

Yufeng asks him, "Where did you get this beautiful cart?"

The man grins and says, "I made it ... myself."

Yufeng senses the lie and asks, "Good, I'll provide the materials and engage you to build me one like it, at the *royal compound*."

Caught in his lie, and fearing the royals, the man quickly changes his story, "Well, actually my *Shifu* (master) made it years ago and when he retired, he gave it to me."

"Your master ... was he a trained physician?"

The man nods.

Yufeng takes out some silver, "I'd like to meet him."

The man's eyes open wide at the silver and starts closing the cart up, "Yes ... master ... we can go right now ... it is not too far."

Yufeng puts the silver back in her pocket and smiles as a plan starts to evolve in her mind. Later she will recount everything to Yufei.

Maybe because her mind is focused on the medicine cart, she is temporarily unaware that other eyes are following her in the streets.

17 Tibetan Buddhism

That night Yufei and Yufeng are discussing each other's adventures ... Panda is spinning a toy prayer wheel which occupies LF's undivided attention ... back and forth ... back and forth ...

Yufeng smiles at Yufei and says, "Your turn ..."

Yufei shakes his head as though clearing out the cobwebs.

"Where to start? Maybe back to the Bon, like Qime explained to us years ago."

"Okay ..." and he tells the stories he had been told ...

The ancient Bon were like our old folk religions, seeing the hand of the gods everywhere ... then they were exposed to Buddhism in the 7th century when King Songtsen Gampo married two Buddhist women, Princess Wencheng from China, and Princess Bhrikuti Devi from Nepal. Towards the end of the 8th century, another King, Trisong Detsen, invited two Buddhist masters from India to Tibet, one was the mystic Padmasambhava, and the other was called, Shantarakshita.

Master Shantarakshita built the first monastery in Tibet, while master Padmasambhava used his power to dispel the *dark forces* preventing the spread of Buddhism.

Yufeng stops him.

"What powers? Did they say?"

Yufei shakes his head.

"They didn't know ... or wouldn't say. I met an impressive young monk, my age, who, I could sense, was enlightened ... his name was Sakya Pandita, of the Grey Earth school, but then, when I started talking with him, he was called away."

"Did Gugu know?"

"I don't think he did ... I think Gugu hasn't searched for the same things that I am."

"Panda, come here."

Panda walks over to them.

"Tell baba, what you told me in the market."

"I saw a lot of dark beings there."

Yufei is instantly alert.

"What happened."

'Nothing ... they seem to be waiting for someone or something."

"Did they see you?"

"No ... I cloaked myself and the others."

Yufei looks at Yufeng who shrugs her shoulders, rolls her head, and stifles a laugh.

"Baba ... why do you look surprised?"

"Where did you learn that?"

"Mama taught me."

Now it is Yufeng's turn to be surprised as Yufei stifles his laughter,

"Of course ... *mama* taught you."

Yufeng asks Panda,

"Panda, when did I teach you that?"

"Do you remember that market day, when you probed grannie Flo, the dried red mushroom seller?"

Yufeng thinks back several months.

"Yes, but I didn't find anything wrong with her."

Panda looks down and says softly,

"She died two days later."

Yufeng is surprised.

"What? What happened?"

"Before you checked her, I probed her inside ... the dark infections had spread all over her inner organs ... she was going to die, but she didn't want you or her family to know."

"What did you do?"

"I visualized healthy organs inside her ... covering the dark ones ... the things you didn't see."

Yufeng starts to scold her, but Yufei stops her.

Panda continues,

"She sensed that I did something, and she thanked me ... remember the large bag of dried red mushrooms?"

"Yes, but ..." Yufeng starts to say.

"Mother ... grannie Flo was not afraid of death ... she was afraid of causing problems for her children and grandchildren."

Yufei nods and tells Panda,

"You did the right thing ... *many times, people aren't afraid of death, but something else* ... now explain to us again how you blocked the dark forces in the market today."

"Okay ... it's not hard ... first ..."

***

Later Yufei and Yufeng talk to the others about what Panda had told them.

Chen says,

"I don't like waiting for someone to attack me ... what do you suggest?"

Yufei tells them,

"You and Dorjie and Panda tour the city like before ... trying to flush out these threats. Yufeng and I will watch sight unseen. If you sense them, signal us, or if we see them, we'll follow them to their hideout."

"At first we'll just watch them and later determine what to do next."

"Sounds good ... Dorjie and I will just act normal ..."

Yufei laughs,

"Yeah ... we know, Tibetan Princess and a normal Pirate captain out for a stroll ... haha."

***

Later Yufei resumes his narrative to Yufeng about the religious beliefs. Padmasambhava (Guru Rinpoche) combined the teachings of tantric Buddhism with the local Bon religion and founded Tibetan Buddhism. He translated numerous Buddhist scriptures into Tibetan. This led to the establishment of the first school of Tibetan Buddhism – Nyingma (Red Hats). Now there are Three Major Sects and several minor ones:

"The Red Hat sect (Nyingma) is the oldest ... they combine Indian Tantric practices with the native Bon beliefs. It was the most popular school until the 11th century when other schools became popular. What I like about the Red Hats is that they look to the inner self for answers, rather than doctrines. There is also a sub-sect of this school called the Black Hats (Kagyu Karma), which passes leadership through reincarnation."

Yufeng stops him again,

"It just seems that the Buddha's simple message gets more complicated and more ritualized as time passed."

Yufei nods, "Yes."

"Did you talk to any truly enlightened masters?"

"Yes ... but ..."

She waits as he gathers his thoughts.

"The few enlightened masters seem to be involved in elaborate rituals which obscure a simple pathway to enlightenment."

"Do you think they do that on purpose ... to make it complicated in order to keep their followers engaged?"

"I don't know ... and I don't understand ... why make awakening to enlightenment difficult ... shouldn't they make it simpler ... to get more people on the pathway?"

Panda looks up and says, "Mama ... today I saw red hats and black hats and white hates and Princess Dorjie told me about the different royal families ... it was complicated too."

Yufeng smiles, "Maybe that's why they make it complicated ..."

"Why?"

"To make others believe that they, and only they, know the pathway to bliss."

"My way is better than your way?"

Yufeng smiles.

"One abbot said ... my way was handed down from the Buddha to our original founder."

"He spoke to Buddha?"

"Kind of ... through a reincarnated Buddha." he smiles, then continues.

"The White Hat sect (*Kagyupa*) rose in the 11th century when a Tibetan named Marpa went to India to learn Buddhism under Master Naropa. He then spread his teachings to his student, Milarepa. Then, in the 12th century, Milarepa's student Gampopa, founded the White Hat Sect. This school stresses the oral communication of knowledge from teacher to the student, rather than written doctrines. It also stresses the more severe practices of hatha yoga. The central teaching is the "great seal" (Maha mudra), which is a realization of emptiness, freedom from samsara, and the inseparability of these two. The basic practice of Maha Mudra is "dwelling in peace," much like the Chinese Chan and Japanese Zen."

"The smallest school of Tibetan Buddhism currently is the Gray Earth sect (*Sakyapa*), which was founded by Sakya Kunga Nyingpo with its main monastery, Sagya Monastery in southern Tibet. The central teachings of the Sakyapa School are based on the Path and Goal, systematic tantrism, and Buddhist logic. It creates a balance between sutra study and meditation. ... the Sakyapa Sect emerged in the 11th and 12th centuries at monasteries where Indian Buddhist texts were being studied and translated into Tibetan. Its most well-known figure is a monk called Kunga Pandita, who is called Sakya Pandita ... he was the abbot I was talking to, before he was called away."

Yufeng holds up her hand again to stop Yufei's monologue.

"So, there are elements of Buddhism and the Bon in all of them?"

"Kind of ... many of the Buddhist practices we saw in China and in India are also in the Tibetan schools ... calm meditation (*shamatha*), insight (*vipassna*), the Mahayana, the bodhisattva vow, mind training methods to awaken compassion (*lojong*) ... also the Vajrayana practices, sacred syllables and verses (*mantras*), sacred hand gestures (*mudras*), and yogic discipline."

"And just as in China there are two schools of the Chan Buddhism, here there are four ... or more."

"More?"

"There are a lot of hidden monasteries in the mountains, with their own believers."

"Are they all enlightened and benevolent?"

Yufei's face drops a bit. Yufeng presses the question.

"What is it?"

"When I ask those probing questions, I often get evasive answers as though there is something they cannot discuss."

"Cannot discuss?"

"I think they have been instructed not to discuss."

Yufeng looks at him.

"Why?"

"I don't know, I need to ask Gugu or maybe Princess Dorjie."

"Okay"

***

18 Theory of Emptiness from the Dalai Lama

Tibetan Buddhist philosophy as summarized by the Dalai Lama, in his book, *The Universe in a Single Atom.*

One of the principal motives underlying scientific and philosophical inquiry into the basic constituents of matter is to find matter's irreducible building block. This is true not only of ancient Indian philosophy and modern physics but also of the ancient Greek scientist, such as the atomists. Effectively, this is a quest for the ultimate nature of reality, however one may define it. Buddhist thought argues on logical grounds that this search is misguided. *Buddhism rejects any notion of independent objective reality.*

In the Buddhist philosophical world, the concept of *time* as relative is not alien. Apart from the temporal phenomena upon which we construct the concept of time, there is no real time that is somehow the grand vessel in which things and events occur, an absolute that has an existence of its own. *Time has been relative in the Buddhist philosophical tradition for nearly 2000 years.*

In Tibet there were myths of creation that originated in the pre-Buddhist religion of Bon. A central theme of these myths is the bringing of order out of chaos, light out of darkness, day out of night, existence out of nothingness. These acts were affected by a transcendent being, *who created everything out of pure potential.*

The Kalachakra system of Nagarjuna presents space not as a total nothingness, *but as a medium of empty space particles.* Space, with its empty *particles (non-physical)*, is the basis for the whole process. *These non-physical particles preceded the Big Bang ... (similar to the quantum vacuum).* The Kalachakra texts *claim that prior to its formation, any particular universe remains* in a state of emptiness. *Where all material elements exist in the form of potentiality as space particles.* At a certain point, when the karmic propensities of the sentient beings who are likely to evolve in this particular universe ripen, the space particles and other elements come together to form the physical universe.

Inherent in this theory is the role of consciousness *...that the formation of the universe is intimately connected with the karmic propensities of sentient beings.* In contemporary terms it means our planet evolved in such a way that it could support the evolution of sentient beings in the forms of myriad of species that exist today on the earth.

19 Lhasa and more ...

The next day, as they walk around the Barkhor market district, in the old part of the city near the Jokhang Temple, with its narrow streets and public square, Panda asks Dorjie,

"Princess. What does *Lhasa* mean?"

"The Place of Gods" Dorjie says.

Panda looks at Chen Er who shakes his head slightly (*don't go there*)

They walk down the busy alleys of Lhasa, merchants hawking their goods, and travelers weaving around each other.

Panda sees a shadow puppet show (Pi Ying Xi) ... which gives her an idea (*hmm ... maybe ... I need to tell mama ... or better, baba.*)

There is a lantern behind the puppeteers, who hold two different cutouts, which they move back and forth before the screen. The spectators, on the other side, see only the shadows acting out the scene.

Chen Er has another thought ... (*not too different from this world ... what was it Su Dongpu wrote? Oh ... I remember ...*

***

I dance alone with my shadow,
* As if in another world.*

***

Much later Yufei would compare these puppet shows with Socrates' philosophic story of the cave people, whose worldview was the shadows reflected on the cave wall by the campfire.

Panda sees some thangkas, colorful woven picturesque hangings, and asks Dorjie what they represent.

"This one is about Chenrezig, the bodhisattva of compassion and with her is Tara, they are two peaceful bodhisattva forms."

The figures are richly dressed in red and blue silks and jewels, symbolizing all the qualities of enlightenment, and their crowns are adorned with five gems, symbolizing the fact they transformed five negative mental afflictions into five types of wisdom.

Looking at another one, she continues,

"This one is Vajrayogini, she is both peaceful and vengeful, and wears jewelry and carries a cup made of human bone. She is the embodiment of absolute wisdom."

Having overcome the fear of death,
she bears the symbols of death as ornaments.

"Her blade held aloft represents wisdom that cuts through delusion, and she is depicted trampling a body—the corpse of ego-fixation."

Dorjie tells more about the history of Tibet ... the old kingdom ... but which is now just powerful families with smaller kingdoms. Her family controls the secular aspects of Lhasa and likewise, other families, other parts of Tibet ... but the Buddhist sects are gaining more political power.

As they stroll. Panda senses a dark presence and clutches Dorjie's arm. The Princess senses the darkness too, even though it is cloaked. She pretends to turn to talk to Chen Er and spots a dark witch following them ... Chen Er understands and signals to a rooftop figure ... then they decide to leave.

As they walk back, Panda points at a large temple on a hill and asks Dorjie,

"What's that big place, Dorjie?"

"That's Mount Portola ... it was a meditation retreat for King Songtsen Gampo, who hundreds of years ago built the first palace there in order to greet his bride Princess Wen Cheng from the Tang dynasty of China."

"What are those people doing on the ground?"

"They are perambulating around the Lingkhor ... the sacred path around Lhasa."

"Why aunty Dorjie?"

"They believe it will bring then good fortune."

Panda looks at her uncle Chen, who shrugs.

Panda laughs.

"People have strange beliefs."

The two older ones think the same thing ... *if you only knew.*

Later, back at their compound, they meet over dinner to discuss the day's events.

Dorjie relates about the dark witch who followed them for a while. Yufei reports that he followed the witch to a temple in an obscure alley. After describing the alley, she dispatches one of her guards to investigate.

Yufei also relates how the other day, he sensed something not discussed among the abbots ... about hidden sects in the mountains.

Dorjie says that she has heard rumors also.

Yufei asks,

"Are they just hermits or is there something else?"

Chen Er asks,

"What do you mean?"

"I've been wondering where all these black witches spawn from ... does anyone know?"

They all look at each other. Finally, Dorjie says,

"We never thought about that. We only see them rarely and it's just a solitary witch ... most people avoid them. Why do you ask?"

"Just as there are the three Buddhist schools here teaching compassion and peacefulness and the elders in Kailash and the different Buddhist schools in China ... I'm thinking there must be some dark monasteries teaching the dark arts."

Gugu asks the obvious,

"Where would they be?"

Yufei looks out the window.

"There are many hidden valleys in these high mountains ... what better place to conceal yourself."

Chen Er looks at Dorjie, who says,

"Interesting ... I'll ask my councilors."

The others didn't have any similar occurrences, but they all agree to leave the next day and travel to Mt. Kailash.

Their plan is to go to Mt. Kailash first, meet with the elders and then travel on to Kucha.

Chen is staying behind in Lhasa with Dorjie ...

"We may meet up in Kucha ... or we may not."

"If I'm not there, don't wait for me ... I'll be around Lhasa ... helping Dorjie prepare for any eventualities."

Then he takes Yufei aside,

"While I'm here, I'll follow up on your idea about some hidden dark monastery."

"Good ... but be careful ... they have some powerful powers and will be able to sense you coming."

"How can I avoid that?"

"Come with me ... we need to talk to Panda."

"Panda?"

Back in their rooms, Chen Er, Gugu, and Yufei practice *cloaking* with Panda.

Panda explains to Chen, "First visualize that you are not there ... that the spot you are in now is empty ..."

They practice for several hours until Chen can master the cloaking technique.

20 Darkness Follows

Before dawn, they quietly leave their quarters and ride out the south gate of Lhasa, before turning west ... silently ... but not undetected, as it's hard to cloak the imprints and dust from horse's hoofs, especially if you want to cover a long distance quickly.

The trip to Kailash takes several weeks and they pass through various towns ... with temples, all of which Yufei and Gugu go to inspect ... as Yufeng remarks to Panda,

"Your daddy has never seen a temple he doesn't love."

Dogging them from behind along their trail ... is another small party, dressed in black kaftans, led by a dark-skinned older woman ... but keeping a safe distance for now.

One evening at their campsite, after all of them finished their meals and were sitting around the campfire, Yufei asks Gugu,

"Who do you think they are?"

"They could be anyone ..."

"Take a guess."

"Your old friends, the Khwarazm ... or maybe some new Yunan or Tibetan enemies ... or friends of Lord Kong's witch ... you are accumulating a long list of enemies." he smiles.

Yufeng looks up and turns to Yufei, who asks,

"Why?"

"Why what?"

"Why are they following us *now*?"

"They must feel you are a threat to *their* plans."

"Which plans?"

"To spread darkness over all of the Kara Khitai, Xi Xia and Tibet."

Just then Panda comes running to them with LF on her shoulder.

"What is it?"

Pointing behind her, she says,

"LF says there is danger behind those hills."

"How ..."

"She flew there and saw them ... she can sense their evil also."

Yufeng and Yufei whisper between themselves. Then Yufei tells the others,

"Build up the fire, leave your sleeping blankets on the ground with brush under them to look like your bodies, wrap the horses' hooves, and let's quietly slip out of here."

They all understand. Panda quickly calls LF, who jumps into her basket. In 20 minutes, they are ready ...

"Panda, we need to cloak our departure ... so the four of us will visualize a scene of us still here ... okay?"

She nods.

At first, they walk the horses, then after 15 minutes, they mount and head off in another direction ... seeking rocky outcrops to avoid leaving tracks. Then they stop.

Panda asks,

"Why are we stopping?"

Yufei looks at Gugu,

"Watch over things here, Yufeng and I need to send a message."

Gugu understands and nods. He looks at Panda.

"We'll continue a slow ride ... they will catch up later."

Panda doesn't understand at first what is happening ... only after they have left does Gugu explain. Panda wants to return to help them, but Gugu prevents her, and they ride on.

***

Meanwhile back at their deserted camp, Yufeng and Yufei, still cloaked, watch at a distance as several black clothed attackers stealthily approach. They attack the sleeping dummies and pause once they discover the truth ... that pause was a mistake.

The bolts from Yufei and Yufeng's crossbows strike their marks with deadly accuracy. All the attackers go down.

Yufei and Yufeng come out of hiding to finish them off.

"Spare one that we can interrogate." Yufei says.

"Okay." Yufeng replies as she slices one throat after another.

Finally, they come to the last survivor. They stand over the man who is slowly dying. Yufei steps on the bolt imbedded in the man's chest. The man screams.

"Who sent you." Yufei asks.

The man doesn't talk. Yufeng tells Yufei to stop. He looks at her.

"I remember a technique your father used once."

Yufei smiles and takes out his knife.

"Before I kill you, I will remove your genitals and then your eyes and then your tongue ... and then we will bury you head down in a pool of horse dung."

The man's eyes go wide as Yufei cuts the man's waistband and his trousers drop.

Just as Yufei approaches with the knife, the man starts talking ... not only one hidden dark monastery but several in the high mountains and although they have their separate rituals and missions, they are allied with the Khwarazm ... through the Shah's mother ... and others ... in Arab lands and even in Latin lands.

When he is through spilling all he knows, Yufei ends his misery.

As they ride to catch up with the others, they don't talk much as they both sense that a black ink-like stain has crept into the pure fabric of their pathless Way.

21 Return To Kailash

We are not concerned just with enlightenment,
but rather its utility to transform the human mind.
Enlightenment is simply a device to change your awareness,
so that you can look at the world in a different way.
We are separated from the Source by our minds.

The next few weeks of the journey are uneventful, but it gives Yufei and Gugu time to explore more the eternities.

Gugu says to Yufei,

"Panda made an unique observation about her Enso."

"Oh ... she has made many about mine too ... which one did she share with you?"

"That she saw no line."

"Oh, that ... yeah, she told me that once too."

"But think about it ... *What if* there is no line ... no difference between the one spiritual Consciousness (the outside) and our temporal world (the inside) ... that there is just one *thing?*"

"And if you observe it without the interference of the mind (the circle), it all becomes one inside and outside."

Yufei picks up on it,

"So, *Consciousness is everything?*"

"Yes ... *It is not that Consciousness is <u>in</u> the universe ... it is that Consciousness is the universe.*"

"*Universe is just another way to say Consciousness?*"

"Yes, and all sentient things have conscious spirits, and they should be viewed this way."

"This physical universe is not everything, *it is just called the universe* to avoid confusion in our minds."

And then it is quiet ... Yufeng and Panda had been listening to this also and they are quiet ...

Meanwhile, LF is clicking her teeth at some unknown bugs in the sands.

***

When they finally get to Kailash, they are pleasantly surprised to learn that their old farm, from their very first stay many years earlier, is waiting for them. The smiling caretaker opens the locks and hands them the keys and they get settled in.

Panda lets LF out but tells her not to leave the walled compound.

This time they are more comfortable walking around the small town, buying food for their visit, and exploring the many temples and small shops in the central town. There also seems to be more pilgrims ambulating around the mountain this time.

Yufei asks Gugu what he thinks.

"Maybe their spirits sense ominous clouds or demons."

The next morning, after breakfast, the four of them walk to the Temple of Wisdom. They are greeted at the door as if the nuns have been expecting them. They are ushered into the rear mandala room where they are warmly greeted by Elder Yeshe and Elder Bim Yi from their first visit many years before.

Off to the side, nuns are working on a new mandala and the singing bowls are playing out their rhythmic sounds as the prayer wheels spin in eternal revolutions.

"Welcome old friends!" Elder Yeshe says bowing in the traditional greeting, and then looking at Panda, she adds,

"And this must be Panda ... I met you once many years ago when you were just an infant."

Panda smiles and bows, "It is my pleasure to meet you again, Elder Aunty."

Then turning to Gugu, the old woman smiles, "Welcome back, old friend."

Gugu just bows with his hands in the traditional Tibetan Buddhist greeting.

Then turning to Yufei and Yufeng, she says, "I'm sure you two have many questions, let's go into the inner room where we will be more comfortable."

***

They go to another, quieter room, where there are many cushions on the floor, around a central fire stove. A nun brings in a teapot, several saucer-shaped cups, and some dried cakes.

After they are settled down on the cushions, and have sipped the tea, they are more comfortable, and Elder Yeshe motions to them.

"Please ask your questions."

Yufeng looks at Yufei. Yufei has a serious look on his face, but before he speaks, he looks at Panda and then at his wife who nods and tells him,

"It's okay. ... she needs to start hearing these things." Panda just smiles but then the smile fades when she looks at her father, whose face has a look of seriousness that she has rarely seen. Yufeng notices it too but doesn't say anything.

Yufei begins, "From Gugu we understand that once trained, we will better be able to navigate in the void, even communicate, go to any place in the physical world, but only subtly be able to effect changes."

"That is roughly correct ... but some parts need to be clarified. The past and present you can see, but the future is still just a cloud of potentialities ... actions or events that are possible, but not certain, at this time."

"But we can see most of the possibilities and the probable outcomes of those possibilities ..."

"Yes."

"And you have had for many years ways to communicate this *information* to us ... if you wanted to?"

"Yes." she answers sensing where this is headed.

Then with a not-too-kind look he asks,

"Then why didn't you warn us of the late winter blizzard that took my father and Qime? If you had warned us somehow, they could have delayed their departure ... it only needed to be by a week or so."

These last words come out harshly as he struggles to control his inner emotions. Likewise, Yufeng is thinking (*and why didn't you warn me about my father?*)

Panda is somewhat frightened by this interchange.

Elder Yeshe looks to Elder Bim to explain.

"But if we warned you, maybe he wouldn't have died the second time and come back with his insight. Sometimes the decisions we have to make are difficult ... very difficult. *Sometimes the most important lessons learned are the hardest.*"

Elder Yeshe continues,

"He had to die again and come back ... to fulfill *his* destiny ... *as he told you.*"

Then she looks at Yufeng who lowers her eyes.

Yufeng can't speak ... she can only mouth the words, "My father?"

Elder Bim sighs, "If you knew they had kidnapped him, would you *not* have tried to rescue him?"

The vision of her father dying in her arms by the coast stirs tremendously sad memories. Panda doesn't understand but she senses her mother's great sadness and holds her hand.

After a pause, Elder Yeshe speaks, "From before you two were born, we knew of your potential and as you both grew, we have watched, trying to not interfere with the divine plan that has been in place from before time ... just nudging a little in hopes that the potential would become favorable ... that you would overcome your trials."

"Can you even imagine the hundreds upon hundreds of ones just like you that we tried to get to realize their potential ... to overcome *their* trials ... all to no avail ... only to watch them become shadow puppet victims of their misguided emotions from the dark forces."

Looking at Gugu, "At times we have sent avatars to offer you guidance and wisdom, but for the most part we have tried to avoid direct interference with your lives ... for obvious and not-so-obvious reasons."

"Not-so-obvious?" Yufei asks.

"Do you remember on your first return journey from Chang An, and you saw Yufeng getting shot with an arrow from the bandit leader?"

Yufei nods.

"And you tried to change that possibility." he nods again.

"And what happened? She fell on the rock and still almost died."

"These decisions to interfere-or-not interfere are wrought with perils either way ... it is a heavy burden."

Elder Yeshe rises and walks out, then after a few minutes she returns with another woman, whom she introduces as elder Yan.

Gently, elder Yeshe removes elder Yan's top robe, revealing that the elder has no arms below the elbow.

Yufeng gasps and tries to cover Panda's eyes, but Panda is mystified and approaches the woman.

"Aunty, can you feel your hands?" she asks.

The older woman nods.

Panda smiles.

"Can I hold your hand, aunty?"

The elder nods and smiles.

Panda closes her eyes and is in the void quickly, where she *holds* the older woman's spirit hands, with her spirit hand.

The others watch, not knowing what is happening until Panda returns and opens her eyes. She smiles at her mother.

"It is like we discussed mother ..."

Elder Yeshe looks at them.

"You have tried this before?"

"Yes ... but just among ourselves ... not with someone else."

Elder Yeshe tells elder Yan she can return to her duties.

After she is gone, Yufeng asks,

"What are her duties here?"

"She teaches the villagers our heritage ... she is one of the gifted Gesar singers."

Panda's eyes light up with this news and looks at her mother, who knows what she is thinking. She whispers to Panda,

"Later Panda ... you can ask her to sing."

Yufeng looks to Elder Yeshe, who smiles and nods.

"Let's take a break for a few minutes ... I need to instruct some elders to prepare a light lunch for us."

She leaves.

***

Later, after she returns, Yufei asks,

"Elder Yeshe, why have you sent for us ... at this time?"

"There is work to be done and it can't wait ... the dark forces are increasing their dark manifestations everywhere ... we hoped it wouldn't happen so soon, but these *possibilities* can turn into *negative probabilities* quickly ... and then it's difficult to reverse things."

"We would like you three to get involved *now* ... we have seen different futures ... ones you are in and ones you are not ... our best chance of success, is in those futures which have all of you working for the forces of good."

"Would we get to accept or reject the assignments?"

"Yes ... but we *hope* that you will not reject."

"If we travel through the no-time ... will our bodies age?"

"No ... you will remain the same age as when you entered."

"When we are not in the no-time, will our bodies age?"

"Yes, in a normal manner ... unless you chose something else?"

"Something else?"

"It's complicated ... we can get into it later ... once you decide."

"Will our bodies be immortal? I mean unable to be killed or harmed?"

Immortality is already yours ...
only your mind is preventing you from this realization.
Whoever you are, you are related to the cosmos,
and the one Consciousness.
And at times, the temporal walls may dissolve,
to reveal this underlying Consciousness.
The whole universe is you.

"No ... only your spirit is immortal ... although your body will heal quickly. You will have no superhuman powers, those are just myths ... even those inner instincts that you have already developed ... everyone has ... you have just been blessed with more and you have activated their potential."

"What about Panda's ability to talk to animals?"

Elder Yeshe looks at Panda and smiles.

"Our first ancestors could all do that ... people today have just forgotten ... the animals have conscious spirits ... Panda touched into that deep memory without a second thought ... as though it was a natural as talking to you ... right Panda?"

Panda smiles and nods.

Yeshe continues.

"Nagarjuna (an ancient sage) likened these natural abilities to an oil lamp concealed inside a vase. When holes are made in the vase, the lamp's illumination is released. In the same manner, when our minds are cleansed through the purification of enlightenment ... we can penetrate to the original nature of our spirit, and the natural power of Consciousness becomes manifest."

Yufei then asks,

"When did it *all* begin? Everything."

Elder Yeshe explains,

"The past has no beginning, cannot have any beginning,
the very idea of a beginning is absurd.
How can things suddenly begin?
It is a beginning-less procession of events.
'Time thinking' is thinking involved in this womb-world.
Such thought does not touch
the realm of Consciousness."

Then Yufeng asks,

"Can you tell us more about the divine plan?"

Yufei is thinking,

RICHARD HOWE

If there is no-time ... then we are in the timeless eternity

22 Divine Plan

In Western theology, *transcendent* is used to mean
outside of the world.
In Eastern theology, it means
outside of thought... that is,
The *absolute* is absolutely *transcendent of all thought.*

The categories of logic, the forms of time and space,
all of these are functions of human thought,
and the mystery that you are seeking lies beyond it.

"So, as I understand it, you want us to be agents in the *Divine Plan* that has been revealed to you and your sisters. Is that correct?"

"What are you saying? You doubt us?"

"I'm just stating something ... is it accurate, or not accurate, or partially accurate, or neither accurate nor not-accurate."

"It's accurate."

"We have one major problem with that. We put our lives, and our families, at risk without knowing if it's the 100% truth ... or it's just what *you* decide to tell us ..."

"What do you want?"

"We need to know ourselves. Too many religions in the world are based on faith and we've seen too many false prophets. We believe in our own instincts, and in their guidance but not so much in the *truthful* words of others ... because sometimes others receive what they want to receive ... and relay what they *want to* relay."

"Just as before you knew about what was going to happen to my father and to Yufeng's father, yet you choose not to tell us in advance ... sometimes you choose to tell us things and sometimes you choose not ... and we're not comfortable with that."

"What are you asking?"

"First, when you receive some directive relating to us or to our mission ... you relay everything truthfully, without your personal filter and we will decide what action to take ... because we are there, in the field and know all the subtleties of the players and conditions."

The elders look at each other ...

Elder Yeshe nods, "We can do this."

"Second, we will need to confirm your messages."

"Confirm? How?" she says a little indignantly.

"I am not sure ... but we will go into the void seeking confirmation ... we hope that somehow you will allow our questions to be answered, truthfully, that is, not changed ... in the same way that you receive your guidance."

Elder Bim starts to object but Elder Yeshe reaches out to silence her and then says,

"We will need to discuss this ... you must realize that this is something we've never done ... so we will need to seek guidance as well."

"We understand."

"Oh ... one last thing ... each of us will make up his or her own mind ..."

"We understand."

"That includes Panda."

They look at the girl who is looking closely at a thangka, smiling, and tracing the outlines of the golden colored threads with her finger, but sometimes the gold thread becomes invisible ... only to suddenly resurface at another spot ...

like a spirit particle.

23 Defeat Dark Manifestations

In the Beginning,
All is emptiness, the very form is emptiness,
no beings, no clouds, no worlds ...
but <u>full</u> of possibilities.

Elder Yeshe begins again to describe the Divine Plan ... first she summarizes the things she's already told them about the universe ...

"In the beginning there were just infinite possibilities ... and infinite *conscious spirits* ... then, through exchanges of information between these conscious spirits, possibilities become probabilities ... and *space* was created ... and with it, *time* ... and then they created worlds and organisms ... and later, when a conscious being entered these worlds, the probabilities interacted with this consciousness and created full histories as well, backward in *time*."

"*Our present awareness of information acts as the catalyst for creation of the past?*"

Yufei asks.

Elder Yeshe smiles and explains.

"*When you throw a stone in the water, it finds the quickest way to the bottom.*

It knows because it has traveled there before ...in no-time."

Yufei then asks,

"*When the universe came into being, it created its own history ... backwards?*"

"*Kind of ...*" *Then pointing to the monks making a new sand mandala.*

"*Inside the timeless Mandala ... the past, present, and future are not three different places ... they are a single happening here and now.*"

When you live in this moment profoundly,
you experience time not serially but simultaneously ...

not as three but as one ... and then ...
you wake up to the knowledge that ... this moment is eternity.

"But what is it all for ... what is the ultimate purpose of the divine plan?"

"For most sentient beings, there is no purpose ... purpose is just a mind game. But for you ... it is to become a celestial being."

"This experience, that you call reality, is just a mind device, like a map, with experiences (symbols on the map), to navigate the illusion ... so you can use these experiences to gain wisdom, and enlightenment ... and evolve beyond them ... it's a conscious universe ... matter is just the background which allows your evolutionary growth experiences. The problem is your mind which, through your eyes, looks outward."

Yufeng starts to ask,

"But what about the Divine ..."

Elder Yeshe holds up her hand to have her hold her thoughts.

"Before going further, this is important to understand ... let me repeat it again a little differently ... those Conscious Spirits were the basic building blocks of the universe ... which, through the exchange of information, influenced possibilities ... into probabilities. Underlying everything is the invisible universal field of Consciousness, which through the conscious spirits ... created matter, light, energy, and everything in the universe."

Yufei and Yufeng look at each other thoughtfully.

Panda looks at them curiously (*Didn't you know this?*)

Later ... continuing the narrative ... the elder explains,

"You went to Gobekli Tepe and learned mankind's history ... and the contamination caused by the dark manifestations. Sadly, since then, the dark manifestations have increased and our efforts to control them have failed to hold them back."

"Control?"

"First, our ancestors built walls, but they failed to protect them. Then they fled south to the lands between the Tigris and Euphrates and created a new civilization ... but the darkness infected the people there."

"Infected? How?"

"With greed, desire, and lust."

"What happened?"

"The civilization died ... just as many others following the same false gods."

"Others?"

"The Osirian, the Egyptian, and others across the seas and inland."

"Even in China?"

"Yes, there are lost civilizations in China ... like Gobekli, that were destroyed and buried."

"Why were they buried?"

"To preserve their memory."

"And now?"

"Now, we are in the final stages of a slowly evolving plan."

"Can you explain it?"

"Certainly ... but you must never reveal this to anyone."

"We agree."

"For many years, our sisters have been advisers to rulers all over the world ... trying to guide them, but with limited success. Now we have a far larger cleansing plan utilizing the Mongols."

"But they are fierce warrior invaders."

"Yes ... but they respect women, especially the mothers and grandmothers ... and they respect *all* people's beliefs and religions ... even those of their conquered tribes ... and they believe in open trade ... which will serve to spread our ideas of women's respect and spiritual beliefs of the Mother Goddess, throughout the world."

"But like Gugu has explained, we can only subtly guide these possibilities into probabilities ... and hopefully into actual beneficial events."

"But everything we've heard about the Mongol warriors is terrifying."

"Not all those tales are true ... many are spread to induce fear, so cities submit to them."

"But ..."

"Do you remember back to that first time you came here from Chang An?"

Yufei and Yufeng remember the Mongols coming to their aid against the Arabs.

Yufei asks,

"We never understood that."

The elder smiles.

"Sometimes it is good to have fierce warriors *on your side*."

Yufeng holds up her hand.

"Can we take a pause for today; we need to discuss some things."

They all agree.

***

On the way back to their farm, they are followed.

Yufei says to Yufeng, "They are getting closer and bolder ... I think they want us to know they are watching us."

Then Panda stops looking at trinkets and just stands still. The parents look at her ... she points to two figures following them from behind. When she points at them, they disappear down an alley.

"We know Panda ... you need to be on alert about them ... tell me or mama if you sense anything ... okay?"

"Okay baba."

***

At their farmhouse, the entire compound is enclosed by a high wall. Feeling protected, Panda and LF play freely inside the walls. At night Panda sleeps inside and LF in her travel cage near the door.

In the mornings, Panda lets LF run around outside while they eat breakfast inside.

On the following morning though, after breakfast, Panda can't find LF ... she runs around, making her clicking sounds and calling but she can't find her anywhere. Gugu goes outside to help. Yufeng and Yufei are cleaning up and getting ready to go to the temple when a heart-stopping scream from Panda freezes time ... and everything in their world changes forever.

They run outside and see Panda bent over, looking at the ground, Gugu is trying to comfort her. Yufeng runs up and sees the tragedy ... LF is lying on the ground lifeless. Yufei runs up, realizes what has happened and starts to search the grounds. He finds some pieces of meat that have been tossed over the wall ... Yufeng sticks a needle into it ... it turns black ...the meat was poisoned.

He goes to Yufeng.

"Talk to her ... console her ... I am going outside."

"Are you sure? Maybe that's what they want you to do .... maybe it's a trap."

When he looks at her, his face has changed ... she has only seen that look a few times before ..."

"I hope it is ..."

"But ..."

"Don't worry ..."

"Gugu stay here ... protect them ... I'll be back shortly."

Then, after getting his weapons he is gone.

Meanwhile Yufeng comforts Panda ...

"Every person and every animal have an eternal spirit ... when my father died, it was just his body that died ... his spirit is eternal and crossed the heavenly bridge ... do you understand?"

Panda nods through her sobs.

"When your grandfather Scorpion died, we had a sky burial, but we will not do that here .... we will cremate LF here and bring her ashes to the holy lake ... would you like that?"

Panda nods but she can sense her inner sadness and something new ... something she had never seen in her ... *vengeance.*

Over the next hour they prepare the fire and anoint LF's body with special oils ... Yufeng knows the procedure and Panda helps her.

When they are ready, Gugu asks,

"Should we light the fire or wait for Yufei?'

Yufeng closes her eyes ... then opens them and says,

"He will be back soon ... let's wait."

***

When Yufei returns there is a tear in his tunic and blood on his clothes.

Yufeng asks, "What happened?"

"There were three of them trying to cloak themselves ... but I can detect their cloaking now, so they were careless."

Then he looks at Panda.

"Panda, the men that killed LF are no more ... do you understand?"

She nods ... understanding that her father has killed the bodies of the evil men.

(*but it won't bring LF back*)

Yufeng tells Yufei to wash up before the cremation ceremony.

Yufei quickly washes up, changes his tunic, and comes outside.

Panda lights the firesticks and the body of LF is quickly consumed in flames.

Panda doesn't cry.

Yufei looks at her and remembers the look ... the same one that Yufeng had after her father was killed by the Kongs.

(*I'll need to talk to her*) he thinks (*but not now ... later*)

The party going to the temple later in the morning is somber. Panda hasn't spoken since they cremated LF's lifeless body and gathered the ashes into an urn.

They all respect her sadness and her internal struggle to deal with it.

When they get to the temple, the elders can sense the change.

Elder Yeshe asks, "Did something happen?"

Yufei looks at her, "We had a warning."

The old woman looks to see if everyone is okay, and seeing them all healthy, asks,

"But no one was injured?"

Yufei and Yufeng glance at Panda ... Elder Yeshe follows their eyes. Elder Yeshe senses tremendous sadness inside Panda. She squats down and faces Panda ...

"How can I help?"

Panda looks into her bottomless eyes, then she holds up a small urn, without saying a word.

Elder Yeshe understands ... rises and says to Yufeng,

"I will have the sisters make the preparations ... do you want to go to the same spot as many years ago?"

Yufeng nods, "That would be nice."

"It will take a little time; do you want to continue our talk?'

Yufei looks at Panda and then Yufeng, who nods.

***

They go into the same room as the day before. It is dimly lit by yak butter candles. There are some whisps of incense smoke visibly swirling around the candles. They sit in a circle and clear their minds.

After ten minutes, Elder Yeshe says,

"We have discussed your concerns and, although we have never consented to this before, but because of the increasing dangers, we agree ... actually, we realized we won't be agreeing to anything that hasn't already been decided by the divine Consciousness."

"So, you can accept or reject any assignment ... obviously we wouldn't ask you unless it was important for the divine plan and your unique skills would offer better chances of success."

"As you know, success is never guaranteed ... all of these outcomes are only potentialities in a universe of infinite potentialities ... our task is to try to nudge the potentialities into probabilities, and then into actualized events."

Yufeng raises her index finger and Elder Yeshe turns to her.

"Because of what happened this morning, we have some heightened concerns ..." she glances at Panda, who feigns not seeing it.

"Could you briefly describe some of the immediate assignments where you feel our talents would be helpful ..."

The elders look at each other, then Elder Yeshe says,

"Okay ... but just briefly for now, until you agree."

Yufeng nods. Elder Bim starts to talk.

"In the near future, the Mongol armies will approach the kingdom of Kucha. The king will have a difficult choice to make ... fight or submit. To fight will be suicidal for his entire people, to submit is to surrender and to some men, that is worse than death."

"So, our mission, would be to convince him of the wisdom of submitting?"

The elders nod.

"But why us?"

"Two reasons we feel you could be effective ... first is your talents ... healing, martial arts and especially your inner instincts ... you will need all those talents."

"And the second reason?"

"Your friend Tarem and his wife Beersheba ... they are well respected by the ministers and the royal family."

Yufei asks, "What are the dangers?"

"There will be members of the royal family who will not want to submit and if that outcomes happen, you will be in the midst of the slaughter and pillage. Also, there is a black witch there."

Yufeng glances at Yufei, then Panda.

"And if we are successful, what then?"

Elder Yeshe speaks now,

"Kucha will be just your first assignment; it is the entry door for the second one."

Yufei motions with his hands to continue.

"Your main mission is to become a part of Genghis Khan's inner entourage ... a confidant, a healer and a respected adviser to him and especially to his sons and their wives."

"Why?"

"Wars of expansion are difficult and cruel ... but after the war, comes the administration of the territories, that's where wise council is important. The great Khan and some around him have some good tendencies ... those must be encouraged and built upon ... and the more destructive elements must be tempered."

"And the dangers?"

"Infinite. Plunder and greed breed especially vicious enemies."

Yufei looks at Yufeng ... then they look at Panda. Yufei shakes his head and starts to decline the assignment ... *it'll be too dangerous for her.*

Panda senses her father's decision and interrupts with a steely look to Elder Yeshe,

"We accept."

They all look at her. She looks at both her mother and father ... they speak without speaking and understand. Panda speaks softly,

"It is all our destiny ..."

Then looking to her mother,

"Can we go to the lake now?"

Panda rises ... the others look at each other and rise also.

Elder Yeshe looks at one of her assistants, who nods.

"We can go now ..."

As they walk out, Elder Yeshe says to Yufei and Yufeng, "We can get into the details later."

They nod and are anxious to put LF's ashes to rest ... hoping to give some type of closure for Panda.

***

At the side of Lake Manasarovar, there are several sacred spots ... the most sacred, from the standpoint of the ancient Bon religion, is a small inlet with a small hill nearby, festooned with a tall pole with strings of brightly colored cloth cascading down the support strings ... this is the same place they scattered Scorpion and Qime's ashes years before.

The small party walk to the pole, Elder Yeshe hands Panda a bright blue piece of cloth to hang on one of the strings ... blue being the color of the heavenly sky.

Then they walk to the beach where the water is gently lapping on the shore. Not sure what happens next, Panda looks up first at her father ... but Yufei is frozen in an earlier memory of this same place when he cast out his father's ashes ... so she turns to her mother.

Yufeng nods and reaches for the urn with the ashes from inside her cloak. She opens the top, and the elders start chanting. Another elder is beating a rhythm on a wooden fish.

Bending down to Panda, Yufeng tells her,

"There are two ways to release her spirit ... one is to empty the ashes along the water line and let the waves gently draw them into the eternal waves of the universe."

"The other, for close family (she glances at Yufei) is to use your hands to reach in and spread the ashes along the water line yourself ... then bow three times in the four directions before washing your hands in the waters."

Then she hands the urn to Panda, and they all wait.

Without hesitation Panda reaches in and grabs a handful of ashes and while she spreads the ashes along the waterline ... she click-talks to LF's spirit ... and as she talks the dam holding back the tears finally breaks ...

But the words she speaks are not human words, they are LF clicking words. It is a very personal and very private final communication.

And no one will ever know what was said that day ... except Panda and LF's spirit.

But in another time ... the prophecy of her last words will come true.

When Panda's spirit and LF's spirit reunite ... on another world.

24 The Messenger

Back at their compound, Panda is somber, as they clean everything up, burning all traces of LF ... except for one ... a small talisman of fur which they liked to play midair catch.

Yufei and Yufeng and Gugu are in another deep discussion.

Yufei says,

"Let's step back and look at what we have leaned ... not just today, but the past few months."

The others wait for him to continue, going over events in their own mind.

"A black witch appeared in our town looking for Gugu. We were attacked at our home by six black assailants. We saw some black spies watching us in Lhasa. We were attacked again on the Lhasa trail coming here and again last night ..."

Gugu adds,

"They are getting bolder and bolder; they know us, and they want to stop us now."

"But not just us ..."

Yufeng looks at Yufei and asks,

"You mean the elders?"

"The elders can protect themselves; I mean anyone associated with us ... Tarem in Kucha, Chen Er, and Princess Dorjie in Lhasa. We will go and warn Tarem, but I think we need to warn Chen Er."

"How do they know these things? Where we are? Tarem in Kucha?"

Yufei shrugs,

"Maybe they receive insight from the dark side, just as the elders receive insight from the light side."

Yufei turns to Gugu.

"You can travel vast distances easier than most ... can you get to Lhasa to warn Chen and Dorjie ... and then meet us in Kucha?"

Gugu nods.

Yufei hands a message to him.

"Give him this ... he will understand ... and one other thing."

"Chen Er is not the type to wait for someone to attack ... I think he will launch his own attack on the dark monastery ... but he needs to be more careful than ever before ... that's why I want to send you, to teach him and Dorjie how to cloak their actions ... to prevent their untimely detection."

Gugu nods.

"I'll help them and then meet up with you later."

Yufeng goes up to Gugu and hugs the monk, who is genuinely embarrassed.

"Be careful, I sense a powerful darkness arising ... like a plague."

Gugu nods and asks,

"So, you'll agree to help the elders and work with the Mongols."

"We will try our best ... We just both worry about Panda."

Yufei looks out the window at Panda. *(so young to be thrown into this fire)*

The next morning, before sunrise, Gugu is gone, having slid out unseen.

***

A few days later on a street near the Lhasa Barkhor market, a nondescript Tibetan monk, like so many other ones, approaches Princess Dorjie with his begging bowl. Dorjie recognizes Gugu but doesn't change her routine, she reaches for a coin and puts it in the bowl as she holds it from underneath ... and a message slip is passes, which she slides into her pocket and continues.

Later that night there is a knock on the side entrance to their palace and Dorjie opens the door for Gugu, who slides in. They walk in the shadows to her quarters.

They exchange quick greetings and Gugu hands Yufei's message to Chen Er, as they all read it.

Princess Dorjie is the first to talk.

"I've heard of that valley ... there are legends and dark stories the grandmothers tell the children about monsters and demons there. Everyone is afraid to even mention it for fear of bringing doom down on their family."

"Do you know where it is?"

"Not exactly ... but once when I was in my rebellious exploring youth, I ventured out to some of the forbidden places."

Chen Er smiles at Gugu. *Her rebellious youth.*

Dorjie pinches him.

"At least I wasn't chasing naked girls in distant islands!"

"Sorry."

"Anyway, once I came upon a valley with ominous signs and warnings to go no further ... many skeletons hanging from trees and tombstones."

"What happened?"

"Well, I was rebellious ... not death defying ... so I rode home to my nana ..."

"That's it?"

"My nana told me never to go there again ... it was the place Yufei mentions."

Chen Er looks at Gugu.

"Did Yufei say anything else?"

"He said you weren't the type to wait for someone to attack you ... so, you would probably organize an attack on the black monastery."

Chen Er smiles,

"He's right ..." then looking at Dorjie, he asks,

"How do you feel?"

"For both me and my people I would like to see it destroyed ... but they have some dark powers."

Gugu then tells them the rest of Yufei's message.

"Yufei told me that if you decide to attack, I was to help train your warriors how to cloak your attack from their senses."

"Cloak?" Dorjie asks

"Hide it from their special senses."

"You can do that? Who taught you? Yufei? Yufeng? The elders?"

"Panda."

There is a pause and then Dorjie laughs,

"That's great ... how is my little niece?"

Gugu's face drops as he tells them about LF.

"They poisoned LF ... Panda was crushed ... they scattered the ashes at Lake Manasarovar."

Dorjie gasps,

"The poor girl."

Then looking at Chen Er.

"Husband, you are the leader, please devise a plan ... I'll organize a small force of my most skilled family bodyguards."

'Okay."

Then looking at Gugu.

"Will you go with us?"

Gugu nods and smiles,

"It would be my fondest desire ... except I am a monk without desire to harm others ... so I will go along for enlightenment purposes."

"But I thought you were enlightened a few lifetimes ago."

He smiles, "I need more experience ... dealing with the black witches."

And their preparations begin ...

After Dorjie selects her warriors for the mission, Chen Er trains with them every day on stealth tactics and silent killing.

In the evenings, Gugu teaches Dorjie and Chen Er more of the cloaking techniques.

Meanwhile ... in another place ...

25 Road to Kucha

From Mt Kailash to Kucha, the family heads north, retracing their journey from years ago towards Khotan ... and then, after Khotan, following the Khotan River north through the desert. It will take them several weeks to cross this lonely stretch of desert, with only a few desolate trading posts and watering holes along the way ... a good time to heal and ponder the words of the elders.

As they ride, Yufei and Panda are silent ... into themselves. One night as Panda is helping her mother clean up, she asks her,

"Is something wrong with father?"

Yufeng looks over and sees the pensive look on Yufei.

"I think I know."

"Can you tell me?"

"It's a long story ... but many years ago when you were a baby, we came to that same spot on the lake and your father cast out your grandfather's ashes onto the waters ... I think the other day, it brought back some memories that he had tried to bury."

"Mother ... can I ask you something?"

"Sure ... anything, what is it?"

"What did father do to the men that killed LF?"

Yufeng's heart skips a beat, as long buried memories surface into her present-day consciousness.

"He killed their bodies, Panda."

"Was he angry?"

"No ... he just separated their bodies from their spirits."

"Is it a bloody process?" (*I remember his clothes*)

"It can be ... sometimes, if they fight."

"Has he done this before?"

"Yes, but only when it was necessary ... in most cases their fates were already determined."

Panda thinks about that for a moment...

"I hope I don't have to do that."

"I hope so too ... but, if you have to ... do it without emotion ... understand?"

She nods, "How did you learn this mama?"

Another drowned memory floats up ... a more painful memory.

"Your father taught me, Panda ... a long time ago ... when my father was killed by an evil man."

"What happened?"

"Your father showed me that the anger and desire for revenge was darkening my spirit ..."

"So, he told you not to kill the evil man?"

"No ... he told me I could kill ... but not out of anger and revenge."

"And what happened?"

"Your father and your grandfather (Scorpion) arranged for me to avenge my father."

"Will you tell me the whole story someday?"

Yufeng nods, "Someday ... but not tonight, it is getting late."

"Okay ... mama ..." then hugging her mother, Panda says, "I love you mama."

Yufeng holds her and says, "I know Panda and I love you too."

***

Whenever they stop to rest, they go over, again and again, the instructions for navigating in the invisible realm. Every evening they review the instructions and then each, on their own, enters into the void.

Later Yufei explains something to them ...

"The thing I've learned while in the void, is that I don't go from one place to the next, to the next, like a journey ... I go from the first point to the final destination ... as though my thoughts collapse at that point, and I am there."

Yufeng ponders this.

"Yes, I have felt that also ... this could be important in many ways."

He looks at her.

"What do you mean?"

"For example, to find a cure for a new disease, I usually go through endless trials with different herbs and decoctions ... however, if I could just leap ahead, think of all the time and lives I could save."

Yufei though, sees other possibilities in this insight ... but he keeps them to himself for now.

At first Yufei and Yufeng stay close to Panda ... but soon she is navigating the void as easily as in the forests around her birth home.

And then one day about a week out of Khotan as they were doing their exercises around their campfire, they hear a scream from Panda ... not really a fearful scream ...more like a joyous shout.

Later when they have all rejoined this world, the adults look at her ... waiting. But Panda is smiling and rocking her head as though she was watching one of the shadow puppet plays. Yufeng reaches over and touches her.

"What is it, Panda? What did you see?"

Panda looks up questioningly at her mother,

"Mother ... Didn't you see her?"

"See who?"

"LF! Her spirit glided to my spirit shoulder ... she was so happy to see me ... and she's fine!"

The others all smile and one heavy burden that has hung over them this past week has just lifted.

***

Later as Yufei and Yufeng are under their furs preparing to sleep, Yufeng senses something bothering her husband.

"What is it?"

"Nothing ... just that back at the lake I thought ... never mind, it's nothing."

"You thought your father might come to you?"

He nods, then says,

"Mysteries upon mysteries ... I don't mind taking on these assignments ... they all seem virtuous and worthy ... it's just ..."

"What?"

"I don't see the ending of the story."

"Ending?"

"How does all this end? When I go into the void, I try to see the ending ... where it is all coming together ..."

"And?"

"There is no ending ... like the universe ... it just keeps going on and on."

"Why does that bother you?"

"In the Snowy Mountains, we planted the seeds in the Spring and harvested them in the Autumn ..."

Yufeng says, "Like the circles in the thangkas."

"Yes ... seasons within endless seasons."

"Is that what is bothering you?"

"No ... something else."

"*I don't think they are telling us everything.*"

The next night after travelling the roads of this world, they enter the pathless roads in the emptiness.

This time it is Yufei who has an epiphany vision.

Yufeng can see the change instantly on his smiling pensive face.

"What was it? What did you experience?"

"Remember when we were at the lake, and I was hoping to see my father?

She nods as Panda comes closer to them to listen also.

"Tonight, he came to me and explained more about his vision."

"Why didn't he come to you at the lake?"

"I don't know but I think it was out of respect for Panda's grieving and LF's funeral ceremony."

"What did he say?"

"He wanted to tell me more about his last words before his death ... do you remember what he said that time?"

Yufeng, who also has a good memory, says,

"Find out the *why* ..."

Yufei adds,

"I often wondered about what he meant ... about the opening in the Enso."

"And tonight, he told me more ..."

"The opening ... is where we must go ... to escape the dark manifestations and karmic reincarnation cycles of this universe *and create a new universe*. The answer lies going *outside the opening of this universe*, where space continues endlessly."

Yufeng and Panda look at each other and then ask Yufei,

"Create a new universe? Why? What do you mean?"

"I don't know ... I have yet to figure out this universe ... but I think it must be important if he sacrificed his life to bring me the message. Remember, he also said he went deeper than any of us ... I think he saw something."

Yufeng is worried about Panda diving too deep into the void. When Yufei looks at Yufeng, she glances at Panda and he understands ... unfortunately so does Panda, who speaks first.

"Don't worry momma, I won't go too deep."

Yufeng wrinkles her eyebrows and tells her,

"Panda, even if LF goes deep, I don't want you to dive deep into the darkness ... your grandfather saw something there."

"Okay mama ... but what do you think grandpa meant about creating a new universe?"

She looks at Yufei, who shrugs and says,

"I think it will come to us when we are ready."

And he was right. Over the weeks on the trail to Kucha, more details to this mystery are revealed to them ... but that is better explained later ...

... when they journey out the Enso opening ...

26 Kucha Reunion

After q few weeks they finally approach the outskirts of Kucha. First, they pass through the archway of an ancient walled city called Qiuci. The walls on either side are about 2000 meters long and 6 meters high, with battlements every 50 meters, but now it is in disrepair. This area used to be the main commercial center hundreds of years earlier. The homes inside the walls are made of dry packed earth with gardens behind them. The people seem relatively prosperous, their long flowing clothes are clean and even the children are well clothed. From inside the homes, they can hear music.

And then a rider whose face is covered by his kaftan, rides up and stops in front of them. Yufei reaches for his small sword, but Panda just smiles.

"It's Gugu, baba!"

They dismount and welcome their old friend.

"What happened in Lhasa? When did you get here? How are the Princess and Chen Er ..."

"Later ... everything is fine ... we can talk later ... let's continue on."

Yufei says, "Okay" ... but still punches Gugu's arm.

"Ouch, why did you do that?"

"I'll tell you later."

As they ride through this first desert village they are struck by the lush gardens and grape vines behind the houses.

Yufeng asks, "Where does the water come from? I don't see canals or streams or even wells."

Gugu points to the mountains, "From there."

Yufeng is confused. Then Gugu points to small piles or earth at intervals leading from the village to the foothills of the mountains.

"Let me show you, follow me." He rides to the nearest pile of earth and points to a hole in the ground from which the sound of rushing water can be heard. They have an underground water system which carries the water under the earth ... from the mountains to the village ... keeping it intact and fresh, all year long."

Yufei smiles, "Ingenious. Where did they learn that?"

"It is said, the grandmothers from the ancient Persian lands taught them."

Yufeng smiles and nods. (*the grandmothers ... hmmm*)

After another 2 kilometers east, they come to the main Kucha city.

Yufei asks Gugu,

"What is the history of these people?"

As they ride, Gugu relates the history of the Uighur Kingdom of Kocho ... how they lived to the far northeast but were driven out hundreds of years ago by the fierce Kyrgyz tribe and finally settled here and prospered.

At the main city gate there are some soldiers, but they are not too alert, just standing there ... once through the gate they go to the first caravansary, get some rooms, stable the horse, and decide to wash up before getting something to eat.

Later they go back to the main dining area and sit at a table with a view of the front gate ... they had just ordered dinner when a wailing cry comes from the gate archway.

Everyone turns as a well-dressed man, whose face is covered by his burqa, is wailing, and wailing ... everyone is mystified. Finally, the owner, recognizing the man ... comes up to him and respectfully asks what's wrong.

Pointing to Yufei's group, the man wails, "It's them!"

Everyone turns to stare at the four new strangers.

Yufei is alert and puts his hand on his killing knife. Yufeng puts her hand over his hand to caution him.

Yufeng rises and approaches the man and then he does something even more strange ... he hugs her and cries out, "My little sister!"

The burqa drops, revealing Tarem and everyone laughs and comes to great him.

Panda is confused.

Yufeng brings her to Tarem and asks her, "Panda, do you remember this smelly old goat? You were just a baby when he last saw you."

Panda shakes her head. (*smelly old goat ... what is mom saying?*)

"This is our dear friend, whom we have come to visit. Tarem, this is Panda, Panda, this is Tarem."

Tarem bows, "From a beautiful mother, a beautiful child."

Yufei asks, "How did you know we arrived?"

Tarem puts his arm around Yufei, "Little brother ... this is *my town* ... Tarem knows everything ... when I heard of your party arriving, I knew it could only be you ... but who is this ... *monk*?"

Yufei introduces Gugu to Tarem and they bow cautiously in greetings to each other.

Yufeng asks, "But why were you wailing ... I thought you would be happy to see us?"

Looking dejected, Tarem lowers his head, "My brother and sister come to my hometown, but they don't come to my home ... but eat in a public tavern ... food cooked by goats! Where are your manners?"

Laughing, Yufei explains, "We just arrived 2 minutes ago, washed, and wanted to get a bite to eat before looking for you ... our humble apologies!" he bows.

"Okay ... but please do not tell my beautiful and gentle wife that you were already eating ... she will beat me to a worthless pulp."

Then reaching out to Panda, "Come little Princess, let me introduce you to all your cousins."

Panda asks, "Mama ... what are cousins?"

Tarem shakes his head, "What can I say ... it seems the old lady drops a calf every year ... I have no idea where they all come from."

Yufei stifles a laugh as Yufeng looks at Tarem and asks,

"Strange, where could they all come from? Didn't you once say your mother had 10 children from 10 different fathers?"

Tarem belly laughs, "These children all look like their handsome dad or their beautiful mother."

They walk out of the tavern and along the way, Yufei asks,

"What's happening here ... I mean with the approaching Mongols. The soldiers at the main gateway arch seemed rather relaxed."

A serious look crosses Tarem's face.

"We have a problem."

Then looking at Yufei.

"Is it a coincidence that you are here, the same time as this ... problem?"

Yufei smiles and Tarem understands ... we can talk later.

27 Panda's Cousins

As they walk to Tarem's compound, Tarem fills them in on the current state of events ... all the time shaking his head,

"It's unbelievable!"

"The Mongols are slaughtering everyone in their path ... and the royals here are waiting for a miracle to spare them."

"There are no war preparations ... no soldiers recruited, no ramparts repaired, no armaments or food supplies stored, ..."

When Yufei asks why, Tarem shakes his head,

"When a minister brings this up to King Barchuk, his Queen shuts him off screaming, "What are you talking about? Those war preparations won't help us! Only *my* miracles will help us."

"Where are they getting this miracle advice?"

"From a black witch who is close to the queen."

"Black witch?"

"They call her the Witch of Subashi ... because she started her following several years ago out of the Subashi Temple, not far from here."

"Buddhists?"

"Originally but now, the place has been taken over by this strange *sect* ... supported by the queen."

Gugu asks Tarem, "But I'd heard Kocho (Kucha) was a Buddhist enclave ..."

"It used to be ... in my grandmother's time, but now there are many beliefs here ... Nestorian Christians, Moslems, Manicheans, Tengriism, and smaller sects."

"Which one do you follow?"

Laughing Tarem says,

"The same as the person I am talking to ... haha."

They arrive at a fairly large walled compound ... not in the wealthy section of town ... but closer the southern merchant's gate.

As they approach, they can hear the shouts and squeals of children fighting.

Tarem smiles, "My little army ...come inside so I can close the gate behind you ... even here ... the walls have ears."

Inside is a strange scene ... two teenage boys are mock fighting with staffs, two other younger adolescent boys are chasing two older girls and in the midst of it all sits Beersheba, holding a newborn and acting as the Goddess Maat, handing out her judgements.

When she sees Yufeng she screams out and almost drops the baby but recovers and hands the baby to her oldest daughter ... and runs to hug Yufeng.

"Little Sister! So long I haven't seen you! Come in, come in ... Jazeel, go in and make a big pot of cool tea for our guests ..."

Then looking at Yufei she asks, "So he is still following you around?"

Yufeng laughs, "Yes, but he is finally trained, and I am getting too old to train a new husband."

Panda looks up at her mother and wrinkles her eyebrows. (*mama, what are you talking about?*)

Yufeng sees this and tells her, "I'm just joking with my older sister dear ... Beersheba, this is our daughter Panda."

Beersheba reaches her arms out and hugs Panda. Panda can easily sense this woman's warm and sincere heart.

Beersheba looks around behind and asks Yufeng, "Where are the rest of your children?"

Yufeng surveying Beersheba's flock of kids just laughs and nods her head at Yufei, "I don't know, my donkey's fault maybe ... or the Mother Goddess put all her goodness in this one special child."

Beersheba, Tarem and Gugu look at Yufei.

Yufei says, "Donkey?"

Gugu tries unsuccessfully to hide his laugh.

Panda isn't sure about what they are talking.

Then the two older boys with the staffs run up to see the new visitors.

Tarem introduces them, "Boys these are those two legendary immortal warriors I've told you about. This is Yufei, and this is Yufeng, and this is their daughter, Panda."

The boys' jaws drop, and they just stare at Yufei. Then the younger one asks him,

"Can you really fly?"

Panda goes up to him and slaps him, "Don't talk silly."

They all laugh and then Yufei says,

"I see you practicing with the wooden staffs ... can you show me what your dad has taught you?"

Yufeng tells him, "Good, and while you boys play, Beersheba and I will get caught up on all that's happened."

Then, the women gather their things and head into the house.

Beersheba points to a small cottage near the back wall, "We have a small guest house for when Harim comes to visit or other travelers ... you can stay there."

Then looking around, "And this man is ..."

"We call him Gugu ... he is an old friend."

"Okay, he can sleep in one of the boy's beds."

"So, tell me ... I am dying to hear all the news ... the last we heard was when you returned to Fujian, a Tibetan princess went with you ... what happened?"

The two women walk to the cottage, chatting, chatting, chatting ... as two sisters who hadn't seen each other in years are wont to do.

Meanwhile in the courtyard, the two older boys are facing off with their staffs.

Tarem says to Yufei, "They are the best fighters in town ... for their age." then to the older boy, Tariq,

"Tariq, you make the first move."

The boy attacks with an overhead blow, but the younger boy parries it and does a sweeping low blow to Tariq's legs ... Tariq senses it and easily jumps over it and comes down again from above ... but the younger boy is quicker and isn't at the same spot any longer, he has moved swiftly to the side ... he thrusts his staff at Tariqs midsection. Tariq turns and is able to dodge most of the force of the blow."

Tarem shouts, "Enough! Stop!"

Then turning to Yufei he asks, "What did you see?"

Yufei has a serious look on his face. He motions for the two boys to sit before him.

"First the good news ... your feet positions and stances are good, you are putting good force into your blows, and you recover quickly ..."

Tariq, the oldest boy says, "Uncle you can be truthful with us ... that is the only way we will get better."

Yufei looks at Tarem who nods and smiles.

"Your skills are good ... good enough for other boys and even good enough for many men ... but ..." he stops and ponders something, then he says,

"Some things are difficult for words ..."

"Tariq ... come here ... give me your staff and you take your brother's staff."

The boy does this and stands opposite Yufei. Tarem, and the other son stand aside and watch.

First though, he asks the youth, Tariq, some questions, "Do you ever sense your mother calling you ... before she actually calls you?"

The boy nods. Yufei looks to the younger boy and asks.

"Just now when you moved to the side, did you sense Tariq's move?"

The boy nods.

"The difference between a good fighter and a great fighter is how he trains and uses his instincts to defeat his opponent."

"Let me show you ... both of you attack me any way you want."

The boys look at each other.

Tarem assures them, "Do what he says ... I want to see you beat this foreigner who comes to steal my gold and rape my sheep ... haha."

The boys shrug and move on either side of Yufei, who has given his staff back to Tariq. Tarem throws Yufei another staff. While they are posturing, Panda strolls out eating a piece of Hami melon and squats near Tarem.

Yufei smiles and tells Tarem, "Tell them to attack when they are ready."

The boys are good and have practiced together for years, so they fight good together ... but Yufei senses everything.

Just as Tariq gets ready to strike, Yufei has knocked his staff away, and struck a light blow to the back of his knees dropping him to the ground. At the same time the younger brother thinks this is an opening to strike a blow at Yufei ... but he is sadly mistaken as Yufei literally catches his staff with his own and twists it out of the boy's hands. The boy knows he has been beaten and submits.

Both boys are in awe. Yufei explains.

"If you use your instincts and sense their moves, you can easily defeat them."

The boys nod, then Tariq asks him,

"What if our opponent anticipates like you?"

"Right now ... until your skills are better, I would avoid that confrontation at all costs."

"Run away?"

"No ... avoid the confrontation ... it's not so difficult ... you also need to use your mind. Fighting should be your last resort."

Just then Yufeng comes out and asks, "Are you finished here? Beersheba has some snacks inside."

"Almost ... I have one more lesson for the boys."

Saying this he turns to the boys, "The other thing is to be wary of *every* opponent, never get overconfident ... understand?"

They nod. Then Yufei hands Panda his staff.

Turning back to the older boys, "I want you two to attack my daughter and teach her how Kucha boys can fight."

They look to the girl ... and then to their father, who looks at Yufei, who smiles.

"Do it boys ... show these foreigners that Kucha boys are the best fighters in the desert!"

"But father ... she's just a girl ..."

Hearing that, Yufeng turns on Tarem and starts slapping him everywhere,

"Is that what you teach your boys ... that girls are weak?"

Tarem defends himself and cries out to the boys,

"For God's sake boys, attack the girl ... teach her a lesson ... before her she-wolf mother kills me!"

The boys turn and face off with Panda, who seems distracted ... this confuses them ... then before they can move, Panda has them both on the ground and their staffs flying off to some other land ... maybe Tibet."

Panda sings and laughs as she goes inside.

"Lalala ..."

Later, when the adults talked, none of them can remember seeing Panda move. Yufei and Yufeng are just as surprised.

Panda smiles and asks her mom, "Mom, can I go play with the girls now ... these boys are boring."

Yufei and Tarem stifle their laughs as Yufeng tells her,

"Okay, but first go wash your hands and come inside and eat something."

Panda skips off as the boys run alongside telling her cordially,

"Here Miss Panda, the wash basin is here, we'll show you..."

The three adults watch them run off.

Yufeng says, "They will be okay now ..." then pausing, she adds, "They remind me of us when we first met ... what was it? Over 12 years ago?"

Tarem laughs then asks more seriously, "Did you see her move?"

Yufei shakes his head and asks Yufeng, "No ... did you?"

"No ... and how did she know ... what they were thinking *before they were thinking*?"

Yufei shrugs ... "*I can sense it once they think it ... but not before.*"

They shake their heads as they walk inside to catch up with all the news.

Later that night as they put Panda under the furs to sleep, Yufeng asks her,

"Panda, what happened in the courtyard today with the boys ... inside your (conscious) mind? How did you know what they were thinking ... *before* they thought it?"

"LF told me ... good night mama ..." then she rolls over and goes to sleep.

Yufeng just smiles, thinking, (*oh ... yes, of course, LF told her ...*)

***

When she returns to the table with Yufei and Gugu, Yufei asks her,

"What did she say?"

Nonchalantly Yufeng says,

"LF told her."

Yufei crooks his head and smiles too, "Oh, yeah, of course ... LF told her."

Then they both stifle their laughter so as not to wake Panda.

Turning to Gugu, Yufei asks,

"Tell us everything that happened in Lhasa ... could you teach them the cloaking? Did they attack the monastery?"

"Yes, yes, and more ... let me start with the cloaking ... they both picked it up quickly, once I taught them how to empty their minds."

"As for the attack, Chen Er is a natural leader, as you know ... the Princess selected five of her most skilled bodyguards and Chen Er trained them to be silent killers."

"The monastery is in a secluded valley in the high mountains ... getting there was no problem but getting inside the valley to the monastery was difficult ... we had to scale down sheer cliff walls to come in from behind ... luckily the Tibetans are used to mountain climbing."

"The cloaking kept the guards in the dark about our approach and they were too overconfident. After we were able to silence their outside guards ... we eliminated their followers and leaders ... some few may have escaped but the Princess has warriors hunting them down and now that the superstitions for the place have been exposed, the people do not fear them anymore."

"What did you learn from them?"

"That was the strangest part ... when we told them we were going to eradicate them all, they laughed and said there were too many dark monasteries in other lands, and we couldn't eradicate them all."

Yufei looks at Yufeng. Yufeng asks,

"Was anyone injured ... on our side?"

Gugu shakes his head.

"Just one warrior."

"How was Chen Er and Dorjie through all this?"

"They fought masterfully ... I knew Chen Er was a great fighter ... but I wouldn't like to fight the Princess ... she is fierce."

Yufei laughs,

"Now I know why Chen Er is afraid of her ... haha."

He laughs until Yufeng punches him.

In the middle of the night Yufei wakes up ... a moment later so does Yufeng. He looks at her.

"Are you thinking what I'm thinking?"

"About LF?"

He nods and says,

"If LF knew what the boys were thinking before thinking, then LF traveled to the no-time."

"Yeah ... that's what came to me too."

"Do you understand it?"

He smiles and she says,

"Me neither ... maybe in the morning ... or the next morning ... or"

Then she is back asleep, but Yufei stays awake a little longer ... pondering.

When he awakens, he knows and shakes Yufeng.

"In the no-time, LF saw all the potentialities and transferred information, to effect the outcome she wanted to happen."

"But how?"

"I don't know ... just as I don't know how Panda can communicate with her."

"Maybe we ask Panda ..."

Then they look at each other and laugh.

"No ... that won't work, she'll just think we are children."

***

28 The Dark Witch of Subashi

The next morning, everyone is up early ... Beersheba and two of her girls are preparing fresh baked flat bread, Hami fruit, eggs, and roast lamb. The boys are clearing away the previous night's debris and arranging the seating around the large central rug.

When the visitors arrive, they are pleasantly surprised by the lavish breakfast.

Beersheba tells the boys to show the guests where to sit. Tariq and his brother crowd around Panda. Tariq speaks first to Panda.

"Sister Panda please sit here next to me ..." but then his brother, Baraq, objects.

"No sister, please sit here next to me."

The two boys are squaring off to settle this with their fists when Beersheba looks over, shakes her head, and tells the boys,

"She can sit between you, okay?" with this decision, they are happy.

Yufeng smiles at Beersheba. They quickly sit down and feast on all the foods.

Tarem asks Yufei, "What would you like to see today?"

Yufei looks at Yufeng ... the night before they had discussed how much to tell Tarem of their mission ... in the end, they decided to tell as little as possible about the elders ... *for now.*

"Like we discussed yesterday, we are merchants looking for new trade routes for our caravans ... so maybe we meet some influential merchants and also one or two influential ministers at court ... that are equally wary of this 'witch' you mentioned and the coming invasion."

"The Witch of Subashi ..." Tarem says and adds, "Good ... I know just the people. In Kucha we have a merchant's guild which meets often ... I am one of the leaders and the others respect me ... also I know the ministers to whom we should talk."

Yufei asks, "The Mongols ... what is the latest news on them?"

"They are at war against the Western (Xi) Xia and should defeat them soon."

"What lies between the Xi Xia and Kucha?"

"Nothing ... we will be next."

"Then we don't have much time."

Yufeng squeezes Yufei's arm. Tarem and Beersheba look at him, sensing their reason for being here is not only for trade.

Beersheba asks the boys what their plans are for the day, and they mumble nothing.

"Maybe you can show Panda our city?" the boys' eyes light up.

"Yes! Wonderful idea mama!" Tariq almost shouts. The adults laugh and the other girls ask to come too.

Yufeng looks to Beersheba, "Will they be safe?"

Beersheba nods, "No problem ... my boys are feared ... and respected here." Then looking at the boys,

"But no fights ... understand?"

"Yes mama."

Beersheba leans over to Yufeng, "I sensed that you two prefer to meet these merchants and ministers alone?"

Yufeng nods, "Yes, thanks" then smiling, "And the boys seem happy with the arrangement."

Beersheba smiles,

"Just like their dad."

***

An hour later, the group of youths ... Tariq, his younger brother, two younger sisters and Panda are strolling through the streets of Kucha.

"And this is the famous mosque .... and this is the famous temple ... and this are the royal palace ..."

After another hour, Panda asks the sisters, "Do you want to see more temples, and mosques?"

The girls don't speak as they are in awe of Panda also ... but they do shake their heads.

"Good ... me neither ..." then turning to Tariq she says, "OK ... now listen ... the first thing I want to see are exotic animals ... falcons, leopards, wolves, things like that ... and I want to see their trainers ... then I want to see your most beautiful gardens ... but not just the pretty flowers ... I want to see where they grow healing herbs ... okay?"

The boys look at each other and their sisters ... they confer a minute and then Tariq says,

"Why didn't you say so in the beginning ... let's go this way to the animal trainers ... but you can't tell our mother."

Panda smiles and rolls her head like her mother.

And off they go ...

***

Meanwhile, Tarem, Yufei, Yufeng and Gugu go to meet various prominent merchants and the lure of additional business from a wealthy foreign trader opens every door with welcome smiles.

At first Tarem vouchsafes for them as very prominent merchants from distant lands. The merchants all know Tarem acquired his wealth in trading in distant lands ... but even to this day, they don't know that it was from the illicit jade trade with Yufei, that made Tarem's fortune.

Yufei mentions traditional Chinese items ... teas, lacquers, silks, etc. ... which are all harder to come since the invasions and tribal wars have disrupted the Silk Road caravans. But when they mention invasions, it's just the opening Yufei was seeking.

"Which invasion concerns you the most?"

All of the merchants that they visit say the same, "Our biggest worry now is the Mongols. Their army will be here soon ... a few weeks, a few months ..."

"But I didn't see any preparations for defense?" Yufei says innocently to them.

"Ha! ... if only it were that easy ..."

"What do you mean?"

The first man is wary, but Tarem tells him it is okay,

"I have already told him about the witch, so feel free to tell him your thoughts."

Then each of them opens up about the dark influence this witch has over the queen and the same influence that the queen has over the king.

"What will you do?" Yufei asks each one.

Looking around, one merchant says in a low voice "Many merchants have started moving their valuables and families further west."

"But isn't that equally dangerous?'

"Yes ... to the west is another unfriendly tribe, the Kara Khitans ... and beyond them, another, the Khwarazm."

"The Black Khitans?"

"Yes ... but we see no choice."

"But what if this witch was ... *gone*?"

The man rises and closes the doors and windows, and in a low voice says,

"She has an army of spies ... they operate out of the Subashi Temple ... many people have disappeared."

Then Gugu asks the man, while making the motion of cutting his throat,

"But if someone were to silence her ..." but the man cuts him off.

"Yes, yes ... everyone would rejoice and support that someone."

They all rise.

Yufei and Yufeng bow and tell each merchant and minister they meet,

"Thank you for your time ... hopefully the gods of good fortune will prevail over the darkness."

***

Meanwhile at the exotic animal grounds, Tarem's children are amazed when Panda appears to talk to various animals ... falcons and steppe wolves ... even the trainers are in awe when she approaches a dangerous snarling huge steppe wolf and gets it to lick her hand. They even accept criticism when she berates them for not caring better for the animals.

Panda gets closer to a falcon and whispers to it.

"What are you doing?" Tariq asks,

"Trying to learn their language ... each animal in different locations uses different *language* to communicate ... like people,"

"Words?"

"Not words ... it's hard to describe ... *sounds* and body movements."

The boys and girls don't understand ... but for one boy ... his life has changed forever ... Tariq will remember this moment for his entire life ... the moment one knows when one's future destiny reveals itself to you.

At the herbal gardens, behind the local clinic, Panda finds some promising new herbs which she collects to show her mother later.

On the way home, they go to the market streets and look at various toys and treats. Tariq is hovering over all of them as though they are his lion cub pride. But as they leave one street and enter another, they are blocked by two carriages passing with armed guards protecting them on all sides. Panda freezes, grabs Tariq's hand, hides behind him, and drags him back into the alley into the shadows ...

"Quick ... all of you hide back here."

They do as she says and peer out onto the street. The carriages stop, a side window curtain is pulled aside, and a dark shrouded figure looks around.

Panda shrinks behind her new cousins, hiding herself physically and non-physically cloaking her spirit. Even though the other kids are blocking her, she *senses* the dark witch looking for her.

Tariq is quick to understand and shouts at his brother,

"I told you no more candy ... when we get home, I'll tell mother ... and you girls also ... I hate being a babysitter every day!"

The witch passes over them and looks further down the road ... thinking ...

(What was that I sensed a moment ago?)

Sensing nothing more ... even with her invisible probing, she tells her driver,

"Continue on to the palace ..." (*something new is in Kucha ... but what? Mongol spies? Kara Khitans? Those stupid old women from Kailash?*)

The carriage moves down the street and out of sight. Only then do the children come out and look at Panda, who has a hardened look on her youthful face. She looks at Tariq.

"We have to get back. I need to tell my parents about this,"

Tariq nods, gathers the others, and tells them all, "Let's go home this way."

On the way back the children don't talk and Tariq, who was in awe of Panda before this, is now committed to protecting her ... *forever*.

29 To Avert Destruction

Back at Tarem's compound, they enjoy another feast but a more subdued one. Panda has explained to her parents what she saw and felt. The boys confirmed to their father that it was the Witch of Subashi Temple.

Beersheba, seeing that some serious, private discussions are enfolding, sends her children outside to do various chores. Her eldest son, Tariq, though looks at his father, who nods.

"Tariq, you can stay ... you're getting old enough to learn these things." Beersheba nods and tells the boy,

"Then make yourself useful, make some mint tea."

Yufei stands up and helps Yufeng up also ... in a corner, they confer privately for a minute and then come back and Yufeng sits down but Yufei remains standing ... and he starts to explain more to them.

"Tarem ... dear brother and friend and Beersheba, sister of my wife and dearest friend ... we need to tell you some things because our presence here could put you and your family in danger..."

With those words, Beersheba slides in next to Tarem and holds his hand.

"We are not here on just a vacation ... or a trade trip ..." then he pauses.

"We are on sort of a mission ... I can't tell you everything as it would only increase your risk ..."

Tarem asks, "What kind of mission?"

"The first part, which concerns your family and all the people of Kucha ... is to prevent their slaughter by the Mongols."

Beersheba asks, "Just you three?"

Panda clears her throat.

Correcting herself, Beersheba says, "I mean ... just you four."

Yufei looks at her and Tarem ... Panda looks at Tariq

"All you can see are us four."

"There are more of you?"

"Not physically ... but that's what's hard to explain ..."

Yufeng speaks, "When something good happens to you, you think it's luck ... or blessings of the gods? ... it is neither ... there is an invisible force underneath this realm which ... *can* enable good outcomes."

Then Yufei pours cold water on this positive thought by saying,

"And there is an invisible dark force which *can* cause dark manifestations ... bad evil things ... this force strives for destruction."

Tarem asks, "The Mongols?"

"No, not all of them anyway ... they are more like a fire on the steppes which fosters a new growth in the spring ... yes, they are warlike ... and there are some dark elements there also."

Tariq asks, "And the Witch?"

Yufeng says, "Panda, tell them what you sensed ... but first let me explain, Panda has special abilities ... like the healing shamans, she can probe inside to heal ... or to learn a person's deepest thoughts."

Panda speaks, "Today in the market, even before she arrived, I sensed an evil ... a constantly probing evil ... like a predator animal on the steppes, looking for its next prey to feed off."

She looks at her mother, who nods, "Tell them everything."

"But not just to capture and kill the prey ... to tear it apart savagely ... and her prey are ... humans."

Tariq says, "Her carriage stopped, the window curtain opened, and she looked out searching for something or someone, but Panda was hiding behind us."

Panda clarifies, "That was just for her guards, the witch can sense through people."

"Then how ..."

Yufei speaks, "We know how to hide ... how to cloak our spirits from these people."

"Cloak?"

"Brother, there are others who help in this fight for light, they taught us some skills ... some we learned from our own experiences (looking at Panda) ... some you saw before when we traveled together."

Tarem nods and looks at Beersheba and then his son,

"If your mission here in Kucha, is to rid us of this witch, we will help ... and others too ... but how will this solve the Mongol problem?"

If the witch is gone, and the queen neutralized by prominent ministers, we hope to convince the king to submit to the Mongols."

"Surrender?"

"*Submit* ... and survive; *submit* and save the lives of all the people; *submit* and spare the city from complete destruction ... it is the Mongol way."

Yufeng adds, "Submitting will allow the king to stay in nominal power and just pay tribute to the Khan and some other bureaucratic duties, like taxes and supplies for his armies ... far, far better than the cemetery."

"Some won't agree ... but that's your job ... to convince them ... they know and respect you ... we will take care of the witch."

Beersheba looks at her friends,

"You must be very, very careful ... she is evil incarnate."

Tariq speaks, "Father ... mother, they will need a local guide ... I would like to assist them."

Beersheba looks at Tarem, Tarem looks at his oldest son who is still a young teenager ... then he sighs and agrees.

Looking at Yufei, "He is a good boy, he has his mother's brains, and my good looks ..." everyone rolls their eyes as Beersheba slaps him.

"You old goat ... I don't know how I put up with you all these years."

Panda smiles, "I can tell you ... it's because deep down you love him with all your heart."

Beersheba smiles and tells Panda, "You're right but ... it's not polite to poke around other people's hearts ... didn't your mother teach you that."

"She did ... aunty ... I'm sorry."

"It's okay ..." she smiles.

Tarem interjects, "Well, we have a lot to do and not much time ... I heard today, the Mongol khan's armies are already at Dunhuang."

Tarem says, "I'll start to lay the groundwork with those merchants and ministers we met with today ... I need to think of a good cover story ..."

"How sure are you that Kucha will be spared if the king submits?"

"Pretty sure ... we even think the Khan will send a message to that effect when they are close ... and he will keep his word."

Tarem is already thinking his plan through and who to line up first ... and then second ... so the others will follow, *if I can get those first few merchants and ministers ...*

Yufei approaches Tariq, "How far is it to this Subashi Temple?"

"About 20 gongli north ... in the foothills .... There are two temples actually ... an East Temple and a West Temple."

"What else do you know?"

Tariq looks to see if his mother has gone, "Well, mother has forbidden us to go near there ...."

Panda smiles and tells him, "Big brother, you can tell them ..."

"My friends and I sometimes ride out to the mountains ... I have a friend who lives further up in the mountains .... maybe two gongli past the temples."

"Is it heavily guarded?"

"Only the East Temple where the witch goes ... the guards sleep in the West Temple."

Yufei looks at Yufeng, "Here's what I think ... we don't know how powerful the witch is so we must be very careful ... Panda sensed her powers but was able to cloak herself and the witch wasn't afraid of Tariq. "

Yufeng raises her eyebrows, "Are you thinking of sending them there alone?"

"Just to scout it out ... they can hide in the hills nearby and watch their movements ... I'll give her my small telescope and they will bring blankets for the night."

"Stay outside in the mountains alone at night?"

"No ... at sunset, make their way up to Tariq's friend's place and stay there. Then come back the next day by another route, avoiding the temple."

"Then looking at the two youth, "Under no circumstances do you go inside the temples or even get close ... understand?"

"Yes, uncle!"

"Yes, baba."

Well ... so much for expecting teenagers to follow their parent's orders ...

30 Subashi Temple

Early the next morning, the two youths mount their horses and ride out ... with two worried mothers wishing their eyes could go all the way with them.

Panda is a pre-teen (twelve or thirteen ... according to whichever cultural calculations you use) ... Tariq is in his early-mid teens (fourteen-fifteen)... but that is where the closeness ends. Tariq is tall and strong for his age ... driven by a desire to be like his father ... who has become a legend in Kucha.

Panda, meanwhile, takes after her mother, and is wiry and strong but not so tall as Tariq. But her looks are deceiving ... climbing through the Snowy Mountain trees with LF and her monkey friends, has given her incredible strength and balance ... along with her hidden inner talents ... she is a formidable fighter. ... exceeding even her parents in some special abilities ... but even there ... many of her talents are, as yet, still undeveloped, or rather, yet to be realized ... whereas Tariq is the outer world guide, Panda is the invisible inner world guide on this mission.

Panda is smiling as they ride out. Tariq asks,

"Why are you smiling?"

"Because of you."

"Me? What about me?"

"You are so shy ... we will never get to know each other unless you learn to talk."

He scratches his head, "I don't know what to say to you ... I guess I'm a little afraid."

"Of me?"

"Not of you ... but I'm afraid to say something stupid."

Then she laughs, "Don't you understand? We are old friends now ... you can talk freely ... who cares if you say something stupid or I say something stupid ... look there ahead on the trail ... isn't it beautiful?"

He looks and smiles, "You are right ..." then he looks at her and asks,

"Can you ride fast?"

Panda laughs, whips her horse, and rides off shouting, "See if you can catch me!"

And the two gallop off ... to their own destiny...

***

About two hours later, Tariq holds out his hand to motion her to stop.

"What is it?"

"We're getting close ... maybe we should go off the trail now."

"Okay." She says, willing to follow him in these new lands.

Tariq leads off to the west towards some low hills. After another 30 minutes he stops and dismounts. He holds her reins, and she dismounts too, then he hands her both reins and says,

"Wait here a minute, I want to see how close we are to them, from on top of that hill." pointing to the hill on their right.

"Okay."

Tariq runs up the hill, looks out for a minute and runs back.

He takes both reins and ties them to a bush, "Come with me ... do you have that telescope?"

"Yes." she reaches into her bag and brings it out.

"Good."

Then he grabs a water flask from his horse, and they walk up the hill. Near the top they crouch down to remain unseen by the guards on the other side, about a gongli (km) away.

Panda scans the temples with the telescope and then hands it to Tariq, who does the same.

"This is a good spot, we can see the entrances of both temples and also their corral, where they keep the two carriages."

"Two? There's only one there now. But why do they keep two carriages?" Panda asks.

"The other one must be somewhere else. I've heard that sometimes the Queen comes out here."

When Panda scans with the telescope again, she notices, "I don't see any local worshippers going there."

"Since the witch arrived last year, the locals are afraid ... they tell strange stories of people in black dancing around a large fire ... chanting ... I don't know if it's real or just stories to keep people away."

"Let's take turns watching with the telescope."

"Okay."

"Let me know if you sense any danger."

"Okay ... but I am worried about probing down there ... I can hide myself from her probing but I'm afraid she may sense my probing and send the guards after us."

They spend the morning watching ... not too much happened ... every two hours the guards changed ... until after lunchtime, when the second carriage returned and the black witch steps down, looks around and goes into the East Temple.

Even though they were more than a thousand meters away, the youths hid behind the hill ... wary of her evil gaze.

After a few minutes, Panda peeks out and sees that she had gone inside, and they had brought her carriage to the corral, next to the other one.

An hour later, three Mongol warriors ride up unchallenged, stabled their horses at the corral ... and stride into the East Temple carrying a packet.

The two watch through the telescope and about 30 minutes later, the three Mongols come out of the temple ... without the packet ... go to their horses and ride off ... towards the East.

A short time later, the witch comes out, gives an order and her carriage is brought around. The driver sets down some steps and she climbs up the portable steps and enters the carriage ... after scanning 360 degrees around. Before she started her scan though, the youths ducked again behind the hill.

A few minutes later, the carriage rolls off down the valley towards Kucha.

Panda looks at Tariq, "Did you see?"

"See what?"

"Those three warriors brought in a packet but when they left, they didn't have it and when the witch left, she didn't have it."

"So?"

'It's probably in the East Temple."

"No ... wait! You're not thinking about going down there."

Panda looks at him like he is a child and as she stands, says to him as she steals around the hill,

"Aren't you supposed to protect me? Come on."

After the witch left, the guards went into the West Temple to rest ... so the two youths were not spotted, approaching behind rocks and bushes. Finally, they steal into the doorway of the East Temple.

Tariq starts to ask,

"Why would they just leave it unguarded?" ... when they hear a low growl.

They turn and face a large crocodile guarding the inner chamber. Although he has one leg chained to the wall there is no way around him and his mouth could swallow Panda in one bite.

Tariq is afraid but draws courage when he sees that Panda is unafraid.

Panda tries different sounds and gestures to communicate with the animal but can't find the right one... LF's spirit comes to her and points out the back leg ... she notices the chained back leg is festering around the bracket.

She reaches into her packet and brings out a small bottle of a milky liquid.

"Try to get his attention so I can put this on his leg."

Tariq, who has not really known real fear up until now, laughs,

"Get his attention? I'm trying to avoid his attention!"

He jumps in the other direction and waves his hands, "Hey ... you ... ugly monster look at me!"

Panda berates him, "Don't call *her* an ugly monster!"

Tariq wonders (*her?*)

Silently though, Pada moves around to the back leg ... if the crocodile turns quickly, she could be trapped ... but she has confidence in her animal instincts and her jumping prowess ... also LF is working behind the scenes to pacify the huge animal. She pours out some of the liquid onto the festering leg wound. As she does this the animal turns and looks at Panda.

Panda does something remarkable ... she reaches out and puts her hand on the animal's back and probes it. The animal responds by closing its jaws and looks at this new creature.

After Panda moves away the animal curls back to investigate his back leg and realizes the pain is less ... and its consciousness connects with Panda's conscious spirit ... not in any communication ... but an emotion of oneness.

Then Panda walks around towards the inner chamber doorway, stops, turns to the animal, and tells it,

"We will go in for only a minute. We mean no harm. We are friends."

Tariq stares at her and the animal, "Do you think it understands?"

"I'm not sure ... but I think we can enter."

Slowly ... ever so slowly they enter the dark witch's chamber and what they see resembles a child's worst nightmare ... skulls on poles, a torture rack in one corner, strange symbols on flags, a large table for dining ... or dissecting ...

In the back is a small bed and a large table with a large wooden throne-like chair behind it. As they approach the chair, they see the packet on top with some parchments sticking out.

Panda holds her hand up to caution Tariq.

"Don't touch anything, she will know. ... let me touch them."

Panda reaches into her pouch and retrieves a pair of medical gloves and puts them on. Then she slides the document out of the packet and tries to read it."

Tariq watches over her shoulder, "It's in Tangut, can you read it?"

"No, but I can memorize it. Do you see any others?" she rolls it back up and returns it to its original spot.

"There in that basket, several more."

She goes there and unrolls 2 more rolled parchments ... memorizing the contents."

After she returns them to the basket, they make one last look around. They both spot a big trunk in the corner near the bed at the same time and go towards it.

Panda tries to open it, but it is locked. She reaches inside her pouch, retrieves an acupuncture needle, and picks the lock open.

When they open it up, they are astonished by all the jewels and gold inside. She reaches carefully to the bottom and slides out a jeweled broach.

"You're taking it? Why?" Tariq asks.

"As proof ... it's one of hundred from the bottom ... I don't think even a black witch remembers the location of every stolen treasure ... or checks them every day."

Tariq looks around, "I think we should leave now ... how about you?"

"Okay ... let's go."

They retrace their steps out past the crocodile and the resting guards ... but don't relax until they are riding several gongli on the way home.

And only then does Tariq's breathing return to normal.

Panda asks him,

"Did you recognize those warriors that rode up?"

Tariq nods,

"Mongols ... *I think from the Naimen tribe.*"

31 "What were you thinking?"

But the #1 thought as
the pair of youths look at each other ...
"Thinking?"

Back home, their thoughts of a warm welcome after a successful mission are quickly dashed when Beersheba starts slapping Tariq and Yufeng berates a bowed Panda for entering the temple.

"What were you thinking?" Beersheba asks as she looks for something to use to beat her disobedient son.

Yufeng is equally enraged.

"Don't you understand how dangerous the dark forces are?"

"Their powers are frightening ... you could have put the whole mission at risk!"

Panda, meanwhile, gets some paper and starts recreating the documents she memorized in this strange script. When she is finished, she hands them to her mother.

"This is what the strange warriors brought. And these were other ones."

Just then Tarem, Yufei and Gugu return. When they hear of the youth's adventure, a new round of scolding has to run its course before they look at the documents.

Yufei looks at it and hands it to Tarem, "Can you read it?"

Tarem scans it and asks Tariq,

"These warriors who came there, did you recognize them?"

"Naimen Mongols."

Tarem turns to the others,

The message is short, "Armies will arrive in a few days. Make sure the king does NOT submit. When we slaughter everyone, *me and my brothers* will share our booty with you ... as agreed."

"Is it signed?"

"No."

"What about the other ones?"

"One looks to be from several months before outlining their plans on attacking the Xi Xia and then Kucha. Asking the kings to submit or be destroyed."

Yufei asks Tarem, "Do you think the ministers will believe these documents?"

"I'm not sure ... maybe if we had something else."

Tariq looks at Panda ... Panda smiles and reaches into her satchel and retrieves the beautiful, jeweled broach.

'Would this help, uncle?'

Yufei looks at it and smiles at his daughter,

"Daughter, what have you been doing? Stealing from the nasty old witch?"

"Sorry baba ... I though the little sisters could use it to play with their dollies."

Then they all finally laugh.

Yufeng asks the other adults, "Well, should we punish them more with sticks for not obeying us ... or congratulate them for bringing back this evidence?"

Gugu suggests a compromise.

"I suggest the two of them go to our room and reflect on what happen and understand the risk they took ... not only to themselves but to the whole mission."

Then looking at them he adds,

"Think about it ... what if you got caught and under torture exposed everything ... and all the people in Kucha were slaughtered including all their families ..."

A little more subdued, the two nod and start to go towards the guest room. Panda stops and turns,

"You are right ... we will reflect on it ... oh ... one last thing ... if you go there, look out for the large crocodile guarding the inner chamber." then the two walk off.

Yufeng looks at Yufei and the others,

"*Crocodile?*"

There is a silent moment of comprehension ...

Yufei says casually,

"Yeah ... of course, look out for the large crocodile."

Then they try hard to stifle laughing.

***

Meanwhile, back at the East Temple, the witch has returned. Immediately upon entering she senses someone has been there. She looks around but can't find anything ... she opens her treasure trunk, but it appears okay ... she looks at the last document, but it is where she left it. She tries to sense another person's presence ... which she does ... faintly.

She calls her head bodyguard and asks him to inquire of the guards if anyone had come in here while she was gone.

He returns shortly and shakes his head.

"And they had at least two guards at the entrance at all times?"

"That's what they said ... but after we left, who knows ..."

'Get them in here ... all of them!"

Once they are all lined up in front of her, she starts to grill them.

"I KNOW one of you came in here while I was gone."

Glancing at the torture rack, "I can get you to talk one way or the other."

"Who was on duty outside my chambers while I was gone?"

Two of the guards raise their hands ... slightly.

"And you were outside the doorway all the time?"

The sweat on their faces exposes the truth. One man says yes, the other says he took a short rest. The witch turns to the one who said he stayed on duty.

"So, you were here all the time?"

The man nervously nods.

"Did you enter my chamber?"

The man shakes his head, "No ... never Mistress."

Now she knows he is lying ... but she doesn't know why ... she goes to the man, places her hand on his head and probes inside.

Inside she sees flashes of memories ... even one from inside her room ... but there are no date captions on these images ... it could be today or a week

149

ago. But she senses no evil connection behind his action, no group targeting her ... (*stupid curiosity ... but I need to teach them all a lesson.*)

Turning to the chief bodyguard she says,

"Show him what happens to disobedience ... feed him to the monster."

The man starts screaming as two men drag him out to the crocodile for ...

... *dinner* ...

32 A Plan

That night, while the two youths reflect on their misadventure, the adults come up with a plan.

Tarem will organize the merchants and ministers behind a campaign to convince the king to submit ... or depose him if he refuses.

"Will they go that far?" Yufei asks.

"If their families and their own lives depend on it ... I think so."

"But it depends on your success in eliminating the Black Witch of Subashi. What's your plan?"

"Yufeng, get Panda and Tariq out of jail and ask them to come here."

When they arrive, Yufei asks them,

"Have you thought about what we told you?"

"Yes baba, and we both now realize you were right ... we saw the opportunity and it blinded us of all the other repercussions."

They look at Yufeng who softly mouths, *the Way* ...

There are many different pathways in this life .... all affected by one's decisions.

"Good ... because now we're getting into a more dangerous part of this mission and many people's lives depend on all of us making smart decisions and working together ... understand?"

They both nod.

"Okay ... Tarem, of all your children, which two are the fastest riders?"

"Tariq and his brother Baraq."

Yufei looks at Tariq, "Is that true?'

The boy nods then glances at Panda.

"What?"

"Actually, she's faster than me ..." they all smile.

"I know but I need her for something else ... the crocodile."

Panda smiles and rolls her head. Then Yufei asks them both,

"You watched them for several hours ... how many guards do you think she has ... in all?"

"Maybe twelve ... we didn't want to go inside the other temple to count the sleeping ones ..."

Gugu stifles a laugh, "Well ... that was smart."

"Where are the stables for the horses?"

Tariq draws a map, showing the temples and the stables.

"Off to the south ... downwind."

"Do you think you and your brother could sneak up to the horses, and steal a couple ... then ride like the wind southward ... without being caught?"

Tariq looks at Baraq and they both smile mischievously, "Well maybe ... if ..."

The adults in the room pause and look expectantly at the boys.

Tarem asks, "If what?"

"If Panda gives us each a kiss."

"WHAT!" shouts their mother.

"Just on the cheek mama ... like a sister ..." he adds defensively.

They look at Panda, who smiles and leans over and kisses them both ... the boys are ecstatic and start running in circles. The women are shaking their heads. Yufei says,

"Just like their dad."

Beersheba grabs the boys and stops them ...

Yufei lays out the plan ...

"Here are my thoughts ... first we need a diversion to reduce the number of guards ... the boys will sneak up and steal two fast horse and gallop off yelling and screaming ... hopefully several guards will follow reducing the opposition ... while the guards outside are watching this, we four will sneak into the West Temple and while Panda watches at the door, we silently eliminate the guards sleeping in there ... then we take out any remaining guards outside and go after the witch ... Panda will take care of the crocodile and we will take care of the witch ... any questions?"

"What if something goes wrong?"

"Something always goes wrong ... that's why we need to be aware in both worlds ... this one and the underlying realm."

Beersheba asks, "What about me and the girls, how can we help?"

Yufei looks at Tarem and says, "We think you and the girls should pack things and head south towards Tibet for safety."

Tarem shakes his head, "She won't ... "

"If you fight ... we all fight ... we will stay here and have some fast horses ready ... in case we all need to flee to Tibet."

They all agree.

Tarem takes the two boys off for a private session on horse-stealing, while Yufeng takes Panda aside and quizzes her about the crocodile.

Yufei and Gugu discuss documents they may need to convey their submission to the Khan.

33 Eliminate the Witch of Subashi

By early morning, the raiding party is already on the knoll overlooking the temples. Down at the horse corral things go *almost* according to plan ...

The boys successfully sneak into the fenced corral, but, unfortunately, nobody told the guard's horse about *the plan*, and they are a bit reluctant to join in ... *ooops so much for the plan* ... the horses all shy away from the boys. One of the guards at the temple notices the horses getting nervous and starts to walk over to investigate. Luckily, before he reaches them, the boys grab two horse, open the gate, and gallop off yelling with some of the other horses following. The first guard alerts the others and 3 more join the first guard, grab their horses, mount up and chase after the boys.

While this was going on, our raiding party entered the West Temple and eliminated the guards sleeping inside. One guard who was watching outside returns early and is confused when he encounters a young girl at the entrance. Forewarned by her senses, Panda has already unsheathed her knife and cuts the surprised guard's throat ... with no feeling of anger ... like she was releasing his body from his spirit ... but under her breath she whispers,

"*This is for LF.*"

Then the four steal to the East Temple and eliminate two guards outside. Inside, the antechamber they are confronted by the fierce crocodile, but when Panda goes up to him and gives him a treat he returns to his resting place.

Inside is just the Black Witch and the Chief bodyguard. Yufeng takes down the bodyguard while Yufei goes after the Witch. Fearless and snarling, she throws up a cloud of blinding powder ... but Yufei anticipated it and blocks his eyes with his baklava and lunges at her, knocking aside her curved knife and grabbing her forearms.

But she fights like a trapped she-cat and whirls and twirls try to bite him or scratch him anyway she can. Gugu comes around behind her and knocks her out with the butt handle of his knife and ties her up.

Yufeng rushes up to Yufei, "Are you okay ... let me look at you?"

She inspects him and sees some scratches on his hands from the witch's fingernails. Then she inspects the fingernails.

"Poison!"

"Panda! My kit! Quick!"

Panda rushes in and brings her small portable medical kit and needles. Yufeng pours white powder on the scratches and places several needles in his arms. Then he pours two white pills from a bottle and gives them to Yufei. After he appears stabilized, they turn to the witch who is wakening.

Even knowing she is trapped the witch is still defiant.

"You will never stop us! We are everywhere and soon the Mongol hordes will wipe Kucha off the earth ... haha!"

Yufeng goes up to her and tries to probe her but can't. She motions to Panda. Panda probes inside the witch's memories and starts to see faces ... Mongol faces. The witch realizes this and bites into a poison tooth and dies quickly.

Knowing that time is precious, they take some original documents and souvenirs and leave ... the same way they came.

Yufei is weak but with Yufeng's help, they manage to ride back toward Tarem's compound ... halfway out of town, the two boys join up with them on the stolen horses.

***

Back at Tarem's, they learn that Tarem has already gone to the palace. They leave the two boys to stay with their mother and sisters and they go to the palace.

Outside, a guard has been alerted to their impending arrival and ushers them into the minister's office where Tarem has gathered some prominent merchants and the sympathetic ministers.

Tarem smiles when they enter, and tells the others,

"These are my friends ... quickly, before the queen comes, tell us your news."

Yufei is still feeling weak and Yufeng is supporting him and adjusting the needles. He asks Gugu to explain what happened. Gugu goes though the events quickly and summarizes everything.

"The Black Witch of Subashi is dead, and we have the evidence of her treachery with us." he holds out the original documents from the Mongol conspirators.

The group reads and passes around the documents. They also realize that if the king doesn't submit, they will all perish ... there will be no alternative then but to depose him ... but they still hesitate as one asks,

"But how can we be sure the witch is dead ... we just have these stranger's words."

Even though he is weak, Yufei throws them a sack ... when they open it, they are shocked to see the witch's head.

Tarem takes that moment to gather their courage.

"We can't wait and debate any longer, the Mongol envoys are waiting for the king's reply ... he must submit or be replaced. Let's go see him."

They all agree and head to the king's receiving hall. The viceroy has been alerted and they are ushered in before the king.

Tarem and the chief minister present the evidence. The conspiracy documents, the sorry state of the defenses, the fate for those cities who defy the great khan ... and finally the witch's head.

Hearing about their activity from her spies, the Queen rushes in and shouts,

"Who are these people? What lies are they telling you?"

"Do you know what the Black Witch will do to you all?"

Yufeng says, "Not much I'm afraid." And kicks the witch's head to the queen who screams and faints.

The Chief Minister says, "Guards take the queen to her quarters and confine her there."

Then looking at the king, he tells him,

"King Barchuk, you have only two choices ... submit to the Mongols or be deposed by the people and flee to exile."

The king recognizes the obvious, "Write a reply to the Mongols ... we will submit."

The minister brings out the document that Gugu and Yufei had already prepared.

"Here it is your highness."

"That was quick."

"We knew how smart you were ... especially with the witch dead and the queen locked up ... we also advise sending the queen on a long trip somewhere."

Seeming relieved, the king agrees.

"How should we send our reply to the Mongols?"

Tarem suggests.

"Your Highness, it was my friends here who alerted us to this danger and who enabled us to find a solution. I suggest we send your reply with them ... and one of our ministers with a royal guard."

"So be it!" the nervous king proclaims, trying to reclaim a sense of control.

***

Before leaving for the Mongol camp, they gather for one last time at Tarem's. The family is sad they will go ... especially the boys.

Panda consoles the boys, "We will meet again."

Tariq asks,

"Are you sure?'

She smiles and nods, "I am sure." then she kisses them both on their cheeks.

Tarem and Beersheba ask the same question, "Will we see you again?"

Yufei is weak but smiles ...

"Yes ... in this world and in the next world."

Beersheba smiles and says,

"I prefer in this world."

They all exchange hugs and mount up as the minister and their escort are waiting.

As they ride, Yufei asks Gugu,

"How did the witch of Subashi compare to the ones outside of Lhasa?"

"*From the same evil spore.*"

34 Genghis Khan

On the journey to the Mongol camp, Yufei asks Gugu and the ministers about Genghis Khan. They tell him that his father was a leader of a small clan. When Genghis was a youth, his name was Temujin. One day when Temujin was still a youth, his father visited another friend on the steppes and they made a marriage pact between the man's daughter, Borte and Temujin. In the Mongol custom, at that point, a boy will live with the bride's family for several years until manhood.

On the way home though, Temujin's father was given poisoned food by another tribal group of riders and died. Temujin learned of this and returned to help his mother, but the rest of the clan shunned them and moved away ... leaving the family to survive by themselves ... just Temujin, his mother, a second wife and several young children ... on the barren steppe.

Against all odds, the family survived and years later, when he became a man, Temujin went back to reclaim his bride Borte, but before he could do so, she had been kidnapped by the Merkit tribe ... and pregnant by their leader.

In time, he would recapture her, and his following of warriors gradually grew in strength. Many warriors joined him because he rewarded them for their abilities, and he divided the spoils of raids equally.

At that time, the Mongols were fearless warriors with incredible durance and riding abilities. As he rose to power, other tribes tried to defeat him, but he kept winning and in 1206, at their kurultai meeting (to select their leader), he was named the Great Khan.

"What spiritual beliefs do they follow?"

"Genghis follows the God of the Blue-Sky, Tengri."

Yufeng asks,

"No woman goddess?"

"Yes ... there's also the Mother Goddess of Nature, Tengri's wife... they are firm believers in the spiritual power of nature."

Yufeng looks at Yufei and smiles ... then Yufei asks,

"How does he control his armies?"

"He has four sons and several competent generals ... he delegates authority to them ... after careful pre-planning every step of a campaign."

"Then he seeks out allies ... other tribes who will fight along with theirs for a share of the plunder."

"And when they fight, their formations are calculated to surprise the enemy or to lure them into traps by feigning a retreat, only to lead them to destruction."

"So, what you are saying is ... that although they are traditional nomadic hunters, they have evolved into a highly organized fighting force?'

"Yes ... and very efficient. They can be incredibly cruel ... or incredibly gracious ... it all depends upon whether the enemy resists or submits."

"Which is why we are here."

Gugu nods but he and Yufeng are worried about Yufei, who is slumping in his saddle from the dark witch's poison.

They pause on the trail several times for Yufeng to treat him. After each treatment he feels better ... but only for a while.

35 The Mongol Camp

With their Kucha flags and white flag of peace blowing in the wind ... their small caravan approaches the Mongol encampment straddling the road to Wuwei.

They explain their mission to the outlying guards and are escorted by a group of mounted warriors to the main encampment.

As they ride through the camp, they notice that everything in this camp is designed to move over land quickly ... once they capture and pillage a city, they pack up, send the bounty home, and move on to the next battle site ... which currently is to subjugate the Xi (Western) Xia tribe.

Like all Mongol encampments, everything is organized by groups of 10, then 100's, then 10,000 warriors (a tumen) ... their horses, women, tents (*gers*), etc. Secure in their knowledge of their own invincibility, the newcomers cause little notice among the Mongols, who continue going about their business of cooking, repairing items, cleaning, feeding the horses, etc.,

The escort takes them up to the main tent, which is much larger than any of the others. Confident in their own immortality, the sentry guards don't even ask them to deposit their weapons ... they know to even grasp the handle of a weapon inside this tent is instant death.

Yufei is weak but still manages to hold himself up unaided, Yufeng is on one side and Panda is on the other side with Gugu. Behind them is the Kuchean minister with the peace submission document. The escort guards remain outside. Upon entering, it takes a moment for their eyes to adjust.

At the very back is a long table and a large man sitting behind it ...
(*Genghis Khan ... they think*).

Seated next to him is a woman (*a wife?*). And along both sides are several warriors standing and looking at these new visitors.

The visitors enter, approach the Great Khan, and bow in obeisance. The Khan says something unintelligible, and they rise. Yufei speaks with Gugu translating into the Mongolian Altaic language ... then the Kuchean minister speaks in the Uighur language, which the Mongols can understand.

"Great Khan, we come from the Kuchean King with his positive response to your message of submission to the Great Khan."

Genghis looks over and smiles to his black robed shaman, Teb Tengeri ... Panda and Yufeng catch the glance and Panda catches her breath and squeezes her mother's hand, and then glances back at this man.

"That is good ..." he says, looking again at Teb Tengeri,

"We had been led to believe your king would not submit."

Teb Tengeri has been the shaman for Genghis for many years ... he has six brothers and they have become a formidable force in battle ... and to some ... a much too powerful force within the camp.

Gugu continues,

"We uncovered a conspiracy trying to turn the peaceful Kucheans against their beloved Mongol brothers ... but we were able to thwart their black plan."

"The minister will present the submission document, signed by their king. The king wishes peace and prosperity between our two people."

The minister hands the document to an aide who scans it, nods to the Khan, and hands it to him.

Genghis smiles and speaks, (translated) "Wonderful ... Wonderful ... my people will welcome this respite before our final push to defeat the Xi Xia."

Then he turns to an aide and whispers something.

The aide says, "Please introduce your party."

Yufei, in a loud voice introduces them,

"I am Xiang Yufei of Wuyi Mountain in China; next to me is my wife, my spirit, my best friend, my confidant, my strength ... her name is Wang Yufeng ... in her own right she is a famous healer, who has traveled the far corners of the world to learn from the great physicians the art of healing ... in this life, it is her mission to help people overcome the diseases which infect innocent people."

"Next to her is our daughter, Panda, a deceptively innocent looking child, whose talents and abilities are only now manifesting themselves."

"On my side, is our companion, Gugu, a learned Tibetan Buddhist scholar ... and good at sweeping out temples."

"Finally, as a token of good faith by the Kuchean king, we place ourselves at your mercy." (*sounds better than hostage*)

One of the Khan's sons approaches Genghis and whispers in his ear.

The Khan asks Yufeng, "Do you recognize anyone in this room?"

Yufeng scans the room with her eyes ... and without her eyes ... and then she smiles as she looks at Ogedei, the Khan's 3rd son.

"Many years ago, this man helped us ... I hope we can repay his kindness."

"This is my son, Ogedei. He tells me that back then you were on a mission for the old women at the Temple of Wisdom ... are you now on a mission for them?"

Yufeng smiles, "It depends ..."

"Depends on what?"

"To enable the Kuchean King to submit, we had to vanquish the Black Witch of Subashi ... in that struggle, she poisoned my husband. I believe the poison came from your lands (she looks at Teb Tengeri) ... if I can find that poison and heal my husband, we will serve you."

"Why would you serve me ... for riches?"

She shakes her head and looks at Borte (the Khan's wife),

"We have no need for riches ..."

Then turning to the Great Khan, "By serving you we serve the great god of the heavens, Tengri."

Startled Genghis asks, "How do you know Tengri?"

"We have traveled to the birthplace of man ... Gobekli Tepe, what westerner's call the Garden of Eden ... we have met the holy grandmothers who continue the traditions for thousands of years in worshiping Tengri and the Mother Goddess of Nature."

Upon hearing this, both Borte and some other women take especial notice.

Borte asks, "You have gone to the Holy Mountain Kailash?"

Yufeng nods.

"You have gone to the legendary valley of the Mother Goddess in the far west?"

Yufeng nods.

"But we have heard it is guarded by the Caliph of Baghdad, the Sultan of the Ayyubids, and the leader of the Brotherhood of Assassins?"

"It is."

"I'd love to hear the story."

"When you have the time."

Borte goes to the Khan's side and talks to him ... after a short discussion, Genghis nods and Borte returns to her seat. Then he motions for Ogedei and his youngest son, Tolui, to discuss something. Then he addresses their group ... first to the minister.

"Please convey my warm regards to the king and hope for a lasting peace between our two peoples. In a few days, I will send a delegation of our officials to go over our peace requirements with your minsters."

The minister bows and says, "I am at their disposal when they come to Kucha."

An aide comes up and leads him outside, where he mounts and departs.

Looking at the remaining members of the peace mission Genghis says,

"I welcome you to stay with us and offer advice and counsel when appropriate. I am assigning two of my sons to assist you ... Ogedei and Tolui ... Ogedei, since you have a little history with him and he can help you with your search for the medicine ... and Tolui because he has a new bride, not much older than your daughter, who just had a baby, and she can be a friend for her."

Borte whispers something to him.

"And my wife would like to tell you that our ger tent flap is always open to you and she is anxious ... as well as me ... to hear about your travels to the far west ... I am thinking we may go there someday also."

Everyone seems happy with the outcome ... everyone except Teb Tengeri, the dark shaman. He stares at Yufei and Yufeng as they depart, probing them ... little does he realize his biggest danger is not from them, but from the young girl with them ...

... *who is probing him as she cloaks herself.*

36 The Mongol Ger

Once outside, Yufei stumbles, and Yufeng grabs his arm to steady him ... Ogedei, sensing the man's weakness, organizes for them to have their ger set up near his and his younger brother's. While it is being organized, he brings them to meet his wife, Toregene.

She is outwardly friendly to please her husband but inwardly wary. Nevertheless, Yufeng is cordial to her. Beside her is a small boy about 3 years old.

"And this is my son, Guyuk ... Guyuk, say hello."

The child looks at one then the other and runs off to play.

Ogedei looks at the ger still being put up and decides to let Tolui introduce his new wife and baby to the visitors.

"Tolui, you introduce them to your wife, Sorkhohtani, I'll push the workers to finish their ger."

Ogedei goes to where they are putting up the tent while Tolui brings them over to his ger. Inside, is his young wife Sorkhohtani and her newborn baby, Mongke, (a future khan).

Sorkhohtani is busy holding the baby when they enter but still smiles a warm sincere smile at the new guests.

"Sorkhohtani, this is Yufeng, her husband Yufei, their daughter, Panda and their friend Gugu."

She bows down to them, and they do the same.

Yufeng and Panda go to look at the baby boy, "How old is he?"

"Almost a year ..."

"So big! My Panda was half that size at one year!"

The two women exchange knowing glances and then Panda also.

With those first few words, glances, and feelings of sincere affection ... they become lifelong friends ... Tolui continues the introduction,

"They are emissaries of the kingdom of Kucha and bring their submission of peace."

His wife smiles ... most mothers are against war, even the wives of fierce Mongol warriors.

"Wait until you hear their stories ... my brother Ogedei met them many years ago in Tibet, where they were helping the Immortal Elder Sisters there. And they have traveled to the far western lands to meet the grandmother guardians in the valley of the Mother Nature Goddess!"

Sorkhohtani cannot fathom all this at first, "It sounds unbelievable! Is it true?"

Yufeng just smiles.

"Will you tell us your stories?"

Looking at Yufei, who smiles, "Sure ... but first I must help my husband recover from a vicious poison."

Just then Ogedei returns and tells them that their tent is ready. They bow and walk to their new home. Ogedei explains everything about their mobility along the way ...

"Everything we own can be loaded up on carts and animals in a short time until we get to the next campground ... there are certain rules that everyone must obey ... like no urinating in bodies of water ... you will learn them quickly" ... then he laughs. Ogedei, she can tell, is well-liked by most of the warriors.

"Or pay the penalty."

Ogedei leaves and they go inside the new ger and start to stow their gear away when Yufei has a seizure.

He collapses to the floor, shaking, Yufeng and Panda rush to his side.

Yufeng tells Gugu, "Close the flap. Panda put something in his mouth to bite on!"

Panda grabs a tent peg and forces it between Yufei's teeth ... the teeth try to bite through the wooden peg. Yufeng is going through her portable medical kit to find the right pill. Finally, she finds it and forces it into his mouth.

Panda is watching ... apparently frozen ... but not really ... she is probing ... Yufeng realizes this and asks,

"What do you see Panda?"

She shakes her head several times, "It's like a lightning storm inside his head ... flashes of lightning ... a violent storm inside ... he can't control it ..."

"Could you do anything?"

"No ... I tried."

Just then Sorkhohtani comes into the tent, bringing extra blankets. She sees Yufei shaking and rushes to help.

"Just hold him down ... I need to insert my needles."

Panda hands her mother's medical kit to her and she starts removing needles and placing them into Yufei's critical qi points on his head, chest, and hands.

"You've seen this before?"

"Yes, in my village there were some who had this."

"Is there medicine there to cure it?"

Sorkhohtani looks at her sadly, "There is no cure ... but the spells can be controlled with an herb."

"He was poisoned by a black witch."

"Poisoned?"

Yufeng nods.

"Has he had these ... spells, before?"

"Yes, but not for a long time. I think the poison is like some of the epidemic diseases I've seen which searches the body for weak spots and then attacks the person there ... some their heart ... with Yufei, his head qi."

Panda asks, "Mother. What can we do?"

"We need to find the poison they used and then find the cure."

Sorkhohtani says, "Maybe I can help you find the poison ... I think it grows on the steppes in the northern lands.

"Thank you."

"Also, I'll send to my village for the medicine we use to control the attacks ..."

Yufeng has known only a few women like her ... her sister, Lanting, Immortal Sister Zhang in Quanzhou, the female doctor Wu in Kochi, India, the grandmothers in Gobekli, and Princess Dorjie ... women who unselfishly are there for other women when they need them most ... just as she has been there for them and others.

After a few moments, Yufei stops shaking and is resting.

They take the wood peg out of his mouth and he sleeps.

Then Sorkhohtani asks, "How did he get poisoned?"

Yufei recounts the story, Afterwards, the woman is in awe.

"Unbelievable ... she sounds like someone I know here."

"Who is that?"

"Teb Tengeri ... maybe you saw him in the main tent ... he always wears black wolf furs and bone necklace."

Panda says in a louder than normal voice, "That's him, mama."

"That's who, Panda?"

The face I saw inside the witch's mind before she killed herself ... I recognized it today."

The two women look at each other and then Sorkhohtani warns them,

"Don't say any of this to anyone. He is very powerful and ruthless. He has six brothers, and they are powerful ... even the Khan is wary of him ... at this time."

**

Meanwhile in another ger, not far away, Teb Tengeri and his brothers are venting their anger at each other.

"You said we would get to plunder this rich city, Kucha." one brother shouts at Teb, the oldest.

"I wanted a new wife ... now, who can I ravish?"

Teb angrily throws a bowl at him, "Go ravish one of the donkeys in the corral."

"Everything was planned and going smoothly ... until these newcomers came along and spoiled my plans."

"So, what are you going to do?"

Thinking of a new plan, "First we need to discredit them in the eyes of the Khan ... and then ..."

"How are we going to do that?"

"Why do I have to do all the thinking ... when I have a plan, I'll tell you ... for now, have someone watch these new people day and night."

"Don't worry ... they will pay for taking away our gold and plunder..."

37 Mongol tales

The next morning Yufei has somewhat recovered and is sitting up in their tent, drinking some liquid ... he asks Yufeng to fill him in on what happened yesterday. She retells the events from the day and night before and also the news about Teb Tengeri.

He looks at Gugu and then Yufeng and finally at Panda.

"Do you all see what I see?"

"Just as the Black Witch was the key to achieving our first assignment to save the Kucheans, neutralizing this evil man and his brothers is one of the keys to our success with the Mongols."

Gugu adds,

"Yes ... and we need to be careful ... he knows now that we are a threat."

"And it's not just him ... what I learned in the mountains with Chen Er and Dorjie ... there is a vast web of these dark centers."

Yufei sighs.

"Gugu, you filter around the camp learning who the key warriors are ... Teb Tengeri's group, the Khan's family and the important generals."

"Yufeng, cultivate, the Khan's wife Borte, Tolui's wife, the physicians, and any others that you sense could be helpful."

Yufei says, "Oh, Sorkhohtani told me her older sister, Chaur, is married to Jochi, the Khan's oldest son. The Khan has some other wives, but Borte is the primary wife and the most influential ... after his mother Hoelun ... and the women can give opinions in the councils."

"Good, try to meet her also."

Panda asks, "How about me ... what can I do baba?"

"Be friends with the younger family members and sons and daughters of the generals ... also with Tolui and Sorkhohtani ... be like a sister. And don't reveal all your skills ... it will just draw attention to you and reduce your effectiveness."

"What do you mean?"

"If they know you can fight, if they know you can communicate with animals, if they know you can sense their thoughts and actions ... they will be wary of you, and you will lose an advantage when we need your skills most ... understand?"

'I understand."

"So ... let's do those things and later we can share what we learn."

"What will you be doing?"

"Tarem told me about one of their young generals, Subedei, I want to meet him."

Yufeng says, "Okay ... and everyone be alert ... don't forget ...we are in a hostile land, in the middle of a hostile camp, surrounded by hostile warriors ..."

Panda laughs, "So what is the problem?" and then the others laugh too.

***

Panda goes to Sorkhohtani's tent ... and the new mother warmly greets her. Panda has picked up several words of the Altaic-Uighur language quickly and can communicate with her.

"Good morning Sorkhohtani ... can I help you today?"

Smiling, she tells the visitor, "That would be wonderful but first you have to start calling me with the name my sister uses ... it's *Sari*."

"Sari? I like it. What does it mean?"

She laughs, "In our homelands, the sari are small animals always causing mischief."

"Haha ... I like it all the more ..." then more somberly.

"I used to have a friend like that."

Sari notices the mood change and asks, "What happened?"

"To warn us away from coming to help you, some evil men killed her."

"I'm sorry ... did you find these evil people?"

"My father did." then Panda smiles,

"Sari ... I like that name ... how can I help you?"

"Can you hold Monke, while I prepare some soft food for him and clean up?"

"Sure, no problem ... come here you fierce warrior."

The baby (and future khan) laughs.

Just then Tolui comes in and looks around, "Where is the guard?"

Sari tells him, "His wife is in labor, I told him to go to her."

A bit angrily, Tolui says, "You should never be without a guard, especially while we are in enemy lands."

"It's okay, Panda is guarding me ... right Panda?"

"Right."

Tolui laughs, "I mean a warrior guard."

Panda tells him, "My father taught me to never underestimating your opponent."

Rebuffed, Tolui says, "And what will you do if an enemy swings his fist at you ... like this."

Surprisingly, to him, his fist just moves the air as Panda sensed his move.

Tolui tries again and again to strike her, but she is never there.

"What if he comes at the baby with a knife?" Tolui unsheathes his knife.

"Please don't do that."

"Haha ... afraid?"

"No ... I don't want to hurt you or scare the baby."

"Sari, take the baby, I need to teach this foreigner some Mongol fighting lessons ..."

Sari says, "Go outside."

Panda says, "No ... in here ... this must be kept private."

Not understanding, Tolui asks, "Do you have a knife?"

"Yes, but I don't need it ..." looking around she sees a heavy wooden ladle.

"This will do."

Tolui laughs again (*I like her spirit ... but still I need to bring her down a bit.*)

Then the fight starts ... Tolui lunges with the knife, but again, Panda is not there and bangs him on the back of his head with the wooden ladle. Tolui makes a sweeping slash, but Panda leaps high and comes down again with the ladle on Tolui's head. Tolui reaches out with both arms to grab her in a wrestler's hug, but Panda knows and slides easily under his legs and bangs him on the head again.

Tolui pauses and rubs his head.

Sari yells, "Stop ... you are going to break my favorite wooden spoon on this man's rock head."

They stop and then all laugh.

Tolui says, "Good ... we have found a new bodyguard for you."

Panda asks them, "But let's keep this our secret ... okay?"

They agree.

***

In another area, Yufeng is attending Borte, who is now almost 50 years old. Life is hard for Mongol women, eking out a living on the steppes, and traveling, usually in the winter, on war campaigns.

Borte is lying on some furs and after inspecting her and talking to her, Yufeng has placed needles at points where her qi is blocked. She turns the needles ever so gently. After about 30 minutes, she removes them and then does a quick moxibustion on other meridians where Yufeng senses blockage to the flow of qi.

Borte asks her, "What are you doing?"

"Your body functions by the flow of qi energy ... through invisible channels inside your body ... sometimes the qi gets blocked or out of balance and the needles help to restore the balance."

"Move your legs now ... how do they feel?"

Borte moves the legs and smiles, "Much better ... much better!"

Then she moves her arms, and they are not stiff anymore.

Then she looks at Yufeng closely and asks,

"It is said that you come from the Immortal Sisters of the Temple of Wisdom .... is that true?"

"Kind of ... my husband and I are from a small village in Southern China ... but we have come to know the elders at Mt. Kailash."

"Are you on a mission for them?"

"I am on the same mission as you ... peace and freedom ... for women, for personal spiritual beliefs, for trade."

"But you've heard the stories of what happens when our armies conquer a people?"

"Yes, but I have also seen how women are respected here, and how different people's beliefs are respected ..."

"Why is that important to you?"

"I've been to many distant lands where women aren't respected ... they are treated worse than slaves ... where people are slaughtered because they believe peaceably in the Mother Goddess."

"You know of the Mother Goddess?"

"I have been there ... to the birthplace ... the grandmothers are still there in the valley ... they all haven't been slain."

"There are stories ... old stories ... of a group of grandmothers who came from the west to teach our people ..."

Yufeng nods.

"Have you told any others about this?"

"No."

"Good ..."

"Why?"

"There are good people here ... many are good ... but like children ... do you understand?"

"Yes."

"And there are some with dark hearts also ... more cunning ... they try to poison people's minds/"

"I know ... those are the people we must defeat."

Borte doesn't say anything, just nods.

"Sister ... of the people around the great khan ... who should we be most careful?"

Borte thinks about it, then looks at Yufeng and finally decides to trust this new friend.

"The most dangerous is Teb Tengeri and his brothers ... they are black spirits."

"We've already sensed that ... we have evidence to link him with that Black Witch in Kucha."

"You do? That is good ... I will try to arrange a private dinner with the Khan where you can tell him this ... he is weary of Teb Tengeri also, but he is cautious."

"The members of your family and their wives and children ... can we trust them?"

Borte thinks longer this time, as though going through the list of names ...

"For the most part ... some are braver than others ... some are smarter than others ... some are a little slow ... there is only one I'd be careful of."

"Who is that?"

"Ogedei's wife, Toregene ... she seems interested in gaining personal influence."

"In a bad way?"

"I don't know, she's clever ... maybe a bit too clever ... it's just a feeling ... you can judge for yourself."

"Thank you for your confidence ... can I ask you one last thing ... how will I find Hoelun?"

"Do you mean where she is... I can introduce you to her ... she has a lot of aches and pains also ... she is almost 70 years old now."

"Thanks ... but I mean, what kind of woman is she? Wise? Kind? Friendly?"

"You will see ... she has had a hard life ... a very hard life ... let someone tell you the story some time about her husband poisoned, her tribe abandoning her, living off small field animals on the cold bleak steppes ... and she survived and raised the great khan ... a remarkable woman ... but hardened by her life."

"And Genghis will listen to her?"

"Absolutely! He worships his mother."

"I would love to meet her."

"Come ... I will introduce you to her ..."

38 Subedei

In another part of the camp, Yufei, feeling much better after Sari's medicine and treatment, walks to where they are teaching some young warriors fighting skills and tactics.

The person in charge is about the same age as Yufei and seems respected by all the warriors listening ... the man's name is Subedei and along with his older brother Jelme, Jebe and Khubilai (not the later khan) ... are called the *Four Hounds* of Genghis Khan.

He is directing them with flags. One group is attacking some stationary defenses ... then Subedei waves different colored flags and the attacking horsemen retreat. Immediately the defending horsemen chase after them. Subedei changes flags again and some of the retreating forces peel off to one side ... then a little later, another group peel off to the other side ... after a few minutes he changes flags and the retreating forces turn around and attack, along with the two groups that had peeled off ... now the retreating forces have the pursuers in a trap. Subedei raises another flag, and the action stops. The commanders ride to him and dismount. Subedei addresses them.

"Good ... good ... of course in a real battle we will draw them back a long way to tire their horses and get them away from their forts."

One of the commanders asks,

"And they will believe our deception?"

"Yes."

"Why? Are they that stupid?'

"Yes."

Just then Yufei steps up and says,

"Your commander is right. I have traveled and fought the Song, the Jin, the Caliphate, bandits, and pirates ... your leader is right ... these armies are not disciplined ... they do not think ahead ..."

Subedei turns to Yufei.

"And where did you fight these people?"

"The Song in my home country of China, the Jin outside of Chang An the old capital, the bandits and pirates on the trails and river in between ... and the Caliphate in the far western lands of Arabia and on the high seas."

"Do you think they can beat our invincible armies?"

"No ... not if you follow your leaders and commanders."

"And have you killed these other warriors that you mentioned?"

"Some."

"We have killed hundreds of thousands."

"50 ... or 500,000 ... what's the difference?" then Yufei adds,

"But ..."

"But what?"

"I think it's better to have these people submit ... if possible ... in any attack you will have brothers who will die, mothers and wives who will mourn and children who will grow up not knowing their fathers."

Most of the commanders' nod, a few don't agree ... one of them, a brother of Teb Tengeri pushes forward and says,

"Well, I don't agree ... we are warriors who survive on plundering everything before us."

"You are entitled to your opinion." Yufei says trying to avoid a fight.

"Are you calling me a liar?" the man says angrily, trying to pick a fight.

Yufei looks at Subedei and smiles, "I didn't say that ... did I?"

Subedei tries to diffuse the situation.

"Bork, he didn't call you a liar and you should respect a guest of the great Khan."

Bork just snorts,

"The Great Khan isn't here, and I think this man is a liar and a coward spreading fake stories of killing these other peoples. If he's so brave, let's see him defeat me."

Then he turns around and those with him shout encouragement.

Subedei looks at Yufei who smiles and shrugs.

Bork has a shield and large curving sword ... Yufei only has his killing knife. Subedei offers him his sword and shield but Yufei declines.

"I'm okay ... just hand me that staff over there."

Others start to hear about the upcoming fight and form a large circle around them.

At the same time, Yufeng and Borte are walking to see Hoelun. They learn what's happening and Borte asks if Yufeng wants to help her husband.

"It's just one warrior? No, he can handle 20 warriors ... let's go."

The other sons of Genghis come out to watch ... Jochi, the oldest son, Chaghatai, Ogedei, and Tolui.

Teb Tengeri also goes to watch ... but from a distance.

Bork is half a meter taller than Yufei and outweighs him by seventy kilograms. While Yufei has been relaxing in the Snowy Mountains, Bork has been honing his fighting skills in countless battles on the northern steppes.

The combatants face off ... Bork roars and charges, Yufei dodges and strikes a blow to Bork's knees, dropping him to the ground. He rolls and is back up quickly. He charges again, a little more cautiously this time, but the outcome is the same and he goes down. This time though, Yufei is on him quickly raining down vicious blows to his arms and head. Bork tries to defend his head with his shield only to have Yufei strike his legs and back.

With the shield blocking the blows, it also blocks his vision, and he doesn't know exactly where Yufei is ... so he slashes blindly as Yufei steps back and watches the warrior fight the air ... finally Yufei mercifully says,

"I'm over here."

Embarrassed from the laughter from the crowd, Bork charges again ... and goes down hard. Yufei is on him again and Bork cannot defend himself and he is getting weaker and weaker from the blows.

Finally, Yufei takes out his knife, grabs Bork by the hair and prepares to slice his throat. Bork is helpless.

Yufei looks at Subedei who shakes his head. Yufei releases Bork who slumps to the ground. A great cheer sounds out for Yufei ... Subedei and Yufei become close friends from that time.

Later ... back at their tent, each one reports on what they learned during their day. Then Yufeng announces,

"Tonight, we will have a private dinner with the Great Khan."

39 Dinner with the Khan

That night they walk through the camp ... but instead of going to the khan's tent, they go unseen to Borte's tent. Borte welcomes them warmly and seats them all around in a circle. Different Mongol traditional foods are brought in, and they engage in some small talk. Borte asks Yufeng,

"Can Panda read and write?"

Yufeng smiles, "Yes ... in several languages ... she has a knack with languages ... not just our human language, but also animal language."

Borte raises her head and looks to Panda, "Really ... you can talk to animals?"

Panda smiles shyly, "Some animals and birds, aunty."

"How do you know what they say?"

"They are conscious, just like us, but their language is simpler, and they use chirps and squeals to indicate what they want to say."

"Amazing! My sons can call to their horses and the horses know their whistle."

"It's like that."

Just then the great khan strides in alone and closes the flap and ties it off.

"They are eyes everywhere ... especially for a khan."

Then looking around, "Ah ... our new guests ... I have heard some amazing stories about you all ...are they true?"

Yufei laughs, "*Life is just a story*, great Khan ... we have heard stories about you too ... that you can fly on the clouds and just shout to the gods and the rains will pour down ... is that true?"

The great Khan laughs loudly, "But I want to hear myself ... did you really defeat the Caliph, the Brotherhood, and the Sultan?"

Over the next hour, they exchange tales ... and with each tale, the Khan becomes more impressed. But then he asks,

"But how do I know these are true?"

Yufei says, "Ask Subedei."

Yufeng says, "Ask your wife and mother."

Panda says, "Ask Tolui and Sari."

Gugu says, "But in the end, go to the holy mountain of the Mongols, Burkhan Khaldun, and ask Tengri."

"And Tengri will confirm all this?"

Yufeng says, "If he doesn't ... his wife, the Mother Goddess will beat him."

There is a pause and then great laughter.

"My wife says that you have some evidence that Teb Tengeri was conspiring with the Black Witch to have the king refuse submission ... can you show me?"

Yufei brings out the documents that they took from the East Temple.

The khan scans them.

Yufeng asks, "You can read? ... I had heard that you couldn't."

The khan shushes her with his finger to his lips,

"It's a secret ... there are lots of secrets here."

"Can you recognize the writing?"

"Maybe ... what other evidence do you have."

Yufeng turns to Panda, "Panda, tell the great khan what you saw when your father was fighting with the witch."

"Sometimes, like my mother, when we heal people, we need to probe to find the cause of the disease."

"And you can also see other things?"

"Yes ... images ... like watching the shadow puppets."

"What did you see?"

"I saw that man Teb Tengeri. Later I described him to my mother and father and when we came here, we all recognized it was him."

Then looking at them again,

"And you come here *for* the Elder Sisters at Kailash mountain?"

"We come for ourselves ... but we share the same goals as the elders of Kailash, the grandmothers of Gobekli Tepe, and the Sky God, Tengri."

The Khan turns to Borte and asks,

"Gobekli Tepe?"

"The western grandmothers at Gobekli are the priestesses of Tengri and the Mother Nature Goddess."

Yufei asks him a question,

"Great Khan, why do you think you, above all others, have been successful in conquering so many nations?"

Without a blink, he says, "I have been called by Tengri."

"Called by Tengri ... to do what?"

"To unite all the warring peoples under one system which protects all peoples, men, women, old, young, Buddhist, Nestorian Christian, Moslem ... all beliefs."

"This is your destiny?"

"Yes."

"How can we help?"

"What exactly is your mission?"

"To help you achieve your heavenly mission, while at the same time, saving as many people as possible."

"We think it's better if a kingdom submits to Mongol rule rather than be destroyed ... do you agree?"

"Yes ... most certainly we need their skills ... we try to convince them to submit but their leaders are too prideful and greedy, and they misjudge their own strengths."

"You have fought the Caliphate Arabs ... what is your opinion of them as warriors?"

"You will not have much trouble with them, they are too complacent after many years of defeating inferior neighbors."

"What about this Brotherhood of Assassins ... did you fight them?"

"Kind of ... they are skilled individual assassins ... I would be wary of them."

"But you are not afraid of them?"

"They will not harm *us*."

Genghis looks at him and starts to ask why when ...

There is a knock on the tent flap ... a message for the khan to come to his large tent.

"Okay ... I'll be right there."

Then looking at this group.

"I appreciate your information and warning. I warmly accept your offer to assist me. I think for now, Yufeng can work with the physicians to keep our people healthy ... especially my wife and mother. Panda, you are tasked with helping Tolui and Sorghaghtani ... he will someday be a khan and his children also."

Yufei, I'd like you to help advise my armies ... I heard from Subedei today and he thinks highly of you, so attach yourself to him."

Then looking at Gugu, "And what am I going to do with him?"

Yufeng says, "He is a good boy and I have some errands for him to do ... finding herbs and cures, praying to the 1001 gods in the world ..."

They laugh ...

"Good we will need his prayers to succeed."

"I must leave ... anytime you need to tell me something, tell Borte, she can always find me."

Then he laughs, "Even when some young girls are trying to distract me ... haha."

Borte slaps at him, and he unties the flap and rushes out.

They all look at each other, then Borte asks,

"Was it a good dinner?"

Yufeng hugs her, "A very good dinner."

"Oh ... there is one thing ... this shaman, Teb Tengeri, if Genghis is wary of him, why doesn't he just get rid of him?"

"It's complicated ... my husband is very loyal to those who supported him when he had nothing. When he was young, the tribe abandoned him and his mother and siblings ... Hoelun taught him hard that alliances were important ... because they had none, they were cast out and almost starved to death."

"Later he had a sworn brother (*anda*), Jamuka, who eventually turned on him. Genghis captured him several times but would not kill him. The same is true of Teb Tengeri, who was his spiritual shaman in the early days ... but now, he and his six brothers are growing more powerful ... and that concerns him. But Tengeri hasn't done anything outright against Genghis, so Genghis doesn't go after him."

"Where are his homelands ... Teb Tengeri?"

"Why do you ask?"

"We believe the poison that attacked my husband came from him ... so it might be some herb from his native lands."

"His family is from the north, near the great lake, a place called Barga."

"Thank you."

Then Borte looks at Panda,

"One day can you show me how to talk to animals?"

"I'd love to!"

"But we have to find a nice gentle animal ... okay."

After that they head back to their tent ... not unseen this time.

***

Back in their own tent, they discuss the day in low voices.

Yufei starts, "They have been re-provisioning themselves for the final attack on the Xi Xia ... I think they will march tomorrow. General Subedei has asked me to accompany him ... and I agreed."

Then Yufeng speaks,

"The medical corps will split up ... some will stay here to attend to the sick and wounded and a few will go with the army to care for the wounded during the battles ... I am not sure which to do ...if I stay here, I will be able to filter around and learn more and make more alliances; however, if something happens to Genghis, I'd like to be there. What do you think?"

Yufei and Panda and Gugu are in a deep meditation. Yufeng waits. When they come out, she repeats the question.

Yufei looks at the others and asks,

"I didn't sense any danger to Genghis on this battle ... how about you?"

The others shake their heads in agreement.

"Good, then I'll stay here and get to know more ... I want to get closer to Borte and Hoelun."

Panda says, "I'll get closer to Sari and her sister, Chaur, Jochi's wife."

"Good." Then looking at Gugu, "How about you?"

"I appear to be free .... for now ... so I'll ride north to Teb Tengeri's homelands and try to find the source of that poison and any antidote."

"Good!" Yufeng says ... relieved of that burden. And since Gugu has access to the wisdom of the universe, she feels confident that he will find the source of the poison.

181

40 Genghis Defeats the Xi Xia

The next day the march is announced, and the camp is a dust devil of activity. The plan is to move the women and children and wounded along with the main battle armies ... but not too close ... following behind at a distance and setting up a new campsite, well behind the conflict lines.

Yufei gets a morning acupuncture treatment and herbal booster from Yufeng. Then he puts on some leather armor that Subedei sent him. As he turns around looking at himself ... he asks,

"How do I look?"

Panda laughs, "Like a toy soldier, baba!"

Yufeng hugs him,

"Take care of yourself, I don't have time to train a new Mongol husband!"

Panda doesn't understand the joke.

Later, in the morning, Yufeng goes to Borte's tent and tells Borte about Gugu's plan ... she understands and arranges to get him some horses and a guide.

Then she tells Borte of her plans to stay with the main camp to tend to the sick and wounded in camp. Borte appreciates that and tells her that she will introduce her to the physicians staying in camp ... who will set up their clinic.

"Good ... years ago, during an epidemic in China, I helped set up a mobile hospital in our village."

"That's great ... the Khan welcomes people with skills like yours."

Panda goes to Sari's tent and offers her services. Sari is relieved as it is a lot of work to get everything folded up and packed for the trail. Panda helps watch the infant Monke most of the time ... except for feeding time. Panda has never been this close to a family with an infant and the experience is awakening to her in several different ways.

Sari travels alongside her older sister, Chaur, who has two young sons, Batu is 5 and Orda is 6 years old ... both of whom are intrigued by this strange new girl that they have heard whisperings about. As they walk along, they ask her a thousand questions ... where are you from, what do the people look like? What is a jungle?

Panda is strong and can carry young Monke and field all their questions ... giving the sisters time to catch up on their gossip. The unfortunate part of following the great army is the dust cloud that follows so many horses and wagons ... so for safety and cleaner air, they let the distance between them and the army, grow longer and also veer off to one side.

The Khan's spies have located the Xi Xia forces about two days away ... so this first march won't be so difficult. On other campaigns, they have marched hundreds and even thousands of kilometers.

It is still winter which is the favored time for Mongol campaigns ... the ground, the rivers and the lakes are all frozen ... making travel easier ... but it is cold on the open steppes ... especially when the wind from the north comes down on them.

Sari and her sister walk together while the boys tag along with Panda. Sari tells her sister some of what she has learned about this new group of visitors ...

"I heard from the monk that travels with them that they are emissaries of the Immortal Elder Sisters ... sent here to help us."

Chaur stops walking and turns,

"Do you think it's true? Every religion respects the Elder Sisters ... even our Nestorian Christian fathers."

"I have met them only two times, but they have an aura about them ... and look ... over there ... that girl is barely ten but has the maturity of an elder herself."

They watch Panda interact with the two boys, whom she has already won over.

Later when they camp, the boys will teach her their favorite game of *knucklebones*.

***

As Gugu rides north with his guide, in search of herbs to combat the dark poison ... Yufei rides southeast with the main forces.

Before the end of the day though, Tolui and Subedei's force (25% of the total force) splits off to the north, in an encirclement strategy.

A little later, Jelme and Jochi's force (the oldest son of Genghis) splits with another contingent off to the south. Each Mongol warrior has three horses close by in order to always have a fresh horse ready.

Genghis has been successful in his campaigns by understanding the enemy and the terrain. He wisely uses spies and scouts to help him, and his generals devise the best strategy for success.

The Xi Xia belong to the Tangut tribe and are also fierce warriors ... and they are defending their homelands. The upcoming battle will be fiercely fought.

Genghis forces have the advantage of a coordinated and disciplined strategy. His four top generals and his four sons immediately obey their commands when they see the signal flags.

The following day they continue the march but stop short of the expected place of battle in order to give the men and horses a pause to rest and the encirclement forces time to set up.

That night Subedei, Tolui, Yufei, and Jochi slip back into the Mongol camp to meet with Genghis and go over the strategy. Later he asks if they all agree ... which they do. Teb Tengeri is in the war council and stares at Yufei ... later he will voice his displeasure privately to Genghis and even later to his brothers.

The plan is to leave half of Genghis' remaining force in reserve, the other half will march toward the Xi Xia ... after the initial clash, the first contingent will feign a retreat. When they get back to the reserves ... they will pause to mount fresh horses, while the reserves charge the enemy, and once the first contingent mounts their fresh horses they will join with them. Meanwhile the north and south armies will form a pincer trap movement and they will decimate the Xi Xia warriors inside their trap ... who, by then, will be on tired horses.

The Xi Xia still fight fiercely but hope drains for them after they realize they are trapped by Genghis' fresh troops and also isolated from their main camp. By mid-day, most of the fighting has worn down ... now it is mostly cleaning up the battlefield. Mongols retrieving any of their wounded or dead Mongols and sending the wounded enemy across the bridge to the underworld.

***

Back at the camp, Yufeng has made friends with the physicians left behind ... one is from Persia, one from India, and another from China ... they all welcome her to their group. Later when they hear of her experiences with the epidemics and traveling to meet the great Moses Maimonides ... they ask her a million questions. Her humble and accommodating demeaner wins her the friendship of these experienced medical colleagues.

As they are setting up the field hospital she makes some useful suggestions, which they all acknowledge. Once the battle starts, the trickle of injured, becomes a flood ... sword cuts, lacerations, embedded arrows, broken bones and more.

Now the work begins ... with her hands full of body parts she smiles warmly when Panda arrives to help. She introduces her to the other physicians who welcome all experienced hands.

Many times, through the day and night when Yufeng is operating, Panda will assist her in *seeing* inside, where the obstruction is located, the bone broken. The other doctors notice this and also ask Panda to *look* inside when they have a difficult patient.

Borte and Hoelun stop by to see if they need any supplies. They see Yufeng and Panda working together seamlessly helping the fallen warriors ... saving an arm or a leg, bandaging an eye, removing an arrow ... they are both amazed.

They call one of their favorite physicians to their side who tells them.

"They are fantastic ... Yufeng's medical knowledge spans the world, and the daughter can somehow see or sense the damaged organ inside. Just watch a few moments for yourself ... and notice one thing ... they both work as one but there are no words ... they sense the other's thoughts."

"And their treatments?"

"Their diagnosis and treatments are the best ... equal to the immortal masters."

Then Hoelun whispers to Borte,

"We must protect them ... people with that much power for good will alienate others ... I have heard the Tengeri are already plotting against them."

"I will talk to Sari and Chaur."

"Good ... and all your sons."

Borte nods.

Yufeng and Panda did not even know that the two women had visited. When you are probing deep inside a man's body to stop a severed artery, you have little time to socialize.

Later when the rush is over, Yufeng and Panda go to wash up.

"You did good today Panda ... your skills improve every day."

"Thank you, mama ... but you are the master."

Yufeng laughs ... "Don't tell your father that ... he likes to think he is the master ... remember when someday you marry ... don't diminish the man's self-esteem."

"I will try mama."

But then something flashes through Panda's mind, and she stops.

Yufeng asks her,

"What is it?"

Pausing to try to recapture that image, she gives up.

"Nothing ... just an image when I said those words."

41 The Aftermath of War

The camp that night is celebrating the victory. There is a huge bonfire, musicians are playing their traditional instrument, the stringed *morin khuur* ... they call it the *horsehead fiddle* because it resembles a hollow wooden horse's head and is played with a bow with strings of twisted horsetail hair.

Groups of men and women are singing ... throat singing ... mimicking the natural sounds of nature ... the winds in the trees, the bubbling streams of runoff water. The melody creates an harmonious feeling with everyone around the campfire.

Panda is with Chaur's two boys, Orda and Batu, and some other children. They are teaching Panda how to play *shagai* (knucklebones) games. The knucklebones are the joint bones of horses about half the size of your thumb ... each side though is different, so, if you throw them on the ground they will roll and land on different sides. Each side is referenced to an animal ... the horse and sheep sides are considered lucky ... the camel and goat sides are unlucky.

There are several games but the boys like the horse race game ... there are 4 boys and Panda. Each has a sack of knucklebones. First, they draw lines in the dirt, then they place one of their bones on each racetrack. Each player takes turns throwing their ankle bones. If the player throws the bones and the horse is facing down, that is one point, and that person can move their racing horse one space. The first player continues throwing his bones until he doesn't throw a horse, then the next boy throws his bones ... and the race is on.

***

In their tent, Yufei and Yufeng are relaxing after washing the blood and dust off their clothes. They relate the events of the day and marvel at Panda's energy to go out and quickly play again.

"Children have all the energy in the world."

"I have to tell you ... in the hospital ... she amazed me with her abilities to not only see inside but instinctively know the right treatment. I was very proud of her."

"How did it go on the battleground?"

"Just as they planned ... Genghis has four able generals ... he calls them his Four Hounds ... they have been with him from the beginning, so they know what each one has to do ... also he has his 4 sons who are equally skilled and loyal ... so the army moves like an intelligent 8-armed force ... like a wolf pack. "

"What about the enemy."

"Their strategy appears to be ... you come - we fight ... they are no match for the Mongols. The Mongols control their horses with their legs, so even in retreat they can turn and launch arrows at the enemy. They planned a huge trap for the Tanguts, and they fell right into it ... and then it was a slaughter ... finally they received a message that their khan had submitted."

"And it's over?"

"Yes, they will provide warriors when Genghis needs them and also tribute."

"But what about their lands?"

"I don't think the Mongols are set up for being landowners, or administrators ... at least not yet."

"How did it go here?"

"It went well ... it's always difficult treating so many injured men, but they are well organized ... I helped a little here and there. They welcome trained physicians from all lands. Genghis knows his people have limited skills and education, so he covets talented immigrants and craftsmen from vanquished tribes or just those seeking to be on the winning side ..."

"Yes, I've even heard of some Chinese coming over from Northern China to escape the Jin ... and offering their services."

They hear the rising voices of singers.

"Maybe we should join the celebration."

"Okay."

They leave the tent and join the bonfire. On the way there, they spot Panda engrossed in playing shagai. They spot Sari and Tolui and walk up to them.

188

"Greetings!"

The couple turn and when they see who it is, smile warmly. Tolui says,

"Greetings noble warrior ... how did you like seeing our armies in action?"

"I was telling my wife; it was like seeing a hunting wolf pack ... circling around ... and all with a single purpose of defeating the enemy."

"Yes ... that's exactly what it is ... my father is a military genius ... don't you agree?"

"I do agree."

Then Sari says,

"And I hear that your wife is a medical genius."

Turning to look at Yufeng,

"Really? What have you been doing all day, while your husband has been off fighting the enemy warriors."

Yufeng laughs,

"Just cleaning up all the damage after you ... right Sari?"

Sari laughs and agrees. This younger Mongol couple now look at Yufei and Yufeng's relationship with envy ... like older brothers and sisters.

"Let's go see the smoke dance."

"What's that?"

Come on ... you'll see ... it's beautiful."

At the campfire there are some dancers carrying a small bellows made from animal skin bladders ... after they deflate it, they go to the fire and suck in the heavy smoke ... then they go to a female partner and she dances around him until he blows out circular smoke rings ... and when the smoke rings expand larger, she jumps through ... then he also jumps through. At the end, he blows out two rings which join into one and they both jump through.

Yufei and Yufeng are captivated by the dance and the rings. When they see the two smoke rings merge into one, Yufeng whispers,

"Like our spirits...." Yufei holds her tighter until Panda squeezes in between and asks,

"Can they make three rings join?"

They laugh and Yufei says,

"If they can't ... we can ... right?"

They all laugh.

Around the circle others watch them. Most admiringly, but a few, like Teb Tengeri and his brothers watch and study them ... comparing notes ... like a predator.

Hoelun and Borte also watch them interact with the families and wonder how they can protect them.

Subedei is on the other side of the fire, drinking with some of his commanders and raises his drink flask to Yufei, who does the same.

Ogedei is close to Subedei and asks him,

"This new Chinese ... how did he do in battle?"

"It was enjoyable to watch him fight ..."

"Why?"

"He fights without thinking, anticipating his opponents moves, and killing without emotion."

"No joy?"

"No ... nor sadness ... like ..."

Ogedei turns to hear better.

"Like it was meant to be ... like the antelope running up the rocks of a mountain ... every foot, sure ... every leap, perfect ... like he had done the exact motion many times before."

Then Subedei turns to face Ogedei, the future khan.

"It is his and our destiny that those three have come here ... we need to protect them."

Ogedei nods.

42 Avarga

The next morning everyone is up early breaking camp.

"Where are we going mama?" Panda asks as they pack all their belongings onto a cart.

"To their homelands in the north."

"Everyone?"

"Yes ... and every animal and cart."

"How long will we go there for?"

"For the summer pasture months."

"And after that?"

"Maybe another campaign."

Panda ponders this a minute, then gathers her things.

"Okay."

"Where's baba?"

"He's with some of the commanders discussing the routes to take to avoid flooding rivers."

"What about all the wounded that we treated."

"Their families will care for them now ... they will call us if they need us."

"What about Gugu?"

"He'll find us there."

"What is the name of the place?"

"It is called ... *Avarga*."

***

They traveled all day, every day, for several weeks. The stop-unload-rest-load up routine becomes a habit after the first week. Panda rides with her mother some days and with Sari on other days. Yufeng rides often with Borte and sometimes with Sari or her sister. Hoelun is a fine woman but hardened through the years, and she is getting old ... and after losing many old friends, is reluctant to make new friends.

Yufei enjoys the camaraderie of the commanders. Many times, when they stopped to rest, they would practice their warrior skills. They are the best horsemen on the planet and their accuracy with the bow and arrow is uncanny.

The only dark cloud around Yufei is the increasing need for Yufeng's healing treatments to keep up his semblance of fitness.

But because of Yufei's excellent fighting skills, he is accepted easily by most of them ... but not the group around Teb Tengeri.

One day, Yufei asked Subedei why.

"What have they got against me?"

"You are everything that they are not."

"Also, at Kucha they had their eyes set on looting and plundering that city ... and you took that away from them."

But Yufei feels there is something else ... something more sinister ... connected to the dark manifestations.

... and the army rode on ... guided by the stars to their northern homeland.

***

In the far north, Gugu had little success at first in finding the poison that caused Yufei's disease. He found the homelands of Tengeri but there were few people still living there.

When asked, his guide told him that they were either with Genghis or with another tribe further west. People didn't linger long alone on the steppes.

(*Maybe I'm doing this the wrong way.*)

One night when they camp, Gugu goes into a deep meditation to find the answers. In the void he sees a group of black witches dancing around a fire. There is a mountain in the background. The witches are brewing some decoction in a pot and adding diseased carcasses.

Then one of the witches sees him and points him out to the others and he leaves quickly.

When he comes out of the meditation, the guide is shaking him.

"What is it? What's wrong?"

"You were meditating and then you started screaming ... I was trying to wake you."

"What did you see?"

"Some witches and a mountain near a river, but the river was dry."

"What did the mountain look like?"

"It had two peaks, one taller than the other., and sharp vertical cliffs on one side."

"I know that mountain ... it is not far from here ... we can go there tomorrow."

"Good."

Gugu tried to rest but it was difficult ... the look from the witches still haunted him.

In the morning they rode further north. Finally, after two days they saw the mountain in the distance.

Gugu exclaimed,

"Yes, that was it. What land is this?"

"The grandmothers tell us to stay away from here. They say it is haunted by evil spirits."

They ride closer and come to a watering hole ... by the side of the hole is the carcass of a dead horse ... rotting away.

"Poison water. Don't go near it." the guide says.

Gugu looks around and says,

"Something else ... notice there aren't any carrion birds eating the carcass ... even the vultures know it is poison."

The guide looks around and nods,

"You are right ... we'd best avoid it."

Gugu gets off his horse and tells the man,

"Not yet ... this is what I came for. Hold my horse so he doesn't spook."

Gugu wraps a baklava around his face and grabs a couple of bags, a small flask, his gloves, and a long sharp knife.

He goes up to the carcass and pries open the mouth ... he notices some grasses ... he takes a sample. Then he cuts open the belly and the stomach ... inside is more of the same type of grasses. With gloves he takes a sample. Then he goes to the water and gets a sample of the water. All of this he wraps again carefully in bladder containers.

"Why are you doing that?"

"Something killed the horse ... I want to find out what."

He loads it into one of his saddle bags and puts the dirty gloves and other items in the same bag. Then they ride on.

"Let's try and find a village or some herders."

"Okay."

> *The holy man, though he be distressed,*
> *Does not eat food mixed with wickedness.*
> *The lion, though hungry,*
> *Will not eat what is unclean.*

***

Meanwhile, advance scouts from the main army have reached the Mongols summer homeland, Avarga.

The Mongol holy mountain, Burkhan Khaldun, overlooks this lush river valley with spring grasses reaching up the rays of the sun. The Onan River flows through the fertile valley ... while on the other side of the mountain runs the Kherlen River.

The destiny of the Mongol conquests ... and the world ... have been determined on this holy mountaintop ... by one man ... Genghis Khan, who was born nearby (as was Subedei).

When he was younger, and attacked by the Merkit tribe, Genghis escaped into this mountain and was sheltered by an old woman. Since then, he has revered this mountain as the home of Tengri, the Blue-Sky God.

> *I went up Mount Burkhan,*
> *Though I was frightened and ran like an insect,*
> *I was shielded by Mount Burkhan Khaldun,*
> *I will honor Burkhan Khaldun with sacrifices.*
> *every morning, and pray to it every day:*
> *my children and my children's children*
> *shall be mindful of this.*

43 Summer Grasslands

From a visitor's eyes, the Mongol camp is a huge, chaotic sprawl of tents, animals, animal skins hanging out, children running everywhere, campfires and more ... spread out, haphazardly as far as the eyes can see. But to a Mongol, everything is in its place. A warrior who has been gone away fighting for two or more years can come back and quickly find his ger.

It is all organized by armies ... and divisions in those armies. Since his assignment to join Subedei, Yufei and Yufeng's ger is close to Subedei tent, which is not far from Ogedei's larger tent. Panda spends half of her time with her parents and the other half with Sari, her sister Chaur, and their children.

Spring is when the steppe grasses spring to life, animals drop their calves, and children play war games ... and in the tents of the commanders, where the adults drink and plan their own war games.

Recently, southeast of them, a new khan has ascended to the Jin throne. Fearful of the rising Mongol threat, the new Jin khan sends an emissary to Avarga demanding that the Mongols under Genghis submit to him ...

That this new Golden Khan of the Jin wants Genghis to submit is taken as an insult ... it is said later that Genghis just spat on the ground. But still ... submit or not ... that was the question of the day ... and night ... for many nights. Even with their conquest of all the nearby Mongol tribes and adding the new Tanguts and Kucheans to their fold, Genghis could only muster a fraction of the vast Jin armies. Added to this mismatch in the size of forces ... was the terrain problem ... to reach the Jin cities, Genghis would have to cross the formidable Gobi desert. So, it was not an easy decision ... all of the gains over the past decade could be lost by a rash unwise decision to war.

During the summer, as the children played and the newborn animals grazed, the debate went long into the nights ... even in Yufei and Yufeng's tent. Yufeng asks Panda,

"What have you heard Panda?"

"The Khan's sons are all for the war against the Jin ... the wives are more fearful but will support their husbands. All Mongol women are familiar with the wars, especially Sari and Chaur ... but I think they would prefer peace to allow their sons time to grow."

Yufei asks Yufeng,

"Have you talked to Hoelun and Borte?"

"Hoelun keeps her thoughts to herself... unless it impacts directly on Genghis."

"Borte will support Genghis in his decision."

Panda asks,

"Baba, when will the great khan decide?"

"Soon ... I understand, when he feels the great spirit move inside him, he will climb the holy mountain to communicate with the sky god, Tengri."

"What do you prefer?"

"Your mother and I prefer peace ... we fight war, only to defeat the dark manifestations."

"But are the Jin people, dark manifestations?"

"It's not the Jin people that he will war against, it is the Jin leaders, the same ones that invaded Song China many years ago and killed the Song emperor and his family and enslaved millions of our countrymen."

"Do you hate them, Baba?"

"No ... no more than I hate the coldness that took your grandfather's life ..."

Yufeng sensing the conversation is headed into uncharted territory, asks Panda to go to ask Borte if she needs any acupuncture treatment for her arthritis."

"Okay mama." and she runs off to Borte's tent.

"Why did you send her away?"

"You know ... why open old wounds?"

Yufei goes up to her, hugs her, and tells her,

"I was so lucky to find you."

She laughs, 'Yes ... you were, you rascal! So how are you feeling?"

"Maybe I could use a treatment also ... I feel weak at the end of the day ... as though my body is constantly fighting an enemy inside."

"Okay, lie down on the furs ..."

She goes to get her medical kit.

"I wonder how Gugu is doing?"

"I was starting to wonder also... I thought he would be back by now."
Yufei smiles a certain smile and asks,
"Maybe your special massage first." he asks.
She smiles and helps him untie his waistband.

***

Gugu meanwhile, is currently not doing so good. After he took the samples from that dead carcass, he fell ill, with the same disease that infected Yufei, but with different organs affected. With Gugu, his lungs are attacked, and he has found it difficult to take a full breath. They camp out near a flowing stream on the sunny side of that twin peaked mountain.

Gugu tells the guide to get him fresh running water and cook some small game in a soup, making lots of broth for him. Gugu spends many hours meditating and trying self-healing exercises. Although his spirit is immortal, his body is not, and he knows he could die.

The guide suggests a sweat house, so they construct a small tent, build a fire inside, and close the flaps with Gugu inside. He does this for two days as the guide replenishes the fire.

A few days later, a herder comes by with his flock of animals, moving to a new pasture. His wife, mother, and children follow him and camp near the same stream, only further upstream. The guide goes to ask them if they have any experience with this type of disease.

The older woman comes down to their camp and inspects Gugu. She recognizes the disease, goes back to her tent, and brings back a herb. She tells them how to prepare the medicine.

Gugu thanks her and asks her where the herb grew, because they have a friend with the same disease. The old lady points to a valley in the foothills on the sunny side of the twin peaks. They thank her profusely and give her some traditional gifts.

The guide tells Gugu,
"These grandmothers can tune into a certain plant and know its healing properties."

"Yes, my two friends, Yufeng and Panda are like that. They seem to merge their spirit with the spirit of the plant."

The guide mixes the herbs like the old woman told them and gives the liquid to Gugu. In two days, he is feeling much better, and they get ready to go search for that valley. Meanwhile, the herder and his family have moved on to a new pasture.

***

On the way to Borte's tent, Panda stops off and sees if Sari needs anything. Little Monke sees Panda and cries out in delight.

"He likes you now more than me." laughs Sari.

"Until he's hungry ... then he cries for you." laughs Panda.

'Where are you going?"

"To see Borte."

Okay ... say hello to her for me."

"I will." then Panda leaves and heads to Borte's tent. Along the way she passes Teb Tengeri's tent. Outside are two of his brothers who start to taunt the girl.

"Hey look! It's the jungle girl ... I hear you can talk to animals."

Panda laughs, "I'm talking to you, aren't I?" then she skips off laughing behind her.

One of the brothers laughs at the other,

"You do smell like an animal."

The first brother slaps him, and they get into a wrestling match until Teb Tengeri comes out and breaks it up.

"What was that about?"

They tell him and he starts to plot a surprise for Panda.

He whispers to the brothers, and they run off.

Meanwhile Panda arrives at Borte's tent, greets her, and asks her if she needs an acupuncture needle treatment.

"Not today, I still feel fine from the last treatment. Can you do the acupuncture treatments too, Panda?"

"Not yet, mama is still teaching me about the points and meridians."

"But they say you can see inside? Is that true?"

"Kind of ... it's hard to describe in words ... mostly I can see disturbances ... like a blockage that affects the balance of the qi ... which causes a problem in the energy field ... I can see that disturbance ... and then my mother can recommend a treatment ... acupuncture, moxibustion, herbs, exercises ... whatever will help restore the balance."

"How did you get this ability? Did your mother teach you?"

'No ... it was just there one day, then my mother helped me to develop it."

'Do you want to be a healer like your mother some day?"

"I think so, but I am not sure what the Mother Goddess plans are for me."

"I understand ... be careful Panda ... even in this camp ... there are people jealous of people like you ... people with special abilities."

"I will ... thank you for being friends with our family."

The woman hugs the girl, and she leaves to go home.

Borte watches her leave ... with an ominous premonition of danger.

44 Wolf Warrior

On the way back, Batu, one of Chaur's boys catches up to her and tells her there is a surprise for her in a nearby tent (pointing).

Panda doesn't suspect treachery from the unwitting boy, and smiles, "Really? Will you show me?"

The boy laughs, "Sure, follow me!"

He leads her towards the outer rim of one group of tents where there is a lone tent set away from the others.

The boy points ... "It's in there!" then he laughs and says, "Go inside!"

As Panda approaches the tent, she senses danger ... she slows down and probes inside.

There is a wolf inside!

She probes further ... trying to communicate with the wolf ... is it friendly or deranged somehow?

When she gets to the tent flap, she pauses again ... probing ... reaching out to the animal ...

"I am coming inside, wolf ... I am Panda ... I am a friend ... I will not hurt you ..."

She opens the flap and enters. Watching from behind some other tents the two brothers and Teb Tengeri stride out ...

Then they hear a ferocious wolf's roar from inside.

Teb says, "One down ... two to go."

The boy, Batu, hearing this, becomes frightened ... and realizes the Tengeri warrior had lied to him!

He runs to tell his mother Chaur, who is frightened by the news and runs to find her husband, Jochi. She also sends her sons to find Sari and Yufeng.

At the tent, the growling has calmed down. The Tengeri brothers slowly walk toward the tent ... when Chaur comes running up.

"What have you done? Why have you deceived my son?" she shouts at them.

They start to confront her when Jochi and Sari and Yufeng arrive.

Not seeing Panda, a frightened Yufeng asks,

"What's happened? Where is Panda?"

They point to the tent.

"These men tricked my son into telling Panda there was a surprise inside the tent ... then when she went in, he heard a wolf's roar ... that's when he ran to find me."

Yufei arrives as well as Tolui and Subedei.

Yufeng goes to enter the tent.

Sari tells her to be careful, "Take a couple of warriors with you."

Yufeng shakes her head, "No it's best if I go in alone."

Yufeng enters the tent ... her eyes adjust ... and then she sees Panda ... on the ground ... playing with a large wolf. When Yufeng enters the wolf growls, but Panda calms her,

"No ... don't growl ... mother ... friend."

Yufeng smiles and asks,

"A new friend?"

"Yes, someone tied her up in here ... as a surprise."

"The Tengeri's ... you have to be more careful now ..."

Yufeng comes closer and strokes the wolf's fur.

"Is she okay?"

"Look." pointing to bruises on the animal's back. And here pointing to her neck where a tight leather collar is almost choking the poor animal.

Yufeng thinks a minute and whispers to her ... she smiles ... then Yufeng leaves the tent.

Outside Yufei and the others are waiting. They ask her what's happened inside ... she shakes her head and whispers to Sari who nods and slips away.

She waits a few moments and then she confronts the Tengeri's just as Genghis arrives.

With each word, Yufeng's voice rises ... "A defenseless little girl!"

She walks around the three of them.

"You are such brave warriors ... you want to kill a little girl!"

She spits on the ground and challenges them, "How about fighting a helpless woman?" she spits again.

One of the brothers' charges at her and she cuts him down easily and while he struggles to get up, she slashes a brutal kick to his head, knocking him out."

Turning to the other brother, "How about you big boy?"

This one is more careful and more dangerous, he reaches for his sword and slashes at Yufeng, who easily ducks under it a kicks the man's legs out ... he goes down and another kick knocks all senses out of him. Yufeng grabs his sword and holds it to his neck.

Just then Genghis comes up ... he already knows what has happened, but he doesn't want a rift just yet ... if he is going to battle the Jin, he will need Tengeri's supporters.

"Stop!"

Genghis goes up to the two brothers and asks,

"What have you done?"

They look guiltily at their older brother, Teb, who says,

"They were just playing a joke ... they didn't think she would go inside."

Genghis looks at Yufeng.

"Where is your daughter?"

She points and calls out.

"Panda, you can come out now. I have taken care of these two animals."

The flap opens and Panda walks out, leading the wolf unchained beside her.

The crowd backs off ... Panda walks up to her mother ... the wolf sees the men and growls.

"Hi mama ... what are you doing? Teaching these children, a lesson?"

Everyone, even the Tengeri's, breathed a sigh of relief to see her alive.

Genghis looks at Yufeng and Panda.

The great Khan asks,

"Panda, what happened?"

Panda explains, pointing to the two Tengeri on the ground,

"These men lied to Batu and told him that they had a surprise for me in the tent. Batu believed them and told me there was a surprise in the tent. Inside I found this poor animal chained by the door, waiting to pounce on anyone who entered ... a child, or even an old woman ... like your mother ... could have entered and been killed."

Genghis looks at the two on the ground and then turns back to Panda and asks,

"What did you do?"

"I talked to her."

'Her?"

"The wolf is a female ... we talked ... she showed me where these men had beaten her on her back ... where they had put a collar that was choking her ... you know it's strange ..."

"What?"

"When someone who has never known kindness, is shown kindness ... they really appreciate it."

The great Khan smiles and nods ... "I think you are right ...but what should I do to those that don't show kindness?" looking down at the two ...

Panda thinks for a minute, then says,

"I know!"

They all look at her.

"The horse stables need cleaning and the camel dung on the steppes need collecting for the winter campfires ... maybe they could help with that!"

The great Khan almost falls over laughing,

"I agree ... but first I need to have a chat with them ... so this doesn't happen again ... okay?"

"Okay ... what about the wolf?"

"Do you want to keep her?"

Panda looks at her mother who looks at her father, who smiles and nods,

"He can sleep in our ger and guard it at night."

"Good idea." says the Khan, then looking at Teb,

"I want to talk to you and your brothers ... NOW!"

As they walk off, the others come up to Panda ... gingerly ... cautious of the wolf.

One of the boys asks,

"Will he bite me?"

"Not now ... I told him you were a friend."

Batu wants to pet him, but his mother still holds him back.

Panda tells her it's okay and holds Batu's hand as he lets the wolf smell him. Once the excitement is over, the people drift back to what they were doing.

Sari walks with Panda and Yufeng ... and their new pet, back to their tent.

Chaur holds Batu's hand and walks back to her tent and the others do the same.

Only in the Tengeri tent is there still an animated discussion.

Genghis is controlling his anger.

"I can't believe it ... attacking a small girl!"

They plead their innocence.

"You two ... clean the stables for a month and scour the steppes for dung ... I want cartloads of it ready for the cold days! Understand?"

They bow to the khan.

"And one last thing ... these new people ... the girl and her mother and father are *untouchables* ... understand? They are like my family ... understand!"

He waits for them all to agree.

"We have a big campaign coming up and we don't have time for this infighting ... understand!"

They all bow again.

Genghis stomps out. Teb tells his brothers to keep their hands off Yufei, Yufeng and Panda.

"I have bigger plans."

His two brothers don't understand ... which probably is best.

Genghis doesn't go back to his tent, instead he walks over to Yufei's tent. Outside he coughs and asks, "Anyone home?"

Then he enters and they all bow to him. The wolf doesn't growl ... just watches.

Genghis walks up to the wolf and asks Panda,

"Is it okay if I touch him?"

"It's okay to touch her ... I told her you were a friend."

Genghis wonders as he reaches out to the wolf. (*When did she do that?*)

Genghis says to Panda,

"The wolf is a powerful spirit animal. In our culture they represent strength, courage, and wisdom. The grannies tell me that I am even descended from a blue-grey wolf and a fallow doe ... haha ... what do you think?"

"Maybe ... great Khan ... is it okay if I keep her?"

"Of course ... I insist on it ... I give you a command to take care of this she-wolf ..."

"Why do you like this wolf, great Khan?"

"I think it is a sign from the Mother Goddess ... we are about to embark on a great mission, and I think this wolf spirit is a sign from the gods that they support us ... that's why it's important for you to take care of it ... understand?"

Panda nods and Genghis continues,

"The ancient legends tell of a fight in the heavens between a good white wolf and a bad black wolf ..."

Panda asks,

"Which one wins?"

"The one we feed." then looking at the wolf,

"I think you have found a good wolf spirit, so feed her for all of us."

"I will great Khan."

Then looking at Yufei and Yufeng he asks,

"Is that why you have come ... to feed the good wolf?"

They smile and nod.

"Good ... if we battle the Jin, we will need all the help we can get."

Yufeng takes a step forward and asks,

"I heard from others that the battle instructions are clear ..."

"Great Khan, if possible, can you spare the peasants, and especially the educated and skilled professionals and craftsmen."

"I will try."

"But I heard that the royalty and government administrators are to be executed ... can I ask why? Why execute these government administrators, couldn't you use them?"

"I spared them on our first campaigns and only left a few Mongol administrators to watch over them. After our armies had gone, they killed our administrators, and turned their backs against us. These privileged elite will not change their ways ... so it is best to eliminate the threat to our rear lines."

Yufeng nods and Yufei adds,

"To administer your kingdom, you will need hundreds of skilled craftsmen, engineers, administrators, scientists, and ..."

Genghis sits, "And on and on ... I know ... but most important are intelligent people that I can trust around me to counsel me ... like you two ... ah, three."

Yufeng crooks her head and looks at the Khan,

"Panda?"

"My sons and grandsons will be khans someday and will need her counsel."

Then looking at Panda,

"Will you help them, Panda?"

Panda smiles,

"If they are not naughty ... *shu shu* (uncle)."

They all laugh, and Genghis stands,

"Okay ... I will warn them that if they are naughty, elder sister Panda is authorized to spank them ...haha."

Looking at Yufeng,

"I'd like you to continue to look over our medical corps ... make sure they have what they need, that each unit has a small medical team ... and my wife and mother also ... and when we conquer a new nation ... quickly enter and protect their physicians and educated."

"And me?" Yufei asks,

"Stay close to Subedei, he will be a great general someday ... he is learning from general Jebe and his older brother Jelme now, but I think he will surpass them quickly. Help them to think creatively and strategically ... employ new tactics if the old ones don't work ... improvise."

"And after the victory, help them to control the men's urge to pillage and plunder ... we need the learning and skills of these other cultures."

Looking up to the sky, "And pray to the Blue-Sky God and the Mother Goddess that we can achieve our mission."

45 Genghis Talks to Tengri

That night, the wolf sleeps next to Panda, near the door flap. In the middle of the night, the wolf starts growling which alerts the others, who grab their knives.

When the flap opens, it is Gugu, surprised to be met at the entrance by a steppe wolf, teeth bared, crouching down ready to leap.

"No ... Lana ... no ... friend."

Yufeng and the others wonder (*Who is Lana?*)

Gugu stops and enters slowly. Yufeng tells him,

"Panda has a new pet."

"Lana?"

They look at Panda, who looks back questioningly.

"What? Wolf in Chinese is *lan* ... so *Lana* ... I liked it and she liked it too."

"Okay ... just asking." then looking at Gugu,

"What happened? What took you so long? Are *you* okay?"

"I'm fine ... I found where the disease came from ... unfortunately it attacked me ... but fortunately we found the herb medicine to cure it ... it grows in a mountain valley northwest of here ... near the big lake, on the sunny side of a twin peak mountain."

He hands the herbs to Yufeng, who inspects it carefully ... probing for its essence.

"I have seen drawings of this in one of the Arab medical books, but I had never seen the herb before or studied its uses."

"The old woman who showed it, told me how to prepare it ... let it soak in fresh pure spring water for two days, then add it to warmed fresh spring water ... not boiling ... cover it for a day in a pot and then bury the pot in the earth for two days. Then after that take 1 mouthful, three times a day for three days."

"Good."

Then looking around, he asks,

"Did I miss anything here?"

Yufei looks around, shrugs,

"No ... things have been pretty slow here ..."

Yufeng smiles,

"You must be tired ... I'll make your bed up over there ... Lana is sleeping in your old spot."

They all laugh and go back to sleep ... except Gugu keeps one eye on Lana and Lana keeps one eye on Gugu ... just to be safe.

***

A few days later, most of the war debates have exhausted themselves and Genghis makes an announcement ... he will climb the holy mountain and talk to the Blue-Sky God, Tengri ... to determine their fate.

When he leaves, everyone can see the burden he is carrying on his shoulders and they know the risks ahead ... either way.

He is gone for several days ... no one can remember just how long, but the one thing they all remember is the look on his face when he strode back into camp ... a determined man, with an enormous burden on his shoulders ... sanctioned by the god of gods, the Sky God himself. And when he talked to the gathering that day, everyone heard ... not his words, but the words of the Sky God telling them what they must do ... to march on the Jin and defeat them ... and then march on other nations to bring them all under the great Mongolian ger.

But before the invasions, there is much work to do ... a multitude of preparations ... as they have learned from their past campaigns.

46 War Preparations

The next few weeks and into the autumn, every morning, there are meetings of the khan's sons and top generals ... and some specialists, ... engineers, weather specialists, allies and potential allies, herdsmen about pastures and watering holes in the desert and mountains along the proposed line of march, etc. Every detail of the campaign is gone over several times at the top level and then to lower levels down to the *tumens* (forces of 10,000). Yufei, healthier now, is allowed to sit in on most of the meetings. He listens mostly, only offering his opinion if asked.

Advance scouts are sent out to check every possible route forward ... and backward (retreat) if necessary. All the watering holes, vegetation, villagers, herdsmen, ... everything!

They will cross the Gobi desert in the winter ... their favored season for warfare ... and the one least expected by their enemies. They will carry their own food as well as the horse's fodder. When the Mongols march, they try to spread out as wide as possible ... first for better foraging and second for better defense.

Their plan is to march three armies ... two main armies through the major commercial passages east through the desert and mountain passes and the other army through a lesser-used passage further west. Once through the deserts and mountains, parts of the main east army will drive west to reinforce the smaller western army while the remainder will turn east to plunder and pillage and to draw the Jin armies out of their fortresses.

Any major well-fortified fortresses will be bypassed and blocked off from any rear attack. Cities and towns will be encouraged to submit first ... if they don't, they will be destroyed and plundered.

Already, months ago, they have sent spies to the northeast ... former Khitan (Liao) areas of the Jin empire and found many dissatisfied Khitans ready to defect to the Mongols. Likewise, their spies found many northern Chinese who were ready to switch allegiance should the Mongols invade. These will be important alliances in the upcoming campaign.

All summer long, the preparations continue ... routes planned, alternate routes scouted, and alternates-to-the-alternate routes scouted. Stores of foods and fodder are stacked and placed on carts. Usually in a Mongol war party, each warrior carries everything that he will need for one to two weeks ... but on this campaign, extra stores are being prepared for the difficult desert crossing.

Yufeng is working all day and night going over the medical teams for each army ... questioning the physicians and reassigning any that she feels are less qualified for the emergency field surgeries. The primary goal is to patch an injury fast so the warrior won't die and, if possible, so he can reenter the battle quickly.

Panda has become the Pied Piper of the royal youths, who follow her and Lana daily wherever she goes. To each of her charges she has made a wolf hair bracelet to identify them as Panda's wolf pack. The parents are happy to have a respite from having to watch them constantly ... allowing them to help in getting their warrior husbands ready.

***

Yufei and Gugu are always close to Subedei and therefore with the Khan's sons and the generals, Jebe and Jelme. From returning spies they discuss all the tactics in their box of tricks for each city, fortress, and Jin formations... plus paying bribes, spreading propaganda, marking river crossings.

Their confidence is overwhelming ... albeit in one regard, misplaced ... how to breech the walls of a strong, well situated, well-defended fortress. Their strategy discussions seem to end though when they get to the walls ... content to waiting to see what happens when they get there. Most of their battles have been fought against other nomadic tribes on the open steppes.

One night when they get to this same fortress wall issue, Subedei turns towards Yufei and ask him if he has any input on this problem.

Yufei, in his own meditations, has tried to find answers to overcoming these walled fortress defenses .... but each time, it is not clear ... he sees strange *machines* that help them break down the walls, but he can't see the details. But he sees something interesting ... a face ... a familiar face.

Yufei rises and addresses the small group of commanders.

"Like you, I have thought about this too. In the past, I usually find my answers inside ... deep inside ... and I have gone there."

Like all Mongols, they respect the seers, the shamans and Subedei asks, "What did you see?"

"Like you discussed ... problems. These walled cities are formidable ... they have food, water and other supplies stored inside to hold out for a long siege. They can hide behind the high stone walls and shoot arrows, rocks, and other weapons down on our warriors ... it will be a big problem."

"Your warriors think they are invincible ... but they are not ... we have all seen death ... so your commanders must be ready for this."

Subedei asks again,

"So, you think the Jin will defeat us at these walled cities?"

"Maybe in the beginning ... but then I saw a familiar face and some strange machines."

"Machines?"

"Machines to break down the walls."

The commanders look at each other. Subedei asks the question they are all thinking.

"Who was the familiar face?"

"A friend called, Chen Er ... he was trained and served in the Song navy defeating the Jin, but more than that, he has commanded a fleet of ships fighting off Arab fleets, and others."

Jebe says,

"But we are on land, not the water."

"Some of the strategies are similar, but also he knows of these new weapons ... weapons to defeat his enemies."

"New weapons?"

"New cannons, exploding cannonballs, fire ships, repeating crossbows and other weapons."

"Where did he get these weapons?"

"From different lands and from a scientist in China ... a friend of ours called, Su Xiao."

There is a silence, then they ask Yufei to step outside for a minute.

Inside he can hear them talking about what he said and whether they can trust him. He overhears Subedei tell them that the Khan visited Subedei one night and told him to trust this man, *Yufei and his family completely.* There is some more discussion until they ask him to come back in.

Subedei asks him,

"Where is this man, Chen Er and do you think you could convince him to come and help us?"

"I'm not sure where he is ... I think he is in Tibet ... at Lhasa."

"What about this other man ... the scientist?"

"He's further away ... in Quanzhou ... along the coast of Southern Song China."

"Are there any others in your past teams, who could be helpful?"

"There's a man called Tarem ... in Kucha ... he has battled with us in the far western Arab lands... I think he would come."

"The machines, the cannon ... who could help us make these?"

"The scientist."

"Who could best teach us how to use them.?"

"Chen Er."

"And this Uighur?"

"He can also help teach your people to use them ... and he could help me find the others."

"How long would it take for you to find these people and bring them here?"

Yufei rolls his head ... then smiles ... and they understand.

"When I get back ... I get back ... maybe a year, maybe two years."

One of the generals, Jelme, Subedei's older brother, says,

"By then we will have defeated the Jin."

Yufei looks at him,

"Maybe ..."

"But even if you have ... there are other kingdoms on the western borders of your lands ... with even higher fortress walls."

They confer some more and then tell him,

"We will talk again tomorrow."

Later, in his tent, Yufei keeps thinking about the implications of his talk ... traveling across the vast desert and mountains to Tibet ... and even larger distances to Quanzhou ... the dangers, the time ...

(*My god, what did I just propose to them?*)

Yufeng just watches, then suggests,

"Maybe you go inside, dear.

He looks at her.

"For your answers."

Later he tells Yufeng he is having trouble sleeping ...

"Oh?"

"Not the sleeping part ..."

"What?"

"The dreams"

"What about them?"

"Strange ..."

"Like what?"

"Invasions and slaughter ..."

"And in other cities, massive welcomes ... it makes no sense."

Yufeng tilts her head and looks at him.

"Are you dreaming the dreams ... or are the dreams, dreaming you?"

"That's the part I can't figure out."

She holds him close ...

"Don't worry, rascal ... what could possibly go wrong?"

Then she smiles and they both break out laughing ...

Panda enters with the wolf trailing after her.

"What's all the laughter about?"

Yufeng hugs her and Yufei scratches Lana.

"Nothing dear ... a private joke."

Panda smiles then goes to her father and asks him ...

"Father, when you go beyond the veil ..."

"No ... I don't go beyond the veil ..."

She tilts her head ... the wolf tilts her head too ...

"It's more like I enter a place between space."

"Between space? What does it *feel like to you* in there ... in this *in-between space*?"

He ponders a moment,

"*It doesn't feel empty ...*"

Panda smiles, "Yeah."

47 After the Weavers Retire

After the tapestry room is closed for the night, Granny Panda retires to her chambers. She stirs the coals in the brazier to warm the room and takes off her heavy fur robe. Then she retrieves a worn leather journal from beneath the blankets ... and opens it.

***

Panda:

I'm writing these things for you ... in case something happens to me or your mother.

Don't show this to anyone ... it could be dangerous. We've seen things ... in other lands ... good things but also some very frightening things.

Kingdoms in the Western lands are growing in strength, but they are afraid of anything they don't understand ... and they certainly wouldn't understand you. Their peasants are dominated by their religious clergy and their feudal lords ... both of whom use superstitious beliefs to attack any perceived enemies to their authority ... enough of that ... just be wary of everyone, especially foreigners.

Let me tell you about the lands and things I've seen. I first traveled to ancient Gobekli Tepe ... your mother and I visited it once, long ago ... and again since then... it was beautiful, and I understand even more, why our mission is so important. You should go there someday.

We saw the origins of what they had described, the invasions, the plundering, the killings. It was horrific and without mercy. After that the remnants of the grandmothers gathered, organized, and spread out over all the lands ... the Diaspora of the Grandmothers ... to Egypt, to the lands in the inland seas, to the Fertile Crescent, to Sichuan ... and to far-off Tibet ... some as sanctuaries, some as places to rebuild.

I went to ancient Egypt and Greece, where science, philosophy, and medicine had flourished once ... until the world forgot it and will need to rediscover it again. Then I followed the Mongol armies on several campaigns with your mother. And that's when ... we saw something interesting ... all the death and destruction is causing change ... to the survivors, it is beneficial change ... caused by the free flow of information and knowledge! But we also saw terrifying dark manifestations embedded in their religious beliefs by evil men trying to stop this rebirth.

Oh ... some people are coming by ... they see my candlelight ...

I'll write more later ... We are going to the land of the ancient Romans...

48 Crossing the Gobi

The next day Yufei meets with Subedei and the other commanders.

Jebe tells him,

"We have talked about what you said last night ... but we've decided not to do anything until after we see what happens at the first walled city."

Yufei nods,

"I understand ... when do we leave?"

Subedei slaps his shoulder,

"Today! Are you ready to travel across the desert ... for two weeks ... with no water and only buzzards circling overhead waiting for you to provide them a meal?"

Yufei smiles and looks at Gugu ...

"Sounds like fun."

They go back to their tent and find Yufeng is already packing everything.

"So, you've heard?"

She nods and points ...

"I've packed your travel kit ... Gugu, you'll have to pack your own stuff."

"No problem ... a fur robe, a bowl, chopsticks ... anything else?"

Yufeng looks at Panda and shrugs...

"Men are such helpless babies sometimes."

Panda laughs,

"I'll help you Uncle ..."

Yufei goes up to Yufeng and holds her close.

"Where will the medical units be stationed."

"Not too far behind the front lines. We need to keep the medical porters close to the battle ... so they can pick up the injured and help them to our mobile clinic where we can repair the least injured quickly and send them back in."

"The others?"

"Some who we think can return in a few days, we'll keep them in nearby tents, where their families must care for them ... the severely wounded we will send for their family who will take them back to care for them."

"What about the others?"

"Sky burial."

Gugu comes up with his loaded pack.

"I'm ready."

Yufei takes a last look at them, starts to walk out with Gugu, but turns and comes back and embraces Yufeng ... not knowing if or when they will see each other again. Panda looks on with immense love for them both.

Yufei turns to her and smiling asks,

"How about you ... what will you be doing while we are working?"

She laughs.

"Haha ... you'll be having all the fun while I'll be watching over my wolf pack ... also helping the women, treating the wounded warriors, cooking, cleaning ... the non-fun stuff."

Then she pouts,

"When can I join you two and play warrior games ... I need the practice."

Yufei laughs,

"You'll get your chance Panda ... sooner than you may want ... for now though we each play our parts ... okay?"

Panda hugs her father.

"Okay baba ... I am just teasing you ... but be careful out there ... use your third eye often ... some of the Tengeri's may be watching for an unguarded moment."

Yufeng is startled,

"Do you know something?"

"No ... just what I feel ... they are our enemies and you taught me not to turn my back on an enemy."

Yufeng turns to Yufei,

"She's right ... be careful."

"I will ... and I've got Gugu here to watch my back ..."

Yufei turns, looks around but Gugu is gone ...

"Well ... sometimes ..."

"Bye ... see you when ..."

Yufeng completes his sentence,

"... when I see you again..."

RICHARD HOWE

***

49 War Mongol Style

Unlike many armies, the Mongols do not march in a file, but rather spread out over the steppes ... for better foraging for the horses and to provide a wider defensive front.

The warriors are aligned by their groups of 100-man, 1000-man, and 10,000-man armies ... the last called a *tumen* force. The first few days of the march are uneventful. Scouts are sent out early to detect any Jin forces and also to scout the route ahead for forage and water.

A Mongol warrior had several spare horses and could change horses and ride for over 100 kilometers if needed. For the first few days of the march though, the main forces averaged about 50 kilometers per day... keeping their horses rested and their forces together in case of an attack ... news of their movements had already spread to the Jin capital.

The next two weeks are a monotonous trek over the desert sands and rock scrabble. Their prior planning had laid out a good route between oasis, and they make steady progress across the desert ... which is both good and bad ... in that any attack is hard to conceal and the desert is like crossing a river ... once across, your back is to the river and doesn't offer an easy retreat.

After another few days, they approached the foothills, behind which stands a line of mountains with only a few passes ... all well-known and well-defended passes with fortifications manned by Jin soldiers. Genghis decides to camp here and have a meeting with his commanders on which routes through the mountains to take.

While they are meeting several local Ongut tribesmen ride up under a peace banner. When they enter Genghis' large tent, Genghis rises and greets their leader, AlaKush, whom he knew from before. After the formal welcome, the leaders sit down.

AlaKush warns Genghis that the Jin are waiting for them at the main passes.

Genghis grunts and nods. Then AlaKush tells him about another trail through this first mountain chain which leads into the Jin lands. As they talked, the other commanders moved forward to listen to the description of this secret pass.

As a show of sincerity, the Onguts agree to stay with the Mongols as hostages. Genghis trusts the man's words, but still asks his commanders their opinions. He knows what he was going to do ... he just wanted them all to buy-into his decision.

At first some fear a trap, but in the end they all agree it could be a fortunate opportunity. When Genghis announces they will use the route, he dresses it as though it was a sign from the gods of their victory.

Later Subedei would go to Yufei and tell him confidentially what happened.

Yufei smiled and said,

"Thanks ... I already knew ... and it is a safe route."

Subedei is amazed and still a bit cautious in believing him.

The next day they split their forces, sending the main, but now much smaller force along the original line of march ... in case any Jin spies were lurking around. Then a smaller force headed through this new pass and bypassed the first line of Jin defenses. Once through ... this smaller, but powerful force will attack the main pass from the rear ... with attacks from the front and rear, the Jin defenders quickly flee.

After this initial victory though they come to the main string of higher mountain pass ... all heavily fortified and defended, with larger numbers of Jin soldiers. The main pass through the mountains before them is called Yehuling. A few gongli before the pass, the Mongols set up camp to decide how to attack.

On the Jin side, the commander watches nervously ... hoping to avoid a battle, even though he has a larger force hiding in wait behind the pass.

Then he makes a fatal mistake ... he sends an emissary to the Mongols to try to lure them into a trap about the Jin only having a "small" force at the pass ... but the emissary defects to the Mongols and tells Genghis the truth about the large force waiting to ambush them.

Genghis uses this knowledge to his advantage ... attacking with a small force at first, leaving his main forces in wait to ambush the Jin when they came out of the pass ... and it worked beautifully.

The small Mongol force attacked, the Jin came out of hiding, the Mongols retreated, the Jin followed them into the jaws of death ... and were decimated.

Next, they headed through Yehuling pass towards the Jin capital at Zhongdu.

But there, the massive walls of the capital stop them ... abruptly.

For days they hurled waves of warriors to their deaths without making any progress.

In Genghis tent, the meetings were getting heated. Genghis wanting results, the commanders frustrated ... and summer was approaching ... where even in the north the weather can turn uncomfortable for these artic-rim warriors.

One night after the other commanders had left, Jebe brings Jelme in and approaches Genghis. Later they send for Subedei and Yufei.

Genghis questions Yufei about these "machines" that he had heard about in his travels to the West.

Jebe was one of Genghis four most trusted generals and Jelme and Subedei were proven warriors who could also think strategically, so Genghis trusted their instincts as well, and they all seemed to respect Yufei ... as he did too.

They talked into the night, decisions were made, rendezvous discussed ... in the morning, Yufei and Gugu traveled west, Jebe traveled east, and Genghis headed north to recoup ... but keeping control of the conquered passes for an easier return the following fighting season.

That night Yufei searched out Yufeng, told her of his plans, and, with Gugu, immediately set out west. There was no time for a last embrace as every moment lost now could mean disaster later.

"Where will you go first?"

"Kucha ... and then Lhasa."

"That seems the long way. Why not just go to Lhasa?"

"I don't know ... just a feeling from what I saw inside."

"If you find him, will you go down the tea-horse trail or the great river?"

"I'm not sure ... that's why I need to talk to Tarem and Chen ... Tarem will know what the Jin are doing along the great river and Chen will know what's happening on the tea-horse trail."

"Do you sense Chen Er is still in Lhasa?"

Yufei just shrugged and rolled his head.

"When I get closer ... but ..."

"What?"

"I feel this is the right path ... not just for us ... so I think I will find them."

"Not just us ... what do you mean?"

"I don't know ... for others too."

"Others?"

"I don't know ..." then he points to the stars in the sky.

"Okay."

They hold each other with their arms and then ... embrace ... inside.

They go outside and Gugu comes up with a large bundle of Jin warrior clothes.

"I thought if we are going to be traveling a thousand gongli through Jin lands, maybe we should dress like them.

Yufei laughs.

"Good idea ... but let's wait until we get far away from the Mongol camp."

Gugu doesn't understand, but they go to their horses and mount up.

Yufei says to Yufeng,

"I think you'll be headed back north for the summer ... I'm not sure when or where I will see you again ... but it will come."

She smiles and says,

"I know."

Then she says to Gugu,

"You take care too, Gugu, and don't forget you both can get killed."

"Say goodbye to Panda ... maybe it's best this way ... she would just want to come with us to protect us."

Yufeng adds smiling,

"And maybe see Tarem's son, Tariq ..."

50 To Lhasa by way of Kucha

Yufei and Gugu travel westward ... at first through the hills ... after a week, they reach the plains of the upper Yellow River, which they follow further upstream for another week ... to a junction riverport which has roads leading to the south ... to Chang An, where they hope to learn more from Harim.

Along the way, they encounter a number of Jin checkpoints, but their uniforms, high rank insignia, forged documents, and stories of the battles enabled a quick passage.

***

Chang An is a different scene from their earlier trips, with more troop activity everywhere ... Jin soldiers on the battlements, new fortifications being built ... and a tightened scrutiny of all travelers. However, their uniforms and forged papers allow for easy passage into the city. If there is any hesitation, Gugu, from his vast knowledge base, reviles the guards with detailed knowledge of their local commanders in the capital.

On the way to Harim's, they walk by Hasan's old shop (the former Khwarazm agent), which has been boarded up since he and his associates had disappeared.

At Harim's they find their old friend ... a little older but still clear minded. He has a young boy acting as an apprentice.

"One of Beersheba's nephews ..." he explains.

Over mint tea they catch up on all the news.

Yufei warns him to leave Chang An.

"And go where?"

"To Kucha .... you will be safer there with Beersheba."

The old man nods ... the war-weary nod of a man who has been through this several times before. Then his head nods up and he looks at Yufei.

Yufei immediately knows the old man's thoughts.

Gugu looks at him questioningly.

Yufei whispers,

"The books ..."

Yufei ponders this for a moment.

"I was thinking about them along the trail. I think you should seal it back up for now ... we will help."

"How? People will see."

"No, tell them you are repairing some inner walls that are falling apart and you want to add a new storeroom. Have the boy arrange for the wall material to be brought and dumped just inside. We will do some visible repairs towards the front but behind the carpet screen, we will wall up the door."

"Forever?"

Yufei shakes his head,

"No ... Yufeng and I both have books in there that we want to explore."

Then instinctively, he adds,

"And someday, China will be safe for them to be rediscovered."

Harim asks,

"When do you want to start?"

"Immediately, send the boy now. We need to go to Kucha to find Tarem ... do you know if he is still there?"

"Yes ... the boy came back from there yesterday."

"Good. Let's get to work ... I want to leave by tomorrow."

Harim calls in the youth and gives him instructions. Hidden behind the rear blanket, Yufei and Gugu prepare the wall.

It takes them most of the night to complete the new wall covering the door.

"Let it dry then cover it up with rugs and shelves."

Harim nods.

"We will leave now. Take care old friend."

"You're not staying the night?"

He shakes his head.

"A storm is coming ... we need to get ahead of it. I think you should come with us now to Kucha."

Harim shakes his head.

"I'm too old to run at every sound of thunder ..."

"This isn't just thunder, Harim ... promise me you will leave before the storm breaks ..."

"I will ... and thank you for everything."

With that they say goodbye and ride out the West gate towards Lanzhou, Dunhuang and Kucha.

Along the way, Gugu asks Yufei,

"Why didn't you bring him with us?"

Yufei sighs.

"He is old now and seen many wars in his time ... and ..."

"*He has earned the right to die where he chooses.*"

***

Chang An > Lanzhou > Dunhuang > Kucha

Outside Lanzhou they discard the Jin uniforms and put back on their "traveling merchant" attire.

Dunhuang is controlled by the Xi Xia now and are friendly towards merchants (and after their defeat are an ally of the Mongols).

But even so, they don't linger in the town ... staying only long enough to replenish their food and pick up on any news of dangers ahead ... and then move on to Kucha.

On the outskirts, Yufei cautions Gugu.

"Be careful what you say to Beersheba."

"About what?"

"Everything. If she thinks Harim is in danger she will go there herself to drag him back to Kucha."

"Would that be so bad?"

Yufei pauses.

"Would *you* like someone to interfere in your life's pathway?"

"What would you do if it was Yufeng?"

"I would try to drag her to Kucha ..."

"Try?"

Yufei looks at Gugu while crooking his head and raising his eyebrows.

Gugu smiles ...

"Oh, I understand ... kind of, but this marriage thing is confusing to me."

Yufei laughs. (*monks*)

***

At Tarem's archway gate, they see some of Tarem's children running in and out of the compound ... but curiously, always closing the gates quickly behind them.

When they get to the gate to the compound, Yufei knocks on the gate.

One of the boys comes ... looks questioningly at the two riders ... then the light of recognition turns on and he smiles.

"Baba ... Baba ... your friends!"

Then he runs inside as the two riders enter the compound and close the gate behind them. They survey the scene of boxes of trade items piled near the gates ready for travel.

Tarem comes out and smiles, with Beersheba following, carrying a new baby.

Yufei smiles, looks at the baby, then at Beersheba, who looks at Tarem.

Tarem holds his arms up,

"What? My mother had 10 children! I am a failure in her eyes!"

They all laugh.

Pointing to the boxes, Yufei asks,

"Going somewhere?"

"Let's go inside."

Inside, they clear off a table and Tarem unfolds a large map of the area. In the center is the Kucha kingdom, on the East is the Western Xia, on the West is the Kara Khitai, on the north are the Mongols, on the south is Tibet.

Then he looks at Yufei.

"We are in the middle. What do you think is going to happen?"

But when he looks at Yufei, Yufei has gone inside. Tarem and Gugu know to wait. Tarem tells Beersheba to get some tea and food ready for later.

About ten minutes later, Yufei comes out of his spell ... he looks at the group, smiles, then points to the map.

"Right now, the Mongol armies are fighting the Jin in Northern China, but in time, they will turn towards the west. The Western Xia are already aligned with the Mongols so they won't pose a problem and if your king continues to submit and support the Mongols, then the Kucha Kingdom will be spared destruction. After that I sense the Mongols will expand their control westward to the Kara Khitan areas."

Tarem interrupts.

"Why? I mean, not why you think that, but why they will expand?"

"The Great Khan firmly believes it is his destiny to conquer the world. That this is the wish of his god Tengri."

"And he believes that?"

"Yes ... most assuredly ... it is what drives him. That and to rid the world of all the wars between petty tyrants ... plus their misguided suppression of their women and foreign beliefs."

Beersheba asks.

"He supports women?"

Yufei nods.

"Women are highly regarded in his camp and the wives of most sons and commanders can speak up at meetings. His mother and wife are like goddesses to him. Yufeng is now a leader in their medical corps."

Beersheba smiles, then stops, and looks at the map again.

"Yufei, what about Chang An?"

Yufei sighs knowingly.

"It will see invasions."

"When?"

He shrugs and shakes his head.

"I can sense events ... but when I go inside, there are no dates. All I know is that it will come to Chang An also."

"My father!"

Then she looks at Yufei again.

"You told him all this?"

He nods.

"And you left him there?"

Yufei looks at her with a saddened face and nods his head.

Her eyes flash but before she can say something she would later regret, Tarem grabs her and hauls her outside.

From inside they can hear them shouting.

Yufei looks at one of the children, seemingly unconcerned with the argument of her parents outside. Smiling she says,

"Don't worry, they do that a lot."

After a while they come back in.

Tarem asks Yufei,

"I agreed to ask you one question. Is that okay?"

Yufei nods.

"Knowing what will probably happen. Why did you leave Harim there?"

Beersheba is silent ... holding her tongue.

Yufei looks at Beersheba and says as gently as possible.

"He knows the dangers ... I explained them in detail."

"He told me that he's tired of running from invasions."

"And would rather die there than someplace else."

"And I felt that *he had earned the right to make that decision for himself.*"

There are tears in Beersheba's eyes as she listens and realizes the truth and also senses the deep affection that Yufei has for her father. She walks up to him and hugs him.

"I know ... he can be a stubborn old goat at times."

Tarem adds.

"That's why we all love him."

Yufei looks at Tarem and asks,

"So, tell me what all the trade goods are doing in your compound?"

"We were planning a trade caravan to Tibet."

51 Kucha & Tarem

"Tibet? ... Great! ... Can we tag along with you?" Yufei smiles.

Tarem looks at Beersheba and Tariq.

"Maybe that can solve one of the problems we have been wrestling with ... Beersheba and the babies ... if you two go along, then Beersheba can stay here and avoid the hard desert-mountain trip."

"Sounds good to me." Yufei says looking at Beersheba,

"How are you with that?"

Beersheba looks at Tarem.

"On one condition ... after you get to Lhasa, you go to Chang An and tie up that old goat of a father of mine and bring him here."

He laughs and agrees.

Then Tariq coughs and Tarem looks at him.

"You can speak now; you are a man."

"After Lhasa, I'd like to go with Uncle Yufei and see more of the outside world."

Tarem looks at Beersheba, who nods.

"It's okay with us, if it's okay with Yufei."

Yufei smiles and reaches out his hand in a handshake.

"But you must do everything I say ... even if you don't understand."

Tariq nods his head several times as he bows down in obeisance.

"Yes uncle, yes uncle."

Then Beersheba asks Tarem,

"When will you leave?"

"Before sunrise tomorrow."

"Okay, then you men finish your preparations and I'll get all the food packed and dinner ready."

It is a busy night, and they go to sleep late, exhausted.

Before they sleep Tarem speaks to Yufei.

"I learned something about those Arabs that attacked us in Chang An years ago."

"Hasan?"

"Yes ... he was an agent of the shah of Khwarazm, sent by the shah's relative the governor of Otar."

"Did you learn anymore?"

"They, the Khwarazm, have been invading the Western Liao and Kara Khitai and taking over parts of their fading empire ... all along the Silk Road and even the Guge Kingdom in the south."

"Which we need to travel through?"

Tarem nods.

"What do you know of this shah?"

"He is a self-centered, pompous ruler full of himself from conquering the diminished Seljuk Empire and his mother is an equally powerful black force in their kingdom."

"Interesting ... rats everywhere."

"Yeah ... good night."

***

Kucha to Tibet

The trail to Tibet follows along the Khotan River south through the desert to Khotan. The trails are less worn lately, due to fewer caravans during the tribal wars.

Gugu asks Tarem,

"Are you worried about bandits or warring parties along the way?"

Tarem crooks his head, in the manner he saw Yufeng do once, and says,

"Worried? ... Would that help?"

They all get the joke except Tariq ... later they explain that it was what Yufeng had told others at a dangerous point in their previous adventures.

It's obvious that Tariq admires his father and also Yufei ... with Gugu, he is more cautious, but still friendly ... it is one of the reasons that Yufei assigns Gugu to teach Tariq about enlightenment and other spiritual matters.

Along the route, whenever he can, Tariq questions Yufei about his adventures and strategies. At first Yufei was reluctant to supplant Tarem's parental authority position until Tarem told him to tell him everything ... even the spiritual aspects.

"The boy is strong, a good rider, a good fighter, and has a quick mind ... always asking questions. I think I have taught him all I can ... it will be good for him to learn from you."

Yufei nods and ponders how to go about it ... then he asks Gugu, who says,

"It must be part of the divine plan ... it will be for a reason, I am sure."

"Okay ... let me think about it."

Later at their campfire, Yufei takes Gugu and Tariq aside.

"Have you studied the Tao?"

Tariq nods,

"A little, but I don't understand everything."

"Don't worry ... no one understands it at first."

Then Gugu explains,

"You can't seek the Tao; it has to come to you. Just be quiet, still inside, and empty ... do nothing and it will come."

'Do nothing?"

"Nothing. Some call it *wuwei* ... no action ... 'stopping the mind' ... think of your mind like a pond ... but the water is disturbed, your mind confused ... first you must still the waters and then you can see the moon's reflection ... only then can you receive the wisdom of the Tao."

"How will I receive it?"

"It is impossible to describe it in words ... the Tao is like the Spirit ... like consciousness ... it can't be explained in words. You will just *know* ... *everything is in the knowing.*"

"But ..."

Yufei holds up his hand,

"That is enough for tonight ... but before you go, I have a question for you."

"What master?"

"What do you dream about?"

Tariq lowers his head, embarrassed by his thoughts of Panda.

Yufei puts his hand on his shoulder,

"It's okay, son ... another time ..."

With that, they retire for the night.

Tarem smiles at Yufei when he climbs into his fur bedding.

***

The next night after dinner, Yufei starts to teach Tariq some fighting skills.

"Get a staff and meet me at that open area."

The two face off.

"Attack me."

But Tariq waits, just making some feints, trying to get Yufei to attack.

"Good ... but let's try some actual fighting." And with that, Yufei launches a vicious attack which crumples Tariq.

Helping the boy up, he explains,

"Always ... always be ready for an attack. Understand?"

Dusting himself off and straightening his bruised arms and legs, the boy nods.

"Okay, now your turn to beat me up."

Tariq smiles ... he has been taught for many years by his father.

First, he feints with an overhead blow, which fluidly converts to a slashing cut.

Yufei blocks it easily.

Next Tariq tries several other tactics which have worked successfully in his fights in Kucha ... all to no avail.

Finally, out of breath, Tariq asks,

"Master, how do you know my moves before I make them?"

Pointing to his heart and stomach, he says,

"Here ... I can sense your move inside ... your instincts are the most important thing you need to connect with ... to listen inside ... to trust your instincts ... and to *follow them without thinking*. Do you understand?"

"A little ... my mother told me something like that."

Tarem smiles,

"I hope you got your mother's instincts, because her instincts are more powerful than mine."

Then Yufei says something Tariq will never forget.

"Yufeng and I were born with enhanced instincts, and they've grown through our experiences ... but Panda has three times our instinctive abilities."

Tariq thinks (*three times?*); then he asks,

"Uncle, how can I *train* my instincts?"

Yufei smiles.

"First follow the exercises that Gugu teaches you, and second, practice awareness every day. As you ride, as you eat, as you do everything ... be aware."

Tariq is taking all this in and resolving to himself to develop these inner and outer skills.

Without thinking he says,

"This is the best vacation ever!"

The three men smile. (*vacation?*)

The next day as they ride, Yufei points to a fleeing steppe marmot. Pointing to it, he says one word.

"Tariq"

Tariq kicks his horse into a gallop, while he brings his bow around and notches an arrow in one fluid motion. The fleeing animal doesn't stand a chance.

Yufei is impressed with Tariq's archery skills and tells the boy.

"That was good ... next time though, we'll try it a little different."

Tariq wonders. (*different?*)

When they stop for lunch, Yufei brings Tarem aside. Tariq watches the discussion ... at the end Tarem nods.

Yufei goes to Tariq.

"Mount up."

After they are both mounted, Yufei tells him,

"Now we will raise the level of training. Your father seems to think you can handle it, but we'll see."

Tariq steals a quick glance at his father, who is blank faced.

"Get out your bow and have some arrows ready ... ride over to that group of rocks ... I'll get my bow and ride over there (pointing to the other side of an open field."

"When Tarem shouts, we'll ride at each other, firing arrows, trying to kill the other rider."

Tariq thinks (*trying to kill?*)

The boy looks at his father, who shrugs impatiently.

"How do you think I learned to fight ... by killing steppe marmots? You need to learn this, and you need to learn it quickly because we never know when an enemy will attack us."

"But I don't want to injure uncle."

Yufei laughs.

"Worry more about yourself boy and remember what we've taught you ... feel the attack coming inside ... sense the arrows *before* they arrive."

Then they ride off to both ends. The boy was a little nervous but still confident ... as youths tend to be.

Once they appear ready, Tarem shouts "Attack!" and they ride at each other.

Yufei launches an arrow on a high arc, then starts to gallop at Tariq, launching two more arrows quickly.

Tariq dodges these two and fires two of his own. Just as he starts to launch his third arrow though, he senses he must swerve, which he does ... instinctively ... in order to avoid Yufei's first high arced arrow. By then they are upon each other and Yufei is smiling.

"Good ... you remembered!"

The boy is excited.

"I can't explain it ... a feeling ... a voice ... telling me to swerve quickly ... I didn't think about it, I just followed the feeling."

The other two join them and congratulate Tariq ... then his father brings him back to earth.

"Good ... tomorrow we can get into knives, and you'll have three attackers."

Tariq frowns and then smiles,

"No problem if the attackers are old goats like you three ... haha."

***

52 Lhasa & Chen Er

They cross the desert, reach Khotan, but don't stop ... just replenish supplies and get information from Tarem's jade relative about any patrols south to Kailash.

"You should be okay ... I heard the shah's forces have gone north to the Fergana."

They look at each other and nod.

"Good ... thank you cousin."

The man then asks,

"Our *other* business ... do we still continue it?"

Tarem looks at Yufei who nods.

"For now ... but stop if you sense anything threatening ... understand?"

The man nods.

They leave early the next morning and retrace their trail from many years earlier to Mt. Kailash.

They avoid the Guge Fort and any soldiers that still might be there and continue past it.

Finally, at Kailash they rest.

Gugu and Yufei go to visit the elders and report their activities.

Elder Yeshe tells them,

"It is good ... you have accomplished a lot since we last met."

Yufei asks,

"What news can you tell us of dangers you foresee?"

"Your news about many black cells throughout the world is something we suspected ... but could not prove ... they must be well cloaked."

She looks at Yufei with a sigh ...

"You must be extra careful ... if we can help, we will, but mostly you will be on your own."

Yufei nods,

"We know. Thank you, elder sister."

Then she asks,

"When will you leave?"

"In the morning ... I feel we must not waste time."

She nods and gives him a package.

'For your wife and daughter."

Then they leave the temple, gather Tarem and Tariq, and ride towards Lhasa.

Only once, a week later, are they stopped by a Tibetan patrol ... Yufei shows letters from the princess, and they are allowed to pass. There are only small villages along their route, so they don't do much trading until they get to Lhasa by the end of the month.

At Lhasa, they first go to a caravanserai, get rooms, wash off and go separate ways. Tarem to the trade markets with Tariq, while Yufei and Gugu to the princess's compound to look for Chen Er.

The guards usher him in and he finds Chen Er and the princess having their late breakfast. They exchange welcomes which are sincere and emotional for all of them.

Then Yufei looks at Chen Er's belly and asks the princess,

"Are you hoping for a boy or a girl?"

She breaks out with a belly laugh as Chen throws some pillows at Yufei.

"I get no exercise ... no pirating ... no sword fights ... I am like that thing you warned me about."

"The eunuch?"

"Yes ... whatever ... what's up with you ... where is Yufeng and Panda?"

"They are still in Mongolia, helping the Khan."

The princess and Chen Er share a quick glance.

Yufei understands and says,

"Let me explain ..."

For two hours, he goes through the mission of the elders, their experiences in Kucha and Avarga ... and most recently with the Jin invasion.

At the end, all Chen can say is,

"Wow! You have been busy!"

There is a pause for them to digest it all, then Yufei asks what's been happening in Tibet.

They tell them about their attack of the dark monastery, but one unfortunate consequence is that the royals' power in Tibet is mostly symbolic now ... once they vanquished the dark monastery, the real power has been usurped by the Buddhist sects ... first one and then another. But they still work together when it comes to defense against outside forces.

Yufei says,

"I saw some Tibetan Buddhist monks in the Mongol camp."

The princess nods,

"Yes, they have emissaries with them to try to avoid an invasion ... what do you hear?"

"Right now, they have their hands full with the Jin ... that's one reason I am here ... after that I have sensed their efforts will be westwards, rather than south to Tibet ... at least, for the near future."

They look at each other and smile.

"So how can we help you?"

"We ... I mean the Mongols, need siege engines and cannons, like we saw in the West, and we know the Chinese have built some ... I want to enlist you and Su Xiao in our cause and bring you both north to Mongol lands."

Chen rubs his chin and looks at the princess who understands, and then laughs.

"You go with him ... you need the exercise. we'll be okay here."

Then she rubs her belly.

Yufei looks at Chen Er.

"What? Are you two expecting a little pirate?"

The princess corrects him,

"I'm expecting a little princess ... just don't forget how to get back!"

Chen Er though looks concerned about leaving her. But she is firm.

"No ... it is foreordained that you should go ... and while you are in the Mongol camp, you can lobby for negotiations rather than invasion of Tibet ... I will get you some formal letters."

Chen Er looks at Yufei.

"What are your plans?"

"You and I, Gugu, and Tariq, Tarem's son, will go down the Tea-horse trail like before and catch a boat to Quanzhou. When we get there, we meet with Su Xiao and then we sail north to meet the Khan's armies that are raiding the Liaoning Peninsula."

"Do you think Su will agree to help the Mongols?"

"I hope so ... after I talk to him and explain things. If not, we get all the plans and leave quietly."

There is silence, then the princess says, she wants to spend a little time alone with her husband before they leave in the morning.

Yufei understands and tells them where they are staying as he leaves to find Tarem and Tariq.

The next morning the group gets together at the inn as Tarem prepares to go to Chang An to bring Harim to safety in Kucha ... and the others to go down the Tea-horse trail to the port and then Quanzhou. The princess is there to see them off and she hands safe passage letters to the two groups.

She also hands a letter to Yufei to give to a Tibetan Buddhist monk from the Sakya monastery, called Kunga Pandita, believed to be in Avarga camp, working for future peaceful relations.

Yufei tells her he met him once before and will deliver the message.

They all bow to each other, Tariq has an emotional farewell with his father, who admonishes him to follow Yufei without thinking ... in everything ... just as you would me. Tariq bows low to the ground before his father and then he does obeisance to Yufei as well.

Then they all mount ... Tarem heads north, the others head east.

They proceed down the tea-horse trail and two weeks later arrive at Yufei's Yunnan compound. The villagers are happy to see them, but sad when they relate what happened to their neighbors. They are also unhappy that their favorite healer, Yufeng, is not with them. Saddened by the news of what happened to their neighbors, they only stay one night and continue down to the Annam port.

Chen Er talks to several captains as well as his agent in the port. They expect one of his ships to arrive sometime next week.

That gives them time to rest and to discuss the next two legs of their journey ... Quanzhou and sailing north.

Yufei asks him,

"Have you ever sailed that far north?"

"No ... some Quanzhou ships used to sail there, but that was about 100 years ago, before the Jin conquered the Liao/Khitan kingdom."

"So there probably aren't any old sailors around."

"No, but Su will have old sailing maps from that time. With those charts we can navigate there ... if there are no big storms."

With the mention of big storms, Gugu explains to Chen Er,

"You know I can die if I drown?"

'What?'

"I thought you were immortal like my friend here."

Yufei punches him. Tariq watches their friendly bantering ... but his mind is somewhere else .... on the northern steppe ... with a certain young female wolf warrior.

53 Quanzhou & Family

After a week's sail, they arrive in Quanzhou, where they meet with Chen's family. Lord Chen is older but still one of the elder statesmen in the country. Chen Yi is an important minister now and spends most of his time in the capital.

Both men are eager to hear about the Mongols and Yufei is eager to hear the news from Wuyi. They welcome Tariq like family and Gugu like ... well ... like a wandering monk.

Over dinner, they are especially interested in Yufei's Mongol news but a little circumspect in relaying the Wuyi news.

Yufei suspects something is amiss.

"How are Anhua and Lanting?"

The elder Chens exchange a glance, then Lord Chen quickly says,

"You can see for yourself ... they are in town for their oldest boy, Chen Ming's civil examination. We are waiting now to hear the exam results before ordering a celebration."

Just then the doors burst open and a very elegantly dressed Chen Anhua rushes in announcing,

"He passed ... in the top three!"

Everyone is happy with the news and Lord Chen talks to Lady Chen about a dinner celebration that night.

So wrapped up in himself, Chen Anhua hardly acknowledges Yufei's presence.

"Oh ... hi Yufei."

A few minutes later, Lanting enters with her oldest son, Chen Ming, who passed the examination. Yufei is shocked at her appearance. She is well dressed, but the lines on her face show years of stress and unhappiness. Yufei immediately senses sadness inside and rushes to congratulate her. It takes a moment for Lanting to recognize this man whom she hasn't seen for more than a decade.

"Yufei? Is it you?" then looking around,

"Is Yufeng with you?"

Yufei shakes his head,

"No, I came alone ... with Gugu and Tarem's son, Tariq."

She lowers her head,

"Oh ..."

Then she recovers quickly in front of the family.

"Did you hear? Our oldest son passed the Jinshi examinations today."

"Yes ... congratulations!"

Then turning to the boy, Yufei says,

"Congratulations."

The boy, Chen Ming, bows to Yufei.

"Thank you, honorable Uncle. I have heard many stories about you."

Yufei turns back to Lanting, who turns and walks away ... avoiding any more discussion, saying only,

"I need to help your grandmother get ready for our celebration meal."

Yufei looks at Chen Er who looks at Chen Yi, who shakes his head slightly.

Chen Anhua meanwhile is effusive retelling the results to his father ... as though it was his own successful achievement.

Yufei wonders if he would act the same if the son had failed.

Something has changed ... but I need to walk on eggs to find out.

Chen Yi breaks into his thoughts.

"Let me show you three where you can stay ... how long will you be here?'

"We're not sure ... not long I think."

He leads them out a side corridor.

"Later, I'd like to learn more about the Mongols ... how they fight, what they think, how we might defend against them ..."

Yufei just nods.

"Okay ..." *if only it was that easy ...*

Gugu and Tariq stay in one room and Yufei and Chen Er in Chen Er's old bedroom. As Chen Yi starts to leave, Yufei grabs his arm and brings him back into the bedroom and closes the door.

"Tell me ... what happened to those two people out there?"

Chen Yi lowers his head.

"It's partially your fault."

"My fault?"

"After you appointed Chen Anhua to be the clan's fund manager ... he slowly started to change ... money and power does that to some people."

Yufei crooks his head to the side.

"My father and I didn't become aware of it until it was too late ... you and Chen Er were gone and Lanting deferred to him too often to keep the peace in her family."

"What did he do?"

"He started dressing differently ... more elegantly, like a court minister. He started flaunting his money ... buying companies and properties with the funds."

"But that wasn't the plan ..."

"We know, but we didn't find out until later and Lord Chen and I have enormous and important responsibilities in the capital ... for all of China."

"I'll talk to him ... he'll listen to me."

Chen Yi shakes his head.

"I'm not so sure ... I tried and he cut me off quickly. Then my mother asked me to go easy on him. ... but it's only gotten worse."

"What about Lanting?"

He shakes his head.

"You saw her ... what did you think?"

"I barely recognized her."

"Maybe you should talk to her first."

"No ... I need to talk to Yufeng first."

Not understanding, Chen Yi looks around the room.

"Older brother-in-law, I need to be alone now ... please tell the others."

Chen Yi nods and leaves, closing the doors and telling a servant not to let anyone inside.

First Yufei gets comfortable. He changes out of his sea-salt smelling clothes, washes, and puts on a fresh tunic. Next, he places some mats on the floor and opens the window in front of them. He takes some deep breathers and sits in the lotus position.

He closes his eyes, empties his mind and, in a few moments, he is gone ... inside, but not into the void like before ... this time he goes to the steppes, to the Mongol camp where Yufeng is walking. She stops, senses Yufei's spirit and goes to her tent.

In a few moments they are connected, and information is shared.

Afterwards, slowly he comes awake but still sits there pondering his potential actions and their potential consequences.

When he enters the dining room, everyone is already seated. Lord and Lady Chen at the head of the table, Chen Anhua on one side and Chen Yi on the other. The rest are scattered randomly with Tariq sitting next to Chen Ming. The youths hit it off and trade stories about their very different cultures.

Yufei doesn't want to ruin the festivities by confronting Anhua, so he relates stories of their adventures in Tibet, in Kucha, and in Mongol lands. Then it is Chen Er's turn to describe his Tibetan adventures and the announcement of another Chen grandchild on the way ... a princess!

Yufei asks Chen Ming about his plans now.

Nervously he says,

"I want to follow in my family traditions and serve the emperor to help the people."

Yufei laughs, "Said like a true diplomat!" then looking at the youth he asks,

"What about following your Uncle and pirating on the high seas?"

Embarrassed the boy says, "No, no, my mother would never allow me to do that!"

Which causes more laughter.

During the meal, Yufei tries to look at Lanting, but she always notices his glances and turns away.

Once the dinner is finished, Yufei whispers to Chen Yi that he wants to speak to him and Lord Chen alone. Then he whispers to Chen Er to keep Chen Ahua with the main party.

Chen Yi whispers to his father, who rises and asks Yufei to come into his private study. The two rise and Chen Yi follows. Anhua starts to rise to follow but Chen Er grabs him and tells him he needs to talk to him privately.

Inside the study, Yufei explains his plan. They agree with Yufei. Then Lord Chen tells him,

"I can arrange it."

With that settled, Yufei asks Chen Yi,

"The boy, Chen Ming, what's he like?"

"He's a good boy ... and devoted to his mother."

"Good ... but we must make it look real ... not planned."

"We understand."

Then the two Chens look at Yufei.

"Thank you for coming at this time ... truly destiny shines."

Yufei is less ebullient.

"Hopefully it works like we plan ... let's go."

Lord Chen tells Chen Yi,

"Chen Yi, you bring Second Son up to date on the plan."

"Okay."

Back at the main table, everything is the same. The two youths are talking about weapons training.

Chen Ming raises his voice,

"Eagle hunting! Really?"

"Yes, it's done in the northwest by several tribes using large golden eagles."

Chen Ming turns to his mother and asks,

"Mother, can I travel out west someday?"

Lanting nods.

"Sure, why not, maybe your father will spend some time with you ... now."

Anhua casts a sharp look at Lanting who turns away.

Yufei speaks to the two boys.

"Many years ago, Chen Er gave me some wushu lessons in the back courtyard ... would you two boys like to match your skills?"

The boys both shout acceptance and jump up.

Chen Er leads them out back. Some, but not all of the party follow them out. The women mostly stay inside to help clean up.

Outside Chen Er shows them where the staffs are stacked. He hands one to each and tells them to fight but not do any major harm.

In a flash the boys are parrying and thrusting ... swinging blows at each other. Although younger, Tariq is more skilled whereas Chen Ming is taller and stronger. They mock fight for a while until it becomes apparent that Tariq is the better fighter and is holding back, but Chen Ming doesn't feel bad ... he is happy to have a new friend. After a while they pause and rest their staffs.

Yufei then grabs the staffs and hands one to Anhua.

"Shall we play ... like old times, friend?"

Unsuspecting, Anhua smiles.

"Sure."

Then Yufei whispers something into his ear and Anhua's face changes into fury. Anhua starts slashing at Yufei who just blocks without attacking. Anhua picks up the fury of his attack and *seemingly* breaks through Yufei's defenses, Yufei goes down and Anhua keeps up the assault. Yufei appears defenseless but Anhua continues to strike him. The others are shouting but no one can stop his fury. Chen Ming runs inside to get his mother. Lanting understands quickly and goes to wrap her arms around her husband to stop him, but Anhua slashes at his wife and she goes down. Finally, Chen Er clubs Anhua from behind knocking him down. Everyone rushes to Yufei and Lanting to see if they are okay.

Knowing where every blow was coming from, Yufei managed to avoid any major damage, although he still will be badly bruised in the morning. Lanting was not injured, and her son and Lady Chen are ministering to her.

But the boil has been pierced.

Lord Chen calls for a family meeting with his three sons and Yufei. Anhua is still angry though, but he will never go against his father.

Lord Chen asks Anhua,

"What was that all about?"

Defiant, Anhua says,

"Ask him, he started it.'

"I'm asking you ... don't disobey me!"

"He said he was replacing me as the manager of the clan wealth fund."

"And that's why you attacked him? Over money? Is that how I raised you?"

"But I control the wealth fund."

"No, you don't ... the family controls it. Yufei and Chen Er set it up that way. You were just a *temporary* steward ... and now you are being replaced."

"Replaced? Why?"

"Frankly because you have abused your power. You have used the funds without consulting others as though it belongs to you and you alone."

"But ..."

"No buts ... this fund belongs to our descendants, not to you! Your misuse of the fund has become a family embarrassment."

"But when people find out I've been replaced, I'll be ostracized."

"They won't find out."

"What do you mean?"

"I'll arrange a reappointment for you ... to the western regions where you can reconsider your priorities. You used to have a happy family and people's respect ... and you've lost it all ... for what? Gold?"

"But..."

Lord Chen slams a piece of hardwood down sharply on his desk.

"Anhua! What can't you understand? You abused our trust, you beat your best friend and brother-in-law, and you even beat your wife! What is it going to take for you to understand? Maybe a few years of contemplation on the frontier."

"That's my decision. Do you agree?"

Anhua slumps lower. Finally, he asks Yufei.

"Yufei, why didn't you fight back?"

Yufei looks at him, shakes his head, and says,

"Since we were kids, you have been my best friend ... my one true friend ... how could I fight you? Especially over gold?"

Anhua looks at his father and says,

"I agree."

And with that the family crisis is over.

When they open the doors, Lanting comes in ... not to see Anhua, but to check on Yufei's injuries.

When they are alone, Yufei explains everything.

For the first time in several years a burden is lifted.

Then looking in Yufei's eyes she tells him,

"Thank you ..." then she adds,

"I miss my little sister ... so very much."

Yufei holds her and tells her,

'Me too."

The next day, Yufei, Chen Er, Gugu and Tariq go to see Master Su, who is older now, but still very active with his experiments.

He is very happy to see them all and anxious to hear about their exploits.

They spend several hours relating their stories ... and Su, being a laboratory bound scientist, is captivated by their exploits. Then he says something which later will haunt him.

"Before I cross the final bridge, I wish I could travel the world like you two!"

Yufei smiles and says,

"That's why we have come to see you ... to invite you to faraway lands ... to lend your skills to further the Divine Plan ... to make a difference in the world."

At first Su doesn't understand; then Yufei explains the divine plan of the elders and the things he's seen of the future possibilities ... should they succeed. A world of free trade, of free beliefs, of women's rights, the end of tribal wars ... and even a unified China!

Su looks around at his familiar home and laboratory ... then at his friends. To a scientist rooted in this world, the decision was surprisingly easy,

"I will go!"

"Tell me more about the siege engines that you seek, the cannon you want, the defenses that you encounter and the lands we will travel to ..."

They talk well into the night and through the next day, going over plans, sketches of fortresses, and maps of western lands.

While Yufei goes through these details, Chen Er is meeting with Captain Ding to pick a crew and provision his fastest ship. There have been several successors to the original *Falcon* ... he is now sailing the *Falcon IV* which has many advances as well as more comforts. Tariq is fascinated by Quanzhou, Master Su, and especially these sailing ships. Chen Ming is his new friend and shows him around Quanzhou while the others prepare supplies and siege engine models.

During this time, Chen Anhua's new assignment has come through and he is assigned to Jiujiang. Yufei writes an introduction letter to Empress Wu for him and wishes him luck. Contrition seems to be coming ... albeit slowly. Lanting goes back to Wuyi and her tea business, but she looks 10 years younger than when he arrived.

At a family meeting she was chosen as the new manager of the clan wealth fund and will train Chen Ming in its operations and functions ... to succeed her if he is found worthy by the clan. Chen Ming is genuinely humbled by the confidence in him, although a bit saddened by the exile of his father. Like most Chinese of the day, he worships his father and idealizes his mother and grandparents.

Finally, they are ready to sail. All the goodbyes were exchanged the night before ... mostly between Chen Er and his family but also with his remaining ship captains about their destination. The boat departs on the morning tide ... their true destination, the Liaoning Peninsula, a secret from all but a few ...

Chen Er, Yufei, Tarem ... together again ... the same confident three that journeyed together to the Middle Eastern lands and overcame the Arabs and the corrupt ministers at Court ... and, as the old folk say ...

... a triple-stranded rope is not easily broken.

54 Panda & Sari

Meanwhile back in the main camp, Panda and Sari are working on some hides, scraping the fleshy inside down to the leather beneath. It can be backbreaking work, but these two have become close and seem to enjoy the work as a time to share thoughts. One would think that it was the older woman teaching the younger girl, but in subtle ways, it is Panda sharing wisdoms with Sari.

Remembering something, Sari asks,

"Panda, how old are you this year?"

"13, 14 ... why?"

"Have you had your woman's discharge?"

"Yes."

"The Naadam festival is coming up this summer."

"So?"

"Maybe I need to talk to your mother ... can you find her?"

"Okay."

Panda runs off as Sari ponders something in her mind.

***

Panda can't find her mother until Monke tells her that she walked by with Borte to the river. When she goes there, the two women are sitting on some rocks, by the water, washing out bloodied bandages.

"Mother ... what are you doing? Don't they have slaves to do that?"

Yufeng looks at her sternly and Panda realizes her mistake.

"I mean other workers, tasked with that work."

"Yes, but these ones are for Borte's son's if they ever get injured, and I wanted to make sure they are *clean* ... do you understand?" as she glances at Borte.

Panda smiles and nods.

"We are almost finished here, what did you want?"

"Sari asked me to find you ... she wants to talk to you about something."

Borte smiles and tells her,

"You go along ... of all my sons, Tolui married the smart one."

"Okay ... are you sure you can carry all these back?"

"I'll be fine ... oh ... there something you should check on with Sari."

"What?"

"Come here."

Yufeng goes close to Borte who whispers into her ear.

Yufeng nods,

"Okay ... see you later."

***

Walking back to Sari, Panda asks what the whispering was about.

"I'll tell you later. I need to ask Sari some things."

Then turning to her daughter, she asks,

"Have you noticed any problems with Sari's health?"

Panda thinks.

"No ... like what?"

"Like her monthly discharge?"

"Strange, that's the same thing she just asked me."

Panda thinks more.

"Hers is different than ours."

"How?"

"I've watched you, and your monthly discharge is like mine and follows the moon regularly ... Sari's doesn't ... sometimes she misses it entirely or it is often late ... why."

"How old is Monke now?"

"6."

"What are you thinking, mother?"

"I'm not sure ... that's why I need to talk to her."

Just then they arrive back where Sari is finishing up the hide and washing off.

Sari genuinely likes Yufeng and greets her warmly. Then she says, jokingly.

"Long time you haven't come by here Yufeng ... have I offended you?"

"No, no, no ... it's that worthless husband of mine ... I told him all the other warriors have many wives to help their primary wife, but he refuses ... so I have to do everything ... men are such boys, aren't they?"

Sari laughs.

"Panda said you wanted to see me."

"Sit down, while I make some of your tea."

Panda tells her, "I can do that aunty Sari, you talk with my mother."

The two women sit opposite each other and wait a few moments for the dust to settle and peace returns.

Sari speaks first,

"The Naadam Festival is coming soon."

Yufeng doesn't understand where Sari is going with this, so she waits.

"At the Naadam Festival, all the families must offer their eligible girls to the khan as a wife."

"Eligible?" Yufeng asks.

"Not married or betrothed to another ... who have had their first discharge."

The two women turn to look at Panda who is pouring more tea.

Panda sees this and asks,

"What was that again?"

Yufeng holds up her hand to her daughter and speaks to Sari.

"I can talk to Borte, the Khan wouldn't take Panda."

"But that won't end it. If the Khan passes, then any noble or high warrior can make a claim."

Panda laughs.

"Ha! I will refuse!"

The women ignore her for a moment.

"Do you have any ideas?"

"There is something in the old legends, but you will have to ask Hoelun about it ... she's the only one who would know and who has the authority in the clan to impose it."

"What is it?"

"Come closer."

Sari whispers into Yufeng's ears but Panda can still overhear with her catlike ears.

Panda hums to herself thinking (*That could work!*).

Then Yufeng asks Sari another question.

"Sari ... you know I have studied medicine for many years ... the old medicines of the grandmothers and the new medicines."

Sari nods.

"I'd like to examine you ... if you agree."

Sari is surprised but agrees.

"Don't worry about Panda, she often assists me. I'd like you to lie down on the bedding and loosen your robes."

Sari does so and Yufeng proceeds with a thorough examination along with many questions. Then she takes out some needles and applies them at certain meridians and pressure points.

"Where is that medicine you mentioned?"

"There (pointing) in that small bottle near my clothing."

Yufeng motions for Panda to get it. Yufeng senses something dark inside the bottle and tells Sari she will go outside to inspect it ...

"Please stay here for a few more minutes with the needles, I'll be right back ... Panda come with me."

The two go outside. Yufeng asks her daughter ...

"Sense the essence."

Panda closes her eyes and then suddenly opens them.

"A dark poison!"

"Yes, but a clever dark poison."

"What do you mean?"

It is weak so as not to kill ... just to damage the balance of the qi ... especially the woman's birthing qi."

"You've seen this before?"

"Yes, some women take it to prevent having babies."

"Then why?"

"I don't know, let's go back inside."

Inside Yufeng asks Sari why she was taking this medicine.

"A few years ago, I saw the shaman and told him my discharge was irregular and I wanted to have more babies ... and he gave this to me."

"The shaman?"

"Teb Tengeri ... why?"

Yufeng looks at Panda and then to Sari.

"Panda, go to our tent and get me the yellow yin herbs in the soft leather bag."

"Okay mama."

She runs out.

While she is out Yufeng explains her suspicions.

Sari starts to rise up in anger.

Yufeng gently pushes her back down.

"No, you can't react. Act as though everything is the same. I'll give you new medicines, which work and let's see what happens."

"But why don't you want me to say anything?"

"It's just my word against him, and I think the Khan wants to maintain peace for now. And don't tell your husband."

Sari nods knowingly.

"Thank you Yufeng ... and thanks for lending Panda to me ... she is like an older sister to Monke and a younger sister to me."

"We like you Sari ... do you come from this tribe?"

"No ... don't you know my story? My uncle was Toghrul, the leader of the Kereyid tribe ... my father was his younger brother, Jakha Gambhu, who befriended Temujin when he was on the run. Later my father gave me and my sister to Genghis, who married me to Tolui, his youngest son."

"You seem different than the other son's wives."

Sari ponders this.

"No one has ever said that to me before ... my mother raised us as Nestorian Christians, but I have often thought I was different, and I want my children to be different."

"I dream that someday my sons will be great khans."

Yufeng smiles.

"Know this Sari ... my husband, my daughter, and I want to help you achieve your dream."

The women hug each other, not knowing the forces that will be unleashed on the world to accomplish that dream.

55 And First Prize - the Beautiful Panda

The following month there is good news in the Mongol camp. Sari is pregnant and Yufeng is administering to her. The news is not so welcome in one tent though ... the Tengeri. Teb Tengeri grabs the anti-pregnancy medicine and throws it into the fire.

"Stupid witches and their stupid medicines."

His brother asks,

"What will you do now?"

"Nothing, they may have discovered this and are watching us."

"We do nothing?"

"I think that Yufeng and her daughter had something to do with it ... they are close to Sari now."

"But we can't touch them ... the khan has warned us."

Teb Tengeri though is foolishly not afraid of the khan and is already devising another plan.

The Naadam is coming.

***

Two weeks later, in mid-August, it is time for the Naadam Festival at which time they celebrate their Mongolian heritage. During the week-long festival, there are many feasts and competitions in wrestling, archery, and horseback racing. After the winter war, the summer respite is a time to relax and celebrate the victories. This festival is also time to honor their shared ancestors as now the Mongol nation is a conglomeration of many different tribes that Genghis molded together to form the Mongol Nation.

There is one custom though of particular concern to Yufeng and Panda, where on the day of celebration, all eligible girls are offered to the khan for marriage. The khan is seated on a large seat on a raised dais ... each of the girls is brought by their mother and presented to the khan. Usually, he declines but then the girl is offered to his sons and top commanders. Typically, they already have enough wives and any new one just becomes a servant to the primary wife. But the girl cannot refuse, unless she has been betrothed to another.

After about an hour, the number of remaining girls is dwindling ... only Panda and two others remain. They select the two others and that just leaves Panda. Yufeng brings Panda before the khan and offers her to him. The khan toys with her a bit ...

"Hmmm ... now this one is different. Pretty and smart."

He looks at Borte, who frowns.

"Ooops ... I guess that settles it ... unless another warrior claims you, you are free to play with your wolf."

Then one of Teb Tengeri's brothers steps up.

"I want to claim her great khan."

This causes a stir in the crowd and the khan is not pleased.

Yufeng steps up and speaks.

"Great Khan, I have heard of a tradition which predates this Naadam custom."

The Khan looks at her.

"From the old ones, I have heard that the woman so chosen can claim the right of combat ... that is, she will accept, only if the suitor can beat her in combat."

The khan looks at Borte.

"Maybe you should ask Hoelun, she knows all the old customs."

The khan looks at his mother, Hoelun, who nods,

"It is as the woman says ... the bride has the right of challenge to combat."

The Khan asks,

"And she can do this every year?"

Hoelun nods,

"As long as she wins ... or agrees to submit."

The Khan looks up.

"So be it!"

"But we don't want anyone killed, so they fight with staffs or clubs ... do you both agree?"

They agree, and then face off against each other.

Yufeng is not worried, she has already beat this Tengeri when he plotted against Panda with the wolf trap. Confident in Panda's fighting skills, she thinks,

It will be a fitting repayment for what they have done to Sari.

The "combat" is over in a few minutes with the larger Tengeri unconscious on the ground. Panda sensed his moves, parried them, and cut his legs out from under him, then a blow to the side of his head bent him over, for an uppercut blow which sent him flying through the air ... where he still lay.

Then she whistles for Lana, her wolf, who comes over to her side and howls.

Everyone, except the Tengeri's laugh uproariously.

Her pride of young wolf warrior children also howl joyously ... and Lana joins the children's' howls in joy.

But not all warriors are howling ... some are silently plotting.

56 Su Meets Subedei

The first part of the sailing voyage north is smooth, with light winds off the coast ... as they head due east from Quanzhou and then turn north on the far side of Taiwan. They stay far off the coast all the way to the Shandong peninsula and then head northwest to land at Su Chou (Dalian), in the Jin Empire. The weather during the last week turned stormier, but Captain Ding was used to even worse and managed the boat skillfully.

At Su Chou they pretended to be merchants looking for new trade. This had been a minor port in the old Khitan-Liao Empire and now there were no Jin soldiers ... only a few hold-over Khitan administrators. Chen Er and Yufei pretended to do some trading and loaded the boat with goods for the sail back south.

Chen Er asked some merchants about the Jin and learned that most people hated them after they deposed the former ruling family, imposed taxes on them, and required the young men to serve in their armies ... many had already fled over to the Mongol side.

Then he asked about the Mongols and learned that they were attacking a city about three days journey northwest, called Mukden (Shenyang).

The group meets that night and decide to journey to Mukden to try to meet up with the Mongols.

"It shouldn't be too hard ... everyone will be fleeing away from the Mongols."

Or so they thought ...

***

As they get nearer to Mukden though, they encounter Jin patrols searching for Mongol spies and Jin deserters. At the first encounter, they are able to talk their way out of it but at the second encounter they had to disarm and tie up the Jin.

Tariq asks Yufei,

"Uncle, why didn't you kill them?"

"Tariq, these men were once like you ... their emperor forced them into the army ... my father once almost died fighting these stupid wars for the emperors."

"But I've heard that you kill without remorse."

"That is different ... when someone threatens me or my family, I will send those people across the bridge." then adding,

"Without anger or vengeance."

Then Yufei and his group come across a Mongol scouting party. They throw down their swords and prostrate themselves before them and ask to meet Subedei. One of the warriors recognizes Yufei and they are escorted into camp where they meet up with Jebe and Subedei. The two commanders welcome their old friend ... and new friends equally ... especially when they learn of the siege machine skills of Master Su. They discuss these machines through the night and decide to send Yufei's party on to the great Khan's army with an escort. Genghis is fighting further west around the Jin capital and can badly use their siege skills.

***

Meanwhile ... back in the main Mongol camp, there were several new babies. One of special note, is a baby boy born to Sari, whom she names Kublai.

"It is a common Mongol name." Sari tells Panda.

Panda though thinks *the name is but a shadow of his future.*

Another lesser-known birth was by Lana, who had four baby wolf cubs, one of which was pure white ... another sign from the gods to the great khan. Later, after it was weaned, Panda would gift the white wolf cub to the great khan.

Also, during this new year, with the new siege machines, the Mongols are able to smash down fortress after fortress ... all those who didn't submit. And as word spread ... more towns, submitted without the slaughter and massacre which followed those first few who defied the khan.

57 Genghis beats Jin at Zhongdu

During the winter campaign, with Master Su's guidance, Genghis built several of the new siege machines and attacked Zhongdu, the Jin capital. These siege machines ... large boulder throwing catapults and tall attack towers, do quick work of tearing down the Jin fortress walls. Even the Mongol leaders are amazed and excited. Many warriors come up to Yufei and his group to congratulate them and ask questions.

Genghis arranges a special private dinner with Yufei's group to allow his sons and commanders to ask more questions ... for example, about dismantling them to cross mountains, about making cannon and fireballs which Yufei had mentioned to him. The news from Chen Er and Master Su gives Genghis renewed confidence in conquering the world.

Yufei though brings him down a bit ...

"In the west other armies have some of these machines."

Genghis laughs and says,

"Yes, but I have my Four Hounds!"

In the face of this ferocious new style attack, the Jin submit. They agree to pay a large annual tribute as well as offer the Jin princess, Qiguo, as a bride for Genghis to solidify the peace. Satisfied with their submission, the large bounty, and thinking the Jin will be a tribute empire of the Mongol Empire, Genghis orders his army to pack up the tribute wagons and head home.

Unfortunately, the Jin have other plans, and as soon as the Mongols leave through the first pass, a powerful general persuades the Jin emperor to break the treaty and kill the residual force of Mongol diplomats. This enrages Genghis, who vows vengeance the following campaign year. On the way back he leaves forces to guard the conquered passes which he plans to re-cross the following year.

Meanwhile the train of tribute bearing wagons stretches for tens of kilometers ... there will be celebrations in Avarga this year.

Along the way, Yufei continues to train and prepare Tariq for the Mongol camp ... and his wild daughter.

The boy's dreams start to become more vivid ...

During the march Yufei cautions him to let destiny unfold itself on its own ... he describes his own early courtship of Yufeng.

Aside from his sisters, Tariq has had little experience with girls ... so although he is fearless around any enemy ... he is very afraid of Panda ... and rightfully so ...

Panda, meanwhile, has her hands full taking care of baby Kublai ... the future great khan.

58 Reunion & Victory Party

When the victorious Mongol army returns to Avarga, there is a huge celebration as the tribute treasures are divided and everyone celebrates.

In Yufeng and Yufei's tent, there is a tender reunion between the two entangled lovers, while outside Panda and Tariq renew their friendship. Yufeng calls out to Panda.

"Why don't you show Tariq the camp, while your father and I ... *talk*."

Smiling, Panda grabs Tariq's hand.

"Come on ... I think they want to be alone."

Tariq thinks (*me too*)

Looking at Lana and her cubs, Panda tells her in wolf language to stay and guard the tent.

The two youths explore the camp. Panda introduces Tariq to Sari, Monke, and baby Kublai. Then they go and pay respects to Borte and Hoelun, the great khan's wife and mother.

Along the way, they tell each other what has happened in their travels. At one point, Panda stops him.

'You say Uncle Anhua beat my father in a fight?"

Tariq nods and adds,

"Viciously."

"Impossible ... no one can best my father ... unless ..."

"Unless what?"

"Unless he wanted it to happen that way."

"I don't understand."

"From what I heard, my uncle was following a dark pathway, but to openly confront him, would only cause a family rift and a public scandal. This way, they created the justification for his reassignment and the change of management of our clan foundation."

Tariq doesn't follow it all, but Panda catches it quickly.

They see some riders practicing archery and Tariq says,

"Let's go watch them."

"Okay ... can you shoot arrows while riding?"

"A little." he says.

"How about you?"

She smiles demurely, "A little."

Back in their tent, after the clouds have spent their rain, the two lovers lie still and go over what has happened.

Yufeng talks first.

"It is good to see Chen Er and Master Su here, I think they will help the plan."

Yufei nods, "Yes ... Master Su acts 10 years younger here than sitting in his laboratory every day."

Yufeng laughs.

"Now we need to find him a local wife."

Yufei laughs.

"Tell me again about my sister ... how did she look when you left?"

"Much better ... relieved, I think."

"And her son, Chen Ming?"

"He seems to be a good boy ... and follows his mother's lead ... I think he knows the truth about his father."

"What about my mother?'

"She didn't travel ... she's getting old now ...you should probably visit her soon."

"I was thinking that too when I got your *message*."

Then she asks,

"What about the Song ... do they understand the danger?"

"Lord Chen and Chen Yi do, but times are good, and people don't want to talk about threats when they are making too much money."

"Fools."

"Yes ... what about the Tengeri clan ... any more trouble from them?"

"Not lately but with this victory behind him, I think the Khan will act ... he's just waiting for Teb to make the first move."

"I want to invite Chen Er over to tell us more about his raid on that dark monastery ... "

"Yeah ... we'll have to invite Master Su also ... but how much should we let them know?"

"About the Plan?"

"Yes ... *and about us*."

"I don't know ... let's see what happens ... but come back closer first ..."
And they talked no more that night.

59 Panda & Tariq

At the training field, Tariq cannot hide that he is obviously smitten by Panda, but after the Naadam experiences, Panda is reluctant to commit to anyone too quickly. They watch warriors show off their archery skills, riding and shooting off arrows, then riding another direction and shooting the arrows behind them as if retreating from an attacking army.

Tariq is impressed.

"Wow! No wonder they are conquering everyone. I've never seen archery skills like that."

Monke, who is 8 years old comes riding up to Panda.

"Elder sister, do you want to try it? You can use my horse and bow."

Panda smiles and looks at the boy.

"You promise you won't laugh at me when I don't hit the target?"

"I promise ... I miss it sometimes myself."

Monke leaps down and Panda leaps onto the horse. Monke hands her his bow and a handful of arrows which she slides under the pommel.

"Which targets do you want me to hit?'

"Those ones over there!" he says pointing to some straw targets propped up on bales.

As she gallops off, Tariq is in awe ... he has never seen a female warrior ride like her before ... she is one fluid movement with the horse ... and it is hard to determine where one body starts and the other body ends.

Panda has often played this archery game with the younger boys ... and always wins. So, it is not surprising to Monke who watches her ride ... racing the wind, horse and rider as one spirit, launching arrow after arrow and hitting the target every time.

Off to the side several warriors watch too and when she rides back, they all cheer.

Then Monke looks at Tariq.

"Do you want to try?"

"Okay ... but I'm not very good."

Panda slides off and Tariq jumps up. They hand him some arrows and he gallops off but instead of riding across the field he rides away from the targets, standing on the stirrups, he turns in the saddle and fires his arrows at the target. This is more difficult because each arrow must have a different trajectory to match the horse's new position.

When he is finished, a cheer goes up as he has landed all five arrows in the target zone.

When he jumps off, Panda runs up and hugs him ... until they both realize the awkwardness of it ... then they laugh while Monke is confused.

Later that night, while they eat, Panda avoids looking at Tariq and Yufeng can tell that Panda is lost in thoughts. When they are alone cleaning up, Panda confesses confusion over her emotions. Yufeng counsels her to wait ... everything will become clear at the right time.

"Don't worry about it."

"What was it like when you first met father?"

"I didn't like him, and we had a big fight ... then ..."

"Then what?"

"We were out on the tea plantation and some men threatened us ... and your father protected me ..."

"And then you knew?"

"Yes ... I knew he and I would be together forever."

Panda hugs her mother.

"Thank you, mother ... I'm going to Sari's now to see if she needs help with Kublai."

"Okay ... maybe bring Tariq with you."

Panda laughs.

"Mother! What ideas are in that scheming mind of yours?"

60 Dinner Talk

The next night they invite Gugu, Chen Er, and Master Su over for dinner. Yufeng has enlisted some aunties to help cook the food, so she can entertain and join in the discussion.

After the first round of drinks and mouthfuls of roast goat, Yufei stands to address them. Tariq starts to stand too but Panda pulls his tunic ... and him ... back down.

"First, Yufeng and I want to welcome you here ... in this new land ... to offer your help in a cause which we feel is important ... but which you still only know a small part."

"I want to especially thank you for your trust in us by coming and lending your skills to their cause."

He looks around. Yufeng is smiling and Panda is very proud of her father.

"We'd like to tell you everything ... but we can't ... mostly because we don't know how all this will end ourselves."

"But I can tell you what will happen if we don't try."

Then looking at Gugu he asks him,

"Gugu, when you went north to try to find the herb to cure my poison, what did you find?"

Gugu describes a land full of rotting carcasses, devoid of life ... not even carrion birds.

Yufei continues,

"And that is what Yufeng, and I have seen ... if we don't defeat the dark manifestations."

"This is not about Mongols or Chinese or Arabs ... it is about all peoples."

Master Su starts to ask,

"But how do you know these things?"

"Master Su ... we have told you about the elders at Kailash and the grandmothers at Gobekli Tepe ... their wisdom goes back before time and their vision forward as well ... they have told us these things and we ... Yufeng and I have seen them for ourselves when we journey into the void."

"You see these events happening?"

"We see possibilities of these things happening ... as well as possibilities of other ... better things happening ... what we are trying to do ... is help the better possibilities ... *become probabilities.*"

"How?"

"By bringing you and Chen Er here with your skills, by counseling the great Khan to spare the skilled people in the lands they conquer ... *information ... information that changes the possibilities into probabilities.*"

He pauses as they digest some more food and his words.

"When you look out your tent in the morning and you see dark clouds ... you bring your rain gear ... it's the information that changed your course of action."

"But how does that relate to what we are doing?"

Yufeng looks at Tariq and Panda.

"We believe that it is important for the Mongols to be successful and unite the tribes of the world."

"Why?"

"To cleanse away the dark manifestations, to bring equality to women, freedom to worship one's spiritual beliefs, to open up trade, and the flow of information to the west, and finally, to unite China again."

Each has seen a part of the plan before, but this is the first time that Yufei has explained it all. He sits down and waits. He can sense their internal debates.

Finally, Chen Er rises.

"So, our job is to help the Mongols conquer the world, and destroy the dark manifestations, to free the people, and encourage trade ... "

He looks around and shrugs his shoulders,

"No problem."

Tariq is new to Chen's humor and starts laughing, then the others all laugh too.

"And temper the destruction ... to save lives ... like we did in Kucha."

"When the other fortress cities see how easy we can destroy their fortifications, we believe more will submit to spare their people."

Tariq looks questioningly at Panda.

Panda puts her finger to her lips and whispers,

"Later I will explain it all to you."

Satisfied with her response, he relaxes back.

Su, Yufei, and Chen Er are in an animated discussion about what happens when they bring these weapons later against the Song.

They go back and forth arguing for or against revealing too much until finally Yufeng rises, and they all pause and look up at her. There is a steely glaze on her eyes.

"We have lived for a few years now with the Mongols and this is what I have seen ..."

"They respect women! Women can speak up in all their councils. Genghis especially worships his mother, Hoelun, and his main wife, Borte!"

"They don't painfully bind girl's feet to make them attractive to some pervert!"

"They don't follow archaic Confucian rites craftly designed to suppress women!"

"When they conquer a tribe, they spare the craftsmen and ordinary people."

"They take the wealth of the rich and establish more fair distribution and taxes."

She pauses.

"I can go on and on, but I tell you all ... I would much rather live under their system, than the corrupt and oppressive Song system."

Then she spits on the ground.

"I've had too much of Song corruptness and oppression. You can make your own choice, but, as for me, after seeing their culture, I have no desire to go back to being a submissive female slave ... if not here, I'll live with the Naxi!"

Then she sits down, and everyone is quiet.

Tariq looks at Panda and mouths *Naxi?*

She pinches him.

Finally Master Su, who is the oldest one there in years, rises.

"What Yufeng says is true. For every honest minister in China, there are nine corrupt ones ... and I don't see it changing. Even our old mentor,

Zhu Xi, couldn't fight it and was accused and exiled several times ... even up to his death."

Chen Er rises.

"It was the same in the navy. The least capable generals were promoted and the most capable sidelined and blamed for any failures. I've watched the Mongols fight and they follow the most skilled leaders, who are battle tested and have absolute support from the Khan."

Yufei rises.

"I've fought side-by-side with Subedei and Jelme ... they are not only skilled warriors but skilled strategists ... they plan every move on the battlefield like a Weiqi boardgame. I believe in Genghis vision ... the Mongols *can* conquer the world."

Then Yufeng looks at Panda and Tariq.

"I know what Gugu thinks, what do you two think?"

Tariq is new to speaking and pushes Panda up first.

Although only a teenager, Panda speaks with a sense of prophecy.

"When I have traveled in the void, I have seen many victories and also some defeats ... I have also seen the darkness spreading in other lands ... from a great distance, we are like ants fighting amongst ourselves ... but what I've seen here are mothers caring for their children and men, willingly, not forcibly, obeying the Khan, and not pissing in their own stream."

Su looks at Yufeng. (*pissing in their stream?*)

"It's a law." she tells him. Then looking at Tariq.

"Tariq, you are a man now and have a voice at our camp ... what do you want to say?"

Tariq rises ... nervously, as he hasn't spoken before people like this before. He stumbles at first but then finds his feet.

"I've hunted on the steppe and on the deserts ... survival is difficult ... one time my brother and I came to a cliff wall ... the only way to get to the top was to help each other ... it was a dangerous climb ... and you can never tell my mother ... but we made it. At the top, we looked back down and then laughed ... not because we felt so powerful, but rather because we felt so stupid. Since then, I try to listen more to my father and now, Yufei and the leaders here."

Then looking down at Panda he says,

"I believe in you."
When he says that Panda smiles, and inside she thought something else
...

This is a man I could follow.

61 New Campaign - Kara Kitai

The next campaign season, Genghis sends his main force back through the same passes to attack the Jin rebellion. He also sends an army under Jebe and Subedei west to fight the Kara Khitai, who are being led by Kuchlug, a renegade from the Naiman tribe. Yufei and Tariq will go with them, Chen Er and Su Xiao will fight with the main army under Genghis.

The Jin armies are a numerically larger force than the Mongols and Genghis spends several campaigns against their armies ... winning and losing through the next few years .... until later when something new attracts his interest out west.

Meanwhile, in the west, Jebe and Subedei achieve success and finally defeat the Kara Khitai and enter their capital of Balasagun. After a few days, Kuchlug is captured and beheaded, ending his revolt, and starting the integration of the Kara Khitai into the Mongol nation.

While Jebe and Subedei are still in Balasagun, Genghis sends a new assignment for Subedei to march with a small force to Kazakhstan and subdue remnants of the Merkit tribe along the Orkhon River.

Genghis had fought the Merkit several times ... ever since they kidnapped his wife, Borte when Genghis was a youth. When Genghis became more powerful, he avenged the kidnapping and rescued Borte. But ever since, Genghis, as he did with other tribes, eliminated their tribal identity to incorporate it into his Mongol Nation; but now some remnants further west are revolting against Genghis.

Yufei and Tariq continue to go with Subedei. Chen Er, Master Su and Gugu stay attached to the main armies, helping construct variations of the siege engines and building cannon, which the great Khan will use later on in his western campaigns.

The main weapon against the strong fortress walls is the trebuchet, a large catapult, which can launch huge rocks from a distance ... safely located beyond the range of the fortress arrows.

Su has come up with some improvements ... first to improve the mobility of the engines for transversing high passes and dry deserts; and secondly to hurtle fireballs into the fortress, causing widespread fear and destruction.

Chen Er has been working with migrant craftsmen to forge a new type of siege cannon ... larger than the ones he had on the Falcon. Su assists him in this, selecting the metals and alloys offering strength and durability. It takes lots of testing and forging but finally they have an artillery corps ready to knock down or blow away any wall in the world.

Meanwhile Yufei and Tariq have gone with Subedei's force over deserts and mountain passes to eliminate the Merkits. From a military perspective, it is a small foray, but it brings Yufei closer to Subedei as they get to talk every evening about life and their experiences.

One night around the campfire, Subedei asks Yufei,

"Why do you have only one wife?"

Yufei looks at him strangely.

"Why? How many do you have?"

Subedei counts on his fingers.

"Four."

"How many children?"

Subedei counts again.

"Five ... maybe one more when we get back."

Yufei frowns jokingly.

"I am a poor farmer with only one wife and one child."

Subedei laughs.

"Haha ... I can fix that ... we'll find you some young Merkit wives for you ... how about that?"

Yufei feigns fear.

"Aeee... Yufeng will beat me to death!"

This makes Subedei laugh harder.

"My brave companion ... afraid of a woman!"

Yufei throws up his hands.

"I confess ... it is true."

Then Subedei looks at Tariq.

"I hear you have eyes for his daughter, Panda ... is that true."

Embarrassed, Tariq stumbles over his mouth.

"I ... no ...I mean ... she is nice ... but ... "

Then they all laugh again.

Subedei gives him some advice about women.

"Son ... when you find the woman you will love for the rest of your life ... don't hesitate ... throw her over your shoulder and take her to your tent."

Then looking at Yufei who is frowning.

"Of course, with her father's permission."

Yufei cautions the boy.

"You'd best be careful about trying to throw Panda over your shoulder."

Then they all laugh and retire for the evening.

Alas poor Tariq doesn't sleep too well. He knows that if he ever thought about throwing Panda over his shoulder, that she would kill him (or at least break all his bones).

After defeating the Merkits, Subedei was attacked on his way back by Mohammed II, the shah of the Khwarazm, near the Irghiz River. The Khwarazm outnumbered Subedei's force by three times, but Subedei's forces were better organized and made the Khwarazm pay a high price before they retreated in the night.

Angry at the damage sustained and the failure to strike a blow against the Mongols, the Khwarazm continued raiding and pillaging the Kara Khitai towns ... slaughtering and enslaving millions of their fellow Muslim Arabs.

Only later did Yufei learn who was leading those attacking forces ... the man who had sent Hasan and his assassins to kill him and Yufeng on their first visits to Chang An.

62 Genghis looks West

With the defeat of the Merkit and Kara Khitai tribes in the west, only the Jin, to the east, remained defiant to Genghis, but, unknown to him, his war with the Jin would last beyond his lifetime. Meanwhile though, even while he was at war with the Jin, he had to manage his empire. And further west of the newly conquered Kara Khitai lay the Khwarazm Empire which was expanding eastwards. At first, Genghis saw them as an obvious trading partner for the western part of the Silk Road.

Hoping to establish a commercial relationship, Genghis sent an official diplomat and multi-wagon trade caravan to the Khwarazm city of Otrar. The local governor, a relative of the shah, had the diplomat killed and confiscated the trade goods. This enraged Genghis, who tried a second mission, direct to the shah, seeking justice. The shah, in a misguided sense of self-importance, humiliated these envoys as well. This led Genghis to leave one army to continue harassing the Jin, while he took his larger force west to conquer and discipline the Khwarazm.

But before leaving, Genghis second wife, Yesui, persuaded him to choose a successor. Previously there had been a small scuffle between his oldest son, Jochi, and second son, Chagatai going back many years to Jochi's paternity. Jochi was Borte's first child but conceived while in captivity with the Merkit leader. Genghis had always accepted Jochi and treated him as his true first born, but some of the other sons of Borte looked on Jochi differently.

Genghis was caught in a difficult spot, because to deny Jochi, would be denying and shaming Borte, whom he forever loved, no matter how many other wives he may have (some say hundreds). The impasse was finally resolved when Genghis, after receiving wise counseling from close friends, named his third son Ogedei, arguably the smartest, as his successor.

With that taken care of, Genghis turns his eyes toward the west.

***

The Khwarazm shah, Mohammed II, had a much larger army than the Mongols but they were widely spread out over his ever-expanding empire ... from Samarkand in the east to Persia in the west. Wary of the Mongols open field battle prowess, the shah concentrated his forces in fortress cities. But this proved fatal as it spread out his large forces into smaller armies inside widely scattered fortresses, which the Mongols and their siege machines could easily destroy one at a time, without having to confront the shah's larger force.

First in their line of march, the Mongols capture Otrar, where the first atrocity had occurred. They capture the governor and other nobles and execute them. Then they planned their strategies to capture the next two main cities of the east ... Bukhara and Samarkand. Genghis would attack Samarkand while Jebe and Subedei attacked Bukhara.

Genghis had great trust in Jebe and Subedei and ordered them, along with Yufei and Tariq, to march a long roundabout trek through the lifeless desert to come around from behind Bukhara and surprise the Khwarazm defenders. After this epic trek ... and their victory, Subedei marched east to rejoin with Genghis, who had just defeated the Khwarazm at Samarkand.

Later Genghis would tell Yufei about one strange encounter at the shah's palace ... when he routed the shah and his retinue, the shah's mother, Terken Khatun, would not leave *her* palace and holed up in her separate quarters ... apparently believing some divine intervention would save her ... which wasn't just the ravings of a madwoman.

Bad news travels fast and after the fall of Samarkand, it spreads to a hidden monastery in the nearby mountains. There, a dark priestess organized a band of her black warriors to rescue the shah's mother in order to continue a guerilla rebellion with the shah's son, Jalal al-Din.

These dark warriors though had only fought frighted superstitious villagers and Yufei sensed their plans and alerted Subedei and the Khan. When these assassins arrived, they were slaughtered along with the evil woman ... but it took several months later for Genghis to run down the shah's son in the highlands of India.

After Samarkand fell, the shah fled west and was pursued by Jebe, Subedei, and Yufei and finally died on a small island in the Caspian Sea.

In the end, a satisfying outcome for Yufei against the man who had sent assassins after him years before on his first journey to Chang An.

The celebrations though are short lived when news comes from Avarga that the great khan's mother, Hoelun, has died. Genghis goes into a deep depression and tells the camp they will leave a garrison force in Khwarazm and the others will march home.

That night he sends for Yufei. When Yufei arrives at the former shah's palace, Genghis sends most of his wives, his generals, and even his sons out.

Yufei bows,

"How can I help you great Khan?"

"Sit here and talk with me."

Yufei sits on a chair along the side of the khan. One of his wives, brings in tea ... then he waves her out also.

There is a silence. Genghis seems not sure on how to proceed, which is unusual for him.

Finally, sensing his apprehension, Yufei asks,

"May I talk first?"

Relieved, the Khan nods,

"Please."

"You and I are different ... I never knew my mother ... she died shortly after I was born ... and for my early years, I never even knew my father ... I was an orphan. What most people don't know is that after my father vanished, he became an assassin with the Brotherhood of the Ismailis until finally after many years his past came back to haunt him, and he was contracted to kill me."

Yufei fingers a ring on his finger ... that Scorpion gave him that last day ... the ring of the famous leader of the Brotherhood, Rashid al din.

"I didn't know that part of your story."

"Few know this ... but he couldn't kill me and when we met, it was as if only a few moments had passed since my birth ... and an incredible closeness was born, from the ashes of tragedy."

"Where ..."

Yufei holds up his hand to stop him.

"But it wasn't meant to last. After Panda was born, he traveled through the mountains on a last mission to the elders at Kailash ... but the dark forces had other plans and he died again ... but I was granted the opportunity to see him one last time before he crossed the final bridge to the underworld."

"But ..."

"I say these things so that you know, I have known this unbelievable sadness ... just as you are now feeling for your dear mother. It was difficult for me to deal with his death for many years ... until I realized something deep inside ... there is a purpose in my being here at this time ... and the same is true for you. Most people have no purpose in life ... you and I, and some others though are different ... we have an important purpose ... and we must fulfill that purpose. It was in my father's final message to me."

"I want to share with you his last message to me, and Yufeng, and Panda. He was in bliss, he had finally dropped all his karma, and for the first time in his adult life, he was free and was looking forward to crossing over the final bridge to the other side."

"Yufeng and I have spent some time with your mother, and I think she feels the same way now ... relieved of all the responsibility which accompanies being the mother of the great Khan ... I read in one of the ancient sutras,

'*What was never born never dies.*'"

"I think her spirit is still alive and it is smiling down on you ... proud of what you have accomplished and excited about you continuing your mission to unite and change this world."

Genghis is quiet ... lost in some deep thoughts.

Yufei sees tears falling from Genghis' eyes for the first time. The Khan stands,

"Come with me."

He goes to a hidden staircase which leads to the rooftop. It is empty, except for some mats on the roof.

"Please stand here but don't let anyone come up the stairs."

Then Genghis goes to one of the mats and kneels. He says a silent prayer and then raises his arms to Tengi, the Sky God and speaks very ancient indecipherable words. Yufeng doesn't understand the words, but he understands the meaning ... an ancient plea to the gods for his mother's soul.

In the distance, Yufei hears the howl of a wolf, which seems to follow the khan's tempo.

Yufei wonders, *is that you, Lana?*

Later Yufei goes down the stairs and outside, where he finds Chen Er, who asks,

"Where have you been?"

"With the Khan."

"How is he?"

"Saddened ... but he will be okay."

"Where is Su?"

"Inspecting the cannon ... they are like his children ... did you know he has names for each one ... even the catapults."

They laugh and walk off into the night to find the old scientist.

Su introduces them to each of his new *children*.

"This one was my first ... I call her *Big Thunder*."

Yufei asks the obvious,

"It's a woman?"

Su looks at him as though a child just said something childish.

"Of course ... haven't you been to the marketplace and heard the grannies there?"

"When I was young, there was one large fat grannie with this booming voice ... you could hear her across the marketplace. We called her Big Thunder."

They all laugh.

63 Scouting Raid

Mind is an arena of virtual possibilities,
and consciousness is choosing among the possibilities.

With the defeat of the Khwarazm, Genghis plans to return to northern China to renew his conquest of the Jin. Jebe and Subedei want to travel further west and are granted permission by Genghis. Yufei, Tariq, and Chen Er decide to go west with them, while Gugu plans to go with the older Master Su back to the main Mongol homelands.

The night before departure, they have a goodbye dinner and wish each other a safe journey. They also give the returning two men several letters for their families back in the main camp.

Later, Gugu walks with Yufei and asks.

"What do you sense happening now?"

Yufei pauses and sits on a rock gazing up at the stars. After a few moments, he looks at Gugu.

"I sense great changes happening ... the world is changing."

"I sense that too ... we have played a small part in this change."

"But there is more to do ... not only with the Mongol Nation, but also with the new nations in the west ... and the philosophers and teachers there ... the scientists, physicians, and leaders ..."

Then Yufei pauses and looks at Gugu.

"But first we have to get there safely, and you must return to Yufeng safely... I fear she will need you before too long."

"What do you sense?"

"Danger from close by ... but I am not sure ... maybe the Tengeri clan."

"Then why don't you return with me?"

"I feel my pathway is out west ... not just to battle alongside Subedei, but to meet the grandmothers again at Gobekli."

"You will go that far?"

He nods.

"Chen also?"

"Yes ... he wants to see more of the world before being tied down permanently in Tibet."

Gugu looks at Yufei, whom he has known now for two lifetimes.

"There's something I need to tell you."

"What?"

"After I return these messages ... my mission with you and Yufeng will be over."

"Over?"

"There is a new assignment waiting for me. Actually, it has been waiting for several months, but I have postponed it."

"Do you know where it is?"

"No ... not yet ... but I know it is part of our overall mission ... to defeat the dark manifestations."

Yufei starts to be overcome with emotions.

"Will we meet again?"

Gugu smiles.

"If it is meant to be ..."

"I will miss you, old friend."

"And I will miss you too ..."

And then ... their spirits followed different pathways ... for a while.

64 The Mongol Empire

With the defeat of the Khwarazm and other nomadic steppe and desert tribes, the Silk Road is essentially controlled by the Mongols, and this reopens the famed road of commerce between the East and West ... not only trade but more importantly, *the flow of information.*

Over the years of his reign, Genghis developed a set of laws for the lands they controlled, called the *Yassa*, which governed everyone and everything in the world's largest land empire, the Mongol Empire.

The Yassa was kept secret and not made public; it was kept by the royal family themselves and contained not only laws but also secret spiritual elements. The Yassa covered many aspects of Mongol life and was designed to keep the peace among the various nomadic tribes, to unify the people behind the khan, and to expand and control the empire.

Different from other country's laws, *the Yassa focused on the people*, not their property. Among the rules ... no stealing, mandatory sharing food with travelers, no kidnapping of women, and no desertion by soldiers ... it was a day-to-day set of rules that were strictly enforced.

Under Genghis rule, people were free to worship as they pleased, as long as the laws of the Yassa were observed. Genghis Khan welcomed spiritual teachers of all religions and beliefs, not only in order to pacify the conquered people, but to better understand them.

Some of the spiritual laws, were centered around Tengri, the Blue-Sky God, but there was also a respect of other beliefs. There were laws regarding the election of new khans, and many rules for soldiers during war, e.g., no pillaging before given the order, rules for negligence, theft, slaves, children born from a concubine, adultery, and more.

Some were for basic hygiene ... like no urinating in the waters or dipping dirty hands in streams and lakes. One law was about eating food offered by another ... which required first having the offeror taste the food ... this goes back to an incident when Genghis was a boy, and his father was poisoned by a group of hunters from another tribe.

The laws protecting women were strong and harsh ... kidnapping a woman against her will, or sexual assault was punishable by death.

Aside from the Yassa, Genghis also established a fast and efficient postal system across all the lands they conquered. There were postal posts a day's ride apart, with free relief horses waiting for the postal rider. Free trade, a postal system, laws to protect religious beliefs, laws to protect women ... and more. The alternative ... mass slaughters from endless regional wars and enslavement by pillaging invaders ... as *slaves were one of the biggest items of inter-regional trade.*

But the success of any system of laws comes from the strength of the central authorities and there, Genghis relied on many foreign immigrants to provide administrative duties ... usually experienced Arabs ... rather than Chinese.

65 Goodbye Teb

Back in the Avarga camp during the summer, Teb Tengeri plots for one of his sons to be the next khan. The son, Zun, is big for his age ... and basically stupid and easily controlled by his father ... which fits his plan. Bribes have been paid, alliances made, but even though secrecy is critical, word gets out ... Teb's brothers like to drink ... and talk.

On one such night, Gugu happened to walk by the drinkers and one of the brothers saw him and shouted demeaning obscenities at him.

Gugu had heard far worse insults in his life and continued to walk ... the brother took this as an insult and rose to challenge Gugu. The others tried to dissuade him, but the drinks only added to his bravado.

Just then Panda ran up to Gugu to tell him that her mother was looking for him. Unfortunately, she was caught between the two and Gugu realized he would have to do something. With one arm he swept Panda behind him and faced the charging Tengeri.

"STOP!" he commanded ... and the man stopped.

"On your knees!" he again commanded, and the man dropped to his knees, unable to rise.

Everyone was shocked, including Panda. Gugu grabbed her hand and they walked away ... leaving the warrior frozen to the ground on his knees.

As they walked Panda kept looking back ... then at Gugu ... then after they were nearing their tent, she stopped him.

"How did you do that?"

Gugu took a deep breath.

"Do you remember how you can cloak your spirit?"

Panda nods.

"It's one of those powers ... everyone has it ... they've just forgotten."

"Can you show me how?"

"Sure ... I'll walk a few steps away and then start to walk towards you."

"Okay."

"And then you visualize in your mind for me to stop and then project that thought ... *throw your thought forcibly at my mind*."

"It's that easy?"

"Well ... it's not that easy ... let's try it."

They try it several times ... unsuccessfully.

"You need to put your desired reality into the projection so there is no alternative for the person. He will think it is his idea."

"Listen to me Panda ... before you speak to me, there are many possibilities and maybe only one of those is me stopping ... you need to exchange information with my consciousness so that only that one possibility becomes probable ... the *only* probable course of action."

"Okay ... let's try it again."

After several more tries, she is able to do it ... to get him to stop walking.

Panda is delighted and wants to continue but Gugu tells him he needs to see her mother.

Inside the tent, Yufeng asks what took so long.

Panda says,

"Nothing."

Gugu says,

"There is one thing ... as I walked here, I overhead the Tengeri planning something."

After he tells her, she says,

"I need to alert the khan."

"Maybe you don't go straight there."

"You're right ... I'll go see Borte."

"Good"

After she departs.

Panda smiles and looks at Gugu.

"Okay uncle, now can we practice more ..."

From Borte, Genghis learns of the plot and having vanquished most of the foes except for the Jin empire, Genghis feels confident at this time in dealing with this long-lingering problem. Genghis calls in his younger brother, Temuge, who is stronger than most warriors, and talks to him.

The next day out in the camp, Temuge picks a fight with Teb ... a wrestling match. Although Teb is bigger, he has wasted away over the past few years and Temuge is all muscle.

Temuge defeats Teb and, in the process, kills him. The others of the Tengeri clan start to rebel but Genghis is ready waiting for them, and the brothers and followers are quickly disarmed and captured.

Afterwards all the Tengeri clan are eliminated. The leaders are all afforded a noble's bloodless death ... their still-alive bodies are placed under the receiving platform where the great khan and nobles feast ... crushing the bodies underneath without spilling blood.

After this, it seems as though a dark cloud has finally been lifted. Genghis prepares for the ceremonial burial of his mother ... and afterwards he is solemn for several days until Panda brings him the white wolf cub.

Genghis laughs,

"Just what I need Panda ... my own wolf spirit beside me ... thank you."

"What can I give you in return?"

"Nothing great khan it is my gift to you."

"Nothing? There must be something?"

Panda thinks for a moment, then says,

"Well, there's one little thing ..." which she whispers to Genghis.

He lets out a huge roar of laughter.

"Consider it done!"

Panda bows and departs.

Yufeng asks her what she asked for.

"Nothing ... it's our secret."

That night the two women, mother, and daughter, climb the holy Mongol mountain. On the top ... under the huge expanse of exploding stars, they sit down and meditate.

Yufeng journeys to visit Yufei, who is somewhere out west on the Silk Road ... they don't exchange information ... they just let their spirits entangle even though they are just spirits, they can *feel* the emotion.

Panda journeys to visit her closest and dearest friend, LF. Panda knows how to make the chirping spiritual calls even in the soundless void ... and almost immediately LF's spirit jumps on her shoulder and starts scurrying all over her. The two ... one human spirit and one animal spirit play like children ... among the constellations of stars.

Later, on the way down, Yufeng asks her,

"What did you do?"

"We just played ... like before ... but you know ... it helps me to understand and use my spirit body better ... I even learned how to project my inner sound-less voice ... you should try it with baba."

Yufeng thinks (*roll around and spirit play ... haha ... your father had other ideas.*)

Then Panda says something Yufeng will never forget.

"Oh ... one thing was strange ..."

Yufeng stops and looks at her daughter.

"What?"

"One time when we were playing ... we pretended it was like at home in the forest where we played hide-and-seek ... but this time, in the void, there are no trees, or places to hide, but"

Yufeng waits as her daughter searches for some words.

"LF knows how to disappear in one spot and reappear in another."

"What's so special about that?"

"She doesn't fly from one spot to the other ... she disappears from one place and then appears in a new spot."

"She what?"

She repeats what she just told her and then tells her something else.

"And there was more ..."

Yufeng waits. Panda continues.

"I saw these strange glowing things ... floating around."

Yufeng tries to correct her.

"But it's the void, there is no light ... light is just a reflection from the sun or stars ... there is no sun or moon or any light in the void ... that's impossible."

Panda shrugs, thinking,

I know what I saw ...

They continue down. Yufeng thinking,

She must be mistaken ... but still, I must tell Yufei about this.

66 The Wolf cubs

Life in the Mongol camp returns to normal. Not many people liked the Tengeri's and the few that did, quietly leave, or wisely remain silent.

Of more concern to Yufeng ... Panda is now a young woman, an attractive young woman, and more men are eyeing her, but she remains aloof from them all.

Yufeng and Sari counsel her to be on her guard, but few men dare approach her, especially when Lana and some of her growing cubs are with her.

Over the past year, in the night, her wolf cubs hear the wolf howls from the steppes.

Panda and Lana talk to them and tell them it is okay if they want to go to the wild, but always remember not to hunt humans, But the cubs are comfortable in the camp and don't want to leave, but then one day Toregene, Ogedei's main wife, is frightened by one of the young wolves and tells her guard to kill it. The man hesitates.

"She belongs to Panda, and the khan has told us not to ..."

Toregene shouts at the man,

"Kill it or I'll have you killed!"

Sensing danger, the young wolf runs off, but news of the incident travels fast.

Yufeng counsels Panda that it's time for the cubs to leave.

"One or two wolves are okay. But more is frightening to many people. And you must be careful of that woman."

Panda nods agreement and that evening she rides out on the steppe with her wolf pack running behind her horse. When she gets a good distance and close to other wolf packs in the foothills, she dismounts.

She leads the two remaining young wolves to a rock defile and commands them to enter and stay. Then she and Lana back away slowly. The cubs start to exit until Lana growls a vicious snarl ... the cubs know the meaning. Panda mounts up as she hears the howls of a nearby wolf pack. From her saddle bag she removes a goat carcass and throws it on top of a rock, the scent wafting through the wind.

"The others will smell that soon. Let's go home Lana."

Lana starts running in the direction away from home but circling around any wandering wolf packs ... she will make sure her cubs aren't harmed.

Panda understands and smiles.

"Good luck young hunters, time to build your own pack.

Later, in the night, Lana returns and crawls into the tent and sleeps.

67 Point of Existence

The next day Yufeng stops by to see how Sari and Panda are doing. As she approaches the tent several children come running out screaming ... inside she can hear Panda and Sari laughing.

"What was that all about? Are you telling the children ghost stories?"

Panda laughs,

"No, mother, we just told them if they weren't good, we would send them to work for Toregene."

Yufeng cautions her daughter,

"Be careful, these children talk too much."

Sari agrees,

"Your mother is right ... be careful of Toregene and her daughter in law, Oghul Qaimish, (the wife of her son, Guyuk) and that other woman."

"Other woman?"

"Fatima, the Arab ... I have a bad feeling about her also."

"Why?"

"They have big eyes." (for power and riches)

***

In another tent Toregene is lecturing her daughter-in-law.

"Be careful of everything that we talk about."

"Why mother?"

"I have plans ... just in case."

'What do you mean?"

"Someday, Ogedei will be the great khan ... and after that ..."

"After that what?"

"We have to make sure Guyuk is the next khan."

"But he is Ogedei's son, who else could it be?"

"Don't be stupid, Mongol politics depends on strength ... we need wealth for strength to make alliances."

"I'm sorry mother but I don't understand these alliances."

"Don't worry child, I'll take care of them."

"But what about Sari? Ogedei listens to her." (*more than you*)

"I can handle her."

***

Meanwhile Tariq is on question 549,365 to Yufei as they ride. Finally exasperated, he asks,

"But if something has no physical body, how can it affect us?"

Yufei reaches in and takes out an instrument.

"Look at this ... my compass ... the pointer moves by invisible forces without touching anything ... something exists there, it is real, but it is not physical or solid, yet it can move the pointer. If a common phenomenon like a compass acting on this metal can do this, could not the spirit be an invisible, intelligent, conscious force that similarly acts on and through the consciousness?"

Tariq ponders this for several kilometers ... until a new question rises to the surface.

"Before you said there was no meaning to life but if there is no meaning to life ... what's the point?"

"What's the point ... of what?"

"What's the point of everything that we do ... of our existence?"

Yufei pauses then retraces his previous words.

"When I said there was no meaning to life ... it was the same as when I said that this life is like an illusion."

"Yeah, I wasn't clear on that one either."

"The ancients aren't saying this life is not real ... it is real ... in a way ... but in another way it is not ... like a rainbow."

"Our eyes were designed to see and to navigate this world ... not the other realm, it's invisible. Our eyes can only see and interpret this world."

"But if I see it, then it's true."

"Not necessarily ... *your eyes weren't designed to see the truth; they were designed to enable you to survive.*"

"Then how do I find the truth?"

"You must go inside ... see without seeing ... not using your physical eyes."

"See without seeing?"

"You see it with your spirit eyes ... you *feel* it ... with your instincts ... in your heart ... in your stomach."

"In my stomach?"

"Yes .... haven't you ever had a gut feeling ... a feeling in your stomach?"

Tariq thinks, *(well yes ... every time I see your daughter!)*

"Your body parts all have consciousness."

"What?"

"They all came from the one egg ... which was conscious ... so each part inherited a form of consciousness ... you need to listen inside."

"But ..."

"Not now, we're getting near camp ... just think about these things and meditate."

"Okay ... thank you master."

When they get back to their army area, they see everyone preparing to move out.

Yufei asks a warrior,

"Where are we going?"

"West."

68 Subedei & Yufei go West

In 1221, Jebe, Yufei, and Subedei set out on a western scouting raid in which they attack the Kingdom of Georgia, and after making their way through the Caucasus, they defeat a coalition of Caucasian tribes and the Cumans, another large nomadic tribe on the western steppes.

Jebe and Subedei lead their small army of 20,000 men, with each general commanding a tumen of 10,000. They leave behind a trail of destruction as they move through Persian Iraq and Azerbaijan, sacking the cities which refuse to submit ... Rey, Zanjan, and Qazvin. The city of Hamadan surrendered without a struggle and was spared ... mostly due to Yufei's efforts. Also, Özbeg, the Atabeg (leader) of Azerbaijan, on Yufei's counsel, saved his capital, Tabriz, and prevented his country's destruction by offering to the Mongols a large amount of money, clothing, and horses, which were the Mongols' most welcomed tribute.

From Tabriz, the Mongols advanced north and made their winter base in the Mugan Steppes. There, the army was strengthened by Kurdish and Turcoman freelancers, who offered their services to the Mongols.

One night, Subedei and Yufei are alone in Subedei's tent.

Subedei asks Yufei,

"I know you have been wanting to ask me questions ... now is a good time."

"It's about the complete destruction of some of the cities ..."

"I understand some of your strategy ... not leaving the enemies in your rear, and the need for booty ... but the complete devastation, I wonder about the strategy."

"Yufei, Genghis told me that it is the only way ... *for now* ...we are a nomadic conqueror ... we are few, they are many ... we cannot leave a few Mongol warriors who are unfit to be administrators ... it will diminish our numbers and encourage rebellion."

"What about the innocents?"

"You know as well as me, there are no innocents anymore ... the evil ones hide behind the ordinary people who are just prey for the dark forces against us."

"But ..."

Subedei raises his hand.

"Like you told me once ... we don't do it out of anger ... the Great Khan sees it as a necessary cleansing."

Yufei nods.

"You understand the main reason my father went to war against the Jin?"

"That they demanded him to submit?"

"That was just the last straw ... we are nomadic herdsmen, we do not manufacture anything ourselves ... everything comes up from the south (China), through Jin lands ... in times past they have cut off this trade to punish us ... treating us like children or slaves ... my father has seen this happen too many times."

"But now with the western and northern Silk Roads under Mongol control, you can get goods that way."

"Yes, but the main roadblock to Mongol growth is the Jin ... and they are a formidable force ... they came from the same northern territories as us, so they are fierce warriors too."

Then he looks at Yufei.

"You and I play a small part in this vast play ... but each part is important."

Yufei smiles.

"I know."

***

While wintering north of Tabriz, Yufei asks for, and receives permission from Jebe and Subedei to scout the west ... actually he wants to go southwest to Gobekli Tepe.

His request is granted but with the provision that Chen Er and Tariq stay with the main Mongol encampment as insurance that he will return.

That night he, Chen Er, and Tariq discussed his plan.

Although he feels it is part of all their destiny, he is not sure how much he should reveal about Gobekli Tepe and the grandmothers.

In the end he decides to avoid it for now ...

Chen Er, who was on the first journey to Gobekli, asks him,

"Do you have any important reasons to go there?"

Yufei laughs,

"Let's see .... this invasion, the fate of the world, any new plagues, how to defeat the darkness ... nothing big."

Chen Er laughs,

"Well, it's just that I need to report to Yufeng if you went chasing girls in some harem."

Then they all laugh ... except Tariq, who doesn't understand some of these two old friend's humor ...

69 Return to Gobekli

The next day, Yufei rides out of camp, crossing through the mountains, heading west at first, then south ... on some invisible magnetic bearing.

Sometimes though, when one is focusing on an invisible bearing, they fail to spot signs of danger close by them. As he rides through one set of hills, he is surprised when a band of Ismaili Brotherhood stop him.

"Salaam Praise to Allah" Yufei offers to the warriors. The refrain is returned ... albeit, warily.

"Where are you traveling?' their leader asks.

Yufei recognizes their tribal clothes and dialect, but he is still cautious.

"Sanliurfa."

"For what purpose?"

"To inspect our trade agreement with the Ayyubids and Ismailis for herbs."

The warriors know of this trade but tell him,

"We will escort you there."

"Wonderful ... I hear there are assassins in the mountains."

The warrior leader glances at Yufei not knowing if the trader is mocking him or not.

"Have you been there before?"

"Yes, many years ago ... my father, negotiated the agreement with your former leader, *the old man in the mountain.*"

The man stops and looks at Yufei.

"You are the son of the Scorpion?"

"Yes." then Yufei holds up his ring finger and the man recognizes Rashid's ring.

The man bows and says,

"I am honored to meet you. My mother often told me stories of your father."

"Your mother is ..."

"Mariam ... the old man's granddaughter and the current leader's wife."

Later when they camp for the night, the warrior fills Yufei in on what is happening in the old caliphate, the Ayyubids, the Rum, and others ... valuable information which he will bring back to Subedei.

The rest of the journey did not take more than a week to get to Sanliurfa and they say goodbye to their escort ... later, after he is sure the Ismailis have departed, he continues to the ancient temple grounds at Gobekli.

He dismounts and grabs his water flask and fills it from a nearby spring.

Then he sits on a fallen monolith and drinks the fresh spring water from his flask.

Hmmm, he thinks, *this water tastes different*. He wonders ... as his memory fades.

"*Where did I get this water?*'

Then he remembers ... over there from that spring.

But when Yufei looks, there is no spring there now.

Whatever ...

Just then, one of the ancient ones appears, walks over, and sits down.

Her translucent body seems to radiate an invisible goodness.

Yufei bows deeply to the older woman.

She starts to talk but, no words come from her mouth ... images flood his mind, different peoples, different lands, wars, then a rebirth, then more wars ... in a seemingly endless cycle. The images flow into his memory banks ... and then he and Yufeng are part of the images ... and then, the images fade and it is dark.

A few minutes later, he wakes up.

"Do you understand better now?" the woman asks.

He nods.

"Is there anything else you want from here?'

"Not here ... but I'd like to go the Valley of the Mother Goddess again."

"Now?"

"No, I'll go early in the morning, so I can skirt around Sanliurfa."

"Okay."

That night he sleeps among the monoliths.

Ancient rites and ancient people fill his dreams.

In the morning he drinks more spring water and feels refreshed.

By the afternoon, he enters the valley of the Mother Nature Goddess.

He rides to the same thatched cabin that he and Yufeng went to years before.

Standing outside, waiting for him, is the same old woman, smiling as if she knew exactly when he would arrive.

"Come inside ... I have some fresh tea for you."

A warm feeling of *coming home* envelops him.

"How have you been grandmother, all these years?"

"Fine ... tending to the flowers, keeping contact with our sisters."

"What do they all say?"

"Some good, some not-so-good ... it all balances out. I have been following you three ... we are very pleased with your efforts with the Mongols ... you have done well."

"Sometimes, when I see all the devastation ... all those deaths, I wonder."

"I know, but it is necessary ... as you know."

"And little Panda, how is she?" she asks.

"She is amazing ... so far ahead of me when I was her age."

"It is good."

"I wonder if she will find someone to share her life, as I have?"

"Why do you wonder?"

He laughs,

"She is fiercer than her mother. All the warriors fear her, even the great khan ... she walks the camp with a wolf companion."

The grandmother laughs.

"Really? How wonderful!"

"But there is something else you came to ask me ... what is it?"

"First is about the poison I was infected with several years ago ... sometimes, my strength still fails me ... do you have any herbal flower to fully rid my body of it?"

"Certainly ... see that flower in the pot behind you?"

Yufei turns and sees a beautiful purple blooming flower.

"Snap off an unopened bud and put it in your tea ... let it steep a moment and then drink the whole cup."

He does what she says and feels better afterwards.

After a moment she asks,

"What was the other thing?"

"Recently, the Khan's mother crossed over the bridge."

"We know."

"The Great Khan, the conqueror of the world was heartbroken and grieved deeply. I tried to help him get past his grief, but words can only go so far."

"Yes ... so you wonder if there is another way to help the grieving?"

"Yes."

"Many prophets and gurus have tried ... and failed."

"Why?"

"People aren't ready for the truth ... that through their awareness they can determine this life ... and the next life."

"Why is it so hard for them?"

"The gods gave them eyes, ears, hands, legs, mouths .... to navigate in *this* world ... it was essential ... but because they can't see the unseen, they don't *trust* the unseen."

"The problem is that they've forgotten the hidden realm behind everything ... the things we used to teach at Gobekli Tepe and the other holy places."

"Could we teach them again?"

The grandmother sighs,

"That is our fondest wish ... that is why we all work to further the divine plan."

Yufei nods. Then he rises to leave.

"Wait."

He looks back at her.

"Sit down, there are some things I need to show you and tell you."

He sits back down.

The grandmother speaks,

"Gugu will soon come back here ... his mission with you and Yufeng is completed. We have need for him in another place."

He nods and the grandmother rises, gets a different flower bud, and brews a new pot of tea. After she gives some to Yufei, his eyes get heavy, but he remembers her last words.

"We want to show you images from a *possible* future, which depends on many possibilities ... but which we hope could happen. Close your eyes and dream."

Yufei drifts off, not down into the void, but up into the skies. Images pass by him, some clear, some faded, he feels he can see the whole world ... or at least this part between the two great oceans. He sees wars, and destruction, and a dark plague spreading over all the lands ... massive numbers of corpses ... and then an awakening ... of sorts. But at the end of these visions there are two outcomes ... one shows a spiritual and scientific awakening towards the spiritual growth that the grandmothers seek ... the other is a scene of far more destructive wars.

Then he wakes ... slowly. The grandmother asks,

"You understand now ... what we are trying to realize happen?"

He nods.

"Did you see yourself in the images?"

"In some, but they were confusing ... I didn't recognize the places."

"They were in the west ... in the old Roman Latin lands."

"Why there?"

"That is where we plan to have the rebirth ... after a great plague."

"But I didn't see Panda with us."

"Her mission will be to stay in the Mongol capitals to counsel their khans."

"Will she be alone?"

The grandmother smiles and shakes her head.

"At first ... she will have a companion, just like you have with Yufeng."

Yufei smiles and asks,

"I saw two outcomes ... which will it be?"

The grandmother shakes her head.

"Even we do not know ... it depends ... on the possibilities."

"Yufei ... you and Yufeng have come a long way ... but it is time for you to consider a leap to another level."

"Another level?"

"In the event that the dark futures are realized in this world ... you need to consider creating *a new universe* ... but to do that, *you will need to change your perspective*."

"A new universe?"

"Yes ... you remember in India, the gurus talking about *samadhi* and *turiya*?"

"Yes ... where the individual consciousness merges with the universal consciousness."

"Yes ... and what do the books or gurus say follows that leap?"

"They are silent ... it is like the salt doll ... who is there to report back?"

She laughs at the metaphor.

"Kind of like that but I can tell you there is more ... much more ... a thousand million times more than the before."

"How so?"

"I can't tell you ... it is beyond words ... beyond thoughts ... all I can say is that you and Yufeng are on that celestial pathway ... remember it when you look up at the nighttime sky ..."

Yufei is confused but remembers a line from an ancient text,

"*The light shines stealthily through eternity ... on the celestial pathway ...*"

"Yes."

Then the grandmother rises and brings out a package.

"This is for Yufeng ... there are some new flowers and instructions ... she will understand ... and give her our love."

"I will ... and thank you grandmother."

"Thank you Yufei."

He walks out, mounts his horse, and heads east ... back towards the Mongols.

The grandmother watches him leave and then goes back inside, where her husband, the old zaria merchant, is waiting.

"Do you think they will succeed?"

The grandmother shrugs her shoulders.

"I hope so ... I didn't think they would get this far."

"But we need to prepare for the worst."

She nods and sighs.

"I think Panda will be the key ... she has seen things her parents haven't."

70 The Venetians

While Jebe and Subedei wintered in the mountains, Yufei returned to report what he had learned from the Ismailis.

While the Mongols were wintering there, the Venetians sent a delegation to them, and concluded an alliance in which it was agreed that the Mongols would support the Venetians over other European trading cities (their main rival was Genoa). As the Mongols pursued the Kipchak tribe, Jebe sent a scouting party to the Crimea Peninsula where the city-state of Genoa had a trading station. The Mongols captured and plundered the Genoese colonies along the south coast of the Crimean Peninsula.

After this skirmish, the Venetians invited a Mongol delegation to visit their city in Italy. Yufei talked this over with the others and also Subedei, who saw the wisdom in scouting further west under the guise of trade.

A few days later, Yufei, Chen Er, and Tariq sail to Venice on one of the Venetian ships.

Chen Er can't believe this is one of the top maritime powers in the Mediterranean.

Yufei comes up to him at the railing and asks,

"What is it? You've been shaking your head ever since we set sail."

"I can't believe it!"

"What?"

"The Venetians ... on these *ships* ... dominate the inland sea!"

Tariq asks, "What's wrong, uncle?"

"It's only fit to haul camel dung. Look at the overlapping boards of the sides, that stupid sail and rudder!"

Then Yufei says, jokingly,

"So, you think it is no match for the Falcon?"

Chen Er gags and spits out some wine he was drinking.

"What do they even call them? *Hulks*? What a fighting name ... haha."

"I'd be embarrassed fighting a ship like this ... it would be like fighting children."

Yufei comes closer,

"Keep those thoughts inside for now ... they may be useful later."

Chen shakes his head one more time.

"The only good thing is this Georgian wine ... it is fabulous!"

They sail out of the Black Sea, into the Bosporus Straits. And stop at the Venetian station in Constantinople ... which the Venetians received after assisting the Fourth Crusade in transporting Crusaders there to pillage the Byzantine capital. From there they passed several islands, the largest was Crete, the site of an ancient civilization. Yufei gets some strange feelings from the island.

Tariq asks Yufei,

"What happened to them?"

"Who knows, they faded over time. Like in the Three Kingdoms, empires rise, and empires fall. The first two generations are usually the best, with strong founding leaders, then after they are successful, they become lax, and a new hungrier tribe takes over ... it happened to the Greeks and Romans also."

"Will it happen in China?"

He nods.

"The Song will be replaced by the Mongols, who will be replaced by Chinese, who will be replaced by other Northern Tribes ... and on and on."

"Then what's the point of all this?'

"There is no point ... aside from what *you* make it."

"But I don't know what I want to do."

"Just be open to the possibilities ... be aware ... and then your destiny will come to you ... and most important ... align your mind to the One Consciousness."

Tariq shakes his head as though the cobwebs only became more confusing."

"Oh ... and one other thing ..." Chen Er suggests.

Tariq looks at him.

"What?"

"You might ask Panda to help you understand better."

Tariq smiles at this suggestion and Yufei punches Chen's arm.

As they pass Greece and head north up the Dalmatian coast, the country seems different ... not just the greenery ...

Yufei senses something in the ether about their destination ... this causes him to heighten his awareness.

He talks to his companions.

"Be alert to everything ... learn as much as we can but always keep up the façade of merchant traders."

71 Venice

When they arrive at Venice, they are amazed. The city is built on the water! Actually, the ancient Venetians drove pilings into the shallow marshes and small islands, creating their own enclosures which they strengthened on the inside wall with rocks and gravel ... and then built buildings and streets and canals and plazas on top of this artificial foundation.

The large ship docks offshore, and small boats ferry them around narrow canals. Their host introduces them to some of the local merchants who all seem interested in establishing trade connections to the east. Yufei defers to Chen Er to discuss trade. And while Chen discusses trade ... Yufei discusses printing and paper making ... and roundaboutly ... religious freedoms. They become instant celebrities in Venice and the city leaders roll out the red carpet.

On the trip there, Chen made friends with the captain of the Venetian Galley, Antonio, discussing ship styles and construction from around the world. Antonio is fascinated by Chen's stories of Chinese trading ships, especially the Falcon.

After a few days of sightseeing, Antonio invites them to the Arsenal, the shipbuilding center of Venice. It is a large fortress like structure ... also built on the water, with towers and battlements facing out to sea, but inside are the kays for building ships where they built many ships in the 13th century ... enough to dominate the eastern Mediterranean sea.

In an informal setting, Chen discusses some of the shipbuilding advances China had made with a rapt audience ... the watertight holds, the extra masts, the rear rudder, the keel, larger and lighter sails, cannons, and other improvements.

Yufei makes many new friends also, one of which is a trading family named Polo. One son, Andrea Polo, is about his age and is keen to hear about their travels. The family set up a trading station in Constantinople, after the 1204 Crusades, and Andrea was planning on going back there and on to the Crimea soon.

Yufei discusses going with him ... as he was thinking of returning to Sudak on the Crimean peninsula to meet up with Subedei for the 1222-23 campaign. One day, Yufei and Chen ask their friends if it is safe to ride out in the countryside to see more of the old Roman lands. Their new friends assure them that it is safe ... *if you have an armed escort*, which they volunteer to provide. The following week, they went riding through the Veneto region and down to the old Byzantine capital, Ravenna.

There, they hear about a new up-and-coming trading, banking, and textiles city-state just over the mountains, called *Firenze*.

Yufei smiles,

"Maybe on our next trip ..."

Chen looks askance at him (*next trip?*)

The countryside around the Po River delta is lush and flat. It is one of the major crop-growing regions and also the scene of many ancient battles between the defending Romans and the invading barbarian tribes.

Yufei senses the past battles and comments.

"There's been a lot of blood spilled over these plains."

Chen nods.

What they are unaware of is the new blood being shed as the feud between the Pope's church party and the imperial (Hohenstaufen) party rises again to cover most of northern Italy and parts of Germany. Most of the city states are independent or under a ruler's protection ... but instead of a unified country as it was in Roman times, Italy and several other countries are made up of dozens (hundreds) of city states. These wars are ostensibly over control of church appointments (bishoprics, etc.) but are actually over the power to rule.

Occasionally as they ride through cities and towns, they see signs of recent battles and an occasional question about which party they support. Yufei can sense the answer they are seeking and always answers correctly ... but still it is a tense situation everywhere. In Veneto, Yufeng hears a sad story of two young lovers, whose families were from different parties, and whose love was doomed.

When they get back to Venice their hosts compete to fete them with sumptuous dinners of lavish Italian foods and wines.

One drunken night Chen says to Yufei,

"I could retire here ... the republic is run by merchants ... not greedy officials or priests ... nice countryside, good food, great wine ... Dorjie and I can build a castle ... what do you think?"

Yufei ponders this and says,

"Maybe ... and Yufeng and I could build our own castle also."

Chen thinks this is a great idea and falls off his chair trying to slap Yufei on the back.

They both tumble to the floor in laughter and their Venetian friends laugh and think they have made new friends.

But as the old saying goes ... *beware of pacts made while drunk.*

Later as they stumble along the streets, trying to remember how to get back to their sleeping quarters, they are blocked in an alley by a small band of five Arab traders ... or at least dressed as Arab traders.

Yufei immediately senses the danger and alerts Chen and Tariq. He whispers,

"Assassins ... act defenseless."

Chen thinks (*act* defenseless? ... *we are defenseless*!)

Yufei spots a sword under the second man's cloak and stumbles drunkenly and pretends to throw up in front of him.

The man automatically moves away from the stumbling drunkard.

And before he realizes his mistake, Yufei has his sword, and has killed him and another attacker. He throws the sword to Chen who catches it and duels with the leader while Yufei and Tariq take care of the other two. Chen feints and slashes the arm off the leader, then chops his head off.

They look at each other. Chen asks,

"What do you make of it? Arabs or Venetians or other enemies of the Mongols?"

Yufei searches them and finds a medallion on one of them. He looks at the strange design, then pockets it.

Chen lights a fire stick and only then can they see that beneath their cloaks, all the men wear priestly garments and have priestly haircuts.

Yufei quickly blows out the flame and tells them,

"Dump the bodies in the canal and let's get away from here. No good will come from this."

They toss the swords onto the bodies and kick them into a canal.

"You were talking earlier about retiring in Italy ... to find some peace."

"Yes?"

"I don't think we will find it quite yet ... at least not in this lifetime."

Chen wonders, (*this lifetime? ... sometimes friend you speak in riddles.*)

They don't mention the attack to their hosts and a few days later, they sail back to Crimea with the young Polo. On the boat Yufei shows the medallion to Polo who shirks away from it.

"It is a secret society. ... mysterious and dangerous."

"Why would they attack us?"

He shakes his head.

"Who knows. They see shadows everywhere. You bring new inventions, new ideas ... to them, anything new is a threat."

"Are they connected with the church?"

"They are connected with everything, be careful ... even on this boat ... don't show that medallion to anyone. When I get back, I will alert my family."

Yufei takes him to the stern ... away from everyone.

"Okay, we are alone, tell me more."

Andrea Polo looks around to make sure, then in a low voice he relates the story of the Inquisition by the Catholic Church.

After he is through, Yufei shakes his head and asks,

"And the merchants and educated people allow this to continue?"

Andrea nods.

"Why?"

"Some see private gain from confiscating a competitor's property, some for settling personal grievances ... others, in the lower classes, are just superstitious and are afraid of the church condemnation."

'What about your family and the merchants that we met in Venice?"

"Most of the top merchants are like my family and don't support this fanaticism ... but ... few are bold enough to challenge the church outright."

"So, this evil is Church sanctioned?"

"Yes."

"And the Church is spreading through all the countries around ... Francia, Germania, Norman lands ... even the Slavic lands?

"Yes."

RICHARD HOWE

Yufei wonders *why the grandmothers didn't mention this.*

72 Battle of Kalka

When Yufei, Chen Er and Tariq return to the Mongol camp, Jebe and Subedei's attention has turned toward Georgia. During the winter, they had made a reconnaissance into the kingdom of Georgia, entering along the Kura River. The goal of the Mongols was not to conquer the country but to plunder it, and their Kurdish and Turcoman allies were set in the front as a (*expendable*) vanguard. However, aware of the danger, the king of Georgia amassed a large force of soldiers and drove the Mongols back near the capital of Tbilisi. The Mongols withdrew but continued to launch rear guard attacks on the Georgian army.

The next month, the Mongols returned to nearby Azerbaijan and besieged its capital of Maragheh, using prisoners again as the vanguard to take the brunt of each assault on the city. By the end of the month, they had captured the city and put most of the population to the sword for refusing to submit. Jebe and Subedei then planned to advance south and capture Baghdad, the Caliphate capital, but then fearing the Georgians at their back, they changed their minds and advanced north again into Georgia.

A 30,000 men strong Georgian army was assembled near Tbilisi. The Mongols numbered 30,000 also and had received further support from local Turkmen tribes. Jebe set up an ambush with 5,000 men while the main Mongol army feigned retreat. The Georgian cavalry pursued Subedei's army after defeating the Turkmen and were destroyed when Jebe closed the trap. The Georgian army suffered a heavy defeat at Khunan, and their king was mortally wounded. Then the Mongols proceeded to plunder southern Georgia.

After making it through the Caucasus, the Mongols were met by an alliance consisting of the several tribes who were living north of the Caucasus who had mustered an army of around 50,000 men. They were joined by the Cumans, a Turkic people who had a large khanate stretching from Lake Balkhash to the Black Sea. The Cumans also convinced the Volga Bulgars and Khazars to join them. The Cuman khan placed his army under the command of his brother, Yuri, and his son, Daniel. The first battle between this alliance and the Mongols was indecisive, but the

Mongols managed to persuade the Cuman to switch sides by reminding them of the Turkic-Mongol friendship and promising them a share of the bounty gained from the other Caucasian tribes (the Volga Bulgars, Khazars, and Georgians).

With this new alliance formed, the Mongols attacked the Georgian army and routed it. The Mongols then proceeded to attack the Cumans, who had split into two separate groups as they were returning home, destroying both armies, and executing all the prisoners before sacking Astrakhan, their capital. Then the Mongols began pursuing the Cumans as they fled in a north-westerly direction.

Meanwhile, the Cuman khan fled to the court of his son-in-law, the Rus Prince, Mstislav.

"Today the Mongols have taken our land and tomorrow they will take yours".

However, the Cumans had been ignored for almost a year as the Rus had suffered from Cuman raids for decades. But when news reached Kiev that the Mongols were marching along the Dnieper River, the Rus rallied to defend their homelands. Mstislav gathered an alliance of the Kievan Rus princes who agreed to support him. The Rus princes then began mustering their armies to meet at a rendezvous site.

Preferring to avoid a large battle, Subedei sent 10 envoys to the Rus ... however the Rus killed them ... after which Subedei sent another message ...

"You have killed our envoys. As you wish for war, so be it. But we have not attacked you. May the spirits be judge of all men."

After surveying the area, the Mongol army decided to battle along the Kalka River. The combined Rus army defeated the Mongol rearguard at first, but then the Rus pursued the Mongols, who were in a feigned retreat, for several days, which spread out the Rus armies and exhausted their mounts. The Mongols stopped and assumed battle formation on the banks of the Kalka River. Mstislav the Bold and his Cuman allies attacked the Mongols without waiting for the rest of the Rus army and were defeated. In the ensuing confusion, several other Rus princes were defeated, and Mstislav of Kiev was forced to retreat to a fortified camp. After holding out for three days, he surrendered in return for a promise of safe conduct for himself and his men. Once they surrendered, however, the Mongols executed Mstislav of Kiev.

At the same time, the Mongol wings closed around the shattered Rus army, cutting off its retreat. The surrounded Rus were hit by volley after volley, accompanied by cavalry charges at any weakness in the formation. As the Mongols were carrying out this annihilation, some of the army – led by Mstislav the Bold – managed to cut their way through the Mongol ring and escape. The pursuing Mongol army caught up with Mstislav the Bold's forces and started to besiege the camp. However, the Mongols were not there to conquer, and merely marched east after plundering.

What the Rus feared most would happen ... the loss of their kingdom ... did not come to pass, as the Mongols plundered a few towns in the south before turning around. The Mongol army crossed the Volga River and passed through Bulgaria, marching east towards their rendezvous with their main armies. The Mongols followed this up by attacking the Qanglis Cumans, who had supported their fellow Cumans in the Caucasus a year before. They fought against the Cuman army near the Ural Mountains, defeating and killing their Khan before making them pay tribute.

Following this victory, the Mongols turned east again to meet Genghis Khan and the rest of the Mongol army on the steppes to the east. Genghis Khan showed great appreciation for his generals' achievements and heaped praise on Jebe and Subedei. The importance of the expedition was immense. The expedition was history's longest cavalry raid, with the Mongols riding 8,900 km in three years. Subedei also stationed numerous spies in Rus, who provided frequent reports on what was happening in Europe and Rus.

And for Yufei, Chen, and Tariq it was a valuable experience.

Each riding home with different thoughts and impressions.

Tariq. *How can I tell her my real feelings?*

Chen. *Let's see ... I can send Ding here, to set up our own kays ...*

Yufei. *The dark Inquisition is even more insidious than the grandmothers said ... How can we battle such a widespread dark epidemic?*

73 Borte dies

The next year on the way back to Avarga, Genghis' beloved wife Borte dies. Genghis goes into another deep depression and nightly confronts his powerful adversary called *Death*.

He sends for Yufeng.

When Yufeng goes to see the khan, he is sitting in his large, darkened traveling tent ... alone. She brings a mint tea and explains that her family raised these tea plants for many years ... but still, the bushes die ...

Genghis sighs.

"Like the steppe grasses."

"Then what's the point."

"Why do you conquer new lands?"

"It is my destiny ... the Blue-Sky God gave me this mission."

"And Borte's mission? What do you think it was?"

Genghis ponders this until Yufeng offers,

"Maybe to be your friend and companion ... and to give you male children to carry on your holy mission."

"But now she is gone."

"Right ... and someday you will be gone ... and who will carry on your mission?"

"My sons."

"Are you sure?"

"What can I do ... I spent all those years uniting the tribes."

'And while she was alive, and the boys were young, she guided them, and they listened to her."

"What can I do now?"

"Help your sons connect with the Blue-Sky God like you did ... admonish them to follow your guidance."

"What if they don't?"

"Then all your efforts will be in vain."

He ponders this, looks at her and asks,

"It is said that you can see the future ... is that true?"

"Sometimes I can see images."

"How much time do I have left to conquer the world?"

"Count the fingers on one hand (*five*) ..." she pauses, then continues,

"but your sons will continue and conquer lands from the outer sea to the inner sea."

"And then?"

"Great Khan, empires come ... and empires go."

"Then what's the point?"

"Great Khan, why do you think you were chosen at this time to conquer the world?"

"I've often wondered that myself ... I've always felt chosen for this destiny ... but I've never known *why me* ..." then he asks her,

"Do you know?"

"Yes."

He waits.

"Because the gods ... and the people believe in you ... and because they need you to rid the world of this darkness."

"Great Khan, there are dark manifestations which are spreading into this world from the beyond. The Great Blue-Sky Spirit has chosen you to battle these dark manifestations. You, your sons, and each of us have specials tasks to perform."

"What do you mean?"

"You know the elders at Mt Kailash?"

He nods.

"Have you heard of the grandmothers at a place called Gobekli Tepe?"

"Yes ... a long time ago ... from my mother."

"Yufei, Panda and I were sent to you by them."

He just looks at her.

"You are not surprised?"

"Borte suspected this and told me to protect you ... that you and your family were sent by Tengri and the Mother Goddess. You have been true friends."

"And we will continue to be ... for many years."

"Yufeng ... are you an immortal?"

"Great Khan ... my body is mortal ... but my spirit is immortal and so is yours ... and so is Borte's."

He sighs and lowers his head, tired ... the weight of the world on this one man.

Yufeng gets up, pulls a fur over his shoulders.

"Sleep well, my khan."

After she leaves, Yesui, Genghis' favored 2nd wife comes out. She goes to the khan who says,

"You heard?" she nods.

"You and the other wives must protect them ... understand?" she nods.

Slowly he rises.

"Where are you going?"

"I need to say goodbye to Borte ... by myself."

Slowly, as though already carrying her body on his shoulders, he walks to Borte's tent, where her physical body lies.

He kneels down and lowers his head ... one last time ... wishing he had done this or done that for her before ... hoping she understands.

74 Feeling Not So Powerful

The next night, the Great Khan invites Yufeng to join his sons and warriors in a meal together. After the food is brought in, the khan asks the others to leave them alone.

Yufeng waits the appropriate time and then asks,

"What is it Great Khan ... how can I serve you tonight?"

"Things I can't discuss with others ... they would not understand."

She waits.

He speaks again as if lost in thought.

"When I go to the mountains to seek guidance from Tengri ... I am not sure sometimes if it is what Tengri wants ... or ... if it is just what I want Tengri to say to me."

"What do you mean?"

"Years back ... I felt insulted by the Jin envoys ... I climbed the mountain, and felt I received Tengri's guidance to go to war against the Jin."

She waits ... then asks,

"And?"

"At first we beat their armies, but that war still continues."

"What is it you want to ask me, great khan?"

"When you talk to the spirits, how do you know if it's the great spirit talking or it's your own desires pretending to be the great spirit?"

Yufeng nods in awareness.

"Ahhhh ... now I understand ... but why do you ask me?"

"Before ... I could talk to my mother or my wife ... they saw me as a man, not as the Great Powerful Genghis Khan."

"And me? You don't think I think of you that way?"

Genghis smiles and then Yufeng returns the smile, then they both laugh.

After the laugh, Yufeng gets serious.

"It is said, '*Truth is not always beautiful, nor beautiful words the truth*'."

"Let me tell you what I have learned from the ancient ones ... when you go inside yourself to seek guidance, your mind must be empty ... empty of everything ... then and only then will you be able to receive the message, which may or may not come ... and which may be something entirely different from what you expected."

"So, I can't ask questions?"

She shakes her head.

"No ... it won't help. The great spirit already knows what you need."

She reaches down for her bowl which is *already full* of their Mongol drink.

"Please give me more."

The khan looks at the full bowl and understands.

"If you seek guidance in the future, just keep you mind empty."

The khan smiles and thanks her.

"I know you are close to my youngest son's wife ... tell me in your honest opinion how she compares to the other son's wives."

Yufeng pauses a moment and says,

"She is different with her children ... especially the boys."

"How?"

"The other wives have their sons learn warrior skills."

"And Sari doesn't?'

"Yes, she does, but equally important is to learn about the native people in their areas and to learn how other people govern ... to learn from them."

Genghis nods silently.

"What can I do?"

"After you have dropped this body, there will be power struggles."

"I know, that is why I have already divided up the empire with my sons."

He looks at her, but she is not nodding in agreement.

"What?"

"You must look further great khan ... to your grandsons."

"How?"

They talk more through the night ... when she leaves, the great khan does a short bow to her.

"Good night wise one."

Yufeng just laughs.

"Don't flirt with me old man ... you already have 1000 wives."

Then they both laugh and Yufeng returns home.

But long after she is gone some of her words linger in his mind,

... defeat the dark manifestations.

75 Greece

Plato believed that the physical senses
clouded our perception of the universe.
Just having bodies
makes our perceptions somewhat distorted,
somewhat inaccurate, somewhat of an illusion.
At the level of the body and the senses,
Plato thought that we could never
quite experience things
as they are "in reality."
He felt there was a more perfect,
non-material realm of existence.

(1224) After the Battle of Kalka, Subedei winters again in the Caucuses. Many evenings, he and Yufei and Chen Er talk strategy while Tariq listens.

Yufei asks,

"They say in the villages that you slaughtered unarmed Rus troops after they surrendered?"

"Lies to prevent more villages from surrendering."

"You didn't slaughter the surrendered troops?"

"I didn't say that ... I said what they said was lies. After one large battle near the Kalka River, one whole army that was surrounded drop their weapons and surrendered."

"But then after we granted them their free passage, their leaders got them to take up their arms again and tried to attack us from the rear ... *then* we slaughtered them."

Yufei looks at his two companions, then Subedei.

"We'd like to travel west again ... do we have your permission?"

"Why?"

"I learned a lot about them the last time ... as I told you ... this time Chen Er wants to look again in more detail at their Arsenal and shipbuilding capabilities ... if the Mongol nation gets to the inner sea, they will need to know the capabilities of the naval forces."

Subedei ponders this and agrees.

'Good idea ... what about the boy?"

"Haha ... my new wolf here? He'll follow along us old goats to see the world."

They all laugh, and it is agreed.

This time Yufei wants to go to what was once the Greek empire, and along the coasts of the inland sea islands to learn more about some philosophers he's heard about ... Plato, Aristotle, and others.

After the disastrous Fourth Crusade ... that is, disastrous for the Byzantine Empire ... Greece and the islands and lands around Greece (formerly Byzantine controlled) were divided up between Venice, Genoa, and various Crusader small kingdoms. One such small kingdom was the Duchy of Athens, where Western philosophy had its beginnings many centuries before.

Before the Romans, the Athenians had enjoyed tremendous growth and importance over a large expanse of the Mediterranean ... only to collapse and be plundered by Romans, Persians, and later Turks. At this time though, in the 13th century, there seems to have been a small rebirth.

Their first stop is Athens ... where the agora or marketplace, which had been deserted since late antiquity, has begun to be rebuilt, and the town is becoming an important center for the production of various soaps and dyes. The growth of the town attracted the Venetians, and various other traders who frequented the ports of the Aegean. This interest in trade appears to have increased the economic prosperity of the former city-state.

The preceding 11th and 12th centuries were the Golden Age of Byzantine culture in Greece. Almost all of the most important Middle Byzantine churches in and around Athens were built during these two centuries, and this was reflected in the growth of the town in general. However, this medieval prosperity was not to last. In 1204, the Fourth Crusade conquered the Byzantine capital of Constantinople and Athens, like many other cities fell under the newly empowered Latin countries.

Sailing on a Venetian boat, the group lands in Athens and start to visit various sites ... one of the most intriguing to Yufei is a tall structure called the Tower of the Winds. Located adjacent to the Roman Forum's Eastern Gate, the Tower of Winds, is an octagonal marble clocktower built around 50 BC. There are sundials on all sides of the tower, and a weathervane in the form of the god Triton on the apex of the conical roof. Greeks invented the weathervane to foretell the weather patterns.

The frieze panels below the roof line are what gives the Tower its name. Here you'll see carvings of the eight wind gods. For example ... Notus, the south wind; Boreaus, the north wind, etc. Merchants in the Agora marketplace would use the tower to read the weather patterns ... that is, which way the winds were blowing ... to get an idea of when their ships filled with goods from different directions might arrive.

The dome was an intricate design of segmented slabs of stone that had lasted more than 2000 years. Yufei is especially intrigued with a hydraulic water clock built inside the tower, which was fed by water coming off the Acropolis.

Also near the marketplace was Hadrian's Library built by the Emperor Hadrian when he came to Athens for his final visit in 131 AD. Actually, the Forum was close to the same size as the entire Agora marketplace. Hadrian's Library was a 122 meters x 82 meters walled enclosure with an open-air courtyard, central pool and gardens surrounded by Phrygian marble columns. The libraries, reading rooms and lecture halls with curved amphitheater style seating were at the eastern end of the courtyard. To Emperor Hadrian, libraries were Temples of Peace and Meditation.

As you walk up the path to the Acropolis, the group first arrives at the 5th century stairs leading up to the Propylaea, a central building with two wings, giving a monumental and controlled entrance onto the Acropolis Hill.

Inside the temple Yufei sees some *teachers* still holding *dialogues* with followers. As he approaches, they notice his different dress and invite him to join them in their discussions.

"What are you discussing noble citizens?"

"The mysteries of the universe ... and you?"

"Haha ... the same ... what can you teach me?"

"Haha ... it is a long story. Two of our ancient philosophers, Zeno and Parmenides postulated that time is an illusion of the human mind and that reality itself is timeless."

"Yes ... I have read that elsewhere and seen it for myself."

They look at him more carefully.

"You've *seen time* for yourself? How is that?"

Catching his slip, Yufei navigates out of the spotlight with a laugh.

"I mean I've *thought* about time to myself ... haha ... how can you see time? In the lands I've traveled, the Buddhist Have similar ideas, that physical things are not real, just projections of the mind."

"Like the prisoners in the cave of Socrates." he adds.

They all laugh with him and relax and continue their discussions. Yufei asks,

"What are your current theories?"

"The foremost philosopher in *our* school was Plato. He postulated that everything starts with ideas (eidos) ... which are non-physical ... some call it *forms*, others call it *ideas*."

"Can you give me an example?"

"Yes .... the idea of a tree is immaterial ... the seed grows into the form of the tree and is actualized when it becomes a tree ... just as humans are actualized when their form materializes."

"So, the *forms* are the ultimate reality?"

"Yes."

"And they are unchanging?"

"Yes, all eternal forms are infinitely eternal."

"And real knowledge is knowledge of the forms."

"Yes. There was a philosopher called Plotinus who followed up on many of Plato's teachings in his *Enneads* ... he postulated that there is a hierarchy of beings ... there was the highest supreme *One*, the source of all existence, and then came the *Intellect*, the realm of ideas, and finally, came the *Soul*, controlling the physical manifestations in our world."

Yufei asks,

"Do you mean the human soul or consciousness?"

"We see them as the same."

"Do you believe that this human consciousness can ascend to higher levels of being?"

"Yes."

"How?"

Just as the Buddhists, by purifying oneself of passions of the mind-body and attaining the spirit of the *One*."

Yufei nods and asks,

"Are there many people in the west that believe this way?"

The man laughs and looks around at his friends and starts counting on his fingers ...

Yufei laughs.

"This Consciousness ... could it be the foundation of life and all there is?"

"Yes ... spiritual existence ... is built from these conscious elements."

"But ... our physical senses cannot see them."

"Correct ... how could they ... they can only see the physical manifestations."

"Yes ... I understand ... thank you for sharing your ideas with me ... might I ask why you had this particular discussion today?"

"We knew you were coming."

Surprised, Yufei looks at the man who smiles and points to another man leaning against a pillar. The man shakes his head.

Yufei thinks, *(Gugu?)*

Yufei leaves the way he came ... in thought. Outside he meets Gugu, and they go to a small café to talk.

"What are you doing here?"

"It's complicated."

Yufei laughs.

"What isn't?"

"Did you hear what they were discussing inside?"

"Yes ... some of my assignment is guiding the discussions here ... which will later find its way to the Latin countries."

"What do you teach here?"

"That these small conscious elements interact with each other to create our perception of reality."

"How?"

"Through an exchange of information."

"Are you saying that consciousness plays an active role in the creation of reality?"

"Yes."

"Like we discussed before ... nudging the possibilities into probabilities."

"But it doesn't always happen as hoped for or planned?"

"Unfortunately ... no."

"But if this vast emptiness is intelligent, and conscious, and through our conscious souls, we can cause possibilities to become probabilities, why can't we eliminate the dark manifestations?'

"I don't know."

"Do you understand how it all happens?"

"Not really ... it's mysterious ... I know when we are aware ... our conscious awareness is *sensed* by other conscious awareness."

"And this causes the possibilities to become more probable?"

"Somehow ... yes ... information is exchanged."

Yufei nods. Gugu asks,

'What is it?"

"Sometimes, Yufeng and I can share things ... even though we are separated by vast distances."

"Really?"

"Yes ... and Panda too."

"Oh ..."

"What?"

"That part about seeing without seeing ... it's not the same kind of seeing as the ordinary seeing. Seeing with the mind and eye is one thing; seeing by one's conscious spirit is another. The act of seeing has a witnessing aspect to it, which is the consciousness. That part is not a physical act for it is not a temporal phenomenon. It is the constant ever-present ground that alone makes sense perception in all our experiences possible; the one consciousness that is everyone's ... and to be consciously aware is not to be in time."

Gugu looks at him and smiles.

Yufei is startled.

"What is it?"

"I have to get back ... I sense important events are going to happen in the east."

"Have you seen Tariq?"

"He's down the steps at the forum marketplace. Do you want me to help you find him?"

"I can do it. It was nice seeing you again, old friend. I hope it won't be the last time.

The two clasp each other's forearm.

"My wishes too. Goodbye."

Yufei walks down the steps and Gugu watches him as he finds Tariq and Chen and heads back to the docks looking for a ship to take them back to the Crimea.

On the boat Chen asks why they didn't continue to Venice.

"I sense important things happening back east ... we need to be there."

Two weeks later they rejoin the Mongols and head home with Subedei to meet the great Khan and their families.

76 Tariq & Panda

On the way back ... actually all the while Tariq has been tagging along with Yufei and Chen Er, Yufei has evaluated Tariq and come to realize that Beersheba and Tarem have raised him well ... he has kept respectfully silent when they are with others ... even among their fellow Mongol warriors. Only later, when they are alone does he ask his questions, which are usually well thought out beforehand ... but many times he rides forgetfully ... trying to digest it all into his Kucha cultural upbringing. His grandfather, Harim, had often brought ancient books from the hidden library to teach the boy.

Often his mind wanders to thoughts of Panda ... he feels a strong connection there and sometimes he even hears her voice in his dreams ... encouraging him to learn all he can. This motivates him even more to ask questions.

To Chen these side trips have been about sailing and trade, to Yufei it's about the invisible ... the divine mysteries ... but to Tariq, all questions revolve around Panda.

"Uncle, how did you find all your answers?"

Yufei pauses as he rides ... looks up at the clouds and answers thoughtfully.

"Tariq, seeking is not about looking for something. It is about changing your way of seeing without seeing."

"Seeing without seeing?"

"In the theater, the players act out the play ... at the end, the players cast away their costumes ... look at life like those players ... it's just a drama."

"Just realize the one mind, and there is nothing else at all to attain."

Once Tariq asked Yufei,

"What do girls like?"

Yufei looks at Chen ER and smiles.

"You should ask your Uncle Chen; he is the Romantic Pirate."

Tariq looks at Chen. Chen says.

"They like many things ... trinkets, jewelry, mirrors ... but most of all they appreciate your sincere respect."

Yufei nods and adds,

"So even if you are not interested in what they are saying ... listen attentively."

Chen and Yufei laugh ... Tariq is confused.

Sometimes, Tariq even follows Subedei around and discusses strategy ... and Subedei doesn't mind because it gives him a sounding board for his constantly evolving strategies. Subedei looks at him one day thinking ... (*I should leave behind more spies ... for our next campaign*)

One asset that Tariq has been able to add to the group is his knack for picking up new languages. Just on the 2-week voyage to Venice and later to Greece, he was able to pick up a lot of their languages.

Subedei thinks *maybe this boy would make a good spy.*

Meanwhile Panda has her hands full helping Sari raise her three remaining sons, Monke, 16 years old now is off to war, Kublai, at 9 years is already showing signs of a deep intellect under Sari and Panda's tutelage, Helegu, at 7 years old admires Panda and his older brothers, and ArikBoke, at 5 years is at the age of getting into everything. Unlike the other mothers, Sari wants her sons to be higher educated ... they all learn to read and write and learn new cultures and, as a Nestorian Christian, to be open about other people's beliefs. In this, she is advanced beyond her times. Many visiting delegations come to admire her intellect as well, as Genghis will call her into his audience to listen to the discussions.

And Panda's thoughts, often wander to this boy, Tariq ...

(*there's something about him ...*)

Slowly ... news of the campaigns reaches the Mongol capital ... victories bring celebration ... defeats bring worry for loved ones.

Whenever there is news of a defeat, Panda immediately goes to her mother and looks at her.

"Father is fine, daughter ..."

Then she adds,

"All of them."

Panda starts to say something, but her mother stops her.

"Give it time ..."

"I know ... but if there is a different pathway before me, I want to be preparing for it."

"The best way to do that is be aware ... of your inner self ... explore the void carefully. Everything is *there*, inside you ... not out *there* somewhere."

Yufeng sweeps her arm in front of her.

"I know, mother."

"It all needs to happen in its own time."

***

Later, Panda goes out with Lana to a small hill and sits to meditate. A short time later another person silently joins her. She smiles,

"You are good ... I almost didn't detect you."

Yufeng smiles and sits down next to her.

"I worry about you often." she tells her.

"I know I have felt your thoughts."

She is silent. Finally, she says,

"Panda what is it you are afraid of? Making a mistake?"

She starts to weep and shakes her head,

"No ..."

"Then what?"

"I'm afraid ..."

"Of what?"

"I don't know ... losing part of me ... hurting him ... I don't know and that scares me."

Yufeng holds her close.

Panda looks up at her mother.

"Did you feel this way with father?"

Yufeng nods,

"But here is the secret ... you will never know your pathway, until you lower your walls and let go of everything ... especially your *self, your desires,* and *your fears*."

"Your father taught me that a long time ago ... when I was injured on our first journey ... he tried to kill himself to save me ... without a second thought."

"But ..."

"No, listen to me ... I've seen inside Tariq ... he would do the same for you ... he is a special person ... you were brought together for a reason."

"Do you know where Tariq is now? Is he still fighting in the west?"

Yufeng shakes her head,

"I sense they are safe. Your father is teaching him ... about the things we know ... about the grandmothers ... getting him ready."

"Ready for what?"

"A different life ... not the life we think we live ... for the future battles with the dark side ... and ..."

"To be your friend ... or more ... whatever you two decide ... but one thing we have seen ... he and you were destined to ride the same pathless pathway."

Panda contemplates this and tells Yufeng,

"Thank you, mother, ... I will talk to LF."

Yufeng smiles,

"That will be good."

Yufeng walks away, Lana sits next to Panda as she ventures into the void, where she meets her old friend, LF.

LF is happy to see her,

"Chirp, chirp."

"LF ... you know my friend Tariq? Well, I ..."

Some travelers are blessed to have a sprit companion while in this life.

77 Genghis heads home

Pax Mongolia opens up trade across Asia ... paper and printing, science, and especially ...information ... allowing the seeds of the Renaissance to sprout in the West.

In 1226, Genghis took a spill from his horse ... as every Mongol does several times a year ... only this time after 60 hard years, he heals more slowly than before. Yufeng watches over him and treats his ailments, but she realizes the damage is more serious than others realize. One day when they are alone and Yufeng treats his body with acupuncture, he tells her,

"No one must know my true condition ... understand?"

"I understand, Great Khan."

Genghis starts to feel his age and finally after much urging by his wives, decides to head home ... but fate intervenes ... they must pass through the Xi Xia lands, which they had subdued many years before.

Only more recently, instead of supporting a Mongol force near Chang An, they turned their backs and went home. This desertion caused the defeat of the Mongol force and angered Genghis deeply ... and so he thought ...

Maybe I need to teach them one more lesson.

The Xi Xia retreated to their fortress capital and successfully resisted the Mongol siege. After being an ally of the Mongols, the Xi Xia had learned the Mongol warfare strategies. In their fortress, they had built walls within walls, so if an outer wall was breached, they just moved to the backup wall and any attacking Mongols were trapped between the walls and became easy prey for their archers.

Wanting to see for himself, the 60-year-old Genghis rode out with his generals. As they approached the walls, Subedei pointed out the problem. But they were still too far, and Genghis' eyes were not as sharp as before. He urges his group closer. These men love Genghis and are wary of getting too close ... worried that he won't be able to react as quickly as before to a flurry of incoming arrows.

This only angers him, and he yells at the generals,

"If you are all afraid, I'll go myself!" and he kicks his horse ahead.

The others catch up, but now they are in arrow range and a flurry of arrows head their way. The generals circle around Genghis to shield him, but when they do that, an arrow strikes a horse's leg, causing it to shy up ... which in turn causes Genghis horse to stumble ... which in turn causes Genghis to fall again ... not a bad fall, but he breaks his hip and cracks some ribs ... this on top of the previous year's injuries.

The generals carry him back to camp and into his tent, where Yufeng and his two wives are waiting. Yufeng can see he is in more distress than he wants to admit or that he wants others to see. She waves everyone out except the two wives.

While Yufeng reads his three pulses, the other women remove his battle gear. The wives make him comfortable on the bed ... then Yufeng asks the others to wait quietly by his side while she invisibly probes his insides ... what she sees shocks and saddens her.

Not only are the ribs and hip broken, but there is internal bleeding ... and a bleeding of his critical qi life force. She uses acupuncture and acupressure to try to regulate the internal qi ... reducing the pressure near the breach to minimize the leakage ... but she knows this will only delay the inevitable.

She sends for Panda, who arrives quickly and probes internally.

After which, with tears falling from her eyes, she can only shake her head and whisper ...

"Mama ... they are all ruptured ... all the blood vessels ... all the qi channels."

Genghis senses her diagnosis, but still smiles,

"What do you think, physician, will I sire more children?"

Yufeng feigns a laugh,

"Haha ... you old goat ... probably not in this world."

"What do you recommend?"

"Great Khan ... maybe it's time we head home."

He nods.

"Thank you for your honesty." then to his wives,

"You heard her ... what are you waiting for ... tell the generals to organize the march home."

The wives rush outside to mobilize the generals who will mobilize the others. When they are gone, he asks Yufeng,

"Will I make it back to the holy mountain?"

Tears well up in her eyes ... she has come to love this fierce old man.

"Come closer, there are things we need to discuss ..."

78 Yufei and Tariq return

That same day that Genghis fell, Yufei, Chen and Tariq returned to the Mongol camp. He hears about Genghis fall and goes to Yufeng's tent to look for her, but she is not there. He goes to ask Panda and she tells him that she is tending the Khan.

"How is he?"

She shakes her head, which says it all.

"Have you seen him?"

"Yes ... but now only mother and the two wives are allowed inside."

"Where is his tent?'

"There, but they won't let you in ... even the generals and sons are turned away."

Yufei walks to the tent, Tariq hangs back to talk to Panda.

When Yufei gets to the tent there are soldiers blocking the entrance. He asks one,

"Can you ask my wife to come out?"

The man says,

"No visitors and ... no messages in or out."

Yufei goes to his tent and sits down, closes his eyes ...

I am back ... in our tent.

And then he waits ...

After 15 minutes Yufeng enters ... she slumps into his arms.

He sits on a fur and cradles her ... in less than a minute she is asleep.

He waits ... he is good at waiting on his wife.

Ten minutes later she wakes with a start and looks around.

"You are here ... I thought I was dreaming ... how long did I sleep?"

"Not long ... ten minutes."

She starts to rise.

"I must get back ... the khan ... he is dying."

Yufei is shocked.

"Dying? The Great Khan? How?"

'A fall, old age, broken bones ... it catches up to everyone ..."

"Even the grasses turn brown in the autumn."

"Can you help him?"

She shakes her head.

"I can relieve the pain ... he wants to meet with his sons and generals soon."

"I must get back."

"Okay ... I will go with you."

"Good ... he likes you and may want to see you ... I will tell him that you and Subedei are back."

Back at the khan's tent, only Yufeng can enter. Yufei waits outside as others gather. Subedei comes near him.

"What do you know?"

Yufei looks around.

"Don't show any emotion ... it is not good."

Subedei's face is emotionless, then he looks around.

"Where is Ogedei?"

"Still in the field ... out west ... why?"

"He will be the new khan."

"What if he is not here for a time?"

Subedei looks around and spots Tolui.

"Tolui ... will act as a regent until a new khan is chosen."

"Not Jochi or Chagatai ... they are older?"

He shakes his head.

"The clan homelands are Tolui's lands ... that is where the khan will be buried, and the new kurultai held."

Images flash through Yufei's mind ... Subedei looks at him.

"What is it?"

"Nothing ... let me ask you ... of all the people, who does Tolui listen to the most?"

Subedei thinks and says,

"After the khan, Sari, his wife ... he would jump off a cliff if she asked him."

"Good. And what about Ogedei?"

"The same."

"His wife, Toregene?"

Subedei laughs.

"No ... Tolui's wife, Sari."

Yufei looks at him in wonder.

"I've talked with Ogedei, he is smart, and he knows of all the women, Sari is the smartest ... he often seeks her counsel. The Khan married him to Toregene, who was the wife of a defeated chief. He loved his first wife, but she was childless. With Toregene, it is not a joyful marriage, but Ogedei obeys Genghis in everything."

Yufei laughs.

"Even better."

Subedei looks at him strangely.

"I'll see you later." he says, then Yufei leaves.

Yufei walks over to Tolui's tent, where he finds Panda helping Sari.

He glances to Panda and slightly motions with his head. She understands and walks a short distance away. Yufei follows her nonchalantly.

"What is it father? Is it about the great khan?"

"Yes and no ... I need to talk to Sari alone."

"What about?"

"The succession."

"How about in their tent ... I'll take the children out and leave you two alone."

"Good."

When they get back, Panda asks the children,

"Who wants to help me find mushrooms? I have a treat for the one who finds the most!"

The children all shout their agreement, and they all walk off.

Sari notices the sequence of events and asks Yufei.

"Maybe we should go inside."

They enter the tent and sit down on the rug as Sari pours some tea.

After a few moments, Suri asks,

"What is it you wanted to talk to me about?"

"The succession ... you must be patient ... here are my thoughts."

They talk for an hour until they hear Panda and the children returning. They rise and Sari smiles at Yufei.

"Thank you for your advice ... I think it is wise ... I will talk to my husband this night."

When they come out of the tent, Yufei smiles at Panda and then he walks towards the commanders who are in deep discussions.

79 Genghis Last Days

Genghis asks his wives to leave him alone with Yufeng. After they leave, she asks,

"How can I serve you great khan?"

"The end will come soon, won't it?"

"Yes, my lord."

"There are some things I want to ask you ..."

"Please speak, but don't exert yourself too much."

"I have always felt a close connection with Tengri, the Sky God ... as we discussed. Many times, I have felt compelled to put the world under one nation ... the Mongol Nation."

"I know, khan ... and you have worked diligently to accomplish this ... but even grass must die in the autumn. Regard death and life as equal, and your heart will not be afraid."

"I know and I am not afraid of death ... just curious about what happens."

"To your spirit or to your empire?"

"Both."

"I can address the spirit part ... maybe Yufei can help with the other part ... he *sees* farther than I do. Do you want me to send for him?"

"Not now ... after we are through ... talk to me first ... about it all ... first about my spirit ... where do we come from? The Blue-Sky God?"

"Yes, Great Khan, in the heavens are spirits ... many conscious spirits, waiting for a newborn to attach themselves to and help it grow and develop."

"Conscious spirits?"

"Yes, some will form arms and some legs and eyes and ears ... and they will all connect into your conscious spirit being."

"What about my mind?"

"The same thing, a conscious spirit will attach to your brain and manifest into a conscious mind."

"Is it inside my body?"

"It is inside and outside. There is a conscious spirit for your heart which attaches to your heart, the same for other parts ... but here is something interesting ... when I've treated the wounded warriors, sometimes, they have lost an arm ... but they can still feel their hand!"

"How? If it is no longer there."

"They feel the *spirit hand*, the conscious spirit that was attached to the hand is still there."

"Then what will happen when I die?"

"Your conscious spirit body will drop the mind and your physical body and enter the *not-so-empty* emptiness ... what they call boundaryless space."

"Will my spirit stay intact, or will it dissolve into the emptiness of space?"

"That depends and it is important that we talk about it."

She gives the khan a drink of her spring water.

"It goes to the fundamental question about our existence ... what is the point of our existence?" Are we like rabbits that eat and reproduce ... or is there some higher purpose?"

The khan tries to sit up but falls back down. Yufeng helps to raise a pillow behind him.

"Yufei and I have traveled deep into the inner realm, and this is what we *think* ... which goes back to what I said earlier about the conscious spirits."

"These conscious spirits communicate with each other ... this is obvious in the body and mind ... but they even communicate with other conscious spirits throughout the boundaryless void of space ..."

"And?"

"This communications often can change possibilities, into probabilities, which can affect events to happen."

"You are saying that we may be able to control events by our thoughts?"

"Not our thoughts, our awareness, our intentions ... information ... even over vast distances."

"You mean my spirit consciousness ... even after death ... may be able to influence events?"

"Maybe ... we *think* this to be true ..."

"Yufei and I have done this, great khan ... communicated over vast distances ... and this communication has affected our actions and events.

When he was traveling out west with Subedei, we communicated. And Panda has communicated with my father and Yufei's father spirits."

"Really?"

She nods.

"But how does this affect me and my question?"

"The Tibetan Buddhists believe that the hours leading up to your death are critical, to focus on the passageway ... and they are correct, but there is more ..."

"You must be especially aware of all the various parts of your conscious spirit ... *so that they stay together* ... so it will pass together over the bridge to the underworld realm. Just follow your instincts ... be aware and be receptive to instructions."

"*So, they stay together*?"

"As *one* conscious spirit system ... try to keep it from separating into its various parts but don't fight against it."

"*When the mystic's life comes to an end, he lays it down like a mask.*"

"What instructions?"

"Once inside, *if your mind is empty*, you can still send and receive information."

"About what?"

"I don't know ... but I will be here next to you, like the llamas and try to guide your spirit intact over the bridge."

"Will we be able to communicate ... you and I ... afterwards?"

"Maybe ... I am not sure."

He is silent. He looks weaker.

"What happens if I don't do these things?"

"Then I think it's what the folk priests call reincarnation ... some of your spirit essence will be reborn into a new body ..."

"Why?"

"To try a second time to reach the spiritual awareness which I just described."

He ponders this, then tells her.

"Please send for your husband."

Yufeng nods.

Your witnessing Consciousness is your immortal spirit,
it is not a part of time.
The body is going to die,
but you have something within you that is deathless.
Your Conscious Spirit

80 Genghis & Yufei

When the mind forgets thoughts,
it transcends the realm of fear and desire.
When the mind forgets objects,
it transcends the realm of forms.
When the mind does not cling to emptiness,
it transcends the formless realm.

Yufeng finds Yufei outside, but before letting him go in she prepares him for the Khan's questions. Yufei asks what she has told him ... she explains quickly in their own way. He nods and they enter.

The Great Khan tries to rise but can't. Yufei goes before him and bows.

"Your majesty, conserve your strength."

Genghis struggles with short phrases,

"I'd like to know ... what you see ... about the future of my Mongol Nation."

"Great Khan, I have traveled East, West, South and North ... no other nation is as strong as what you have built. Most of the other nations are weak and divided ... your armies will conquer them."

"I sense that too ... but then what?"

"In the beginning, while your sons and grandsons remain true to your vision, they will prosper."

"And then?"

Yufei looks down.

"And then ..." Yufei pauses,

"And then, a change will occur ... instead of a warrior nation, it will be replaced by an affluent hierarchy fighting against each other ... based upon wealth, position, and greed. And that is when the decline will start."

"Is it inevitable?"

Yufei shrugs and nods.

"Power and greed are used by the dark manifestations."

"Dark manifestations?"

"Dark manifestations which try to corrupt and destroy this world."

"Why?"

"To prevent the evolution of our conscious spirits to more advanced cosmic beings."

"Like the black and white wolves?"

"Kind of ..."

He sinks deeper into the cushions ... deeper into his innermost thoughts.

"What can I do to defeat the dark manifestations."

"You have already done much Great Khan ... you have freed women, freed people's beliefs, opened free trade, which has enabled the transfer of knowledge ... and more ... all of these things will promote an awakening of new thinking."

"But I haven't spent enough time teaching my sons how to govern, how to balance life."

"And what about after I die ... what can I do ... what can we do ... to continue this work?"

"Yufeng and I have thought about this and here is what we think ... even our spirit bodies can affect events in this world."

"What do you mean ... will my spirit self be able to help guide my sons and grandsons?"

"Maybe ... in subtle ways."

"This is what we think ..."

"First prepare your spirit body parts to stay together for your journey."

"How can I do that?"

"I will teach you ... lying there flat, tense your entire body ... keep it tense ... now relax it ... now tense it again ... hold it ... relax ... one more time.'

"Next we will start with your feet and work our way up your body ... tense just your feet ... hold it ... ok, relax ... tense again ... hold it ... okay relax ... one more time ... okay now your calf muscles ... tense ... "

They do this for another twenty minutes ... then Yufei adds something new.

"Great Khan, when you die you will drop your mind and body ... and with your mind, will drop your memories and other useless knowledge ...

but not your knowing ... you must focus on this ... the knowing ... knowing how to defeat your enemies, knowing how to govern different cultures ...

Knowing isn't just knowing good from evil.

But knowing how to deal with people and different cultures and beliefs.

Knowing ...

Before long, the khan drifts off to sleep.

***

In the evening he calls his sons and generals into his tent. His wife, Yusei, speaks.

"The khan wishes to speak to you all ... but his voice is weak, and he has asked me to add strength to his words."

"Please sit comfortably."

They all form a semi-circle around the khan's bed.

Genghis talks softly to Yusei, and she speaks,

"Soon, my spirit will join Tengri, the Sky God, but before that I must give you my last commands."

At this, there is a wailing until he holds up his hand.

"Be silent ... it is of no concern ... and *my spirit councilor* here, (pointing to Yufeng) has prepared me for the last campaign."

They all look at Yufeng. *(Spirit councilor?)*

Yufeng bows her head.

"You all know the lands you will inherit ... and the people you need to support you."

"You must remember this ... one of the reasons we have been successful is that the rulers of the other lands were greedy and oppressed their people."

"So, when you conquer, rule fairly and justly ... so the people support you."

"In the beginning, conquering was the best motivation ... it provided goods to our people ... in the future it will be trade ... so trade must be open and free."

"We are a nomadic people, so seek out the best educated talents in foreign lands to help you govern and prosper."

Then he whispers to Yusei, who whispers to Yufeng, who slides out of the tent. A few moments later she returns ... with Panda.

The khan whispers to Yusei, who motions for Panda to come closer.

"The Great Khan designates this woman, Panda as the *new shaman* of our nation ... all heed her words and advice. That is an order of the great khan. She will be at the side of all future khans."

Panda bows her head thinking, *a promise kept.*

They look at the young woman and then at Yufei and Yufeng ... a bit confused.

Genghis whispers to Yusei, who retrieves a gold tablet.

Yusei motions for Yufeng and Yufei to come forward.

"These two will help you learn more about the new lands and cultures of the west. I am giving them this royal passage tablet. All shall help them in their journeys and provide whatever they may ask ... in all our lands."

There is a murmuring.

"Is there a question?"

One of the generals asks,

"Why? Why these two?"

The khan shows some anger,

"Why does it thunder before the rain? Why does the sun shine?"

"Because it is the will of the Blue-Sky God and my desire also!"

'These three have come from the holy mothers to help us. They have devoted their lives to helping you ... *as long as you are worthy*!"

"Focus on helping the people in your lands, with their crops and herds, education, trade, health and medicine ..."

"Beware of greed ... beware of greedy people ... beware of the dark manifestations!"

The listeners think the same thought, (*what are dark manifestations?*)

The great khan slumps into his cushions and is silent.

Panda comes to his side, takes his pulse, and talks to Yusei, who tells those present,

"That is all for now ... he must rest."

They all file out except for Panda and Yufeng and Yusei.

The older women look at Panda, who shakes her head.

Yusei tells Yufeng to alert Sari and the other older women to get ready to prepare his body for the final journey.

Once Yufeng has left, Yusei collapses. Panda rushes to her, props her up and gives her a drink.

Panda takes her pulses.

"When is the last time you have slept?"

"Several days ago."

"Sleep now ... I will watch things ... if something happens, I will wake you."

"But I can't ... I must ..."

Then Panda, puts her palms on Yusei face and massages her temples until the woman is asleep.

After an hour, she wakes up and sends Panda back to her tent to rest.

Later Yufeng returns and stays there until the end.

81 Genghis Dies

Yufei and Panda are sleeping in their tent when they hear the wailing begin and then know ... the Great Khan has died. Lana starts to join in the wailing with her own howling, as does Genghis' white wolf. They quickly get dressed and rush to the khan's tent where already hundreds of women are prostrating and wailing. Even the fierce warriors are crying at the loss of their leader ... some are slashing themselves with cuts on their arms to memorialize him and to remember this day.

Yufei and Panda go to the entrance flap but only Panda is allowed in. There she sees the wives anointing the body with oils and preparing the khan's body for final display and internment. She spots her mother off to the side and goes to her.

"Can I help?"

Yufeng shakes her head.

"No ... just watch everything. Is Sari here?"

Panda looks around.

"Yes, she's over there."

"Quick, without causing attention, bring her to me."

Panda makes a roundabout walk to Sari, greeting others and then she greets Sari, and whispers into her ear. When Sari looks at her, Panda glances towards her mother. She nods, finishes what she was doing and also walks a roundabout way to Yufeng. The two women go over to a wash basin and appear to be washing some of the ointment rags.

"Have you talked with your husband?"

"Yes ... he understands."

"Good."

"I worry that Ogedei's wife will try to wrest control until her husband can get back."

"Don't worry ... I talked to the khan, and he instructed Yusei what to do and say."

"Can we trust her? She is from a different tribe."

"We all are ... but yes, I think so, she was committed to the Khan and has been the closest wife to him since Borte died."

"Where is your husband?"

"Outside with Chagatai ... Ogedei is far out west, and we haven't heard from Jochi, but there are rumors."

"Rumors?"

"That he was marching here with an army but died of a strange illness along the way."

Yufeng raises her eyebrows as she looks around and asks,

"Why strange?"

"They say he was coming here to confront the Khan."

"And?"

"The Khan would never allow that to happen ... even on his deathbed."

Yufeng pauses, thinking,

"I don't think Chagatai is a problem, he seems content with his lands."

Sari nods.

"So, it is just, Toregene, who was from the Merkit tribe, which Genghis always hated after they kidnapped Borte."

"I'll talk to Chagatai's wife; she is my friend, and Jochi's wife is my sister."

"I'll have Yufei talk to Subedei and the generals."

"Good."

***

They break camp and Genghis begins his last march ... a funeral march.

Pursuant to his last instructions, the new shaman, Panda, rides a decorated horse following close behind the rolling Great Khan's tent.

She is the lone horseman ... so close ... but she seems *changed*.

In the evening along the way, she takes her meals alone and even when Tariq approaches her, she shakes her head slowly, and waves him away.

Many wonder what she is doing ... only Yufeng and Yufei know. And they, when they are alone, will walk away from the camp and sit under the stars of the steppe.

Because of a promise made ...

Three Immortals trying to guide the Great Khan's spirit ... across the bridge of the underworld.

***

After 3 weeks, just before entering the Angara valley, the caravan stops. A small detachment of the most loyal soldiers escorts the body wagon (and Panda) in a different direction, only known to a few, to a spot already chosen years ago and prepared as the Great Khan's last resting place.

Later when the burial soldiers return, they first enter a special tent with Yufeng and Panda and are given drinks to erase the memory of the location of the burial site.

Whenever they are asked, there is a blank spot in their memories. At first, the Khan's instructions were to kill them all to preserve the burial spot. Yufeng, however, convinced the Khan that she could erase all memories of the location.

The rest of the caravan had continued to their home campground to prepare for the kurultai and the selection of the new Khan.

82 Kurultai

Two weeks after the burial, a kurultai is held. Everyone knows that Ogedei is the heir apparent, but he is still way out west and may take months or longer to return. So, the question remains ... what happens in the meantime? Ogedei is well liked by most. Although Tolui is a better commander, Ogedei gets along with everyone and was Genghis favorite son and chosen successor.

Toregene tries to put her son Guyuk forward as temporary khan until Ogedei returns, with her as the temporary Regent, but the other leaders don't agree, and it is decided by the generals, the sons, and other elders that Tolui will act as Regent and manage the Mongol nation until Ogedei returns.

Toregene is furious at being outmaneuvered, but she bides her time in the misbelief that Ogedei will soon return ... not knowing that it will take Ogedei two years to get back and be crowned khan. To Ogedei, Toregene was just a breed cow for sons, as his first wife, whom he loved, was childless.

Sari, the wisest of the sons' wives, starts to make her own alliances with other princes and commanders ... just in case the stars shine on her ambitions to have her sons sit on the Mongol throne.

Most of the commanders, Subedei included, take this time of Tolui's regency, as a welcome respite from the campaigns ... time to foster more children, teach existing children, repair their campaign equipment, renew old alliances, and make new alliances ... especially with the merchants and ambassadors from other lands.

Two years later, upon Ogedei's return ... he first has several meetings with Yesui and Sari, as instructed in secret messages he'd received from his father before he died.

At the Kurultai, Yesui, reads a last message from the Great Khan ...

"To follow and support his sons on their divine mission to conquer the world as he would have if he were still alive."

In a separate confidential message to his sons and generals, he tells them to pay head to the guidance of Yufei, Yufeng, and Panda. That this is not only his command, but the command of the Sky God, Tengri. The generals agree, as most know by this time, the good advice and loyalty of these three.

Later in their tent, the three discuss what happens next. Panda will stay with Sari and serve Tolui, and Ogedei, and all future khans, some of whom may be Sari's sons ... Mongke, Kublai, Helegu, or Arik Boke.

Yufeng cautions her to advise Sari to beware of Toregene. Panda nods knowingly. After they prepare for sleep, Panda steals outside to see Tariq.

Tariq would like more from the relationship now, but Panda is reluctant to give up her independence and also, she is aware that her new shaman responsibilities will demand a lot from her. Tariq is frustrated and Panda cares deeply for him ... but she has conflicting emotions. One is her emotional heart, another is her spiritual heart, and also for her mission, which, with the Khan's last instructions, hopefully will save hundreds of thousands of lives and bear fruit in the years ahead.

"You must choose one!" Tariq says as he walks away.

Panda lowers her head as her mother walks up and holds her.

"Mother I love him, but I can't give up our work now ... it is more important than him and me ... he just can't see that."

"Just give it time ... you are ahead of him on this journey ... he needs to catch up to you."

"I never expected the Khan to appoint me as the shaman ... I told him as a joke years ago. I am not sure what to do."

"Just follow your heart ... and you will be okay."

"Can a shaman get married?"

"Yes, of course."

Yufeng looks at her daughter, who is now a grown woman in the prime of life.

"Here's what I suggest ... you find Tariq and you go somewhere sacred for a few days ... purify your bodies and spirits ... and enter the void together, as your father and I did when we first met."

Panda looks at her mother who adds,

"That's where you will find your answers ... for both of you."

Panda nods and hugs her mother.

Meanwhile Chen Er has been found by the very person he has been looking for ... the Tibetan monk, Sakya Pandita, of the Grey Earth sect, who was sent to the court of the great Khan to smooth relations and try to prevent a devastating invasion. They walk together and Chen Er invites him to his tent, then he sends for Yufei.

When Yufei enters the tent, he is surprised by the presence of this monk whom he had briefly met in Lhasa years ago. The monk recognizes Yufei and bows to him in the Buddhist fashion.

"A mi tou fo"

Yufei asks him,

"You remember?"

The monk smiles.

Then Yufei looks at Chen Er, who says,

"We were just discussing how we can protect Tibet from the Mongol invasion and pillaging ... if it happens."

The monk offers a suggestion,

"We must use all our influences here to protect Tibet."

Yufei replies,

"Not just here."

"What do you mean?"

"In Tibet as well ... if there are self-important royal officials who offend the Mongols, it will lead to pillaging ... if there are minds-in-the-clouds abbots who think they, and only they, hear the voice of Buddha, the Mongols will wipe out all the monasteries ... do you understand?"

He nods knowingly.

"So, we have two tasks ... advise both the Tibetans and the Mongols. On the Mongol side, my family and I have influence and will do all we can ... it is for you and your sect, as they gain power, to control the responses from Tibet."

Chen Er speaks,

"Princess Dorjie is connected to many of the old royal families, and she can talk to them. What she is worried about is the rivalry among the Buddhist sects which can create chaos."

Yufei adds,

"And although the dark monastery was eliminated, there are more in the mountains ... they will try to sow discord."

Then he summarizes,

"So, if Tibet is to be spared, we must all work together ... agreed?"

Sakya Pandita then explains more of his mission ... to get appointed viceroy for Tibet by the khan so he can exert control ... for the good of all Tibetans.

"In Tibet, my sect is rising."

The monk smiles and a pact is made that hopefully will spare Tibet from the ravages of a devastating invasion.

Afterwards Chen Er tells Yufei that he will travel back to Tibet with Sakya Pandita. Yufei nods and clasps his old friend and brother-in-law.

"Can you tell Yufeng?"

Chen Er nods,

"Okay ... I will do it this very night."

83 In a Holy Valley

Later that night Panda finds Tariq and tells him about her mother's suggestion. He agrees immediately ... of course ... if Panda asked him to bite off a rat's tail, he would agree ... such is young love.

Panda is told about a quiet canyon behind the Mongol Holy Mountain with a running stream ... and they say goodbye to her parents and head there. It only takes a few hours and while Tariq clears a small campsite, Panda starts a fire and boils some water, then she adds some tea and herbs that her mother gave her.

Before they journey inside, Panda explains to Tariq the usual advice ... sit comfortably, drink the *tea*, close your eyes, empty your mind, be aware ... be aware ... be aware ...

Tariq follows her advice and starts to drift into the void ... he feels disoriented at first ... *what was in that tea?* ... but he empties his mind and is aware of the canyon and the stream and ... Panda.

He tries to talk but there are no words in the void.

He tries to reach out for her but even that is impossible.

She starts to move (*float*) away ... but he can't stop her.

Then he finds his spirit floating after her.

They come to a clifflike apparition and stop ... side-by-side now.

Panda's spirit is pointing, and Tariq looks to see what it is.

Below them, on the grass steppe, are two riders, racing the wind across the steppe.

At first, they think it is Yufei and Yufeng who are leaving camp soon .... They try to wave to them.

The two riders stop and turn around and look up ... but it is not Yufei and Yufeng.

It is Tariq and Panda ... who wave and smile up at them.

And now they know ...

They have seen the future ...

And they are riding together in the future.

Their spirits hold each other's invisible hand.

It is enough.

For now.

Part 2

The Journey to Sanxingdui

Snow Fox

Male: Xiongxing xuehu ... Female: Cixing xuehu

Sanxingdui - an ancient civilization buried in the forests of Sichuan, just north of Chengdu. The bronze artifacts found in later times are incredible, testifying to the artistry of this advanced ancient civilization.

Wisdom is the oneness of mind,
that guides and permeates all things.
(Heraclitus)

84 Author's Preface to Part 2

People ask me where I got the idea for this novel. Actually, it was easy, as most of it is the culmination of my life's quest into the mysteries of the universe, the purpose of life, and what lies beyond. It is the capstone of my previous 3 novels and my personal roadmap for going into the beyond.

Sanxingdui is an amazing archaeological site, and the ancient artifacts are mind blowing. I traveled to Chengdu about 25 years ago and visited the old Sichuan Museum where I first saw these artifacts ... dusty and forgotten among numerous artifacts. Many years later I visited the actual archaeological site about an hour north of Chengdu where a new Sanxingdui museum had just been finished ... and on display were those amazing artifacts of a forgotten civilization.

In the central atrium of the museum, is a 5m tall bronze *tree*. Maybe you will be struck as I was by how all the ancient myths revere the tree as the symbol of life.

In Book I, there was the grandmother tea tree ... In Book II, the heroes went to the legendary Garden of Eden; in Book III, they sheltered and gave birth in the jungle tree forests of Yunnan under the majestic snowy mountains. In Book IV, they journey with the Mongols, whose Tengri religion honors a tree with two branches and nine leaves as its symbol under the vast blue sky. In this Part II, the missing Tree of Life appears in the Mother Nature Garden, at Gobekli, *and* at Sanxingdui.

All things in life are connected ... but we often fail to see it at the time.

I hope to finish this book soon and publish it ... and then go beyond the beyond.

In any event, my life has been a great journey and I hope your journey is equally exciting and fulfilling.

Cheers,

Richard Howe

Postscript: This is just a fictional novel, with fictional people. It is not a condemnation of any peoples or beliefs; it is not meant to overlook the atrocities committed by invading and plundering armies ... those things are just in the background for the real story of our heroes and their companions.

85 Life is just a story (continued)

The Tale of the Two Legendary Immortals
As told by Granny Hong Xiongmao (Red Panda) –
during the Yuan Dynasty

"But Granny, what happened to Yufei and Yufeng?"

"And Panda and Tariq?"

"And Chen Er and the Princess?"

"Later children, I am tired now ..."

"Granny Panda, did you know Grandpa Genghis?"

"Yes, child ... we were both wolf spirits."

"Was he an Immortal too, like the Legendary Immortals of Wuyi?"

"Yes, of course, he did many extraordinary things in his life."

"Like what?"

"He brought the world together under one banner of the Mongol Nation ... no one had ever done that before ... or since."

"Granny, what happened to Tariq?"

A sharp pain grabs granny's heart and she almost collapses.

The other weavers see this and dismiss the children for the day ... then they help her to her room.

When she is alone ... she starts to write in her journal ... then she feels a breeze from the unopened window.

Before turning she knows it is her mother.

"Mama."

"Panda."

"Is anything wrong?"

"No dear ... your father and I have been busy ..." then handing her some papers ...

"Here, it's all in here. I wanted to bring you these for your journal."

"Is my journal important?"

"More than you realize."

"One day, it will be 'discovered' ... along with the tapestry."

"Why is that important?"

"The people's minds are currently subject to wild swings of beliefs and superstitions ... in the future, science and reason will prevail ... but the desire for spiritual fulfillment will lie dormant."

"And then?"

"And that is when your father's work will resonate with a new generation of scholars and turn them back to the spiritual world for their answers ... and that is when the 'discovery' of your journal will help them answer some of their questions. Then maybe the scientific and spiritual worlds will join."

"Mother, How do you know all this?"

'Haha ... it is why we are all here."

"How long can you stay?"

"Daughter, I am in no time now ... I can stay forever."

The next day back in the weaving room ...

"Granny Panda, can you tell us another story?"

Then, not waiting for an answer the princess points to a spot on the tapestry.

"What's this tree Granny Panda?"

"I don't remember seeing it before."

Granny Panda's eyes, which aren't as sharp as before, looks closely.

"Hasn't it always been there?" she asks one of the weavers.

None of them remembered weaving it.

Then a spark lights up in her eyes,

"I remember ... it is the tree from Sanxingdui."

The children look at each other, "Sanxingdui?"

"Where is that Granny?"

Granny shakes her head.

"It was a civilization that was lost long ago ... and then found buried deep in the forest of Sichuan."

"Can you tell us the story?"

"Certainly ... everyone get comfortable because this story starts long ago, and crosses vast continents,

And continues through time and eternity ..."

***

ENSO - THE JOURNEY BEYOND

Time is a game.
Played beautifully,
by children.

86 Being & Non-Being

Given that we can live only a small part of what there is in us,
what happens to the rest?
Paul Mercier

When Panda and Tariq come back to camp, Yufeng and Yufei can see the change in their faces ... they are very close to each other and comfortable with each other's bodies. Panda's fears have dropped away and Tariq's frustration also.

Over the next few days, Yufei and Yufeng prepare for their next journey ... they plan to travel to the Latin kingdoms by way of Gobekli Tepe. They both want to talk to the Mother Goddess' grandmothers again and then journey on, drawn by some invisible force, to the lands further west.

Chen Er and Sakya Pandita will travel to Tibet to prepare it for their future struggles. One evening they have a small dinner and Yufei and Chen Er get drunk and pass out lying next to each other. The monk didn't drink the fermented spirits, so he is sober. Yufeng just smiles and tidies up. She asks him why he had so many questions of Yufei earlier.

The wise-before-his-years monk replies in an epithet,
"Without questioning a wise person,
One cannot measure their depth.
Without striking a drum with a stick,
One cannot distinguish it from other drums."

"Well said, monk ... and what measure of man do you gauge my husband?"

Sakya just smiles,

"I think you already know."

Sari and some of the other women have a private dinner with Yufeng and Panda ... while Yufei has another drink fest with Subedei and some of the commanders. They are sad to see these new friends leave, but it is the way of the nomadic life ... pasture for a season, then pack up and move on.

Yufei and Yufeng travel light. Just the two of them, but with two extra horses and a packhorse ... like old times. They bring their own provisions and supplement that with small game. At night they talk ... which comes easy, even after all these years.

"Do you think she will be okay?" Yufei asks one night.

Yufeng smiles.

"She'll be okay ... she is further along than we were at that age ..."

"Tariq is a good boy ... I mean, man."

"I know."

"If left alone, they would have no problem."

"What do you mean? Is someone pressuring them?"

"Not someone ... society ... just as it did me when I was younger."

"Tariq feels like they *should* get married ... because that's what everyone else does."

"But in many cultures that I've seen, the shamans don't get married ... they are already married to the gods."

"I know, but Tengri isn't like that ... they have no priest class or celibate shamans."

She holds him closer under the furs.

"Don't worry, they will figure it out ... but, I feel a chill, can you hold me closer old man."

"Old man? Haha ... I'll show you an old man."

And they talked no more that night.

***

But each night the talk would revolve back to the central questions of their quest, always in their minds ... and then they would go deeper ...

What did the grandmother mean by a new universe?

One night, coming out of the void, Yufeng says,

"Well, that was strange ..."

"Those ... shiny things ... what were they?"

"They seem to have an awareness."

"Yes ... and did you see what happened?"

361

"Yes, but I didn't quite understand it ... some seemed to combine first with each other and then attach to something ... something else ... what did you think? You've studied many of the ancient texts."

"All the ancients talked about an invisible conscious spirit element ... the ancient Egyptians called it *heka* or *ba* ... an invisible force that created the universe and allows the great spirit *to communicate* with humans."

"Communicate?"

"Exchange information."

"Does this ability survive the body's death?"

"Yes ... and the Greeks had a word, *suneidon*, which means to be aware *together with* ... the gods."

Yufeng shrugs, then remembers something.

"Oh ... I forgot to tell you, Panda said something, she followed LF into the void and saw those glowing spirits."

"So ... what you're thinking is those shiny things were these conscious spirits?"

He nods and says,

"The Greeks and even the Chinese and others believe that everything starts from some small elements ... the Greeks use the word *atoms*."

"But you don't agree?"

He shakes his head.

"Maybe for rocks ... but how can you get a bird, a horse, or a baby ... from the same basic element as a rock? When we go into the void, we don't see rock spirits ... we see conscious spirits ... *conscious aware* spirits."

"What was that joining that we saw?" she asks.

He looks at her with a smile and rolls his head, then she laughs.

"Oh, I see ... just like all the different parts of the body are connected into a larger system ... these conscious spirits attached to the different body parts and combine to form the spirit body at the same time ... and it's inside *and outside* of the physical body ... just like that warrior who lost his arm."

"Yes! And before the before, there were just these conscious spirits throughout the not-so-empty emptiness."

"Yes! And you think they created the physical universe?"

"Maybe ... but I haven't worked that out yet."

"But that answers one of our questions ... what is a conscious *being* ... it is the combination of these small conscious spirits into a conscious spirit being ... which is attached to our physical bodies."

"But what is the point of it all?"

"And how could we see them glowing? There is no light in the void."

"That is what I want to ask the grandmothers in Gobekli Tepe. I think they are not telling us everything."

"And I think it has something to do with what Scorpion learned ...
outside the Enso gap."

87 Gobekli Tepe

When we leave a place like Mother Nature's Garden,
We leave a part of us behind, in a deep memory ...
And only by going back,
do we find that golden thread again.

The golden tablet from Genghis Khan allowed them quick passage through the Mongol conquered lands. The long trip to Gobekli took several months; fortunately, the lands around Gobekli Tepe had not been invaded by the Mongols and looked much the same. It consisted mostly of small hillside villages ... the larger cities having already capitulated or destroyed.

Even when they were approached by Arab soldiers, the Great Khan's tablet carried the threat of impending death, plus they still had papers from the Sultan from their first trip to these lands ... thus they were allowed to pass easily to their destination ... the Garden of Mother Nature and the grandmothers ... where the old women welcomed them like their very own grandchildren.

They enter the grandmother's home, and it looked the same as on their first visit ... the same flowers and plants and the grandmother herself appears the same ... ageless.

Yufei starts to say something, but the old women held up her hand.

"Relax, breathe our fresh air, drink our fresh spring water first ... let your spirit flow and merge ... then the words will come."

They do as she instructs, and their bodies, minds, and spirits enter into a comfortable relaxation zone ... relaxed and aware ... of everything around them.

Their eyelids become heavy, and they close them ... and then ... without realizing how ... they are in another *place (they are not sure of the words to describe this as a place, or a space?)* ... but it's not their physical bodies, it's their spirit bodies, which are more apparent now to them ... and the *place*, is not a physical place, but rather a dimension-less *space*.

Then a *message* comes to them ...

"You have done well."

"You have placed the Divine Plan before your own needs."

"We will answer your questions."

This later is not a question ... rather a statement.

There is a pause as Yufeng *connects* to Yufei and they become united. Then *they* ... as one spirit ... think ...

"Who are you?"

"We are all those flickering lights you saw in the void ... but we are not separate, we are all connected ... we are One Universal force."

"We are many, but we speak as One."

"We understand about the need to defeat the dark manifestations, but what is the point of our being?"

"What do you really want to ask?

"If we can't defeat the dark manifestations, what is there?"

"As you work to defeat the darkness, you will become more like us."

"And what is that?"

"We are the cosmic beings of the universe."

"The stars and bodies?"

"No, no, no ... much more ... we create the stars and bodies ... we are the vastness, the infiniteness ... the one consciousness ... that creates and shapes the universe."

"What will happen to us?"

"You will be like us."

"But we will retain our knowledge?"

"You will know all knowledge, but more importantly you will retain the knowing ability ... like how to carve jade to expose the beauty inside ... but without the confusion of the mind, you will see the beauty clearly ... you will see and understand everything."

"What will we feel?"

"Everything like before ... even though you will have no body, everything will feel real."

"It's like your drawing ... that we embedded into your mind from birth."

"What drawing?"

"The Enso ... don't you understand what your father was trying to tell you?"

Yufei shakes his head, not sure.

"Inside the circle is this temporal-world illusion ... outside is the real 'conscious universe' ... this world of matter, the circle, is just the illusionary background which enables your experiences ... like the shadow puppet screen ... the screen is immortal, but your shadowy experiences allow you to grow."

"You cannot comprehend the spiritual universe with your physical senses ... you must go outside the Enso ... to see reality without the interference of the mind."

"Here you have form ... there you are without form ... and are immortal."

Yufei smiles,

"Like Plato's cave."

"Yes"

"And the end result of the Divine Plan?"

"Isn't it obvious? Just as animals and plants have evolved on earth, so man must evolve ... once the potential has built up to the tipping point."

"You will make that final jump beyond thought to becoming ... a celestial being ... like us ... without form ... immortal ... didn't Gugu tell you?"

Yufeng looks at Yufei and smiles,

"He must have forgotten."

"And then what will happen? ... What if the Darkness prevails over this world?"

"Then it will be up to you to create a new galaxy of stars."

"Your perception was distorted before ... 'you,' your spirit ... was never inside your body ... that was an illusion ... it was always outside ... you just couldn't see it before ... you must change your way of thinking ... you must change your perception."

"When you change the way you look at things, the things you look at change."

"You will realize that you are a consciousness that lives in space ... like LF."

Then they both laugh, "Of course ... like LF."

"This is the Secret Pathway."

"Secret Pathway?"

"After death, the departed spirit can be reborn/reincarnated, or the spirit agents can disassemble and later become a part of a new spirit body or ... as a few have done, start a new galaxy of stars and worlds."

"How?"

"To create a new galaxy ... you must understand the things you've learned and then dive deep (shedding your form) and pass through the Enso opening."

"And then, first you visualize space, which in itself, creates time, then you visualize the already pre-formed new galaxy ... of stars and planets and organisms."

"Already pre-formed?"

"Yes, of course ... just like the rock finding the shortest way to the bottom ... we have been teaching mankind for eons, but they fail to see."

"You must sense it without the interference of the mind *(or any physical perception) and then ... you will enter into your new Conscious galaxy, where, as of yet there is no past-present-future ... then the worlds will form, and their histories will unfold backwards."*

"Just like that?"

"I am simplifying it for you ... it will take eons in regular time, but in our Consciousness, there is no-time, so it will seem to happen quickly."

"At first, within this new galaxy. there is just a vast void filled with an infinite number of conscious spirits with an infinite number of possibilities and then, through altering their awareness, you cause an exchange of information with some conscious spirits ... you influence those conscious spirits with new information containing new possibilities ... about the new galaxy ... which will lead to desired probabilities (outcomes which have not yet been actualized)."

"These probabilities are of pre-actualized events, which manifest as new worlds, organisms, plants, animals, sentient beings ... a new galaxy full of life ... when you provide the awareness, the conscious spirits cause the manifestations. Therefore, you must learn how to modify your awareness in the way that you recognize what you want to occur."

"And we are the key?'

"Yes, because there is no new galaxy without your awareness, and no awareness, without your conscious spirit."

Later ... they don't know how much later ... they awaken in the grandmother's cottage. There is some food waiting for them and they are both very hungry. They eat ... without talking. Then they get up and stroll outside. The scene is the same as when they arrived. Some elderly ladies tending their gardens, flowers blooming, butterflies and bees flying from bloom to bloom.

Their steps take them to the mountain spring where they cup some water in their hands to drink. It refreshes their minds and bodies.

Finally, Yufeng looks at Yufei and says,

"Well, that was a lot to digest."

Yufei laughs,

"So, what now?"

Looking around, he spots the grandmother walking towards them.

"I think we're about to find out ..."

They rise and greet her, and the elderly woman asks,

"Did you find your answers?"

They nod. Yufeng says,

"It's hard to comprehend."

"Don't try, dear."

Yufei asks,

"What now ... for us ... and Panda?"

The woman smiles.

"Panda will be fine ... she will have her own tests, and she will guide the khans for many years, helping to open up the flow of information to the west."

"And us?"

"For a while, I think your pathway leads to the west, to try to help them."

"Help them ...?"

"Become more enlightened ... less superstitious."

"Why?"

"Their countries and their minds have been overcome by the dark manifestations ... you need to help open their minds ... to let in some fresh air and sunlight."

"Us?"

"And others ... like your mentor, Gugu ... we have cells in all lands fighting the darkness ... working together."

Yufei looks at her and asks,

"But it is not going so good?"

She sighs and shakes her head.

"Not now ... but we look at things in the long term."

Then she holds Yufeng's arm and walks her over to some new flowers.

"Let me show you these flowers, they may be helpful when you travel west."

After they leave, Yufei stares at the spring water flowing down the slope ... remembering all the connections with water in the ancient beliefs.

88 And Then

As souls change into water
on their way through death,
So, water changes into earth.
And as water springs from earth,
So, from water does the soul.

After they leave Gobekli Tepe, they journey west to Antioch on the coast and take a coastal trader to Constantinople first. There, they visit the Venice trading station and book passage with a boat going to Venice.

First the boat stops at the island of Negroponte, then sails around the Peloponnesian Peninsula to another Venetian station at Koron, then Korfu, Ragusa and finally Venice. For Yufei and Yufeng, time seems to fly without really touching them.

Yufeng is amazed at the city built on the water. They stay at an inn near San Marcos piazza and then go visit the Polo family, who welcome them warmly.

Andrea asks them,

"What are your plans?"

Yufei tells them confidentially,

"I'd like to travel to Florence and Rome to learn more about them ... maybe later to some other western nations."

Andrea cautions them.

"You must be careful. Many of these people are suspicious of strangers ... especially enlightened ones."

"In Rome, who is in control?'

"Nominally it is the Pope, but in reality, the nobles and cardinals are equally powerful and many a pope has mysteriously died ... it is a political maze."

"Who is the current pope?"

"He is an Italian, taken the title, Gregory IX. Be very careful of him ... he just authorized an expanding *Inquisition* of heretics."

"Heretics ... what are they?"

"Anyone who opposes the church of the One True Merciful God, Jesus Christ. They are crucified or burned at the stake."

Yufei looks at Yufeng, shrugs and shakes his head. She is thinking ...

(*another kind of epidemic*)

First though, they ride to Florence, stopping at inns along the way, through the Po valley and through the foothills where they meet some skilled pre-Renaissance craftsmen. Along the way and in Florence, they avoid the churches and Florence is one of the commune cities that governs itself. With the bloom of trade, Florence has prospered in textiles and especially banking ... many think that Florence was the birthplace of the Western Renaissance, but it happened in the whole of northern Italy ... Pisa, Lucca, Modena, Parma, Ravenna, Bologna, Cremona, etc. ... *but aside from the pre-Renaissance activity, they also see the Inquisition rearing its dark head everywhere.*

Florence is a bustling and rapidly growing city center. Curiously, they notice many (over 150) high towers scattered all over the city. When asked, a local tells them that they were each built by a prominent family as a show of status ... or by a group of merchants or even just a neighborhood ... and they give the towers nicknames (Black Rooster, Wolf's Head).

While traveling, they don't go unnoticed and narrowly avoid some traps. Later they will be far more cautious ... after they attract a network of clergy spies looking for them.

They circle back to Venice and meet the Polo's again.

"We want to head back east. We feel we are needed there, and your western worlds are all new to us and we need time to understand them."

"No problem, there is a coastal trader heading to the Crimea tomorrow ... I'll talk to the captain ... but rest assured he will have a space for you ... so tonight we can have a dinner together.

"Great!"

Later in their room at the inn, they discuss the real reason for leaving so soon.

"Did you feel it?"

Yufeng nods,

"Yes, in every town, it felt like there was an epidemic there but not a physical disease ... a spiritual one."

"Yeah ... I just wanted to get away from it."

"Me too ..."

"Let's rest."

"Okay."

But sleep is hard to come that night as each one wrestles with how to battle a spiritual darkness.

The next day they sail back to the Venetian's station in the Crimea, buy some sturdy horses, and catch a trade caravan heading to Karakorum.

Meanwhile, after they leave, the new Pope, Gregory IX, pushes his dark manifestation called the Inquisition to cover all the Latin countries, ... to root out and incinerate all unbelievers of the one true faith ... *Christianity*.

Meanwhile, Tarim saves Harim before some very destructive battles in Chang An between the Mongols under General Muquali and the Jin ... although he did have to tie him up, gag him, and lead him out in the night on the back of a donkey. It took Harim three days to stop cursing his son-in-law ... and that was only after Beersheba admonished the old goat for causing so many problems ... *but that is another story ...*

And in Lhasa, one of Dorjie's bodyguards gives Chen a map that he found when they raided the dark monastery. The soldier didn't understand the writings or the significance but in their private room, Dorjie helps Chen translate it.

It identifies other dark cells in other cities ... Kucha, Samarkand, Merv, Kabul, Baghdad, Constantinople, Kiev, Novgorod, Rome ... so many across the worlds.

Chen ER is first to realize the importance of this information.

"We need to get this to Yufei."

"I'll go with you. The kids will be safe here."

"Rather than go all the way to Avarga, maybe we go first to Kucha to ask Tarem where they are now."

"Okay."

89 Tolui Regency

Good and ill to the physician
surely must be one,
since he derives his fee
from torturing the sick.

In the Mongol camp, things settled down during Tolui's regency. No new war campaigns are planned ... awaiting the formal appointment of the new Khan. Everyone tends to mind their own families and personal business.

When Yufei and Yufeng return, there are some small 'welcome back' dinners ... and then their lives settle back into their previous routine as well.

Yufeng and Panda refit and resupply the medical teams. Yufeng holds some meetings to share medical lessons of the field hospitals with the other physicians ... while visiting the still-recovering warriors.

Yufei and Tariq practice with Subedei on the training grounds but Yufei seems distracted about something.

"Is something bothering you uncle ... is it me?"

Yufei is startled by the question.

"No ... no ... it's nothing about you ... there's just something in my mind I can't reach."

"When that happens to me, I talk to Panda ... why don't you talk to Yufeng?"

Yufei smiles at the youth.

"Good idea ...see you later." then he walks off towards his tent, hoping to find Yufeng there. Luckily, she is there, having just returned herself.

Yufeng senses her husband's mood and asks,

"What is it?"

"Those things the grandmother told us in Gobekli ..."

"What about them?"

"I still have a hard time getting my arms around them ... how about you?"

"Me too but we are different."

"How?"

"I don't worry about it ... I think it will rise up into my awareness when we are ready."

He smiles and hugs her.

"You are right ... sometimes I struggle to find the answers too quickly."

"I have an idea ... but I need to talk to Subedei first."

"Okay ... I need to talk to Panda and Tariq too."

His eyebrows rise.

"Oh ... any problem?"

"The usual between two young people who love each other."

Yufei laughs and hugs her.

"You are better at those things than me. I am just a traditional country boy."

She laughs and kisses him, and he leaves.

I wish it were so easy ...

***

Later Yufei finds Subedei on the training fields, directing his commanders.

"Still drilling them?"

Subedei turns and smiles.

"Never enough time. I feel we will need all our skills soon."

"The Jin?"

"And out west."

"I want to talk to you about that."

"The west?"

"Yeah ... I'm thinking of making another spying mission with Yufeng to the Latin countries."

Subedei is warm to that idea but asks.

"Didn't you just come back from there?"

"Yes, but it's a big area and there are parts I haven't explored. We need to discuss the likely targets."

"Yeah ... I was thinking the same, but I didn't know who to send ... you two would be good for that."

"What things are you most interested in learning?"

"Let's go to my tent and talk ..."

They talked well into the night and the destiny of Yufei and Yufeng took another turn back west.

90 Yufeng and Sari talk

Hungry livestock,
though in sight of pasture,
need the prod.

Yufeng has found Panda working with Sari.

Mongke, the oldest son, is 21 years old and a young commander now, and is off training his warriors.

Kublai, the second son is 14 ... and divides his time between warrior training and, at his mother's direction, reading the various tomes from the captured lands. He is good at both.

Helegu, 12, is a want-to-be warrior who admires his oldest brother, Mongke, and follows him around to learn warrior skills.

The youngest, Arik Boke, is 10 and still learning basic warrior skills. Panda assists in their training on several levels.

On this day, the children are busy, as is Panda, which is how Yufeng hoped it would be so she and Sari could talk.

Sari has a warm smile when she sees Yufeng walk up. They exchange sincere and warm greetings.

"Greeting to you too, Sister ... no children?'

"Ha ... the one minute in the day! Are you looking for Panda? I think she's giving Arik Boke more bruises near the river ... haha."

Smiling, Yufeng shakes her head.

"Actually, I was looking for you."

More alert now as the two women share a cautious awareness ever since Tolui was appointed Regent ... much to the displeasure of Toregene.

"Oh ... maybe we should go inside."

Yufeng moves closer.

"Outside is okay ... easier to spot someone coming near."

Then Yufeng goes straight to the point,

"Toregene wasn't happy with Tolui being appointed Regent."

Sari just smiles and Yufeng asks,

"Should we worry?"

Sari shakes her head as she pretends to look around.

"Tolui can handle her ... and we have allies with some of the other princes."

'And when Ogedei returns and is khan."

"Ha! Probably even better ... he hates her!"

"He's told you that?"

Sari moves closer.

"Several times ... and that new girlfriend of hers, Fatima."

Then she says something that will come back to haunt them.

"Don't worry about them as long as Ogedei lives."

"What about their oldest son, Guyuk?"

"He hates his mother also ... she's such a witch."

"Okay but we still need to be careful."

"I know ... was there anything else?"

"Well, there is one other thing I'd like your advice on."

"Panda and Tariq?"

"Yes ... what do you think is the problem? Maybe I am too close to her and can't see the obvious. Is it her role as shaman?"

"No ... that's just an excuse she uses. Panda is afraid."

"Afraid? Panda?"

"Yes ... of losing something ... maybe her independence ... or having to compromise her life for a man."

"Haha. I've raised a fierce warrior instead of a traditional girl."

"Haha ... she's just like you!"

"Any ideas?"

"Well Tariq can't use the traditional Mongol method."

"What's that?"

"Grab her, throw her over his horse and ride off to ravish her."

The two women roll over in laughter thinking of poor Tariq.

'Any other ideas?'

"Maybe ... they have to work it out themselves, but around camp, there are too many distractions ... here's what I think ..."

And they talked for another hour before embracing and Yufeng walking back to her tent to mull over how to implement the plan.

ENSO - THE JOURNEY BEYOND

(first Yufei needs to talk to Tolui ...)

91 Panda & Tariq go north

After talking to her co-conspirators, Yufeng is ready to execute her plan.

Tolui sends a message for Yufeng and Panda to come before him. On the way there, Yufeng slips and twists her ankle ... *apparently* badly.

Panda is helping Yufeng, who is limping with the injury, into the leader's tent.

Tolui welcomes them and explains to them.

"We have reports from the grandmothers that there are some forests to the north that have some miracle herbs ... while we are at peace right now, it is a good time to scout this out."

"You two are the most knowledgeable herbal experts, can you go?"

Panda looks at her mother who is having trouble standing.

"My mother injured her leg .... but I can go."

"Alone?"

"I have no problem going alone."

Yufeng speaks up,

"You shouldn't travel alone ... you should bring someone with you ... maybe Tariq."

Before she can object, Tolui says,

"Good it's set. You and Tariq set out tomorrow to the north forests ... Sari will give you a map and direction."

They bow and leave. Yufeng's leg starts to feel better.

Early the next morning the two set out.

They ride north for several days into the frozen lands (Siberia). Lana runs next to them but sometimes, hearing a silent call runs off to investigate but quickly comes back.

After a few days, they are riding with no thoughts, carefully watching the ground ahead for any animal holes when Panda pulls up short with a blank expression.

Tariq asks her, "What?" but gets no response ... then he realizes she's somewhere else.

Inside ... Panda's former pet, LF's spirit, comes to her with a flash warning,

"Danger coming!"

Panda comes out of the trance, looks down at Lana who is looking back behind them and growling. She turns and sees ominous black clouds behind ... coming quickly towards them.

"Black Blizzard!" she yells at Tariq, and they gallop fast to try to outrun it, but the darkness keeps gaining on them.

They franticly look around for shelter on the open steppe, but there is none.

Then Panda gets another visit ... from LF ... showing her the way.

"There! Behind that low mound."

Panda rides to the mound but only sees a small animal hole on the downwind side. Pointing to the hole she commands the wolf,

"Lana dig it bigger! ... Quickly."

Lana furiously widens the entrance and continues inside until she stops and backs out slowly.

They dismount, grab their packs, and let the horses loose.

Tariq is immediately at the small hole, making it bigger using his knife as a shovel ... as the snow falls faster and faster.

Finally, it's big enough for them to crawl inside, opening into a snow fox den.

They enter cautiously as they spot pairs of eyes watching them.

Tariq lights a small torch, and the sight surprises them.

Lying on the ground is a dying female silver snow fox, and next to her, trying to feed, are two newborn cubs.

Panda makes some animal sounds to calm them. The mother fox has no energy and welcomes the strange help, but soon passes away. Panda scoops up one cub and hands it to Tariq and then scoops up the other one.

"Life is hard on the cold steppe."

Tariq asks, "How did you know this hole was here?"

"A friend."

Tariq asks no more and sets out to block the entrance with their packs and other brush.

When he is done, he turns and sees Panda giving the cubs to Lana for feeding ... then afterwards lying back with the two cubs sleeping on her lap.

Tariq smiles, "We have to get married now ... we have two children."

Panda smiles, "Maybe you are right ... it is a sign."

"Tomorrow, I will pray to the Blue-Sky God."

The next day, the sun is out, and Panda goes on top of the mound and offers prayers and a burning offering to the Mother Goddess. She starts a small fire with some birch branches that she found and watches as the smoke rises in a thin straight plume.

When she comes down, she smiles at Tariq, who is holding the two white cub foxes ... they make a high-pitched sound, which sounds like human babies.

Referring to the straight smoke plume, she says,

"It is a good omen."

And that was how they got engaged ...

However, fate has different plans ... for when they return to Avarga, *Tariq's younger brother, Baraq, is waiting there ...*

92 Beersheba dying?

Tariq's younger brother, Baraq, has a sad face. Yufeng gives Panda a serious look.

Tariq runs up to him and asks,

"Little brother why are you here? Is something wrong at home?"

The youth tells him that he must come home ...

"Mother is dying."

'What? How? She was strong when I last saw her."

"I don't know ... she told me to find you and bring you back."

Tariq turns to Panda,

"I must go home."

She nods and tells him,

"I will go with you."

She looks at her mother.

"Your father and I will go with you. We were planning a new trip west."

Although Tariq might have preferred to travel alone, Panda welcomes her mother's company, and they talk constantly about marriage.

Tariq is preoccupied with thoughts and emotions about his mother though and keeps aloof ... even from Yufei.

Yufei is left to spend time with the younger brother, asking questions about his mother and father. The boy seems evasive at times, leading Yufei to suspect the youth is not telling the entire truth about his mother.

Later when he is alone with Yufeng, he passes on his suspicions. Yufeng looks at him and says quietly,

"You think he's lying? But why?"

Yufei shrugs,

"I don't know. We'll find out next week when we get there. How's Panda?"

"She's okay ... she worries for Tariq, but the marriage decision is behind her and it's like a huge weight removed from her shoulders."

"She is happy with the decision?"

"Yes ... immensely ... it was like a small animal dam holding back a large river of emotion ... once a small branch was removed, the water rushed through, and she realized the beauty in it."

Yufei hugs Yufeng,

"I remember that feeling."

Yufeng smiles,

"You mean when my mother told us we *had* to get married?"

Yufei smiles,

"Yes ... after that I felt that same rush of floodwaters that Panda is feeling ... how about you?"

"Yeah ... it was the same."

Then looking around and seeing the others busy, she says,

"Come closer husband ... it's been several hours since I felt your embrace."

Yufei laughs,

"You sound like Lana when she has her itch."

She laughs and goes to slap him, but he catches her arm and embraces her.

93 Wedding Plans in Kucha

From the strain of binding opposites,
comes harmony.

When they arrive in Kucha, the whole family comes out to greet them ... including a *healthy* Beersheba.

Tariq runs up to her and prostrates before her in obeisance.

"Mother ... I am so happy to see you well! What happened? Did you have a miracle cure?"

Beersheba raises him up as the others are watching ... a bit confused, except for the younger brother who is stealing away ... slowly.

"What do you mean?" then with a dawn of awareness, she spots her younger son and asks him,

"Baraq. What did you tell Tariq?"

"You told me you were dying ... to see Tariq."

Beersheba shakes her head and rolls her eyes.

"It's been years since we've seen him. I told you to try to get him to come home *before* I die."

Tariq wants to strangle his younger brother ... the others are stifling their laughter. Yufeng goes up and hugs her *sister*.

"It is good anyway ... our two children have decided to marry ... this would be the perfect spot to do that."

Beersheba looks at Tariq,

"Is this true?"

He lowers his head shyly and nods,

"It is true ... if you and father consent."

Then she looks at Panda.

"And you agreed to marry my lazy son who is always riding off chasing horses?"

Panda bows before her soon-to-be mother-in-law,

"It is my wish too mother and we believe we are blessed by the gods."

Tarem steps forward and announces,

"Then let's get this wedding celebration organized! Yufei and I will be in charge of the spirited drinks ... you women take care of everything else."

Yufei and Yufeng laugh. Beersheba looks at Panda.

"Do you see what you are getting into."

Panda smiles as she and her two mothers go into the house to plan a wedding ... but just then a knock is on the outer gate.

Tarem tells one of the children to open the gate.

Standing outside is Chen Er and Princess Dorjie. This just adds to the celebration and confusion for Chen when Yufei asks him,

"You've come for the wedding?"

Chen is confused but goes along with the bantering.

"Of course! Did you think we would miss it?"

Dorjie is confused until Yufeng explains that Panda and Tariq will get married.

So, while men do what they do best ... boast and drink; the women plan a wedding for Tariq and Panda.

And while they are drinking, Chen shows Yufei the map of the dark cells.

They talk late into the night and from it, *a plan evolves* ...

Later, in their room, Yufei shows Yufeng the map and points out the black cells along their route west.

"But we can't attack them by ourselves." she says.

"No ... but look ... many of them are where the Mongols have already conquered and have garrisons ... we can utilize them."

She sighs and he asks,

"What?"

"Is this going to be our life ... a life of war?"

He sighs as he holds her.

"I think we have been given this map for a purpose ... and it's part of the Way."

"But where is it leading?"

"I don't know ... and that is what has been troubling me for some time now."

She sees the concern on his face and notices the wear on his body also ... comforting him she says,

"Let's get through the wedding first and take each day as it comes."

"Okay."

They talk no more that night, but the wolf's ears perk up through the night on every new sound.

94 The Wedding

Harmony needs low and high,
as progeny needs man and woman.

To Yufei, it seems like the entire town of Kucha is at the wedding ... merchants, princes, craftsmen, and common people ... and whether it is the lavish spread of free liquors and foods or the musicians and dancers ... everyone is in it for a good time and to wish the bride and groom well wishes ... everyone is happy ... and most are drunk, including the proud parents. Yufei and Tarem seem to be leaning against each other holding each other up. Yufeng and Beersheba may laugh at them, but they appear to be slurring their words a bit too. Only Panda and Tariq seem to be holding themselves sober ... for later.

Wine makes the soul succumb to joy.

From being an only child, Panda now has two additional parents, two more brothers and 4 sisters. Kucha custom (at least Tarem's family) has it that after the traditional Kucha ceremony, the wedding couple is to ride off to the hills with a tent and fur bedding to consummate their union. Before they depart, Yufeng has some last words of advice for her daughter.

"Panda, when it happens it is wonderful ... there is a little pain but then the joy is overwhelming ... your husband may not know what to do, so it up to you to help him ... understand?"

"Yes, momma, Mother Beersheba and the local grannies have been talking to me for days now. It seems all their husbands were inexperienced donkeys when they got married."

Then they both laugh as Yufei staggers up.

"What are you two laughing at?"

Panda hugs her father and says,

"Nothing baba, just how lucky us women are to have brave men to protect us ... right mama?'

Yufei turns to his wife who is stifling her laughter. Then she hugs Yufei.

Beersheba comes up and hugs Panda and tells her,

"Oh ... one last thing, don't make an announcement when you are going to leave, just leave ... it'll be better that way ... for you, believe me."

"Okay ... I'll go find Tariq now. We will leave soon."

Just then Dorjie comes up and hugs Panda,

"Fierce Panda ... be gentle on poor Tariq this night ..." then she stifles her own laughter.

Panda bows down to the ground to these three ladies.

"Honorable mothers, aunties, sisters ... I am blessed to be related to all of you. I wish fortune, blessings, and happiness for all of you and your children."

Dorjie raises her up,

"Rise Panda, enough of that ... go find your husband and enjoy a dance before you sneak out."

Panda bows and walks off.

The women look at each other and then to Yufeng.

"She is a good girl ... you are fortunate."

Yufeng smiles,

"We are all fortunate ..." then adds laughingly,

"And Tariq is the most fortunate ... come on ladies, I think we need to go take care of our husbands ..."

As the celebration and dancing continues ... and no one seems to remember when Panda and Tariq disappeared. One moment they were there dancing and the next moment they were not ... but their absence didn't slow down the partying ...

That only stopped when all the guests were gone, and the three men were drunk asleep in a pile on a rug. The women gently dragging their inert bodies off to their separate beds.

Meanwhile, after making their escape almost without notice (one younger child started to shout but stopped when Lana stared at him with a fierce look).

They rode for over an hour into the hills to a small tent that Tariq had erected during the day. Inside were lavish furs and enough supplies for several days.

Panda was pleasantly surprised.

"Our new home, husband?"

At a loss for words, he mumbles, "For a few days."

Panda hugs him warmly,

"It's beautiful." Then a bit teasingly she asks,

"But husband what will we do here all night?"

That completely freezes Tariq's vocal cords until Panda comes up and slides his outer clothes off.

"Don't worry husband, I think we will be fine."

No more is written of that night except that the clouds discharged the rain many times.

95 Plans

The river, where you set your foot just now is gone -
those waters, giving way to this ... now this.

The first morning after the wedding, everyone is recovering slowly ... except the women who rise early and get the children to start the cleanup while they prepare a late breakfast.

Around midmorning Yufei, Chen Er, and Tarem stumble out of their bedrooms, shading their eyes from the much-too-bright desert sun. Their mouths move but what comes out is incomprehensible. The wives help them to their seats and offer some warming tea to settle their headaches.

By midday, the yard is cleaned up, the children fed and the men able to converse in sentences. The discussion quickly centers on the map unfolded on the rug before them.

Chen Er looks at Yufei and asks,

"What do you think?"

Pointing to the map, Yufei says,

"This is Samarkand, the Mongols have conquered it, and we can get support there for an attack on the black cell near there."

"Who's in charge there?"

"Batu, Jochi's son ... a good warrior and ... a friend."

Chen Er asks,

"What else do you know?"

"Subedei thinks that when Ogedei returns and is chosen as khan, he will launch campaigns further west."

"So, some of these other cells may fall within the Mongol campaigns?"

'Possibly ... but not directly as many of the cells will be off in remote areas ... so we will need to get their assistance."

Tarem adds,

"A cornered animal is most dangerous."

The others agree and nod.

Yufei adds,

"Yufeng and I will head west on a *reconnaissance* mission."

"How far west?"

"First across the steppes, the old Khurasan lands and then Gobekli Tepe, then Arab lands, Greece, and finally to the Latin countries."

"Wow!" then seeing Dorjie outside, Chen Er rises and goes talks to her. When he comes back, he is smiling.

"Count us in."

Yufei is confused.

"In what?"

"Dorjie and I will go with you."

"What about your children?"

"They are old enough now to seek their own destinies ... they will be fine."

Then they both look at Tarem, who shrugs and smiles.

"I'm getting too old for this ... my body aches every morning ... some of my body parts aren't working properly ... who will take care of all my girlfriends ... maybe it will rain ..."

Finally, Yufei says,

"Good, Tarem is in also."

Tarem holds up his hand in desperation.

"But let me tell my wife ... she may kill me!"

They all laugh.

Later around their dinner, Yufei lays out the plan to the wives ... omitting Tarem's participation. Beersheba knows her husband and offers him his face-saving escape.

"Husband, are you going to let your friends face these dangers alone? Or are you going to stay and sit in the market with the other grandpas boasting about how virile you still are?"

The others stifle their laughter as Tarem gives in.

"Okay ... if you insist, I will accompany them ... only because you wish me to protect them."

That taken care of, Beersheba asks,

"What about the lovers?"

Yufeng tells them,

"I talked with Panda before they left .... she and Tariq will go back to Karakorum to counsel the new Kahn ... Sari will need her help to counter that witch Toregene."

"Will she be safe?"

"We think so ... everyone knows she was chosen by the Great Khan and Ogedei and the other princes are fond of her."

Meanwhile in their honeymoon hut, Panda and Tariq are packing up also. They have already discussed their plans to return to the Mongol camp. Panda will stay close to Sari, while being available to Ogedei for counsel. Tariq will continue his training under Subedei.

Panda is happy ... not just because of the weight being lifted from her, but also seeing the confidence grow in Tariq after the wedding. He is even more protective of her now ... even though in a fight, she would be the stronger adversary for any foe.

They let their Mongol horses follow their inner instincts home to Karakorum and their destiny. Camping each night in a different spot, usually close to a stream ... with Lana guarding their tent through the night ... her ears perking up with each strange sound from inside and outside the tent.

96 Samarkand

The eye, the ear, the mind in action,
these I value.

After Kucha, the Silk Road runs on to Kashgar, then to Samarkand, Bukhara, Merv, Isfahan, and Baghdad. Along the trail the travelers relate tales of their recent exploits and marvel at each other's stories.

A month later, they arrive at Samarkand and are warmly welcomed by Batu, Genghis' grandson, an able leader, and one of Panda's original wolf kids. Over a private dinner, they discuss the map of the dark cells and their mission to destroy them.

Batu is excited to assist them and asks them to go along when they execute their first raid. Yufei agrees but warns him to keep everything confidential because these dark cells have spies everywhere. Batu nods in understanding.

"Just let me know what you need."

Yufei smiles and they clasp arms Mongol-style in agreement.

After settling in, they go out to the streets to see what they can find out about this monastery, as the map was vague about the exact location.

In Turkic Samarkand, Tarem is best suited for this type of intelligence gathering. He quickly makes friends with other merchants, who have heard his name in Kucha. During an all-night drinking bout, after the liquor has loosened their inhibitions and fears, he learns everything they know about the monastery.

He learns that the monastery is in the hills, about half-day ride west towards Bukhara. It is set on the side of a mountain with a steep cliff in the back ... hills on both sides and only one narrow trail leading up to it ... making it a difficult place to attack. However, Tarem has learned that there are some small trails up the backside of the mountain, which would give them a possible access point above the monastery.

They start to organize the raid with the help of Batu ... who suggests they send a reconnaissance party first.

Yufei asks Batu,

"Have you met any locals who you can trust?"

Batu thinks for a minute, then smiles.

"No ... but I have an idea ... here's what I propose ..."

They talk well into the night considering all alternatives to ensure none of the rats escape the trap.

The next day, Batu brings a local herder, Ahmed, to Yufei.

"He will help you."

Yufei asks, "How do you know we can trust him?"

"I have his wife, mother, and children as my guests, until the mission is over ... and if successful, a nice reward promised."

Yufei smiles.

Yufei tells the others,

"I'll go first alone with Ahmed."

Yufeng starts to object but Yufei assures her it is the least suspicious way.

Later that day, the two men ride out, one posing as a merchant, the other, a goat herder ... traveling on the same road to Bukhara. The herder is very nervous and afraid for his family ... Yufei tells him everything will be fine as long as they complete their mission without getting noticed. They ride the well-worn trail for several hours and then take a less-used side trail north into the hills.

About an hour later he halts and motions for Yufei to dismount ... they are getting close and there may be guards. They walk off the trail and tie off the horses behind a rock outcropping.

Yufei asks about the layout of the canyon ahead. In the dirt the man draws a crude map ... steep hills on every side, which offers protection from a mounted assault, guards posted on some of the hills, but they change often ... and in the middle of the valley, on the side of the tallest mountain, is the monastery, which has two wings, one for living and the other for worship.

"Can we see everything from one of these hilltops?"

The man nods.

"Yes, but we need to pick one without a sentry."

Yufei rolls his eyes (*smart for a herder*)

"Okay, let's bypass the first hills and approach the second line of hills slowly."

The man nods and they steal around the first line of hills ... which they see are guarded. The second line of hills are not guarded, and they offer a good spot to canvas the entire canyon. Yufei starts to draw a detailed map while Ahmed keeps watch. Early in the morning the sentry guards are refreshed, and the replaced guards retire to the secondary administrative building.

Yufei pauses and considers everything again before folding up his map and indicating to Ahmed to go down the mountain ... that they are done. The herder has a weak smile, for to him, it won't be over until he and his family are away from this dark place.

Later Yufei will tell the others that although it is guarded, he didn't sense a heightened alertness with the guards. On the way back he devises a strategy which he now shares with Batu and the others.

"We bring 10 warriors with us ... more will just cause attention ... and they ride out the East gate and circle around to meet our smaller party on the West road."

"Tarem and I will each take out the sentries on the left line of hills, while Chen and Yufeng take out the hill sentries on the right side."

"Once they are eliminated, half of Batu's men, ... will rappel down the back side of the mountain with long ropes and attack the monastery from the back, while you and your remaining men charge up the trail yelling. When the dark men come out the front to defend against you ... that's when all of us will cut them down with our crossbows.

Batu smiles.

"It is a good plan ... Subedei has taught you well."

Yufei smiles ... *Subedei and many other hard lessons.*

The next day everything is ready, and the first contingent of warriors rides out the East gate heading east towards Mongol homelands, while a small group of *merchants* ride out the western gate towards Bukhara.

A few hours later they all meet up and head northwest on the trail heading north. After another hour they stop and go over the plan again. The first group to depart are the five warriors going around to the back of the mountains. Yufeng and Chen will each go around the east set of hills to the peaks and eliminate the sentries there. Yufei and Tarem will give them all an hour and then eliminate the sentries on the west peaks.

Then he tells his group of four, that once they've eliminated their sentries to work their way to either side of the monastery with a clean arrow shot of the front of the monastery. Then Batu will charge up the valley, to start exterminating the rats. Then he tells Batu that his men are welcome to all the spoils except any documents which may be valuable in finding other cells.

Batu smiles.

"They will appreciate that."

The mission goes according to plan ... almost ... some dark warriors fight better than others, but in the end, they all perish. Only the local witch proves especially difficult ... as witches tend to be. When Yufei and Yufeng enter her inner sanctum, it is dark and they don't see her at first, dressed all in black and blending with the darkness. Then all at once a series of torches are lit, momentarily blinded them ... they quickly recover their senses and see the black witch holding a shiny bronze *fengche*, much like a child's play windmill, only larger, and shining a flickering light at Yufei's eyes.

The witch starts chanting incomprehensible words. Yufeng just laughs and tells her to submit but this just causes her to laugh and spin the windmill faster.

Yufeng is amused until she looks over and sees Yufei writhing on the floor in the middle of a seizure.

Quickly connecting the events, Yufeng launches several arrows at the witch killing her and causing her to drop the windmill.

Batu enters and seeing Yufei, asks,

"What happened? Was he shot? Poisoned?"

Yufeng tries to usher him out,

"Please keep the others out, I will take care of him."

Batu sees the tears in her eyes and quickly turns and pushes the others out to plunder.

Yufeng kneels down and takes his pulses, then makes him comfortable as the seizure recedes.

(There must be a connection between that flickering light from the windmill and his seizures.)

After five more minutes, Yufei starts to come around but is still groggy.

"What? Where? What happened?"

"It's okay, all the bad guys have been killed."

"The witch?"

"She joined the others."

"What happened?"

"I think it was that flickering light from the windmill ... it triggered your seizures."

He tries to stand but is still weak .... When he has the seizures, every muscle in his body goes rigid ... now, afterwards, they are weak. He leans on Yufeng, and they walk out. Batu is there guarding the door and looks at Yufeng.

"He'll be okay ... your men can plunder that room but be very careful of traps and poisons ... and save any documents or maps for us."

"Okay." he says, then turning to one of the warriors,

"Arin, help Yufei back to his horse ... don't worry, you'll get your share of the plunder."

The warrior knows that they always divide up any plunder fairly, so he gladly agrees to render assistance.

After removing any treasure and documents, they put a torch to the monastery.

From scanning the documents, they realize the threat is bigger and better organized than they first realized.

All-in-all though they are pleased with the mission and Batu is impressed with Yufei's strategy and execution. On the ride back to Samarkand, there is the usual warrior after-battle bantering about who killed the most enemy ... when they ask Batu who he thought killed the most, he silently nodded towards Yufeng ... and their respect for her grows a hundred-fold.

As she rides, her thoughts go backwards to her father, an innocent man killed, by similar sinister men that she killed today ... without anger.

Later at a victory dinner, Batu tells them they are all welcome to campaign with him when he goes west against the European kingdoms. They acknowledge the complement but inside secretly hope it doesn't come to pass. During the party, Batu brings out the herder, Ahmed, and rewards him with gold and silver and reunites him with his family.

Yufei tells him.

"My advice is not to show anyone your wealth and to move your family to distant lands."

The man bows several times, amazed at his good fortune and that he is still alive. He gathers his treasure into a sack and leaves.

Yufei remarks,

"A happy man."

Batu laughs, then asks Yufei,

"What are your plans for these other cells ... they seem to spawn everywhere."

Yufei shakes his head.

"It's a bigger problem than we imagined ... I'm not sure."

Then looking at Yufeng,

"We need to discuss it."

(... *with the grandmothers*)

97 Ogedei & Panda

Things keep their secrets.

In Karakorum, Panda and Sari are at the side of Ogedei every day ... usually just sitting there ... only speaking when the khan asks for their advice ... either collectively or individually, on whatever topic the khan desires.

Ogedei is a good man, very humble, and freely takes the advice of Sari, Panda, and the seasoned generals ... especially Subedei. He respects all beliefs and is a big jovial man ... who likes to drink, a little too much, with fellow warriors and always with his younger brother, Tolui, whom he loves.

Toregene, however, is a constant irritant ... she has her own personal agenda and is furious when Ogedei listens to others instead of her. And by her side is an equally sinister woman, named Fatima, a Central Asian captive in the service of Toregene, and now given broad powers by Toregene.

Ogedei appoints capable administrators from the various captured and migrant scholars. One such adviser is Yelu Chucai, a Khitan refugee from the Jin empire, who joined the Mongol administration. After judging each other up for a few weeks, he and Panda become mutually respectful friends.

After one regular strategy session, the two stroll out of the khan's tent together. Yelu asks Panda if they can talk privately ... as he wants to learn more about her views. They find a quiet spot near the river. Karakorum is now the new capital of the Mongol empire and undergoing a building boom, funded by endless wagonloads of tribute and treasure. Palaces are being built as well as mosques, churches, and temples.

With a wide sweep of his hand, he asks her,

"What do you think of all this?"

Panda reaches down to pet Lana and the two white foxes.

"We prefer the open steppe ... don't we Lana?"

"Lana?"

"The wolf's name."

"I've heard that you have a gift with animals."

She laughs,

"And I've heard you have a gift of speech."

He looks at her questioningly.

"You don't trust me?"

She looks straight into his eyes, probing inside ... causing him to blink.

"I trust animals more than people."

"Why?"

"They are less devious."

"Do you think I am devious?"

"I think you can be if you want to be ... like now."

Taken aback by the woman's frankness, he asks her,

"Now? How so? What have I said or done?"

"It is what you haven't said."

"Like what?"

"Like why you wanted to talk to me ... like what you want for your people."

Protesting, his voice raises a bit.

"But I haven't ... you cannot know what is in my heart!"

She smiles a knowing smile ... and then he knows ... the stories about her are true ... she can see into a person's heart.

But then she adds,

"But I haven't seen or heard you give false advice to the khan ... but if you do, I will alert him."

She smiles again.

Then he clears his throat and tells his story so that she may understand him better ... about his Liao-Khitan homeland in the northeast, invaded by the Jin, about his father and grandfather who were generals and ministers for the old regime ... and then under the new Jin regime, in order to help their people ... about his acceptance of the reality of the Mongols spreading over the lands and his desire to make it less destructive as possible.

In the end they establish a friendship of sorts ... sharing some similar goals to protect the ordinary people as well as the educated and crafts people.

As he walks away, Sari walks up and asks Panda,

"What do you think of this Khitan?"

"I'm not sure ... I don't sense any evil ... his words though sound too perfect though ... if they are true, he could be a good ally to have ..."

"Ally? Against what?"

Panda motions with her head towards Toregene and Fatima walking in the distance. Sari nods and Panda asks her,

"What do you think ... will they overplay their hand?"

Sari shakes her head.

"She's too cunning for that ... just be alert."

Then Panda asks,

"What else do you hear?"

"Ogedei is planning a major campaign to the west."

Panda thinks ... *(mother and father are on the way there)*

And then another thought enters her senses ...

And Tariq will go ...

98 Return to Sanliurfa

Many who have learned from Hesiod,
the countless names of the gods and monsters,
never understand that night and day are one.

Our western travelers don't stop in Merv or Isfahan but continue through the foothills of the Caliphate, avoiding Baghdad, and on to the headwaters of the Euphrates and Tigris Rivers ... to the ancient lands of Gobekli Tepe.

First, they go to Sanliurfa and get rooms in the same crude *expensive* hotel as before. The small town seems unchanged from their earlier visit, decades ago. The postmaster has changed ... the old one retired with his family, richer than when he arrived. The traitorous prostitute left one night after she realized she had alienated both Arab kingdoms *and* the Brotherhood. Many new faces ... and one old familiar face ... Ahmadil, the zaria merchant's shop is in the same spot and he is sitting outside ... looking the same, with a welcoming smile on his face.

As they walk up to him, he rises and greets them.

"Last night my wife told me we would have guests soon."

Yufei and Yufeng's eyes water as they greet him like their own grandfather.

Yufeng hugs him and says,

"You look the same grandfather! How do you do it?"

"Haha ... you are teasing this old man ... I just ride my donkey to the valley every day and drink the delicious spring water. Will you go there?"

"Yes, soon ... but first my husband wants to go to Gobekli Tepe."

"Oh ... so you married him?"

Then looking at Yufei he asks,

"Is he trained?"

She laughs,

"Almost." and then they laugh except for Yufei, who asks.

"All these years you still make the zaria shipments to China?"

He nods.

"They are my best customer."

"Not to the west?"

"Ha! They still think diseases are the punishment of the gods for their sins."

Then he stares into the clouds and adds,

"But their day is coming ... when even their gods won't be able to help them."

"The invasions?"

The old man shakes his head.

"Worse ... a black plague ... but don't worry ... it is still many years away."

Then looking around at the others, he says,

"I remember these two, but who is this beautiful princess with them."

Yufeng laughs and introduces Princess Dorjie.

"This is my brother Chen Er's wife, Princess Dorjie from the mountains in the sky."

The old man goes to bow but the princess stops him and instead bows to him.

"It is my honor grandfather; my husband has told me how you helped him years earlier. Our lands will be forever grateful to you."

Embarrassed, the old man says,

"It was nothing ... a small business dealing ... merchant to merchant."

Then looking around he asks,

"When will you bring the children?"

Yufeng is surprised.

"Our children?"

"Of course ... who else's children ... and the grandchildren too ... they all must be taught."

Looking at Yufei, she says,

"Soon grandfather ... it is still dangerous traveling and that is why we have come to talk to the grandmothers. We have information on many dark cells across the lands. We are not sure how to deal with them all and seek advice."

He sighs knowingly.

"It is what we have feared ... you go to Gobekli ... I will tell the grandmothers that you will be coming soon."

Yufeng then takes the old man by the hand as though walking with him towards her horse, but in reality, wanting to ask him a sensitive question.

"Grandfather ... only my husband and I have gone to the valley ... what about our friends ... can they come with us?"

The old man turns and asks her,

"Do you trust them with you daughter's life?"

She nods.

"Then it is okay. But please explain the importance of secrecy to them ... for many other people's lives also depend on it."

"I will and thank you grandfather."

"Thank you for all that you have done my child."

99 Gobekli Tepe

Many fail to grasp what they have seen,
and cannot judge what they have learned,
although they tell themselves they know.

After they leave the old trader, Tarem, Chen Er, and Dorjie retire to their rooms to rest, while Yufei and Yufeng ride out to Gobekli Tepe. There they find the same monoliths as before and sit at the same spot as the first time.

As they sit a *spirit* elder walks up silently ...

"*Welcome.*"

The two smile and bow to the elder sister.

"*You two have done well ... but, you have questions?*"

Yufei asks,

"When will it end, this struggle with the dark?"

"*It may never end ... can you accept that?*"

They look at each other and shake their heads.

"No ... that is why we have come ... can you help us?"

She quotes a saying from an ancient philosopher ...

The cosmos works,
by harmony of tensions,
like the lyre and bow.
Therefore, good
and ill are one.

"*Now do you understand?*"

They shake their heads, still confused.

"They are the same?" Yufei asks.

"*Don't worry so much ... it will come to you ... in time.*"

Then she points to a unique looking tree carved in the stone ...

Strange, Yufei thinks ... *I don't remember that tree from before.*

"When up was named, down was created.
When yin was named, yang was created ...
and when the Tree of Life was named,
the Tree of Death was created."
"Where there is life, there is death.
where there is good, there is evil ...
it is one of the laws of this universe."

Yufei asks,

"So, we can never rid this world of evil?"

The elder sister shakes her head and says,

"The best we can do is to try to control it ... like a gardener does with weeds."

"But why ..."

"Why was it this way?"

"Yes."

"It wasn't intended ... it came about as a consequence of setting up the universal natural laws."

The elder woman sighs, shrugs and asks,

"Do you have any other questions?"

Yufei looks at Yufeng who asks,

"And us ... do we fight the darkness through eternity? Is that our destiny?"

The elder smiles,

"No, child ... when you go to the valley tomorrow, you will learn more."

With that final comment she fades away, and they stare at each other.

Finally, Yufeng asks,

"What do you think?"

Yufei shakes his head.

"I don't know ... let's head back to town."

"Okay ... but first I want to burn some incense."

"Okay."

After lighting the incense, she places it near one of the monoliths and notices the carving of the strange tree on the side of the stone stele.

She asks Yufei,

"I don't remember that carving from before ... do you?"

He looks at it and shakes his head.

"No, and I think I would because it is a strange looking tree."

Then he asks her a strange question.

"Does this happen often to you too?"

"What?"

"That events from the past seem to change ... from how you remembered them."

She thinks about that for a moment and says,

"Sometimes ... what does it mean ... we are getting old and forgetful?'

"Or maybe the past is changing ... because of some new future."

100 The Grandmother

Under the comb
the tangled and the straight path
are the same.

The next day, with the others, they visit the grandmother in the Mother Nature Valley.

She is waiting for them and she too, looks ageless.

"Welcome back ... come in ... bring your friends ... have some cool spring water."

They go inside and sit on some mats, relaxing and drinking the cool spring water.

As their minds drift, they see in the back, a tree, which neither remembered from before, like the one carved on the monolith.

When asked, the grandmother says it has always been there.

Then Yufei remembers a legend Moses told them from their holy book ... about a tree in the Garden of Eden ... but he can't remember the significance of it.

Yufeng asks,

"Grandmother, people ask us why there so much conflict in the world?"

"Child ... it is as the ancients say,"

> "Dogs bark at what they cannot understand."

"But sometimes, when I see all the dead from the invasions, I wonder when it will all end?"

"Do you still have the bracelets?"

Holding out their arms with the bracelets they both say,

"Yes."

"Look at them ... closely."

Yufei has a gold dragon ouroboros bracelet with a zig zag lines (water flowing in a stream) on one side ... and the dragon is coiled in a circle, like the Enso ...

Yufeng's is a similar silver snake ouroboros bracelet with circles carved in it ... like the ripples when you dive into the water ... and like the ripples of time in the fabric of life.

They show the others their ouroboros and the grandmother asks,

"Where is the beginning? Where is the end?"

Yufeng replies,

"There is no beginning ... no end."

"In the world of no-time," she explained, ...

Eternity is not endless time ... Eternity is no time.

Look outside the circle,

This inside world is just a drama.

Only by going beyond the Enso,

can the essence of time be grasped.

From outside the Enso ... the past, present, and future

are not three different places ...

They are a single happening here and now.

When you live in this moment profoundly,

you experience time not serially but simultaneously,

not as three but as one ... and then,

You wake up to the knowledge that this moment is eternity.

Yufei then understands something ...

"Those lines ... like the stream from Siddhartha."

Yufeng's eyes also light up,

"And the circles ... like ripples in the water ... from the stone tossed into the stream ... remembering from the future, the shortest way to the bottom."

Looking out at the Tree of Life, Yufei adds,

"Endless ripples of time."

"It is not possible to step into the same river twice."
(Plutarch)

The others remain silent until Princess Dorjie says,

"In the high mountains, near Mt Kailash, the rivers of the world are born from beneath the earth. The waters have gone in all directions to form mighty rivers since the beginning of time. People have come and people have gone ... but the rivers continue to flow."

As she finishes, the others wait for her to continue. She pauses and looks at the grandmother.

"Will it always be so?"

The grandmother looks at her and says,

"No one has ever asked me that question before."

They all wait as the grandmother chooses her words carefully.

"For you and your children and their children ... and even their children's children it will be so ..."

"And after that?"

"Beyond that, it is unclear ... a fog of war and of new weapons of destruction beyond description ... there are different futures ... people could destroy even the planet we all live on ... or ..."

There is a gasp from the visitors.

"What? The evil could destroy this world?"

"Evil, ignorance, greed, ... and a lack of wisdom."

This is not the news they came to hear as each one tries to digest a lump in their stomach.

The grandmother breaks the mood and invites them out into the garden. There ... in the center ... is the tree they saw engraved on the monolith. Tall ... maybe 4-5 meters high, with many branches with a large fruit on each branch. They all stare at the fruit.

The grandmother tells them,

"You can pick one and eat it if you want to."

They each pick a fruit and try it ... the taste is sweet and delicious ... more delicious than any fruit they have ever tasted before.

And their lives changed without them knowing ...

Inside ... they seem at peace, and ... out of the time field. Individually, their minds drift ...

RICHARD HOWE

Is this the same fruit
that Adam and Eve were forbidden from eating?

Is this the same fruit
that Sun Wukong was forbidden to eat.

101 The Ortogh

Without injustices,
Justice would mean what?

Back in Sanliurfa, they say goodbye to the old trader, and head to Acre along the eastern seacoast to catch a ship to Venice.

In the port, there is the same mix of pilgrims headed to the holy city ... and more merchants taking advantage of the opening of the Silk Road. Chen Er and Tarem mingle with these traders, learning what items are being traded now ... and what dangers still arise along the trade routes. The traders are all in awe of the Mongol ortogh and ask how he obtained it, but he dodges the question like any trader would.

Dorjie and Yufeng wander the streets looking at personal items, jewelries, and any medicines. Yufei tags along with them but occasionally stops to talk to some pilgrims and ship captains. Finally, he finds a Venetian ship captain who knows the Polos and is sailing the next morning back to Venice ... with stops along the way.

That night, over dinner, they discuss the next part of their journey ... port-hopping to Venice. observing the trade opportunities, as well as the port defenses, troop strengths, etc. Just then though the captain of the Venetian ship finds them and tells them some bad news.

"A ship collided with my ship on the dock ... I have to stay and get it repaired ... it could take weeks ... but I found another ship for you ... it's Venetian"

Handing him a paper,

"Here's the ship name ... the captain is expecting you."

Yufei thanks the captain for finding them and after he leaves, they all look at each other. Yufei says,

"I don't like last minute changes caused by accidental collisions ... do you?"

They all shake their heads.

"We don't have to leave quickly ... let's check out this new ship tomorrow."

"Tarem, you ask other traders if they know this ship. Chen, you and Dorjie do the same. Yufeng and I will meet the captain."

The next day, while the others go about their tasks, Yufei and Yufeng board the ship and find the captain, who seems to be a genial man.

They explain their desire to go to Venice and the captain agrees to a price ... he tells them, that he will also stop at several of the Venetian stations along the way.

After they leave, Yufei looks at Yufeng, who says,

"I couldn't detect any darkness or evil intent in him ... he seems honest. How about you?"

"Yeah ... that's what bothered me ... he seemed like someone else I met a long time ago."

"Who was that?"

"A religious pilgrim along the road to the Holy City."

"But what bothers you?"

"I can't explain it ... it is as though their individual minds have been *washed away.*"

"Did you sense a darkness?"

"No ... let's talk to the others and see what they've learned."

They meet up in a tavern near the port. The others all came up positive for the ship and captain. Chen, though, senses Yufei is looking for something.

"What is it? Did you find something about the ship?"

He shakes his head.

"No ... more of a premonition."

"Do you want to find another ship?"

"We asked ... there isn't another for at least a week here ... maybe longer. We could travel up the coast to Constantinople and find one there ... but it's longer."

Yufei looks at Yufeng and the others and they decide to stay with this one.

The next morning, they leave the tavern and board the ship. The captain is pleasant and welcomes them warmly. The crew seems typical, and they cast off.

The ship stops at various Venetian stations along the route: Rhodes, Crete, Cephalonia, and Corfu.

At all these stops, Yufei takes copious notes about fortifications, pastures, and other trading opportunities.

Instead of continuing to Venice, the captain makes an unplanned stop at Split, also a Venetian station, but a smaller port set up against steep seaside hills.

Yufei asks the captain if he normally stops there.

"Not usually, but I received a message before we left to pick up some passengers here."

"Oh ... anything that will delay us?"

"I don't think so ... it was just some church envoys."

"Oh ... how long will we be in port?"

'Just overnight ... I'd recommend staying on board though ... this port can get rough at times."

"Okay ... thanks."

102 Split

That night, based on the captain's warning, they decide to stay together as they wander through the town ... until they find a nice local restaurant on the side of the slope, overlooking the small bay. It is early so they get the best table on the deck railing, facing the sea with a fantastic view.

Dorjie laughs and says,

"I'm dying to try more of the Venetian food ... it is so different from my roasted yak meat."

They all laugh.

A waiter comes to the table, and they ask what the special is tonight.

"Fish, fish, and fish ... clams and pasta ... fish in tomatoes and cheese ... and fresh vegetables with squid fried in olive oil."

Chen Er says,

"We'll have them all!"

Just when the waiter leaves to place the order, a group of clerics arrives. They start to look for a large table, but our party already has the biggest and best. One of the clerics goes to see the tavern owner ... there is an argument ... the cleric points to one of their group who is dressed more elegantly and then he points to Yufei's table. The restaurant owner shakes his head. The cleric raises his voice and slides the man a gold coin. The restaurant owner looks beaten and approaches our group's table.

"I'm sorry but I'd like to ask you to move to another table ... we can put two tables together over there ..." he says, pointing to a side corner.

Dorjie is the first to erupt.

"Do you realize I am Princess Dorjie of Lhasa, and these are emissaries of the great Khan!"

"Yufei show him your tablet!"

Yufei pulls out the tablet and the man is terrified but the Mongols are far away, and the church ever-present.

"I'm sorry but ..."

Then Chen Er and Tarem stand and brandish their swords.

"Let them take the table from us ... if they can."

Now the owner is fearful of an even worse outcome.

Yufei tries to diffuse the situation by walking over to talk to the cleric.

"I'm sorry but that table is already taken."

The cleric is boiling now.

"What? Do you know who this man with me is? He is the archbishop of ..."

Before he can finish, Yufei thrusts his sword at the man's throat.

"Look ... I don't care who he is ... we can kill all of you in 2 minutes ... so what will it be die here or eat at another table?"

The prelate, hearing this, whispers to his cleric and they back off but not until the prelate casts a searing glance at Yufei.

Back at the table they ask him what he told them. He laughs and says,

"I told them to back off or I would send my wife at them."

They all laugh and enjoy a sumptuous dinner. When they leave, they give the owner a large tip. The owner gives Yufei a message,

"Be careful of those men ... *they are from the Inquisition.*"

Yufei shrugs it off ... *I have defeated far more dangerous men.*

And they all leave to board the boat for the night.

The next morning though they are in for a surprise.

103 Venice

*Sound thinking
is to listen well and choose
one course of action.*

As the boat gets ready to part, Yufei asks the captain how long it will take to get to Venice.

"Half a day ... if the winds are good."

"What are you waiting for?"

"Our other passengers aren't here yet."

Just as he asks,

"What other passengers...?" the group of clerics from the night before, arrive and board the boat.

The others of their group watch the clerics board also as Yufei says a silent prayer for favorable winds.

During the short sail to Venice, the two sides avoid each other on purpose ... however, if glances could kill, the decks would be awash with blood.

The captain doesn't understand until Yufei explains what happened.

The captain then makes the sign of the cross several times saying a prayer.

"You must be careful of that man ... he calls himself Cardinal Ripaldi ... and claims he is a relative of the new Pope Gregory."

"These are men of the all-merciful Jesus Christ?"

"You know our savior?"

"A little ... but why should I fear a priest?"

"Have you heard of the Inquisition?"

"A little."

"This man is thick in it. Ask your friends, the Polos ... they will explain it ... just be careful, this is not Mongol lands."

In Venice ... the two groups disembark and go their separate ways. Yufei's group heads to meet Andrea Polo, and immediately renews his friendship with the entire Polo family. Andrea asks the purpose of this trip.

"Chen and I are merchants, with a Mongol *ortogh* (trading authorization), while Yufeng is interested in learning more of your medical practices."

Chen asks what the Venetian buyers are looking for.

Andrea replies,

"Mostly gems, pearls, spices, ceramics, lacquered items ..."

Then Chen asks if they accept notes and paper money.

They tell him yes and direct him to the Jewish Quarter where later he finds an intermediary branch of the Jewish money-exchangers from their earlier trip to India and Damascus.

As they walk around separately, they see signs of the Inquisition ... and it's not a pleasant site ... families dragged out of their homes to be tortured. Their property confiscated by their accusers.

They learn that the new pope, Gregory IX, is spreading this scrounge throughout Europe. For now, though, trade trumps theocracy in Venice as Venice is a republic run by the trading merchants and a noble hierarchy ... not the clergy.

They wait until they return to their hotel rooms to discuss their findings.

Yufeng relates about their medicine ...

"They are way behind the Arabs, Chinese and Indians. They still believe diseases are caused by sins."

"Did you encounter any trouble?"

"Only once ... when a cleric started listening while I was describing an operating procedure. When the physician saw him, he cautioned me to be quiet. Later he said, operating on people was condemned by the church ... and there were no women physicians."

Yufei's eyes grow large,

"You didn't do anything ... did you?"

Smiling demurely,

"Of course not, my little rascal ... your little obedient wife cause trouble?"

He rolls his eyes as the others stifle their laughter.

He turns to Chen,

"What's new at the Arsenal?"

"The Polo's introduced me to a ship builder, and we have a meeting tomorrow ... before you came back here, I was sketching some ideas ... this inland sea is not as fierce as the open oceans so I think I can make an even faster ship than the newest Falcon."

"And then?"

"I'll check the costs tomorrow, but I think we brought enough jewels to finance it. Then once it is built, we search for a captain and crew ... the Polo's can help with that ... and then we make a trading run up through the Venetian stations to the Crimea, Acre, or Constantinople."

"For trade?"

"For fun ... and trade ... and scouting the territory ... they won't suspect a Venetian trader."

The next day, Chen heads off to the Arsenal, Yufeng and Dorjie to the medical monastery, Tarem to the markets to see what items are best for trade and Yufei to visit the city leaders with the seal from the khan and then to see an eminent scholar trained in Greek and Roman philosophy.

104 Venetian politics

As all things change to fire,
and fire exhausted falls back into things,
the crops are sold for money spent on food.
How, from a fire that never sinks or sets,
would you escape?

In 13th century Venice ... and much of western kingdoms, there is the overall regional politics and there is the local city politics ... the former under the auspices of a king, princes, large landowners, or a papal legate, and the latter organized as a commune made up from the local populace.

Venice, as well as a few other northern Italian cities, is different in that it is a republic which also has a local hierarchy, all controlled by various factions of trade merchants ... each seeking increased power and wealth at the expense of the other.

In other regions, power and wealth is based on the land holdings, with the two largest landowners being the king and the church. The church though, through various family appointed 'bishops' sometimes extends its influence over the lands of the wealthy families.

In Venice though, the merchants who trade over the seas are the major force in the city and their wealthy merchant families who sell the goods to the northern lands select the city leaders.

In other Latin lands, there are the few royal kings (Francia, Germania, England), local barons, and then there are the papal states controlled by the Church, and finally the communes ... free cities controlled by the locals ... and on the eastern horizon ... the ever-present Arabs.

It is easy to say that all are corrupt ... just as it easy to say that a pack of wolves are vicious ... or it's just their survival mechanism. But they seem to be all currently flourishing from new trade and banking, especially in the northern Italy cities.

At first, Yufei's group is welcomed and are protected by virtue of the letter from the Khans and because they helped the Venetians against the

Genoans in the Crimea. Later though, jealousies surface and ... they become targets. Not that the church or the leaders are all inherently corrupt ... just that darkness uses greed and lust for power to corrupt people.

Some days, Yufei accompanies Tarem as he scouts for trade merchandise ... other days he watches Chen and the shipbuilders who start to build a new ship from Chen's plans. Chen has already hired a captain, recommended by Andrea Polo, to select a new crew for the sea trials. As the ship is being constructed, many ship builders stop by for a friendly glass of wine and to make mental notes.

Wary of the Inquisition, both sides avoid questions of religious beliefs ... in the Arsenal at least.

One day the group decides to take a two to three-day reconnaissance inland ... ostensibly to see the historical sites. They ride a few hours and rest in Padova but continue on to Verona for the night. They tour the ancient Roman ruins, many of which are still intact. The next day they ride to the south of Lake Garda, to a small, fortified peninsula called Sirmione. They spend the night in a small hotel there, next to the fortress and, in the evening, go out in a small boat to enjoy a beautiful night on the lake.

Yufeng cuddles next to Yufeng and Dorjie to Chen ... Tarem watches from the back working the oars.

Yufeng says to the others,

"I could live here ... the people are friendly, the food is different, but delicious and the countryside is breathtaking."

"Me too." adds Dorjie.

Then Yufeng notices that Yufei, Chen, and Tarem haven't joined in their assessment. She asks,

"What is it ... you men don't agree?"

Chen speaks,

"Many of the things you mention are true but ..."

"What?"

"Yufei, can you explain it to them?"

Yufei says,

"All the things you mention, we agree on, but there's something underneath that makes us less comfortable."

"What?"

"The culture and belief systems are different ... particularly their church, which is very powerful, and can destroy any dissent, quicker and more ruthlessly than a Mongol horde."

"Even the people are afraid to talk about certain things ... and the stories of the Inquisitions are frightening."

"But we've battled darkness everywhere."

"But not like this ... it's a darkness wrapped in spirituality. To fight it, you appear to others that you are fighting their god, which makes you a heretic."

Dorjie nods and says,

"He is right ... in Tibet, we can't openly fight the sects ... it's seen as going against Buddha ... and if we do, we are cast as the evil ones."

"So, if we try to save them from their misguided beliefs, *we* will be cast as the dark ones."

"Do you think it's like that everywhere in the west?"

"From what I hear, the church is gaining acceptance and power throughout all the western kingdoms now."

Yufeng adds,

"At least in the Arab lands, they were tolerant of other people's beliefs."

***

In another part of Venice, the prelate Ripaldi is screaming at his acolytes.

"You haven't found them?"

Prelate Rinaldi is tall for an Italian, with a thin narrow face with a mustache and goatee, pointed on the downward end. He throws a candlestick at one of them, who easily ducks as he is used to the prelates' tantrums.

"One of them was at the arsenal for the past two days, others went to the markets, and then this morning they all rode out over the causeway to the mainland."

"Where did they go?"

"We don't know ... we're not allowed to have horses ... so we couldn't follow them."

He throws another large object from his desk.

"I want to know everything about them when I return from Rome ... do you understand?"

"Yes, your highness."

A vicious sneer crosses his face as he tells them,

"When I come back from Rome, I hope to have incredible power to crush all heretics and anyone else standing in my way."

Evil comes in all forms ...
even draped in the sacred spiritual garments
of the loving Savior.

105 Venetian sailing

The wolf was a symbol of Mars,
the Roman god of war.
Rome's founding myth tells of
a wolf bringing up Romulus and Remus,
the founders of Rome.

When they return to Venice, Chen's new boat is ready for its first sea trials. The captain, Mario, has assembled a skilled crew and they have been getting familiar with everything while still resting in the Arsenal slip.

Two days later ... an auspicious day ... the boat is blessed, wine is poured over the bow for good luck, and they sail out in the calm seas that day. Everything goes smoothly ... some leaks in the watertight holds are discovered and quickly patched. The sails and fittings are tested and found to be of good quality. Mario is very happy that he signed up with Chen as this is the fastest boat on which he has ever sailed. Later in the day, they return to port and plan the next day's sailing.

They gather in the evening in their rooms and Yufei brings out several maps.

Chen asks,

"Where did you get these?"

"Don't ask."

"This I brought from Master Su, this one I acquired from Damascus, this one in Crimea, and this one, secretly from the Polos."

They start to study the maps.

"Beyond the western seas it is largely blank ... so I don't see any point in sailing off the end of the world ... at this time."

Tarem laughs and adds,

"The goods from the Silk Road go through the Levant ... (pointing) here, here, and here ... then to one of the city states on the peninsula ... Venice, Genoa, Naples mostly ... then they head west and north to the buyers there."

"Our trade contacts are all from the east ... since we can't sail on land, we should cover all the waters along the eastern coasts of the Inland Sea and the sea around Crimea."

Yufei adds,

"Let's save Crimea for another trip ... I think we should explore along the coast to Greece, the eastern islands, and then to the west."

"What about Egypt?"

"Maybe later ... Mario can make a run there."

'Why west?"

"Maybe we can bypass the city states and reach the northern buyers direct by sailing out the Pillars of Hercules and up the Francia coast."

Chen looks at the maps.

"Maybe ... it could work ... but we would need to build a fleet for protection ... or cooperate with an existing fleet .... like Venice or Genoa."

Yufeng looks around.

"So, we go tomorrow?"

Everyone smiles and say,

"We go!"

The weather the next day was bright and sunny. They have all come to like Captain Mario, a happy, jovial, short but well-built man ... a man well-respected by the other captains of Venice and by his crew. They efficiently load all the supplies for their trip as well as some trade goods ... textiles from northern Italy and ceramics from nearby Faenza.

The Polos are there to give them a good send off as well as several other merchants ... and ... some dark robed clerics, concealed in the shadows.

Chen Er has gone over the general route they want to take, and Mario is familiar with all these waters.

Yufei asks him,

"Which ports will we be stopping at?"

"The Venetian stations along the east side of the inland sea (Aegean) ... Split, Ragusa, Corfu, Modon, Crete, Rhodes, Antioch, Cyprus, ..."

"How long will it take?"

"Depending on the winds and how long you want to take ashore ... three to four weeks."

"Good ... can you show me on my maps where these places are?"

"Sure ... my uncle is starting to make maps of this area too ... when we get back, I'll introduce you to him ... he would be interested in the lands to the east."

"Good!"

Chen has designed this ship to be his new flagship, and a comfortable trader for him and his friends ... so, there are three sets of living suites ... one for him and Dorjie, one for Yufei and Yufeng ... and Tarem will bunk in the captain's cabin with Mario ... they make quick friends and Mario looks up to Tarem as an older brother.

Although the watertight holds are not as large as his Falcon, there is more deck space for easy on-loading and off-loading of goods which they buy and sell in the various inland seaports.

Finally, they embark ...

Their first stop is Split, the small port along the coast they visited on the incoming journey, with trade routes going inland all the way to the great inland river, the Danube. Over dinner at the same local restaurant, they discuss their plans. The owner is effusive in welcoming them and rushing the service on them ... probably hoping no church spies see them.

Yufei starts off,

"Chen, your new boat is fantastic! The most comfortable and fastest boat I have ever sailed on!"

The others quickly agree as Chen is embarrassed by the compliments.

"Actually, it wasn't all my ideas, a lot of it comes from their long experience in these inland seas ... there are still some fierce storms that come up quickly when the boats are further offshore."

Dorjie says,

"Then let's stay close to shore on this trip honey ... I only know mountain gods to pray to ... I have no sea gods."

He laughs and hugs her.

"No problem ... I know all the sea gods."

Yufei teases him,

"She said sea gods ... not goddesses!"

They all laugh and then Yufei gets serious.

"So, what have you gleaned about these Latin lands so far?"

Yufeng starts off,

"Well, their medicine is ancient and superstitious ... they have forgotten all that the Greeks had passed on ... there's little I can learn here ... and I'm a bit afraid of sharing my heretic views."

Yufei agrees,

"The same spiritually ... it's this one church belief or we burn you ... after we take all your properties ... there's little individual spiritual quest ... that is the exclusive domain of the priests ... it is disgusting and I am afraid, it will take centuries to outgrow ... but maybe ..."

"What?"

"Maybe if the Mongols conquer all the western lands, they can open up the people's beliefs and usher in a new, more open thinking."

Tarem speaks up,

"As far as trade, I see it mostly coming from east to west ... going back in the other direction it's mostly gold and silver heading east ... and some finished goods ... if you are interested in trade."

Tarem asks Chen a question.

"Chen ... why were you so interested in building a ship here? Are you interested in opening a trading business?"

"Only as one option ... my main reason was to pick the shipbuilder minds about their ships ... if we need to build ships to defeat them, we will need that knowledge."

Yufei asks him,

"And what do you think?"

"I think it could be done ... we capture a major port, one that's close to forests for timbers ... like this one ... bring in the craftsmen and start building a fleet of superior ships. We could control the inner sea lanes and with that choke off the lifeblood of the city states, communes, and western kingdoms."

"The Latin Peninsula is completely fragmented since Roman times into city states, communes, and some encroachments by western and northern kingdoms ... and Rome is a powerless papal state. They could never hold back the Mongols. Give me one tumen of warriors and I could conquer the whole peninsula."

The others are quiet and just stare at Chen. He pauses and looks around.

"What? You asked me what I thought."

Yufei laughs,

"You sounded like Subedei."

Then they all laugh ... except for Yufei who has spotted a cleric watching them from a distance.

"Don't turn, but we are being watched ... by a cleric."

Dorjie asks him,

"Are you afraid of one cleric?"

"No, but the insidiousness of their Inquisition makes me uncomfortable."

"But what can we do?"

"I don't know ... if the Mongols don't sweep through all these lands ... then I fear the darkness will only spread further."

Yufeng mentions something,

"Do you remember what the old grandfather said in Sanliurfa?"

They look at her.

"He mentioned a devastating plague sweeping through these lands in the future."

They nod ... remembering something they hadn't focused on before.

Just one of the many cleansing possibilities.

106 Papal Politics

If everything were turned to smoke,
the nose would be the seat of judgment.
Thus, in the abysmal dark,
the soul (and evil) is known by scent.

In Rome, after a week of impatient waiting, Prelate Ripaldi finally gets an audience with his *'cousin'*, the new Pope Gregory IX.

Ripaldi bows to the aging pope, his eyes searching for any signs of weakness.

"Your Eminence ... congratulations on your elevation to the seat of Saint Peter."

Gregory just shrugs as he reads some documents that Ripaldi had submitted.

"How is your health *cousin*?"

Gregory looks up wondering if it's still accurate to call a person nine generations removed as a cousin.

"So, your proposal is to unify all the Inquisition activities under one bureau ... which you call the *Holy Order of the Inquisition?*"

"Yes, your Eminence ..."

"How will you operate the activities?"

"Similar to the civil authorities for cover, but more thoroughly ... to root out all heresy."

Gregory knows the man's ambition has no bounds, but this one thing coincides with Gregory's ambitions also ... but he fears Ripaldi a bit.

"And you want to lead this new bureau?"

'Eminence, there are many qualified people ... I am just offering my services to the Church."

Gregory nods and calls to his scribe and hands him Ripaldi's proposal.

"Prepare an official papal bull following these guidelines ... but with a few changes."

Ripaldi's ears perk up. (*changes?*)

Both men look at the pope.

"Put the Dominican Order in overall charge for executing the order ..."

Ripaldi starts to object but stops.

"Have *them* select Grand Inquisitors for the various kingdoms and countries ... and offer our recommendation of Prelate Ripaldi to the Master of the Dominican Order as one of the primary Grand Inquisitor for the Latin Countries ... but for the overall Inquisition work, the Dominican order is under the Master of the Dominican Order and his Dominican Provincials (ruling council)."

Then looking at Ripaldi,

"Is that satisfactory with you?"

Feeling trapped he agrees.

"Most assuredly Eminence, appointing the Dominicans is a masterful choice to lead this ... they are highly respected by the lay people for their ascetic frugality, teachings and empathy."

What he doesn't say ...

And are easily manipulated... like sheep.

107 The Inner Sea

Pythagoras may well have been
the deepest in his learning of all men.
And still he claimed to recollect details of former lives,
being in one a cucumber, and one time a sardine.

The other Venetian stations are similar ... Ragusa, Corfu, Modon, Crete, Rhodes. Antioch is an open city, still run by Crusaders with a large and influential Greek colony. They also see there some of the once-feared Templars ... but the city is trade oriented and is a major port now for the east-west trade.

Chen ventures into the Jewish quarter and finds bankers who belong to the same guild as the bankers he found in India, Damascus, and Venice. Yufei bumps into many pilgrims headed to the Holy City. Yufeng meets some physicians where she learns of Moses Maimonides passing away several years earlier ... they discuss medicine, but she learns nothing new ... the Arab Spring of medicine and learning has faded ... replaced by religious mandated medicine ... only prayer to Allah will heal you from the diseases caused by your sins.

Yufei studies the fortifications and the Templars ... remembering their fierce reputation ... but the ones he sees, seem less fearsome ... the good times taking more toll on warriors than the hard battles. These Templars seem more interested in strengthening their personal fortunes than their fighting ability.

Later, after a nice dinner, they retire with their own thoughts. Chen and Tarem thinking trade, Dorjie about her country's future in a changing world and Yufei and Yufeng having their own bedroom discussion.

Yufeng picks up on Yufei's earlier musings.

"You are still hung up on the alure of paradise?"

He nods.

"Yeah ... today I asked some pilgrims in town ... discretely ... and they didn't understand my question. To them paradise is the one-all reward of everlasting enjoyment at the feet of god."

They look at me like I am an imbecile,

"What could be better than Paradise?"

Yufeng holds him tenderly and explains,

"My little rascal, you have to understand ... it's not *them* ... it's us! We are different."

He shakes his head,

"It's not just us ... I think of Master Su, Chen Er, Panda, Subedei, Genghis, ... and others ... they wouldn't be content sitting around in luxury every day, with everything given to them ..."

She smiles,

"But the other millions of people would be. So, do you create a better world for the 1% or offer paradise for the 99%?"

"Maybe that's the answer."

"What?"

"If we can't stop the dark manifestations of the Inquisition ... and if the Mongols don't come this far ..."

Yufeng adds,

"And if the plague doesn't defeat them ..."

"Yeah ... that too ... then what do we do?"

"I think the grandmothers hinted at it ... we start a new cosmos."

She laughs but then sees that he is not joking.

"What? You're not serious!"

"Couldn't there be another cosmos? This one and a new one, outside the Enso ... not with all the dark manifestations?"

Yufeng wrinkles her eyebrows,

"Hmmm ... interesting. But first come here my fierce warrior."

They both laugh and no more is discussed that night.

The next day they stop briefly at Cyprus and then start the sea journey back to Venice ... without as many stops ... just two stations they didn't visit on the way out ... Cephalonia and Durazzo, which are similar in makeup.

When they get back to Venice, Andrea Polo is there waiting for him with a serious look on his face.

They raise their voices,
at stone idols
as a man might argue
with his doorpost.
They have understood,
so little of the gods.

108 Time to Flee

Stupidity is better kept a secret,
than displayed.

Andrea Polo rushes up to them.

"Come over here." ushering them around the side of a warehouse building.

"You can't go back to your rooms ... don't worry, I have all your personal items at my home."

"Why?"

"The Inquisitors have a new sinister leader ... his clerics are searching for you to arrest you, Yufeng, and the others for heresy."

"What?"

"Don't ask ... it is just a sham ... certain people don't like new ideas which weaken their superstitious control over the people ... or maybe you offended someone."

"You must leave immediately. I'll talk to Captain Mario to get the ship provisioned at Split and then head for our station on Crimea ... they can't reach you there."

"Quick, in the meantime stay on board your ship and have it ready to sail ... or even better sail offshore ... I can send a skiff in the morning with your things."

Yufei and Yufeng confer with the others ... Tarem has no problem leaving ... Chen and Dorjie too. Chen adds,

"Well ... there goes my Italian winery and villa overlooking the sea."

Dorjie laughs.

"You old goat, you just want to sit in the village piazza drinking wine and boasting about your adventures with pretty girls to the grandpas."

Chen laughs.

"See what happens ... I just get settled and ... this fox spirit has snared me again."

Chen tells them,

"I'll talk to Mario to turn the ship around and anchor on a nearby island for the night until we get the things from Andrea."

He goes off to talk to Mario while the others talk about their new prospects.

Dorjie asks,

"What about the boat and the trade business you wanted to do?"

Yufei already has an idea.

"I think we can bring the Polos in on our *Mongol ortogh* and use the new boat for moving goods over the inland seas."

Then Dorjie asks Yufei,

"What do you sense ... is this Inquisition something temporary or will it last a long time?"

"Polo said that the pope has given the authority for overseeing the Inquisition to the Dominican order ..."

"Who are they?"

"The Dominicans are mendicant friars ... that is, they sustain themselves by begging."

"What will that mean?"

"They are not the usual corruptible preachers. Yufeng and I sense this Inquisition will last for a long time, driven by their religious zeal and accumulation of power through superstition."

Just then though they are spotted, and a band of armed friars surround them. Yufei and Tarem grip their swords, but Yufeng has a different idea as she reaches into a side pocket.

She cries out in a loud voice,

"I command you in the name of the Mother Goddess to stand back!"

The attackers stop and look at her ... and so do her friends. What they don't see is her hand coming out with the Tibetan fire jewel in it as she holds it up to the sunlight and the rays burn the clothes of the attackers and blinds them if they make the mistake of looking at the crystal ray.

Soon they all flee and Dorjie hugs Yufeng, who tells her.

"A little magic always helps."

After that, they board the boat and sail offshore for the night ... they all turn back and look at Venice receding in the distance.

Yufeng asks what they are all thinking,

"Do you think we will come back here someday?"

Yufei shrugs.

"We can fight a black witch and even an entire black monastery ... but a false belief followed by millions ... how do you fight that?"

The city gets smaller and smaller as they sail around an offshore island for the night.

Later, Andrea Polo comes out in small skiff with their belongings.

Yufei asks him,

"Will you get into trouble?"

He shakes his head,

"We have influence as well and Venice is still run by merchants."

"The Pope has appointed a prelate named Ripaldi to cleanse the people's faith ... he's the one that's after you ... do you know him?"

They look around and Yufei suggests,

"Maybe ... we had a run in with one on the way here ... over a dinner table."

Then looking at Andrea he asks,

"Will you come to China to visit us?"

He laughs.

"My brother and I were just talking about that ... maybe in the future we will do just that."

After the personal goods are transferred, he gives them some trade goods from Venice as gifts to the Mongol leaders. Andrea and Chen talk about cooperating on the trade business and an unwritten pact about using the new boat is made and the men shake hands. Mario will be the captain of the new boat ... the Polos are free to use it and will save a share of profits for Chen ... Mario will be the intermediary when shipments arrive from the east ... they will set a post station at the Venetian stations at Crimea and Constantinople. Even though their plans have been cut short, most of them like the idea of returning home.

The next morning the journey home begins. Yufei spends most days on deck, drawing maps and details of the various cities. In his mind, the immediate solution to the Inquisition is for the Mongols to destroy the Church hierarchy ... and he plans to help them.

Meanwhile one impatient Grand Inquisitor is not happy learning that his prey has evaded him again.

"Where did they go?"

"We don't know ... the boat docked and departed immediately thereafter ... probably to another trading destination. "

"Alert all Dominican orders along the coastal cities about them ... to capture and detain them."

"Yes master."

I will find you and when I do, you will beg me to release you to heaven.

What is not yet known,
Those blinded by bad faith,
Can never learn.

109 Karakorum

The sun is new again,
every day.

Meanwhile, back home, in Karakorum, Ogedei had decided to send Subedei & Tolui to invade the Jin from the south, by first going southwest and then east and north up through Song lands. Upon hearing the news, Tariq talks to Panda, and they agree he probably should go with the warriors with Subedei and Tolui.

After he leaves, Panda visits Sari and tells her that she is pregnant.

"Did you tell Tariq?"

"No ... I want him to focus on the enemy before him, not on me back here."

Sari smiles and nods.

***

On their return journey, Yufei wants to stop in Athens, where he goes to the Acropolis hill again, while the others sightsee and shop in the agora marketplace.

He sees the same scholars from his last trip debating philosophy.

As he gets closer to listen, this day they are talking about Heraclitus, one of the founders of Greek philosophy.

He overhears ...

"Applicants to wisdom,
do what I have done:
inquire within."

Some of the debaters aren't sure of the philosopher's meaning,

"Is he talking about finding one's psyche?"

Another comments,

"No, no, no ... it's not your mind or thoughts ... don't you understand?"

Just then the speaker notices Yufei.

"Let's ask this newcomer ... what do you think he meant?"

Yufei speaks,

"I am not familiar with this philosopher, but to me, the words mean to seek the eternal answers inside ... from the eternal conscious sprit."

A murmur arises as they discuss this. Finally, one man says,

"Would you like to join us and discuss some of his other words ... for example, he wrote that ...

"*Time is a game played beautifully by children.*"

Yufei smiles,

"That is a beautiful way to say it ... but let me ask for your thoughts ... how did the worlds begin?"

One of the scholars rises and asks Yufei,

"Have you read our classical books?"

"Only a few ... could you enlighten me master?"

"One our first philosophers, Anaximander of Miletus, argued that the *Boundless Consciousness* had no origin, because it is itself the origin."

Another scholar added,

"You see ... *everything either has an origin or is an origin.* Since the *Boundless Consciousness* has no limits, then it is an origin ... furthermore, it is beginningless and immortal."

The first scholar adds,

"Consciousness is real. It exists independently of all phenomena ... like Plato's cave wall in relation to the play of events on it created by the shadows. Like the wall, also it does not move, change, or cease to be there.
"

Yufei says,

"But it's hard to sense this One Consciousness."

"Yes, you must change your perception. One of our scholars put it this way."

"Such things as colors, tastes and smells *are no more than mere names,* he declared, for *they reside only in the Consciousness.*"

440

"These qualities aren't really out there in the world, he asserted, but *exist only in the minds of creatures that perceive them.*"

"*Hence if the living creature were removed, he wrote, all these qualities would disappear.*"

"For ultimately the world of sense perception is unreal, not in the sense of not existing at all *but of having no existence independent of the Consciousness that sustains it.*"

Yufei says, "Then it is also outside of time?"

"Yes, *Consciousness* is indeed outside of time. it is not possessed by an individual nor indeed by anything, for it is not an attribute. It does not come and go, however much it may appear to do so. All these so-called features of *Consciousness* are illusory; they belong to the world of appearances and not to reality."

"Parmenides and Zeno, Greeks from the town of Elea roughly 1700 years ago, held that *time* is an illusion of the human mind, and that reality itself is *timeless.*"

Yufei has an epiphany,

"Then the human perception of *time* in terms of past, present and future is illusory."

The scholars smile and nod as the stranger understands more of the mysteries of the universe.

Then Yufei's spirit connects with something inside and he starts to walk away ... turning, he says,

"Sorry ... excuse me, I must find my friends ..." but when he looks back, the scholars are not there.

Confused, he walks away and finds Yufeng, who looks at him closely as Yufei has a distant look.

"What is it?"

"I found another piece to the puzzle."

"O God! I could be bounded in a nutshell,
and count myself a King of infinite space..."
Hamlet

441

110 Tolui poisoned

The habit of knowledge
is not human but divine.

Meanwhile, in Karakorum, Toregene has an argument with Ogedei, demanding he appoint one of her confidants as a tax administrator.

"What? So, he can skim everything off for himself and you? Never!"

Then he laughs at her and derides her pompous appearance.

"Why do you wear those foolish clothes ... we are on the Mongolian steppe not Hangzhou."

Just then Tolui enters by ill fortune to tell Ogedei they must leave now.

Tolui sees Toregene and avoids her venomous glare.

Ogedei sees this and asks his favorite brother,

"Look at this old crow brother ... do you know what she is planning?"

Tolui tries to avoid getting involved and waves his hands ...

"It doesn't interest me."

His next words though are poorly chosen ... for Toregene.

"What's wrong now?"

Toregene fumes

"NOW? What do you mean by that?"

Realizing his poor choice of words, Tolui tries to back out of the tent.

"Nothing ... nothing ... older brother, I'll meet you at the horses ... don't take too long."

Then he retreats out the door.

Ogedei goes up to Toregene and slaps her.

"Don't ever talk that way again to my younger brother! Do you understand?"

Toregene though is defiant and starts to pour oil on the fire.

"You worthless camel turd, everyone is laughing at you!"

This time Ogedei doesn't hold anything back from his blow and she crumples to the floor unconscious. Her aide, Fatima, rushes up and picks her up to carry her out.

"Put a muzzle on her mouth or I will throw the both of you to the slavers ... understand?"

Fatima lowers her eyes, to shield the hatred in them.

You will pay Ogedei, you will pay for this ... and so will Tolui.

Later in her room, Toregene is recovering, but still seething. Fatima tries to caution her.

"You can't attack the Kahn ... he's too powerful and Guyuk needs more time to become acceptable to the other princes."

"But I have an idea how we can weaken two problems at one blow."

"What are you thinking?"

And the two evil women plot through the night.

Meanwhile Ogedei and Tolui ... along with Subedei, Mongke, ... and Tariq have begun their new campaign against the Jin by splitting up into a pincer attack ... Tolui taking a southwesterly route which eventually goes back north through Song lands in Sichuan ... but at the last minute, the devious Song ministers deny the access route.

Not to be deterred, the Mongols simply march around the Song lands and over the mountains to attack the Jin.

Later they link up before the walls of the Jin capital and crush the Jin armies there.

Near Beijing, Tolui joins Ogedei for a victory celebration, but Tolui is poisoned. Some try to blame Ogedei, but everyone knows he truly loved his younger, very capable, brother. Ogedei is very distraught with his younger brother's death, and he senses Toregene had something to do with it ... but she was many kilometers away ... it had to be one of her agents ... but who? He sends his spies to find out as they head back to their homelands carrying Tolui's body.

Meanwhile Yufeng and Yufei have returned to Karakorum and unite joyously with Panda and their new granddaughter, BaiHu (White fox). The entire camp is charged when they learn that Ogedei and the victorious armies are returning.

However, on the day they return, Sari learns the terrible news of Tolui's death. She wails at the news, becomes depressed, and then, sensing treachery, very angry; she wants to attack Toregene but Yufeng counsels her to be careful ... she has her sons to protect now. She advises her to work with Ogedei to find the killers first.

Yufeng talks to Ogedei, who is still depressed about Tolui's death. She tells him that if she was there, she might have been able to save him ... she suggests setting up an Academy of Medicine in Karakorum ... he agrees and along with Yelu Chucai's support, one is started. Meanwhile Yelu, Yufeng, Panda, and Yufei start to investigate the death of Tolui.

"Have them bring the body into my clinic."

Yelu objects,

"But you can't ..."

A forceful Yufeng tells him,

"Just do it or get out of our way!"

She turns to Yufei,

"Make sure he does it."

Yufei leaves and Panda, nursing her baby, asks,

"Then what?"

"Then we find out the type of poison and where it came from ... that will narrow down the number of suspects."

"But mother, don't you already know it was Toregene?"

"Yes, but we need more proof before accusing the khan's wife. You've seen how she has built up her own power base with the nobles and commanders."

Once the body is brought in for "burial preparation", Yufeng works furiously to open the insides to find the poisons. Inside the stomach she finds what she was looking for ... a dark fluid ... wearing gloves, she takes a sample out and carefully puts it into a glass bottle. Then just as quickly she stitches up the opening and calls the other women in to prepare the body for burial.

Yufeng meanwhile goes with Panda to her own tent and makeshift laboratory where she starts her analysis.

"Panda come here ... what do you sense about this poison."

Panda puts the sleeping baby down and holds her hand over the bottle to sense its essence. Then she closes her eyes ...

In her trance she sees a river valley ...

"Mother, I saw a river in Khorasan (Persia)."

Yufeng pauses for just a moment then says,

"That witch Fatima, wasn't she a captive from the Khorasan campaign?"

"Yes!"

Then she looks sharply at Panda,

"Keep this our secret for now ... we don't want Sari to fall into Toregene's trap."

"I understand mother. Oh ... where is Tariq and Subedei?"

"I heard they continued to Kaifeng to finish off the Jin."

Panda looks at her mother and asks,

"Can you watch the baby? I'll try to warn him."

Yufeng takes the baby outside, leaving Panda in her meditative trance to try to connect with Tariq.

But these non-physical communications don't always connect over long distances ... especially with those new to the hidden non-physical senses.

111 SanXingDui

By cosmic rule, as day yields night,
so, winter summer, war peace, plenty famine.
All things change.
Fire penetrates the lump of myrrh,
until the joining bodies die,
and rise again in smoke called incense.

It took another two years for the Jin to finally collapse. With the help of two Song armies, Subedei captures the Jin capital, Kaifeng.

But after the Mongols leave, the two Song armies seize Kaifeng and Luoyang for themselves and loot them.

Angered, Subedei returns, and crushes the Song armies. Then the victorious army returns with even more treasure wagons.

Subedei honors Tariq at a warrior's dinner and Panda is very proud of him. Later that night, in their tent, she showers her warmth to him.

A few days later, Yufei sends a message to warn their Fujian family against trying any similar Song treachery.

The next spring, Panda has another baby, a son, and names him Heihu (Black fox). The following winter, Ogedei leads an army south into Sichuan. Yufei and Yufeng go with him.

One day, while the army is camped north of Chengdu, Yufei and Yufeng ride out to scout the area.

At a place called Three Stars Hill (Sanxingdui), they come across some buried ruins of an ancient civilization and are amazed.

They decide to camp there for the night.

During the night they are joined by a spirit sister ...

"Look around ... what do you see?"

They see many bronze artifacts that they hadn't noticed when they camped.

"Dig." the elder spirit says.

They dig and finally uncover the top of a large, beautiful bronze tree!

A familiar looking tree.
Yufeng looks at Yufei,
"Do you remember ... in the grandmother's garden?"
He nods.
"This must have been one of their centers ... long ago ... before the Han, before the Shang, before the Xia ..."
"But people say the birthplace of the Chinese people is up north along the Yellow River?"
"Maybe there was more than one birthplace."
Then turning to face the spirit elder, Yufei asks,
"Why ... why did you show us this?"
"*I didn't want you to miss it ... it is important that the ancient sisters are not forgotten ... and for people to know, their work continues ...*"
Yufeng asks,
"Are there more places like this ... buried in time?"
The spirit elder nods.
"*Many.*"
Yufei is confused.
"But what's the point? They obviously didn't defeat the darkness ... how many have failed?"
"*Almost all ... you have done well ... but that's not the point.*"
"Then what is?"
"*What do you think the world would be like now if we hadn't tried to hold back the darkness all these millennium?*"
This causes Yufei and Yufeng to pause and reflect.
Then Yufeng asks,
"So, the battle against the darkness is never-ending?"
"*Yes, but it also allows time for man to evolve ... spiritually ... and to eventually undertake the next leap.*"
"The next leap?"
"*To create a newer, better, universe.*"

The poet was a fool,

RICHARD HOWE

who wanted no conflict,
among us, gods, or people

112 Eastern Europe Campaigns

Give me one man,
From among ten thousand,
If he be the best.

After the Jin, Ogedei tuns his attention to Eastern Europe. In 1236, Subedei and Batu (the son of Jochi) lead an army of 150,000 to the Volga River in the Rus kingdom. Ogedei also sends several Mongol princes along with them to learn warfare.

In 1237, Bulgar falls, and in 1238, Novgorod submits. The following year, 1239, Georgia and Armenia surrender, and in 1240 Kiev submits.

Following these victories, they attack Hungary and Poland with two armies ...

In 1241 Prince Kadan defeats the Poles at the Battle of Liegnitz ... and Subedei defeats the Hungarians and their allies much further south at the Battle of Mohi, coincidentally, a few days later.

They continue their pillaging through the summer and pull back to winter in the Caucus mountains again. It is while there that they learn of the death of Ogedei and although Subedei wants to continue with the campaign, most of the princes want to return to the homeland for the anticipated kurultai.

After that though, the Mongols battled the Knights Templars and the Knights Hospitallers, both formidable Teutonic knights in Eastern Europe; Subedei wants to crush them, but his forces are weakened after the princes take many good warriors back with them ... so, Subedei decides to withdraw also.

When the dead wood of the bow,
springs back to life, the living must die.

113 Ogedei Dies

Not to be quite such a fool sounds good.
The trick with so much wine
and easy company is how.

In December 1241, Ogedei dies ... whether from too much drinking (as claimed) or poisoned (as others suspect). The night before, it is rumored, he had a big fight with Toregene over Fatima. Ogedei blamed Fatima for poisoning Tolui and wanted her arrested. Toregene protested and they fought until he went off to drink with his commanders.

After he left, Toregene sent for Fatima, and they hatched a quick plan ... Fatima will get rid of Ogedei, while Toregene organizes to take over as regent until Guyuk is selected in a new kurultai.

Ogedei dies that night and Toregene spreads the rumor that it was from over drinking, but everyone suspects foul play. Toregene, however, has prepared for this day, and quickly launches her plan to take over ... she calls a kurultai where her bribes and other persuasions pay off and as Ogedei's wife, she is elected regent until Guyuk can be chosen. Once in control, she and Fatima immediately purge Ogedei's followers from leadership positions.

Only Temuge, Genghis younger brother, objects and tries to seize the throne, but Toregene is ready for him, and he is arrested and executed by new *khatun* Töregene.

These are dark times in Karakorum. Everyone is on edge, fearing the next death sentence. Yelu Chutai comes to Sari and Panda and advises them to flee.

"Many others have already gone back to their tribal lands ... or further."

Panda thanks him but tells him,

"Tariq is still with Subedei, I'll wait for him to return ... Guyuk and I are good friends."

"Ogedei was the khan, and he wasn't safe."

Panda looks at Sari, who says,

"I can't leave … and although Toregene hates me, I don't think she will try to come after me."

Yelu asks,

"Why not?"

"She's afraid of me."

"Afraid of you? Why?"

"She thinks my Christian god is more powerful than her superstitions."

A few months later, Subedei returns, along with Yufei, Yufeng, and Tariq. For a while anyway, things return to normal …but there is a tension throughout the camp between the Toregene faction and the non-Toregene faction.

Everyone is waiting for Guyuk to return to be elected as the new khan.

However, Toregene is not waiting. She's bribing all her cohorts and placing them in positions of power … and reaping the spoils.

Chen and Dorjie decide it is a good time to go home to Lhasa. Tarem also heads home to Kucha. For each of them, they have a parting dinner celebration and promise to see each other again soon.

For the others … Yufei, Yufeng, Tariq, Panda and her two kids … and Sari and her children, Subedei, and others … it is a waiting time … and a time to help Sari build her alliances.

"A man with outward courage dares to die;
a man with inner courage dares to live."

114 Tariq dies

The luckiest men die worthwhile deaths.

One night Tariq goes out with three other warriors while Panda stays in the tent with the children. Later in the night she hears a flurry of activity outside.

Yufeng and Yufei rush into the tent, start packing everything and tell Panda she must flee south.

She looks around and asks where Tariq is.

The look on Yufeng's face tells it all.

Then a scream comes from the tent.

Meanwhile, Yufei has tracked down the warriors who poisoned the small party. Before killing them, he gets all the information he seeks ... as his father taught him many years ago. It was as he suspected Toregene and Fatima, who had paid them.

Yufeng tells Panda to leave ... she will bury Tariq ... she needs to try to protect her children while she and Yufei protect Sari and try to hold the good parts of the Mongol nation together ... they've worked very hard these past years cultivating everything for the divine plan.

Sadly, Panda and her children (now 10 yrs. and 8 yrs.) flee south to Yunnan, through Sichuan. They are alone on the trail for 3 weeks, accompanied only by children, their animals, and her grief. Finally, they reach the outskirts of Chengdu. She remembers her mother telling her about this area and she finds the ruins at Sanxingdui.

They see many artifacts ... the children and animals marvel at the large masks and but there is no tree, like the one her mother mentioned.

She thinks ... *that's curious ... is it only visible to some?*

Her two white foxes play among the ruins and find burrow holes.

The children extract some other ancient artifacts from the holes, some smaller masks with strange eye sockets.

The next day, they continue traveling on to Yunnan ... to her childhood family home below the Snowy Mountains. The wild animals remember

Panda and are excited to see her but sad when LF is not with her ... some of LF's relatives often come to play with the children. The wolf and foxes slowly venture into the forest ... less quickly it seems than the children ... sadly though, for Panda, a light has gone out in her life.

Without the sun, What day? What night?

115 Guyuk is Khan

Poison travels faster in these times.

In 1246, Guyuk (the oldest son of Ogedei and Toregene) becomes the khan. Guyuk is not a bad person and sees through his mother's evilness. One of his first acts is to purge all of Toregene's appointments. Guyuk has a younger brother, Koden, who tells Guyuk that Fatima is a witch and is poisoning those around the court that she wants deposed ... including poisoning him.

A few months later when Koden mysteriously dies, Guyuk blames Fatima and orders her arrest and death.

Fatima is disposed of in an especially unique manner ... every orifice in her body is sewed up and then she is rolled up in a rug and thrown in the water.

After this, Toregene is exiled and mysteriously dies shortly thereafter.

Unfortunately, there is a rivalry between Guyuk and Batu, his brother, the khan of the Golden Horde. In 1248, Guyuk marches west to destroy Batu, who is marching east; Sari sends a message to warn Batu, a close ally and supporter. But then Guyuk mysteriously dies along the way.

And then more chaotic times follow ... no one knows who the new khan will be ... many assume that the next khan will come from Ogedei's line, but his children have little power and Sari and Yufeng have been preparing for this day.

Sari gets Batu to nominate Mongke, Sari's oldest son, who is an able miliary commander and respected by most commanders. Meanwhile Sari, Yufei, and Yufeng have lined up other princes and commanders to support Mongke.

They organize a quick kurultai on the steppes which choses Mongke, but many princes are not there ... so, they convene another kurultai later in 1251, at Karakorum, where Mongke is finally selected as the new khan.

***

Shortly thereafter, Yufeng and Yufei ride out one day to the holy mountain. They make camp intending to spend a few days there. The purpose of their trip though is not an outdoor journey, but rather an inner journey.

Once everything is in order and the horses hobbled, they meditate and travel inside to try to resolve some lingering questions.

Yufei wants to learn what will happen now to the Mongols under Mongke and also to the lands west of the Mongol empire.

Yufeng wants to learn more about the coming epidemic, the Black Plague, that the grandfather mentioned years ago to her.

Their inner journeys, which span hundreds of years, lasts several hours. First Yufei comes back to this world, looks over at Yufeng and decides to make some tea.

While he sips from the first brew, Yufeng wakens and welcomes the freshly made tea.

"Thanks ... I needed that after what I saw."

"What was it like?"

"Terrifying ... half the people everywhere dying ugly painful deaths ... the epidemic spared no one ... and they had no cures ... only stupid superstitions."

"Where did it come from?"

"Some thought from rats on the ships that traded in the east ... but no one really knows."

"Did it change the spread of the Inquisition?"

Sadly, she shakes her head.

"No, the Church used it to justify their Inquisition cleansing ... they came out stronger afterwards."

She sips some more.

"What about you? What did you see?"

"The same ... Mongke expanded the empire but finally the smaller European kingdoms gathered together and brought in the Teutonic nights to defeat the Mongols. "

"They defeated the Mongols?"

"Not them ... the Mongols defeated themselves ... they were divided by their own rivalries ... one khan didn't support another ... so their forces were smaller and after the defeats, they decided the Latin Kingdoms weren't worth it."

There is a silence as they digest it all, then Yufeng asks Yufei,

"So where does that leave the divine plan?"

He throws some branches into the fire, and they watch the smoke rise straight up.

He holds her and softly says three words.

"A New Cosmos"

116 Mongke Khan

The blossoms of the nutmeg tree, though dried,
Diffuse their sweet scent in all directions.

Mongke is a good ruler and removes many of the inequities held over from the Toregene-Guyuk years.

Sadly though, the next year Sari dies ... this causes a nationwide mourning as she was beloved by almost all Mongols and even foreigners who visited the capital. Fortunately, though, in her time, she had secured her sons hereditary rule over the empire.

Months before her death, Yufeng had sent a message to Panda to return to Karakorum. Panda and the kids had returned a month before Sari died and she was there to see her over the final bridge to the underworld.

Later Yufeng says,

"She was a brave and intelligent woman, who steered her sons on paths of wisdom."

"The Mongol Nation ... and the Divine Plan have been well-served by her."

Afterwards, Yufei carves a wooden funerary tablet, which they place on their altar ... to honor her in the years to come.

As one of Mongke's first acts, he orders his younger brother Kublai to subdue the southern tribes. Kublai organizes a 50,000 strong force to head south, marching through Sichuan to Yunnan.

Before Kublai's army leaves, Mongke visits Yufei and Yufeng and gives a secret letter from Sari to Yufeng. In it, she asks Panda to be the shaman-adviser to her son, Kublai. After reading it, they visit Panda, who then goes to visit Kublai. When she stands before him, he asks her,

"What ... you don't bow before me?"

Panda laughs,

"Would that make you feel more powerful?

Kublai laughs,

"They say you can heal without touching."

"They say when the great Kublai yells, the world trembles."

Kublai laughs.

"Will you come with me?"

"Maybe ... I have to ask my mother first ... she's very traditional."

Panda goes home to see Yufeng.

"Mother ... I am still in a cloud of confusion."

"About?"

"I'm not sure ... I think it's about life and death."

"Maybe you should talk to your father ... he's over there teaching your son how to fight with staffs."

Panda walks over and watches them fight for a while.

Yufei is a patient teacher, he knows the boy's moves before he moves ... just as Panda does, so he focuses his training on the inside ..."

"Sense it! Sense it! .... yes ... better. Again, use your instincts." Yufei turns and parries, then empties his mind, and does a low sweeping blow which catches the boy's legs, knocking him down.

Helping the boy up he asks,

"What happened?"

"I don't know ... it was like my instincts stopped sending messages."

"This is what you have to be extra careful of ... some opponents can cloak their intentions ... so, if your instincts stop ... use other senses."

"What do you mean ... my physical senses?"

"Maybe ... but also your mind ... think, if you were the opponent, and he was cloaking his instincts, which blow would you use at that moment. This could be the best time to defeat him because he won't expect it."

Panda coughs to interrupt them.

"Oh ... hi Panda ..."

"Hi father ... can I talk with you for a moment."

"Sure, Heihu, go attack your grandmother ... haha."

They walk to a fallen tree and sit down. Panda explains her confusion. Yufei holds her hands in his and explains.

"Panda ... life changes ... it is a universal fact. One of the Greek philosophers said it this way ..."

Just as the river where I step,
is not the same, and is,

so, I am, as I am not.

"We can't know the unknowable ... we just know ourselves ... hopefully."

"All we can do with our lives is to add beautiful moments together and make our own melody. I don't know if Tariq will come back in another form like Gugu did or if he'll be waiting for you at the side of the bridge ..."

"Father ... you have seen the future further than anyone alive ... is there an ending to this story?"

Yufei smiles.

"Yes ... but it is difficult to explain in our language."

Panda explains about Kublai and asks him,

"He wants me to go with him. Sari wanted me to go with him too. What do you think?"

He asks her the same question.

"What do you think?"

"I think about staying to help Mongke ... and my children."

Yufei shakes his head.

"They are ready to leave the nest and find their own destiny. Is it Kublai?"

"No ... he and I always had a close relationship ... and he's a good man."

"Then what?"

"I don't know ... it's just these wars against the darkness seem endless ... and pointless ... and, as you have said ... we will never fully defeat them."

Just then, a poison arrow flies at Panda who dodges it easily.

Yufei tells the grandchildren,

"Get your grandmother back to our cabin. Your mother and I will follow."

Yufei motions for Panda to go around the left side of a line of trees while he circles around the right side.

A few minutes later they meet up on a rise overlooking their last spot.

Panda holds up 4 fingers, Yufei does the same. Then Yufei makes a motion slicing across his throat ... Panda understands, and they each steal back down their paths.

The attackers are overconfident ... and overmatched ... and they join their ancestors one-by-one.

Panda asks her father,

"Did you learn anything?"

"They are from a cult of Dai Viet Black witches far south of here."

Panda asks,

"What should we do now?"

"You go warn Kublai, I'll make sure our family is safe."

Meanwhile Kublai is mobilizing against the Yunnan Dali kingdom.

When Panda hears this, she asks him to send her as his emissary to the Dali king. He agrees and Panda rides out to the Dali kingdom.

Panda has met the king and queen several times and is welcomed into their palace.

Panda lays out what will most certainly happen if they refuse to submit.

This sobers the king and queen up from the delusions cast about from their over-confident ministers ... in the end, the king submits, and the Dali kingdom is spared.

Then Kublai turns his army against the Dai Viets and destroys them in two decisive battles.

With Tariq avenged ... that is ... Fatima and Toregene dead ... her children ... Beihu (white fox), 21 and son, Heihu (black fox), 19, ready to go out on their own ... Panda is alone ... so, with her parents urging her for the sake of protecting China, their motherland, she accepts Kublai's invitation to stay with him as his shaman-councilor.

Before departing she goes off with her children. Although little has been said about them to protect them ... their education through life has been by some of the wisest teachers of the world. As young adults physically and wise adults spiritually, they are better equipped at their age than their parents were to confront a challenging world.

Panda tells them,

"Minimize what you seek, and you will have what you need."

"What about you and father?"

Wistfully Panda looks up at the clouds,

"When form disappears, your father will become the universe, the boundaryless, formless ... the infinite."

"When I attain to that state you will say ... I am no more ... because without a boundary how can an I be?"

"Someday I will join with your father in the cosmos ... to meet your grandparents ... and wait for the time when you will join us."

117 Sanxingdui 2ⁿᵈ Visit

The way up the road is the same as the way back.
The beginning is the same as the end.

After defeating the Dai Viet and with the Dali king submitting, Kublai turns his attention back eastward to join with Mongke to attack the Song. When he leaves, Panda goes with him as his shaman-adviser ... and then summer comes, and the heat halts the Mongol war machine.

Rather than return to their cooler northern homelands as usual, Mongke stays in the south ... *this is a mistake* ...

Many of his northern steppes' men, not used to the tropical heat, get sick from an epidemic ... as well as Monke.

Everything Yufeng and Panda try cannot stop the spread of the new disease and Mongke dies on the field. What remains of his army returns to Karakorum for another succession fight ... this time between Kublai and his brother, Arik Boke.

Before Panda leaves, they gather at home to discuss their plans ... Kublai must return to protect his claim to the Mongol throne, and Panda will go with Kublai. Yufei tells her, the Song will fall soon, and he and Yufeng will try to protect the family there after the kurultai. Beihu and Heihu will travel together ... first to Lhasa to see Uncle Chen and aunt Dorjie, and then to their grandparents in Kucha; Yufei and Yufeng will take a different route back to Karakorum to be there for the kurultai.

Yufei and Yufeng travel back a different route though ... they want to visit Sanxingdui again. They find the tree that wasn't there on the first visit and make camp nearby. While they camp there, they are visited by a spiritual sister.

"I've been waiting for you. You are getting closer to the beginning."
"Beginning?"
"Of your final destiny ..."
"Final destiny?"

"After you discard your mind, and body, and all conscious thoughts."

"What will be left?"

"Pure Consciousness ... untouched by any trace of bodily, or mental inhibitions ... such as the belief that 'I am this consciousness.'"

"But this world?"

"This world is the dream of Consciousness ... the grand illusion of the world which contains all that people want to believe to exist. But all of that, in fact, has no independent reality. Insofar as it exists, it does so only as a manifestation of Consciousness itself. In other words, the world that you experience is a construct seen through your human perception, the means of which - sense organs and the mind - are themselves all part of the illusion."

"And our part?"

"The ancients in India wrote, 'You do nothing at all' what means is that everything that is done by the body, senses and the mind are only as instruments. Your spirit conscious - does nothing. It merely observes, for observation is not itself an act. Do you understand? We are one Consciousness rather than numerous disparate ones ..."

"Everything in the universe is Consciousness?"

"No ... Consciousness is the universe and not just the universe ... it extends beyond the universe ... beyond space itself; nor does it exist before and after all things in time. It endures beyond time itself."

Yufei looks at the metal tree and asks,

"Can the present create the past?"

"Of course ... isn't it obvious?"

Yufei crooks his head like a dog.

"But ..."

The sister continues,

"Consciousness is infinite, boundaryless, timeless and everything in this world that it created is finite and exists in time. Your senses, right now, are finite and can only see finite things. What you call time, is just a way for your finite mind to arrange things."

"But that will change?"

"Yes, once you make the leap out of this universe, out the gap of the Enso, you will be one with the Consciousness ... you will be immortal Consciousness ... in no-time."

"Consciousness is like space ... the space inside the Enso, is the same as the space outside the Enso ... one Consciousness."

"The Gita portrays the universal self (Consciousness) as imminent in all things, as the spirit of the world, animating all that lives, residing even in the rocks of the earth, in the heavens and in the souls of men ... but not in time ... you will be that overseeing Consciousness for your new universe."

"The problem right now is your mind ... it is still in this linear space-time world. You think of time moving in one direction."

"But ..."

"Throw a rock in the stream ..."

Yufei picks up a rock and drops it into the stream ... it finds the quickest way to the bottom.

"Do you now know what you just did?"

Yufei ponders this and his face lights up. He says,

"In the world of no-time, it journeyed endless pathways to the bottom and afterwards, the event coalesced on the quickest one ... instantaneously in no-time."

She smiles and nods,

"To view the infinite, you must use different senses, for example, you must use the conscious witness behind your eyes ... to see the world differently. It shouldn't be difficult since, in the end, Consciousness is you!"

With this confirmation a huge weight is lifted.

"So, after I leave the Enso opening ... the way to create the new universe is to ..."

The sister smiles.

"Imagine it and then it will create itself ... just like the rock."

She smiles,

"Out of billions of sentient beings ... only a few have reached the point that you have reached."

"What now?"

"Tidy up your affairs here and then join us ... outside the Enso ... in the dreamless dream called Consciousness."

"Why do you call it a dream?"

'*It all started like a dream ...*"

"Do you ever remember the beginning of a dream?"

Yufei looks over at Yufeng and they shake their heads.

"Don't worry, your wife will come with you and your daughter ... later the grandkids have their own journey to experience first."

Yufei looks over at Yufeng and motions for her to come over to him.

When she does, all that has just occurred to him is transferred to her and she smiles.

"It's like you've envisioned ..."

"Sister, can you help me go through the steps we must take now?"

"No ... this new perception must come from inside you ... but I can tell you that you have already commenced many of the steps ... events that you have experienced or thought about since the beginning ... you just need to change your perception ... think back Yufei ... what is your first memory?"

"The Enso."

"And what can it explain to you? You should activate your mind without dwelling on anything Yufei."

"Like what the Hindu call *Samadhi*?"

"Kind of ... but go deeper ..."

Yufei goes deep inside ... at first there is just the emptiness ... then he sees the Enso ... and then he realizes something he hadn't realized before ... he is now outside the Enso ... and everything else is inside ... this world is just a dream like Buddha said it was.

"Just realize the one mind, and there is nothing else at all to attain."

Yufei understands this now.

"And after that there were many other stages of enlightenment which you experienced ... the sacred spring water near the grandmother tea tree and also in the Valley of the Mother Goddess ... all those sacred waters changed your inner body to better harmonize with your spirit body ... and then there was the fruit from the sacred Tree of Life."

"You were chosen before you were born ... but even so ... you had to experience all these things and discern the underlying meaning yourself."

"Now let me show you something ..."

After she says that, suddenly there is a flash of light and billions of light-like *beings* appear ... reflecting the light ... and once the flash is over, they disappear.

"Wow! What are they?"

"*Those are the conscious spirits ... they are invisible ... you only see them when the light reflected off their invisible formless form.*"

"And these conscious spirits can communicate?"

"*Kind of ... it's difficult to explain ... they exchange information ... and they are all connected to the One Consciousness ...*"

"*These billions of Conscious Spirits are the building blocks of the universe. And underlying everything is an invisible universal field of Consciousness with infinite conscious spirits and infinite possibilities. These spirits are a form of energy, and they create matter, light, and everything else.*"

"And a*wareness* is the tool I must use to transform a possibility into a probability. And I must alter my awareness in a certain way ... I must develop a new way to perceive non-physical things ... *like in dreaming inside a dream.*"

"*Buddha said, It is nothing - just dreams, just dreams.*"

"I remember reading an ancient text ... t*urning the light around* means turning your attention from involvement in mental objects *to focus on the source (essence) of the mind (Consciousness).*"

"*Yes ... now you are getting there. Remember just now when I flashed the light to illuminate the conscious spirits?*"

"Yes."

"*Just as I used the reflection of light to illumine these formless forms in darkness, you must use your experiences to illuminate your pathless pathway ... and then ...*"

"It won't be an invisible pathway any longer."

"*Yes. You will be able to see it clearly. And just as the stone knew the fastest pathway to the bottom. Your new worlds will create their own prior histories ... you just need to create the space.*"

"And once I create the space, time is automatically created, and once I create the space, the conscious spirits will manifest the worlds and stars and organisms, from all the possibilities."

"*Yes. And you know how to create the space?*"

"Yes."

"*There is one thing I must warn you about.*"

"What is that?"

"*To realize your destiny, you must go outside this universe ... outside the Enso ... and once you go beyond this Enso, and create your new Enso (galaxy), you may not be able to return.*"

Yufei looks down,

"You said *may*."

"*No one knows for certain ... I'm just a messenger ... when you reached a certain awareness, I was told to tell you this.*"

"Thank you."

"*Thank you Yufei ... and on behalf of all my sisters, we welcome you and Yufeng to the cosmos.*"

"We are honored venerable elder."

That which always was,
and is, and will be ever living fire,
the same for all, the cosmos,
made neither by God, nor man,
replenishes in measure,
as it burns away.

118 And Then ...

The prophets voice possessed of god,
requires no ornament nor sweetening of tone,
but carries over a thousand years.

European countries learn from their experiences .... they build better fortresses ... drop their local enmities and unite to form larger armies ...and they utilize the Teutonic Knights and Knights Hospitallers as a shock force. They win some key battles and ... in time, the Golden Horde Mongols, under one branch of Genghis sons, decides it's not worth the hassle and settle into the Rus territories.

The Persian empire ... now referred to as Il Khanate, administers the middle eastern countries for another branch of Genghis progeny.

And Kublai settles into his eastern, mostly Chinese-Mongol-Tibetan territories ... and after another brief internal challenge, declares the beginning of the Yuan Dynasty. Panda stays with him in his new capital of Xanadu (Beijing) ... counseling him and teaching his grandchildren.

Yufeng and Yufei return to their Yunnan home. They spend the first few days repairing windows, doors, stables, corrals, roofs, etc.

Finally, when the repairs are done, they take a respite and sit by the pond, reminiscing about when Panda would play with LF out there.

Yufei reaches down and picks up a flat rock and throws it skimming across the pond. It reaches about halfway and sinks; then he throws another which goes further before, it too sinks. Finally, he throws one harder, which reaches the other shore.

Yufeng looks at the ripples, then her bracelet.

"Like us."

Yufeng smiles and asks him,

"So, have you figured it all out?"

"I think so ... do you remember when we sat up on Manting Peak near the Grandmother Tree and I told you the ancients' said life was an illusion?"

She nods,

"Then I explained that their meaning was that it was not a real illusion, just *like* an illusion, like a rainbow, because it all came from the mind ..."

She smiles.

"And then we had more experiences and had further insights ... and more experiences ... and then we met the grandmothers at Gobekli and the elder sisters at Mt. Kailash and Sanxingdui ... and we understood more."

She nods.

"And then all the experiences fighting the darkness while assisting the Mongols ..."

She smiles and holds his arm.

"I remember all those things ... can you answer my question before winter?"

He smiles then says,

"Finally ... after all the things we experienced, I am back to the beginning."

She looks at him in amazement and asks,

"It was all just an illusion?"

He smiles and says,

'Yes ... but this life we share is our story ... understand? Panda will have her story, the grandchildren theirs ..."

"So, life is just a story."

She hugs him and then a thought enters her mind, and she asks,

"And then what?"

He smiles,

"It's simple ... like the spirit mother said .... we will start a new story (universe) ... only this time we will hopefully make the story better."

"Make the story better?"

"The histories, the events, the players, the probable outcomes ..."

"Sounds challenging."

"But what about everyone else ... who live and die without ever learning why?"

"They made their choice ... all of us come into this world without prior knowledge ... then it is up to us to pursue the mysteries ourselves ... or to rely on their superstitions to save them."

"When do we do this?"

"Well ... I think that this current reality is doomed ... the darkness is too powerful."

"I have read all the ancient texts and in some of the Indian myths it describes the various ages and epochs."

"Rather than wait for the end ... I think we start now to create our new galaxy."

"How will you ... how will we do it?"

"We need to internally develop higher powers of our awareness and when we go into the void, we will venture out the Enso Gateway, connect with the conscious spirits there and try to affect the infinite possibilities ... into ones we desire ... we will imagine a new space for a new galaxy to arise in the void ..."

"Our awareness, and the conscious spirits, will cause the space to form and then time will follow automatically ... and then we will exchange information by our spirits to the conscious spirits who will exert their influence over an infinite number of possibilities to create the stars, and worlds, and organisms ... and the natural physical laws ...."

"This new galaxy will populate itself and create its own history ... according to universal norms and celestial laws ... *backwards in time forming a concise even development socially, scientifically, and spiritually.*"

"What about the darkness ... the evils that came with this universe?"

"We cannot eliminate darkness entirely, but hopefully we can weaken its destructive forces by making the good forces stronger and more aware there."

"How can I help?"

"I believe the power to heal is stronger than the power to destroy ... you need to develop your inner healing powers ... use your medical knowledge base ... to purge the evil poisons out. Approach the task as though the evils are a deadly epidemic."

Later Yufeng asks Yufei ... "If it works ..., will we be their ... *Gods*?"

"No ... the causal laws of nature will take over the course of the natural world... people will support the Mother Goddess of Nature ... just as we did."

"Consciousness will only manifest itself through us."

***

Meanwhile Panda is focused on a different world ... the underworld ... where Tariq waits for her.

In her private room not far from the Khan's, Panda often ventures deep into the void to meet Tariq's spirit, which stayed intact following her instructions.

There are no words to describe what happens between them ... spirit-to-spirit ... the duality is transcended.

For now, Panda has led Tariq to a different bridge at the base of the Tree of Knowledge, where, if ever he is to make the spiritual jump as her mother and father have done (and Panda will do someday), he needs to continue his spiritual growth ... and what better place to do this than under the Tree of Knowledge in the *pure buddha-field (viśuddhabuddhakṣetra)*.

Here he has shed his old mind with its limits ... and his spirit can soar higher than the eagles here.

Panda knows that, here next to the tree, he is still a spiritual acorn, but someday, she feels he will be a full-grown spiritual tree like her father.

But she also knows ... he must accomplish this himself. The Buddhas only point the way.

Sternly she *asks* him ...

"Why did you come with all this crowd of people?"

Tariq looks around seeing no one except himself ... then he realizes ... all this baggage must be discarded before he can join her.

And it is this hope that sustains her through the years serving the great Khan.

After several years she is able to create a tulpa in the image of Tariq ... a Tibetan tulpa is not real, it only appears real, and she only does this in the privacy of her secured private room ... but she feels more comfortable exchanging information with this tulpa. It feels more real to her ... and feeling is important in every story.

119 How will you …

Gods live past our meager death.
We die past their ceaseless living.

Yufeng asks,

"Before you create *space*, where are we in this new universe?"

"We are really nowhere … just celestial beings … awaiting the space to form."

"Then what?"

"The conscious spirits will create the space … like a school of fish, separating in the middle … and then they will create an explosion of stars, planets, the elements, organisms for life."

"An explosion?"

"Yes … it's part of a natural law that happens when you create space … and that's when *time* is created and since space dislikes a vacuum, the conscious spirits create the stars and worlds and organisms… everywhere life can survive … millions of worlds."

"And these will evolve into peaceful civilizations?"

"No, that method didn't work … you saw our world."

"Then how?"

"We will have the conscious spirits create the future first … the peaceful, evolved, advanced civilizations."

"So, you will create the end first and then the beginning, and they will grow towards each other … one forward in time, the other backward … resolving any issues by themselves … or by the conscious spirits."

"Yes … like the jeweler whom we gave the jade rocks, who exposed the priceless jade carving hidden underneath the rock."

"But how will you model the enlightened civilizations?"

"By using the few wise models which our world has created … Laozi, Wenzi, Mozi, Plato, Aristotle, Socrates … using their conscious systems as the molding material like a potter … but with a few changes so everything is not the same."

"Molding them physically?"

"Non-physically."

"And the worlds?"

"They will follow the same universal natural laws as all galaxies ... we don't have to get involved ... nature has its own laws."

"And the aberrations?"

"Hopefully, they will be eliminated ... by your knowledge and others ... now that their evil effect is recognized by all ... the fierce grandmothers will help this time."

"What about compassion ... like before?"

"Compassion is not harmful ... just misguided compassion."

"So, where will this new universe exist?"

Yufei draws an Enso in the water.

"Here ... did you think there was only one universe here? Do you remember when we went into the first mandala?"

She nods.

"I've been back there ... there are many different rooms ... one for each universe ... that's where we will build our new universe."

"But ..."

"I've talked to the Kailash elder sisters ... they have started to draw our new mandala ..."

"What about Panda, the grandchildren, our family ..."

"I think this world has only a few thousand years before it destroys itself ... hopefully we can teach our loved ones how to evolve spiritually in that time ..."

"What will it be like ... do you know ... our new world?"

"I have some thoughts ... some people will have a connection with the land, like your father did ... so there will be farmers and growers, but their lives will be easier with new machines. There will be craftsmen and merchants with open markets; there will be teachers, scholars, and scientists ... but no soldiers as there will be no wars of destruction ... and no priestly class ... instead, those resources will go into medicine and science. Everyone will have a home and as they fill up their home world, they will set out to settle other uninhabited worlds."

"An age of discovery."

"Yes. Don't you see?"

"What?"

"This is why everything happened?"

"What do you mean?"

"To prepare us for going out the Enso ... to prepare us to understand creation."

"To prepare us to start a new world story."

Then he holds her closely ... and vanishes.

At first, she is surprised ... then she smiles ... knowing that he has gone on ahead,

Time flows past without touching him.

120 The Waking

Of all the words yet spoken,
none comes quite as far as wisdom,
which is the action of the mind ...
beyond all things that may be said.

He woke up feeling especially refreshed ... the most refreshed he's felt in a long time. He lies there thinking about what has happened. He remembers most of it ... his last thoughts were about their old cottage in Yunnan ... then he looks around ... he is in a similar cottage now ... in their old bed?

He rolls his feet out to the floor, then realizes he is naked, and then a new shock as he sees a clump of his old skin lying lifeless on the floor.

His eyes quickly scan his new skin ...

Then he remembers a line from a book he read somewhere ... about a snake shedding its old skin before it can be reborn.

Hmmm ... no scars on my body, he looks in a bronze mirror ... no sagging skin under the chin ... then he realizes what has happened and quickly gets dressed.

In the large great room of the cabin, a younger Yufeng is busy making breakfast when she sees him, she remarks,

"Who is this nice-looking young man in my house ... have you come to ravish a defenseless young woman?"

'Haha ... you wish!" then he adds,

"I like these new bodies, how about you?"

She answers as she throws an apple at him.

"No, I preferred the sagging breasts and wrinkled skin ... you country oaf!"

"Oh ... and throw the old *you* out in the bin with mine, we'll burn them later."

"Okay. What's for breakfast?"

"I thought I'd make your favorite ... Wuyi porridge, bread, and fruits."

"Sounds great ... why are you up so early?"

"Did you forget old man? The grandchildren are coming today to help with our work."

"Oh ... yeah ... it's just the sight of a beautiful young maiden in my kitchen made my mind go into a fog."

She throws another fruit at him which he catches and asks,

"So how many others do you think will come to our new world?"

As he eats, he recalls his conversations with some of their friends and relatives ...

"I think Chen Er and Dorjie will come soon, maybe Master Su ... especially after I promised him a new body ... haha."

"Any others?"

"I talked to Tarem and Beersheba ... but they choose to stay in Kucha with their kids ... maybe later, when they are all grown."

Then turning to her, he asks,

"Did you talk to your sister?"

She nods.

"She's like Beersheba ... I don't think they understand what we are doing here."

"It's okay ... for most people, *one life is enough*."

"What about Panda" he asks looking at her.

"Did you talk to her again?'

She nods,

"She's waiting to make the leap with Tariq."

"This isn't easy for some."

"She's okay with that ... *if it's meant to be, it's meant to be* ... her words."

"I told her more of what we've experienced ... to leave the old illusion, the old story with the dark manifestations behind."

He shrugs and rolls his head.

"Let's eat ... it's going to be a busy day."

***

Far, far away ... in the old world, Panda is sitting alone in her room, looking out the window and thinking over everything ...

Panda pulls out an oft viewed picture of Tariq ... and her mind wanders further out of this world ...

The soul is undiscovered,
though explored forever ...

***

Years later, the Polo family was granted an *ortogh* partnership with special trade rights across all Mongol lands. On one trip, Andrea brings his nephew Marco Polo with them, and he meets the daughter of his father's old friend, Panda ... *but that is another story ...*

And finally, years later, under Kublai Khan, the Song Empire is defeated and the Mongol Empire spans from coast to coast ... the greatest land empire in the world ... and one of his spiritual advisers is Sakya Pandita, of the Grey Earth sect, which helps spare Tibet from destruction ... *but that is another story ...*

Subedei continues on to exceptional Mongol glory, conquering every force he encounters on his campaigns through eastern Europe, to become the greatest general of all time ... *but that is another story.*

Before that happens the Wuyi branch of the Chen-Wang families have successes and tragedies. Chen Anhua is killed over unpaid gambling debts while stationed in Jiujiang. His oldest son, Chen Ming becomes a prominent leader in Fujian and has several sons and daughters for Granny Lanting to watch over ... *but that is another story ...*

When the Mongols take control of Song China, many intellectuals cannot accept being under such barbarian foreign dominance and commit suicide. Lord Chen (Chen Yi now) and his sons though accept reality and work for the good of the Chinese people ... *but that is another story ...*

Galileo talks about a wine's good taste does not belong to the objective determination of the wine, but the special taste is from the senses of the person who is enjoying its taste.

That everything we perceive is, in some sense, just a creation of our senses (minds)... Reality (life) then ... is just a mind story.

***

In the book *'Night Train to Lisbon',* the author, Pascal Mercier, wrote of life ...

"Life is not what we live.
It is what we imagine we are living."

The End

Writing these books has really been a preparation for the actuality of my own exit from this dream. Not that I fear death, but rather I feel a need to prepare myself for the next phase of life. And as I come to end of this book, I come closer to the end of my personal journey.

And then ...

I will exit the Enso gateway and create my own new universe.

###

About the Author

I graduated from Bowdoin College in 1967 and spent most of the next 30 years as a real estate developer. In 1998, I moved to China. and over the next 25 years, traveled throughout the country and studied the history, culture, and philosophies of China, India, and other regions of the world (the Middle East, Christian lands, etc.).

I have had a life-long burning desire to understand the mysteries of life. This quest has led me on many pathways ... from acquiring and reading thousands of books, to trips to ancient temples, to solitary meditations on mountaintops and even visiting an ashram in India ... and finally, one day, after all the many years, I found *my* answers.

Then, in 2020-22, during the pandemic lockdown in China, I was invited to translate several Chinese historical books to be published in China. I enjoyed the endeavor so much that I embarked on writing about my search for the hidden meanings of the universe - hidden within the ancient texts ... but set in an adventure novel story during Song Dynasty China. Fortunately, from my readings, I had a large database of ancient wisdom.

During the epidemic, I wrote three books, The Enso Trilogy, which are the culmination of my life's golden thread. Each book in the trilogy focuses on a critical aspect of a spiritual life: enlightenment, fulfillment, and the afterlife.

In Jan. 2023, while I was finishing the 3rd book, I contracted COVID. A few months later, a heart specialist told me I had a major problem in my heart valve which would require surgery to fix. I told her that I had done everything in my life and with the completion of these three books, I was ready for the next life (Socrates said it better).

I read the other day, '*Sometimes we're afraid of something, because we're afraid of something else*'. I think death is like that ... people are afraid they won't finish something, but this fear is just a creation of our mind.

I just finished Book IV (publish date Jan 2024) which delves into the backside of the universe's tapestry, to understand the divine purpose of it all. In this book, I write a lot about possibilities becoming probabilities and then becoming reality. It's about the journey after death and the purpose of my life.

Thank you for reading my books.

Read more at www.rhowe-haozi.com.